THE LAW OF ANGELS

Hildegard of Meaux – sleuth, spy and now an abbess of the powerful Cistercian Order – has found refuge from a world of violence and blood feud at her new home in Yorkshire. But by taking a bonded maid into the fold, Hildegard has made a dangerous enemy, an enemy who thinks nothing of destroying her sanctuary to further his own ends. Meanwhile her own history, and her possession of a priceless relic, threatens to drag her into the schemes of traitors to the crown who seek to overthrow King Richard's regime – including the ruthless Henry Bolingbroke.

THE LAW OF ANGELS

THE LAW OF ANGELS

by

Cassandra Clark

Magna Large Print Books
Long Preston, North Yorkshire,
BD23 4ND, England.

British Library Cataloguing in Publication Data.

Clark, Cassandra
    The law of angels.

        A catalogue record of this book is
        available from the British Library

        ISBN   978-0-7505-3530-4

First published in Great Britain in 2011 by Allison & Busby Ltd.

Copyright © 2011 by Cassandra Clark

Map on P9 based on one of the series produced by John Speed in the early seventeenth century.

Cover illustration © Margie Hurwich by arrangement with Arcangel Images

The moral right of the author has been asserted

Published in Large Print 2012 by arrangement with Allison & Busby Ltd.

LP

Magna Large Print is an imprint of Library Magna Books Ltd.

Printed and bound in Great Britain by
T.J. (International) Ltd., Cornwall, PL28 8RW

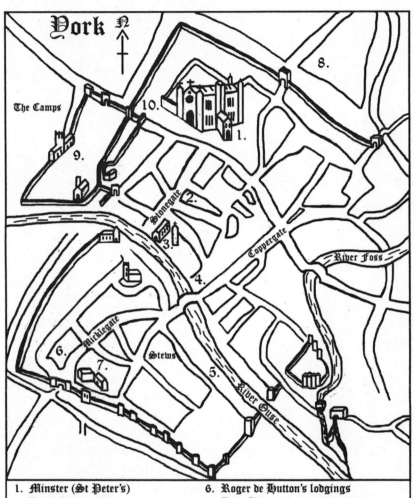

York N

The Camps

8.

10.

9.

1.

Stonegate

2.

3.

Coppergate

River Foss

4.

Micklegate

Stews

6.

7.

5.

River Ouse

1. Minster (St Peter's)
2. Danby's workshop
3. Guildhall
4. Exit of underground passage
5. Sisters of the Holy Wounds
6. Roger de Hutton's lodgings
7. Holy Trinity, first station of the pageant
8. Where Hildegard lost her hat
9. St Mary's Abbey
10. Bootham Bar

Prologue

The heat in the small attic under the thatched roof of the guildmaster's house was stifling. It reinforced a feeling of intimacy. The distant sounds of the market added to the sense that the two of them inhabited a private world.

'Compare the price of swans,' suggested the girl lightly as she sprawled across the bed wearing nothing but her cotton shift.

The young man grinned. 'Swans! Compared with what?'

'Books, you sot wit! Haven't you been listening?' Sitting up to tug the hem of the shift over her head she gave him a challenging look then flung her head back to allow her long hair to trail radiantly over the pillows. She was in all the pride of her youth and beauty. Smiling indulgently she said, 'I've just been telling you, dunderhead. They're saying King Richard has bought two books for twenty-eight nobles!' She couldn't keep the awe out of her voice.

'What's that got to do with swans?' he demanded.

'Think about it! You can get two dozen swans for only three nobles. Which is the better bargain?'

'Depends what the books were,' he teased. 'Me, I wouldn't give a farthing for a hundred books but I'd give a pouchful of groats for a swan with all its feathers on. Anyway,' he continued, 'what would you be doing with another swan? Surely one's enough?' As he spoke he raised both arms.

Attached to them was a pair of wings. They were of such length they trailed round his ankles as if he was crossing the floor on a cloud. With his bright hair and dancing eyes he looked less like a swan than an angel.

Smiling softly the girl reached out, 'Are you keeping them pageant britches on for ever?'

They were stitched all over with white goose feathers and he pushed them roughly aside as he climbed onto the bed.

'At least take your wings off,' she advised.

He began to tickle her. 'It's not a sin to wear wings, is it?'

'No, but this is!' she teased, sliding more comfortably beneath him. 'Are you married?' she whispered. 'No? Then sin!'

'Is this your wife?' he murmured.

'No. Then sin!'

He cloaked the wings over them both by stretching her arms above her head so that they were lying inside a feathered cave with sunlight filtering through the quills. Splinters of gold leaf seemed to gild their skin.

'Is it a fasting day?' he whispered.

'Sin!'

'Is it daylight?' he continued.

'Sin—' She tugged hurriedly at his britches. 'Sin ... sin ... a thousand times sin. Take them off!'

As he struggled out of the offending garment he began to recite from the forthcoming mystery plays in a large, false voice. 'Doom nighs near and—'

'Shush!' she murmured, pressing her fingers to his lips. 'You're all talk and no action today. Whatever's the matter? Are you still worried about your lines?' She pulled him closer.

At that moment the door of the attic flew open. Three men entered.

They had hoods pulled well down over their faces and carried drawn swords. One came straight over to the bed. A thrust of his blade into the white feathers brought a gasp from the youth and he stared at the steel tip protruding from between his ribs in astonishment. A gout of blood appeared. The girl's eyes widened in horror as gore dripped onto her breasts and as she was dragged out into the flash of daylight she gave a shriek of fear. Behind their masks the men said nothing. She began to plead for her life.

Meanwhile, in another part of the county, two men are sitting on the battlements of a castle commanding a view over the royal forest. A blizzard of gulls, driven inland by a glittering easterly, swirls above their heads. Out of this avian storm one bird detaches itself, alights on the parapet and struts confidently towards them.

Fixing it with an interested glance, the elder of the two men asks, 'Do you think they can be trained to hunt like falcons?'

His companion assesses the bird, its weight, heavier than a barnyard cock, its white breast, grey wings, its raptor's beak marked at the tip with a red spot like a drop of blood, and observes that the creature clearly regards the men as naught. Both watch as it turns its head to display

13

first one yellow eye and then the other. 'Everything living can be trained to kill,' he concludes. 'Whether they'd return the prey to you is another matter.'

A second bird detaches itself from the flock and alights with a struggling herring in its grasp. The first gull makes a grab to claim the fish. At once a squabble breaks out. Yellow claws draw blood until the attacker flies off clutching its stolen prize. With a shriek of rage the second launches itself in pursuit.

'How like men,' observes the elder of the two.

'Only the prize is different,' replies his companion, narrow lips twisting with amusement. He watches the fight continue in mid-air.

'An omen?' His companion follows his glance. 'Young Richard and brave cousin Harry?'

The fight continues. Blood is drawn. The white feathers are streaked with red.

'No doubt it's treason to compare the crown to a herring,' the younger man remarks.

His companion spits over the parapet. 'No doubt.'

Chapter One

Some days before this, in the deep peace of a summer morning, Hildegard was lifting skeps in the lower meadow at Deepdale. She wore a white mesh veil and padded gauntlets and worked to the sound of contented bees murmuring within the hives.

Three years had passed since King Richard and Mayor Walworth had outfaced Wat Tyler's shocked and betrayed countrymen at Smithfield. In fact the third anniversary of Tyler's murder fell on the Feast of Corpus Christi in scarcely a fortnight's time.

And it was two years since Archbishop Courtenay had received the pallium from Pope Urban VI in Rome and had emerged from Canterbury with new powers, stamping hard on the Oxford dissidents and scattering them like ants about the realm.

But it was only one year since Hildegard had been given leave to move into the grange at Deepdale in the north of the county and turn it into a minor cell of her mother house at Swyne.

It had been a hard year but now the fruits of their endeavours were beginning to show.

As she worked in the drowsy heat she was sharply aware that it was also a year since the Abbot of Meaux, Hubert de Courcy, had abruptly left on pilgrimage, putting the running of the abbey in the hands of his cellarer, Brother Alcuin.

The honeybees flew serenely in and out of the hives, their king royally at ease inside his straw-stitched palace. Their skeps were upended baskets of woven blackberry briars placed on wooden stands as protection against predators. Conical reed tents called 'hackles' kept them from rain and the heat of the sun. During the previous week several frames of wax had been taken out for delivery to a chandler in York, leaving some skeps empty, but the rest, today,

15

were buzzing with life.

Hildegard was busy hefting the remainder of the skeps so that she could judge how much honey was in them. She worked alone while the two other sisters who had joined her at Deepdale busied themselves around the house and kitchen garden.

It was a sad thing, she thought with a glance at the empty skeps, that the bees had to be destroyed in order to remove the honeycomb. She pondered the possibility of trying a method she had observed in the abbey hives at Meaux. There a straw cap was put on top of the skep and the bees were encouraged to take up residence in this new place. It allowed the honeycomb to be removed from below without killing the bees themselves. That would be worth trying, she decided, as she finished her task and began to walk slowly back up the meadow.

The sisters at Deepdale were lucky to have received a request for beeswax from a chandler in York. He had been tearing his hair out because an expected consignment from the Baltic was delayed in the Humber estuary by a dispute over port taxes. It was his privilege to supply the guilds with their Corpus Christi candles and his reputation would be in tatters, as well as his hair, if he couldn't deliver. A call had gone out to all the local beekeepers to spare what they could. Deepdale made an offer at once. They could use the income.

At a safe distance she took off her protective veil and removed her gauntlets. A year ago the grange had been nothing but a wilderness of nettles and ground elder. It had taken six nuns seconded from the priory at Swyne, together with Hildegard, a lay sister called Agnetha, and a couple of strong Dalesmen, to bring some order to the place. Now they were almost self-sufficient.

As she made her way through the long grass she gazed up towards the scar at the dale head where the sheep were being rounded up.

The high-pitched whistle of Dunstan, the shepherd, and the bleating protests of the sheep themselves floated down in the hot silence of mid morning. The shearmen must have finished their work. Soon the shorn flock would be brought down to start the long journey to summer pasture on the banks of the Humber. The wool clip meant more vital income. There might even be a profit by the end of the summer if the crops didn't fail in the present drought. It was hard work, trying to survive in the wilds, but it would be worth every blistered palm and cricked back for the harvest that must surely follow.

Her thoughts were interrupted by the sound of a man's voice hailing her from the orchard. Assuming it was the shepherd's lad, she lifted her head. But it was a monk in the familiar white robes of a Cistercian who had called out, and now he came striding energetically through the grass towards her.

'Brother Thomas!' she exclaimed with pleasure. 'How good to see you. But what brings you over to Deepdale so soon? Surely it's not time to hear our confessions again?'

Based at the Abbey of Meaux, he was the newly

ordained monk given the light task of attending to the community's spiritual needs. Tall and broad-shouldered and no more than twenty-five, he now removed a wide-brimmed straw hat to reveal a bony, intelligent face, lightly tanned by the weeks of unending sunshine.

He greeted her with a somewhat apologetic expression. To her surprise she saw two young women standing at the gate. In fact, on closer inspection, she realised that they were little more than children. One of them wore a battered straw hat with a stylish tilt to the brim and a chain of daisies round the crown, while the smaller of the two had a hood pulled over almost concealing her face. Both looked dusty and dishevelled from their journey.

'Come into the kitchen and have a beaker of ale,' she invited, leading the way through the trees towards the house. Two ponies and an old ambler were already being installed in the cool of the barn by the stable lad.

'This heat seems endless,' Thomas said as he fell into step beside her. 'The wells are dry as far as Beverley.'

'How about Swyne? Are they coping?'

'Doesn't your prioress always cope? I think she's conjuring water out of the sun itself.' He chuckled. 'But I have something to tell you.' He glanced back at the two girls who were trailing at their heels and lowered his voice. 'You have your first guests.'

Hildegard gave him a startled glance. 'Guests?'

'Your prioress sends them with her kind regards.'

'For how long?'

'She didn't say. There was some haste in her decision.'

'Whatever possessed her to send them here?'

Thomas shook his head.

'What else did she say to you?'

'Nothing – other than to make sure they arrived safely.'

She gave him a sharp glance. 'So what's their story?'

'Can we talk somewhere in private?'

By now Agnetha, the lay sister, had appeared from the dairy. After greeting the girls, Hildegard turned to her. 'I wonder if you'd give our guests something to eat and drink, Agnetha? I'm going to whisk Brother Thomas away so I can catch up on news from Swyne.' She led the way into the house.

The young monk sat down on the bench opposite Hildegard. They were in the small chamber off the main hall where she did the accounts. It was scarcely big enough to swing a cat in but it gave some privacy during the daily comings and goings in the rest of the house and now, too, it was a refuge from the blazing sun. She offered Thomas a mazer of ale from their brewhouse.

'This is good stuff,' he observed after taking a long drink. 'Almost as good as ours at Meaux!' he teased as she refilled the vessel.

'It's Agnetha's latest project,' she smiled. 'If she ever leaves here she'd make a good ale-wife. In fact, there's nothing practical she can't turn her hand to. I don't know what we'd do without her.'

'And the two nuns?'

'Marianne, solid and sensible, and Cecilia, thankfully given to poetic flights that transform the mundane into something beautiful, with a voice that makes us feel we're in heaven already!'

'And all three the perfect helpers to establish a grange like this. You've worked hard this last year. The brothers at Meaux are impressed. Every time I visit I see changes for the better.'

'We're so fortunate. Soon we'll be able to take in our first orphans.' Hildegard gave him a straight look. 'Or are these they? From what you've hinted there's obviously more to them.'

'It's as I told you. I really know nothing else. The prioress came to me as soon as I'd said mass and instructed me to escort them here at once. She was in a hurry. She said, "See what Hildegard can make of 'em."' He lowered his voice. 'I believe her haste came from the need for one of them to be hustled out of the clutches of some horsemen who had just ridden onto the garth. The talkative girl, Petronilla, tells me she's an heiress and was about to be married off to an old man she hates. In fact, she wants to become a nun, or so she says.' He gave a small jerk of his head as if to show his scepticism. 'Maybe the prioress fears her guardian will try to snatch her back before the child has had time to decide matters for herself?'

'She's a pretty child.' When the straw hat had been swept off, Hildegard had caught a glimpse of a pert face under a cloud of dark hair. She looked about sixteen or a little younger. There had been a delicate silver pin nestling in the curls. If she wanted to he a nun, she thought, that would have to go. She gave a smile to indicate she shared Thomas's scepticism and asked, 'So she's an heiress, is she? And the one in the hood?'

'Not a word could we get out of her.'

'Is she dumb?'

'No. She made an ill remark about her pony before we set off but that was it, all the way here, mile after silent mile. Of course,' he added with a long-suffering shrug, 'it would have been hard to get a word in edgeways with Petronilla present, as you'll shortly discover.'

The conversation moved briefly onto other issues. Thomas asked if she had heard anything of the Scots since the truce ended at Candlemas but she shook her head. 'Just that assault on Annandale, taking back what was taken from them, to be taken and retaken for generations to come, no doubt, unless everybody changes their attitude.'

'I hear Lord Percy has introduced the death penalty for breaking the truce – a turnabout in his thinking that's had us all open-mouthed at Meaux. He must be worried about this renewed alliance with the French. He could lose every-thing if the Scots and French make a concerted attack.'

'That's what we feared last year but luckily it came to nothing. But it's not only the Duke of Northumberland who could lose everything. If the north's taken, those in the south are going to suffer as well. The Londoners would do well to remember that.'

Thomas nodded in agreement. 'It's high time

21

we got some action from those in Westminster. They're too busy feathering their own nests to rule the country properly. The barons should be defending the realm, not bickering over who gets the biggest slice of its wealth. We need proper leadership. Gaunt should step aside and let King Richard get on with the job. He's seventeen now. Of age. But Gaunt must rule the roost, mustn't he?'

Hildegard had never heard Thomas so incensed.

He was frowning. 'All that aside,' he went on, 'we brothers at Meaux are worried about the safety of our outlying granges should the Scots reappear. We worry about you nuns, Hildegard. This is such an isolated part of the county.'

'We're safe enough as long as the Scots don't call Northumberland's bluff and start raiding right down into Yorkshire again. Besides, nobody knows we're here, it's so remote!' She leant forward, 'But tell me, any news from Meaux, Thomas?'

He understood instantly what she meant. 'He's absent still.'

There was silence.

Eventually Hildegard said, 'Safe, one trusts?'

Thomas was quick to reply. 'Be assured, we would hear if there was anything to hear, and so would you. He is our abbot. The name Hubert de Courcy is constantly in our prayers.' He gave her a soft look. He was her confessor and guessed whose name lay deep in her heart.

She poured them both another beaker of ale. 'Are you having anything to eat before you leave?'

'I'd like to get back before vespers if I can.'

'Take a pack of bread and cheese with you, then. I'll get Agnetha to make one up.'

He leant forward. 'I know you haven't been out of Deepdale since moving in here last summer. That's almost a year. I said as much when I was over at Swyne.'

'And?'

'Your prioress mentioned Archbishop Neville and the possibility that you might have to seek an audience with him in York.'

She gave him a hurried glance. 'Is that all she said?'

He nodded.

'I expect she'll be more explicit when it suits her.'

Thomas knew about the quest to fetch back the Cross of Constantine that had sent Hildegard to Tuscany over a year ago. Perhaps he suspected the prioress had yet another mission for her along the same lines, but if he did he was tactful enough not to probe any further.

He could not help adding one thing, however. 'If you feel you need an escort at any time, Brother Alcuin will give me permission. I'd be glad to accompany you.' A disarming smile lit up his features. 'Alcuin is less troubled by the strictures of the Rule than Abbot de Courcy. He lacks the abbot's ruthless sense of purpose. We're enjoying his easy-going rule while we can, expecting to pay for it a hundredfold when the abbot returns from Jerusalem. Meanwhile,' he looked hopeful, 'if I can be of any assistance, I am yours to command.'

'You missed your vocation, Thomas. You'd make an admirable knight. I may yet call on you. If the prioress really does have some errand for me, I shall be glad of your presence.' They exchanged warm smiles but just then Hildegard happened to glance out of the window to where the newcomers had appeared.

They had gone to sit on a bench in the yard and were turned slightly away from each other, the silent one staring at the ground from under her hood while kicking at a stone with the toe of her boot. Her companion, hair shaken free to catch the sunlight, had broken off one of the briar roses and was holding it to her nostrils with evident pleasure at the scent.

Hildegard stood up. 'No doubt I shall discover in good time why the prioress has seen fit to send me a couple of guests without warning! I'd best attend them.'

When Thomas left he was carrying a bundle wrapped in cheesecloth for his brothers, and something for himself to eat on the ride back, and had strung the two ponies together the better to lead them. Hildegard, accompanied by her hounds, Duchess and Bermonda, walked with him as far as the domain gate. A few yards after starting down the lane he turned in the saddle to raise a hand in farewell and was soon out of sight.

By now the sun hung like a bloodied orange behind the topmost branches of the trees. When Hildegard turned back she could see the grange at the head of the dale. The tumbled buildings shimmered as the sun's rays sparkled on the shards of feldspar within the stones. From the kitchen chimney a thread of smoke crawled into the luminous sky. She paused with one hand on the gate as a figure clothed in white drifted outside and knelt among the herbs. The frail and yearning cries of the sheep floated from the upper pasture.

Unexpectedly she was moved by a feeling of happiness.

After everything that had happened since her knight-at-arms husband had gone missing in the French wars nearly ten years ago, she suddenly realised she had managed to find a haven and a purpose at last.

This is home, she thought with a start of joy. Peace, beauty, order. A refuge in a world gone mad with violence, with schism and with blood-feud.

She made her way back at a leisurely pace towards the house with her hounds ghosting through the arching stems of barley grass at her feet. Languidly content, she followed them along the bank of the stream where glistening buds of anemones and wild garlic grew. She would go back to the house now and see what more she could do for her guests.

Chapter Two

Agnetha was busy in the kitchen when she entered. The remains of two boiled eggs and some crumbs of bread were on the table. Petronilla was standing beside her regaling her with some story or other, but she stopped when Hildegard appeared and turned, as if caught doing something wrong.

Her cloak was thrown carelessly over the bench and she hurried to retrieve it. She was wearing a linen shift in a pretty shade of blue over a white undergarment with fashionably long sleeves that she had looped up, bunching them over her elbows as if she was about to set to work. It was a most stylish effect as she probably realised.

Agnetha gave Hildegard a wide smile. 'Just in time, Sister. Petronilla is going to show me how they make pastry at her father's great house over the other side of Galtres Forest.'

'Really? Well I won't interfere, then,' said Hildegard, keeping the smile off her face. The prospect of anybody teaching Agnetha anything about pastry was amusing, it was yet another of her practical skills, but before she could turn to address the silent girl, Petronilla interrupted.

'Well, of course they don't make pastry now,' she said. 'They don't make anything. The whole place is gone to wrack and ruin. It's probably crawling in weeds with rats in every chamber, now that father has died and my ridiculous guardian has stepped in. But that's what it used to be like. It was very grand before that foolish man ran it into the ground. I wonder–'

'I should like to hear more about that,' Hildegard broke in. 'Perhaps when you've finished helping Agnetha she'll spare you for a few minutes and you can come to my little chamber across the hall to tell me about it?'

She bent to the more silent of the two. 'Meanwhile, let me show you where you're going to sleep, my pet. Did you bring any belongings with you?'

The girl nodded and produced a small bundle from inside her cloak. Hildegard recognised the cloth as a spare from Swyne. It seemed that the child had arrived with nothing of her own except what was inside the bundle.

Without speaking she followed Hildegard obediently into the hall.

'Your name, my little one?' she asked when they were alone.

The girl mumbled something, then cleared her throat, which had become gruff, and mumbled it again.

Hildegard bent closer. 'Maud, did you say?'

The girl nodded under her hood with her glance fixed to the floor.

'Then come with me, Maud, and we'll find you a comfortable corner of your own. That must have been a long, hard ride from Swyne, especially in this hot weather.'

Again the girl made no reply but, head bent,

followed in Hildegard's footsteps up the wooden stairs.

'A perfect summer's day!' exclaimed Cecilia as she came outside to join the others after finishing her morning chores. The nuns had been working hard since prime and had stopped now in the heat of the day to sit under the trellis to eat some bread and cheese.

'No promise of rain tomorrow,' agreed Sister Marianne, passing a platter to her. 'It's getting serious.'

They were all well aware that in many parts of the county cattle were dying, people were succumbing to a strange falling sickness and the wandering preachers were predicting the end of the world as usual. Even here in the dale, despite the lush grass on the banks of the stream, the meadow was beginning to look parched and they were starting to worry about the crops. Most evenings now they were forced to fetch water from the stream to feed the plants in the kitchen garden.

'It'll be a good thing when Dunstan gets the sheep away to summer pasture,' remarked Hildegard.

They sat in silence for a while. A shrike was heard in the woods. A fox barked.

The two girls were visible over the picket fence bordering the garden. Petronilla's lips were moving but she was too far off for her words to be audible.

When it was clear no one else was going to bring the subject up Agnetha flung out her arms and exclaimed, 'So? What are we to make of them?' She turned to Hildegard. 'What do you think, Sister?'

Hildegard shook her head. She had had a word with Petronilla but had only learnt all over again about the guardian from whom she had absconded.

'And the heiress is serious about joining us?' asked Marianne sceptically. She was the eldest of the four, sold into the nunnery when she was nine but, it seemed, with no regrets.

'She's a puzzle, isn't she?' Agnetha commented.

Hildegard was quiet while the three others speculated on the nature of the guardian who had presumably tried to marry her off in order to increase his own fortune. It would be the old story, they agreed. A headstrong young girl coming into a sudden inheritance and resenting being told what to do with it. No doubt such wealth represented ribbons and fine clothes. Not the sober prospect of marriage to a probably older man, a widower even, followed by the task of running his household and bearing his children.

'Maybe she imagines we're like the Gilbertines at Watton,' mused Marianne. 'She'll expect to be able to take a little lapdog into mass and play the lady. If she thinks that she'll have another thing coming if she stays at Swyne.'

'Or with us,' murmured Agnetha. 'We're not living out here in Deepdale for that.'

Hildegard let them talk without contributing anything. It was little Maud who worried her.

Neither girl, it transpired, had ever been to York,

the great capital of the North.

Both of them had emerged a few minutes later from the kitchen garden with full baskets to join everyone else under the vine trellis. The bread and cheese were passed around and beakers refilled with small ale.

At first the conversation dwelt on matters to do with the grange, but when somebody mentioned York and the forthcoming Corpus Christi pageant to be held there Petronilla announced that her father's lands had been miles from any interesting town, let alone York, the greatest city in the world.

'...excepting possibly Jerusalem,' she added. 'I have, in fact, ventured as far as London, a very fine place, too, in its way. It was when I was ten. Father took me to see the coronation of King Richard.'

She described how she had been held up above the heads of the crowd so she could have a better view. 'So close,' she said, 'I could almost touch the king's robes as he went by. He was such a beautiful boy, all dressed in white silk and jewels and riding a little white horse caparisoned in gold and silver. He was dazzling! And, in fact,' she lowered her voice as if to impart a secret, 'we were so close to the king that a man standing next to us caught one of the gold leaves that the four maidens in the towers threw down as he passed underneath the arch. And he gave it to me! I have it still. Or had,' she corrected, 'but sadly I had to leave it behind when I fled.'

She turned to Maud. 'Have you ever been to London, Maud?'

Maud shook her head.

In a tone clearly showing she judged herself more interesting than anyone else Petronilla continued, 'Of course, at that time I was a mere child and I–'

'Seven years ago,' Hildegard interrupted, 'so that makes you seventeen, the same age as the king himself?' Her expression was enigmatic.

'Not quite. His birthday's at Epiphany and mine isn't until midsummer's day.'

'Soon, then.'

Petronilla looked thoughtful but before Hildegard could say anything else she started up again. 'To have witnessed such a magnificent spectacle as the coronation,' she continued in awed tones. 'Fountains running with wine, the beautiful boy-king, the rapturous cheering of the crowds, that's something that has impressed itself on my mind for ever!'

She paused for breath, but before her audience could contribute anything she was off again. 'I tormented myself over how I could ever become queen of England. It seemed hopeless. I was in complete despair! What chance did I have, hidden in my moated grange! It was a living death! To die unknown and unseen! That's when I determined to make my escape as soon as I was old enough and–'

'So that's why you ran away!' Agnetha broke in with a kind smile, 'not to escape your guardian but to become queen of England? It's a pity, then, about Anne of Bohemia!'

Petronilla's eyes flashed for a moment but then she burst into peals of laughter, along with every-

31

one else. 'It does sound ridiculous now, I grant you! But I was only…' she hesitated, 'I was only … I was only ten, don't forget. I knew nothing. I was far too young to know it would be impossible–'

'And now I suppose you know everything, you scamp.' Agnetha gave the air of rescuing her. She seemed to have taken a liking to her, despite her vanity.

Hildegard studied her carefully. The girl was never seventeen.

Maud, as usual, admitted to very little.

They returned to the original question.

No, she had never been to York.

An animal suddenly shrieked from the undergrowth. She gave a little jump and a cry of alarm escaped her. Hildegard patted the back of her hand. 'It's nothing,' she reassured her. 'A fox finding its midday repast. Aren't you used to the countryside?'

She didn't reply.

'I thought perhaps you might have always lived in a town, where sounds are more human and familiar?' Hildegard persisted.

Maud shook her head. With an effort she muttered something about being used to the country.

Petronilla interrupted again. 'We're miles from anywhere. That's why we were sent here. But I still expect my guardian to come crashing after me with his men-at-arms. He's bound to track me down. But if he does I shall tell him I won't go with him. I want to stay and be a nun. You'll support me in this, Sister, I trust?'

'I will indeed if that's your honest desire,'

replied Hildegard.

It was going to take time to get Maud's trust. The poor child was a bag of nerves. Somehow she had brought a sense of unease with her. It was like a dark cloud over Deepdale.

It was true the grange was well hidden.

A path led back down the valley alongside a beck, although the sound of water bubbling over the rocks was inaudible from where they sat. A few miles downstream was a vill surrounded by arable strips belonging to another manor. Then came woodland and after that open countryside and the Vale of York. At the back of the house they had stables, at present without horses, and there were a couple of store-sheds and beyond those the sheep pens. The path crossed the bottom of the meadow and snaked all the way to the cliff at Dale Head and only petered out in the vast desolation of the moors.

Several shepherds lived up there, their own man Dunstan included. They seemed inured to the privations of such inhospitable terrain. Winter and summer alike, the men tended the flocks belonging to different owners, some to the abbey at Meaux, some to Roger de Hutton, yet others to more distant lords. Dunstan, a tall, vigorous fellow with straggly fair hair and far-seeing blue eyes like the rest of the Dalesmen, kept himself to himself. On the rare occasions when he had anything to say to the nuns he stood a few paces off with arms folded across his chest, offering no sign of deference. Two sheepdogs shadowed him wherever he went.

When Hildegard took the tenancy she had been

told that Dunstan had tended sheep in Deepdale all his life, like his father and his grandfather, and even when the buildings had been left derelict for many years he had continued to tend the sheep. By law, of course, the flock belonged to Lord Roger de Hutton who granted rights in the wool crop to Hildegard and her sisters. In essence, however, it was owned by Dunstan. They were well aware of that and let him get on with the job without interference.

Now the shearmen had finished it was time to bring the sheep down to start on the long journey to their summer pasture at Frismersk on the banks of the Humber. They would reach their destination on the first day of July shortly after the feast of Corpus Christi.

Hildegard rose to her feet. 'If you girls have finished your bread and cheese maybe you'd like to come and help me catch some fish for supper?'

The upper waters of the stream lay across a meadow filled with buttercups. When they reached the far side they had to scramble down a grassy bank to the water's edge. Although shallow, the stream ran fast over many-coloured stones. It was so pure they could see right into it. A waterfall cascaded in a noisy slash of white down the limestone crag above. Both girls gave a gasp as they caught sight of it through the trees. Over the centuries the force had worn a smooth basin where fish liked to gather. It was secluded enough for the nuns to use as a bathing pool.

Here, just where the stream narrowed, they set a net from one bank to the other. With trees growing self-coppiced on both sides, the grove was filled with the constant murmuring of wood pigeons.

Petronilla pulled off her boots and slipped her feet into the cold water as soon as the net was set. For once she had stopped talking as if in awe of the serenity of the place. As silent as ever even Maud undid her laces and tugged off her boots, cautiously dangling her toes over the edge of the rock where she was sitting. Her hood was still up. Hildegard waded into the shallows to adjust the net, then went back to sit on the bank beside her.

They sat for some time in silence. The echoing grove enwrapped them in a drowsy cocoon.

Hildegard opened her eyes. The grove was filling with shadows. She realised she must have fallen asleep.

Maud was trailing a stick in the water and Petronilla was standing knee-deep in the pool trying to catch fish in her cupped palms. The choirs of birds had fallen silent. A flock of starlings rose abruptly with a beating of wings and flew off.

Hildegard gave a quick glance round. There was something amiss. It made her skin prickle. Torn between the desire to stay where she was and a sense of unease she got up to investigate. Now the birds had flown the silence of the grove seemed strangely ominous.

A swift inspection revealed nothing alarming so she scrambled to the top of the bank. The grange lay on the far side of the meadow. It glimmered peacefully in the afternoon sun.

Then she noticed a glint of something close to one of the barns. As she watched it flashed again. There were several horses in the yard. It was the winking of sunlight off the buckles of their harnesses that had caught her eye. Of their owners there was no sign.

Before she could move she heard a burst of shouting from the direction of the house. It was followed by a distant crash. A man came running outside. He crossed the yard. Deciding she had better take a closer look she slid down the bank to retrieve her boots. Maud scrambled to her feet in alarm when she noticed her haste.

'Stay here,' Hildegard told her. 'We have visitors. I'm going up to see who it is.'

Maud didn't reply but she was already thrusting her wet feet inside her boots.

Hildegard climbed back up the bank to the meadow. More shouting became audible. One of the voices was Agnetha's. The one that answered was male. To Hildegard's alarm a plume of smoke suddenly rose from the hay loft above the stable.

A second man appeared. He came from inside the house. Sunlight glinted off the sword he carried. By now flames were beginning to shoot from the roof of the stable in thickening plumes. Hildegard's first thought after the shock of seeing an armed man in their yard was, thank heavens we have no horses. Her second was for her hounds. They were both chained inside to keep them out of harm's way when the flock came down. She began to run.

Petronilla, barefoot, was scrambling up the

36

bank behind her and gave a shriek.

Hildegard glanced over her shoulder. 'Get back into the trees!' she ordered. 'Stay out of sight until I tell you to come out!' Bunching the hem of her habit in both hands, she started to sprint across the meadow towards the barn.

She had just reached the kitchen garden when a man appeared between the standing canes of beans. As soon as he saw her he took long strides to bar her way. In the moment it takes to assess danger she noticed a mail shirt under his black linen tunic and something white at his throat. He wore a leather casque with a guard over his nose concealing the upper part of his face, the lower part hidden by a thick heard. In his hand he, too, carried a sword.

Through the slits in the casque his eyes appeared bright but without warmth or welcome. 'Who the hell are you?' he demanded without any preamble.

'More to the point, who are you?' she answered tartly.

He forced her to a halt. 'Are there any more of you?'

'What's it to you?'

He raised his sword. 'I don't like your manner...'

She stepped back. 'I'm not keen on yours either. What are you doing on our property?'

Out of the corners of her eyes she realised that the bean canes had been broken and the plants, so carefully tended, now lay in tangled heaps. Rage surged through her. But her focus remained warily on the knight.

37

He continued to wave his sword about, barring her way, so she sidestepped, taking him by surprise, and ran on briskly into the yard. She knew he had followed her when she felt something snag at her skirt. Before she could turn she was jerked to a stop, but finding that the stranger was trying to drag her back towards the garden she kicked him with the back of her heel under his knee cap. He was not wearing greaves and the blow made him flinch away with an oath, but he regained the initiative by grabbing the front of her habit and spinning her round to face him.

'You nuns don't eat enough,' he growled, running his hands over her body while she tried to struggle out of his clutches, 'there's no meat on you.' He brought one hand up and ripped her head covering to one side, then gave a smirk. 'Norse, are you?' His own hair was as black as Whitby jet. 'I like the look of your lips,' he muttered bringing his face close to hers.

Hildegard brought her hand up to the white neckerchief protruding from under his black beard with the idea of getting a grip on it, but before she could grab hold of it he jerked back. A silver emblem on a chain round his neck slid through her fingers as he uttered a snarl and hit her on the side of the head with the flat of his hand. She turned with the blow and ducked under his outstretched arm.

There was a shout from the direction of the orchard. It was accompanied by a roaring sound like a continuing rumble of thunder. Another stranger appeared pursued by a swarm of bees. Evidently noticing the smoke billowing through the door of the barn where his companion must have set fire to the hay store, he veered towards it and threw himself inside. The bees, stalled in their rage by the clouds of smoke, changed direction and vanished in a whirring cloud towards the woods.

Momentarily forgetting Hildegard, the knight gave a bellow of laughter. 'You sot-witted bastard! Why the hell did you touch the bloody hives?'

The man cautiously reappeared in the doorway, coughing and smacking at himself, but instead of replying he merely raised one hand and pointed silently towards the cliff with his mouth dropping open.

From the lip of the ridge the first of the sheep was starting to cascade down the side of the hill towards the grange. The whole flock began to follow. It looked like cream spilling over the rim of a jug. Ever faster and more furious, the sheep kept on coming and within moments the entire yard was engulfed by a sea of rams and ewes and their terrified yearlings.

Hildegard skidded for shelter behind the barn and watched as the yard filled. Soon the stampeding animals were packed tight. They were the long-legged black-faced sheep of the high moor. No harmless pets, they were used to defending themselves against predators and stood waist-high, the rams wielding huge curled horns that could batter a man to the ground.

There were three intruders, she noticed now, and they were caught helplessly in the tide of sheep. The one that had been standing in the relative safety of the barn door had been forced out by the smoke and now he was knocked to the ground, disappearing under the sharp hooves of the seething mass until his companions forced a way through the flock to his aid. It was only with an effort that they were able to haul him to safety by pulling him up by both arms. They dragged him to his feet and set about struggling free of the flock of sheep.

The noise was deafening. It set the intruders' horses into a panic. Bucking and snorting, they fled and in moments had vanished among the trees.

With a curse the knight in black ordered his men to get off after them. All three struggled as best they could towards the boundary fence, but the entire flock swept on, taking the men with it, running on down the side of the beck into the woods with Dunstan's collie dogs yipping at their heels and Dunstan himself striding along with grim purpose in their wake.

The stable loft was well alight by now. Still chained, Duchess and Bermonda were dimly visible through a haze of smoke when Hildegard entered. She had no option but to run under the burning roof timbers that supported the hayloft to reach them. Wisps of flame fell like feathers over her shoulders. The hounds were rigid with fear. As soon as she slipped their chains, Duchess gripped Hildegard's hem in her jaws and bounded for the open door with little Bermonda scurrying after them.

Hildegard ran her hands over their coats as

soon as they were safe outside. There was a smell of burning dog hair. As she straightened, the grain store erupted and brought the whole roof down in a great roar of flame.

Agnetha appeared round a corner of the house. She looked aghast at the blazing barn. Her hair was awry and she had a cut on her forehead. With a cry she ran to Hildegard and gripped her by the arms. 'Thank Mary in heaven you're safe!'

'Who were they?' Hildegard demanded.

Cecilia and Marianne emerged from the house. They looked equally dishevelled. Smoke came from inside the kitchen behind them and the roof beams were smouldering. 'Have you seen what those devils have done?' Cecilia marched over to Hildegard, and instead of being frightened as she might well have been, she was in a fury of indignation. 'They've smashed the hives, uprooted the plants, pulled the doors off their hinges and even ransacked your chest in your little chamber, Hildegard. We couldn't stop them!'

Marianne was fingering a large bruise on her cheek. 'They've wrecked everything they could lay their hands on!' she confirmed. 'Every crock, every pot, every pan. All smashed to smithereens because they couldn't find who they were looking for!'

Hildegard went cold. 'Petronilla?'

The women glanced at each other.

Agnetha stepped forward. 'I'm afraid they were after Maud.'

Chapter Three

When the men first appeared their leader had been all smiles, telling the nuns that he only had the welfare of his little kinswoman at heart, but when they failed to offer her up he ordered his men to search the place, if necessary to turn it inside out.

'They even dragged the mattresses off the beds and stabbed their swords into the corn bins,' Marianne said in a disgusted tone. 'As if she could have been hiding there!'

'Did any of them wear livery?' Hildegard asked.

The women shook their heads.

Hildegard recalled the emblem on a silver chain worn by the knight in black. It was like ones worn by the barons' retainers but she couldn't place the symbol. 'At least you're safe. And it was lucky the sheep came down just then,' she added.

Agnetha shook her head. 'It wasn't luck. It was Dunstan's quick thinking. He was on the ridge and when he heard me shout he realised something was wrong. The flock had already been gathered and he just told his dogs to run the whole lot down at once. When he followed them he said he'd block the dale end to prevent the men coming back – although,' she added, 'I doubt whether they'll bother to return. I think they were eventually convinced Maud wasn't here.' Despite her words she glanced fearfully towards the woods.

'Did they say anything else?'

'One of them muttered, "All this way for bloody nothing." He was in a fine rage,' Marianne shuddered.

'Dunstan was magnificent,' Cecilia added.

'He saved us.'

It was obvious the women were in shock. Hildegard listened to them go over things again as she poked among the wreckage. They were right, though. Every pot had been smashed. The bench where they sat in the evenings was broken. The vine trellis ripped from its moorings. Plants uprooted. When she looked into the orchard she noticed the upended bee skeps.

Why do that? she wondered. It was sheer malice. Everywhere the air was thick with smoke.

The house itself had taken the worst of the attack and the thatch on the kitchen roof was smouldering. She went across the yard to have a closer look but there seemed nothing they could do to stifle it.

Agnetha followed. 'We emptied the entire water barrel on all the timbers we could reach but it's useless in this weather. Everything's too dry. But then they came back in and stopped us anyway.'

The nearest water source was across the meadow at the stream. The thatch would have to burn itself out. Hildegard brushed her hands over her eyes. It had happened so quickly. She couldn't grasp it all at once.

A sudden thought struck her, however. Ignoring the women's warning shouts she ran inside the house and began to feel her way through the smoke until she reached her small chamber at the end of the corridor. Cecilia had said her chest had been rifled, its contents thrown to the floor. It was true.

Rummaging amongst the debris her fingers closed over a small leather bag and she dragged it from the smouldering ashes. Inside the bag was a missal. Small, with a cover of tooled leather, the text on its vellum pages was written in black and red, the capital letters decorated in gold leaf. It was wrapped in a piece of ancient linen embroidered in one corner with a motif of blue borage flowers. Miraculously both seemed undamaged by the smoke. If she possessed anything precious it was here. She rewrapped the missal in the cloth and briefly pressed her lips to the bundle before clawing her way through the smoke. Outside she gasped in great gulps of fresh air.

Agnetha gave her a sharp reproof. 'That was foolhardy of you.' She, alone of the others, would know why Hildegard had risked entering the burning house.

Avoiding her glance, Hildegard cast a bleak eye over the ruins. Shame stung her. What had happened was her own fault. In her pride she had assumed she could protect her little community. But she had failed. Hubert de Courcy had been right all along. He had objected to her wish to establish a grange in the wilds but had only given in because she had been so insistent. But she was wrong, wrong, wrong. She couldn't protect anyone. Tears stung her eyes.

Miserably she went over to the others. 'Roger de Hutton will have to be told what has happened to his property. We had better return to

Swyne. We'll send a message to Castle Hutton when we reach the priory.'

She felt dazed. A year's work gone in minutes. It was difficult to know what to do next.

'Why don't we have another look to see what we can salvage?' she suggested. 'We have a long walk ahead of us. We'll need food and drink. I'll go and fetch the girls. Maud has some explaining to do.'

Grim-faced, she set off across the meadow.

She reached the bank overlooking the pool. There was no sign of the girls. Then she noticed a bush stir and scrambling down she found them huddled together in a hawthorn brake. When she called they emerged with white faces. Evidently they had risked having a look to see what was going on by climbing to the top of the bank. Now they were both staring with frightened expressions at the burning grange.

Hildegard put a hand on Maud's shoulder. 'So who were they, Maud?'

The girl gave a little shriek and tried to break free but Hildegard gripped her shoulder more firmly. 'Do you know them?'

'I didn't do anything! I didn't!'

'It's all right. Nobody blames you. But we need to know who they are.' Hildegard bent down, but Maud gave a sharp cry and, swivelling on her heels, slithered back down the bank towards the stream in evident panic. Hildegard followed. She caught up with her on the edge of the falls.

For a moment the girl struggled, her hood slipping back to reveal her frightened face be-

45

neath a tightly tied headscarf, but then she kicked out, giving Hildegard a blow on the shins and, almost breaking free, she teetered on the edge of the pool as if to throw herself in. Hildegard managed to grip the back of her kirtle and pull her from the brink.

Raising her voice above the roar of the waters she asked, 'Who are they? You must tell me!'

'Let me go!' Maud shouted above the noise. 'I hate everybody! I want to die!'

'I'm sorry you hate us,' Hildegard panted, still gripping hold of the struggling girl, 'we don't hate you–'

'You would if you knew!' she shouted, red-faced.

'Knew what?' demanded Hildegard.

'Nothing...' the girl mumbled, suddenly backing away with her eyes wide with fear.

'What do you think's going to happen to you? You can trust us.' Maintaining her grip, yet seeing the fear in the girl's eyes, Hildegard spoke as gently as she could above the roar of the falls. 'Tell me, Maud,' she insisted, her voice dropping further with compassion. 'We have to know who they are and what they wanted you for, otherwise we can do nothing to help. Whatever it is you are surely forgiven.'

At her tone Maud drew in her breath, and when she realised that Hildegard was not going to loosen her grip she began to weaken. She stifled a sob. Soon harsh, dry sounds were being forced from her throat, but she did not speak even now and her eyes remained dry, as if the depths of her grief could not be plumbed. She stared fixedly into the trees as if willing herself elsewhere.

Hildegard put a sheltering arm round her shoulders. 'My dear little Maud, you're safe with us. You know that. We'll do everything we can to protect you.' She felt the hollowness of this remark in the circumstances but could think of no other way to comfort the child. 'It's best if you tell us what you know so that those men can be found and punished.'

'Nobody will punish them,' the girl muttered. 'They're protected by a great lord. They told us so. I know they won't be punished.' There was anger as well as heartbreak in her voice.

Hildegard walked her safely away from the water's edge. 'Why would they follow you, Maud? What possible reason could they have?'

Maud scrubbed at her face with her knuckles. More coaxing and the obvious fact that Hildegard was not going to give up without some sort of explanation elicited a small, wounded voice. 'They'll be the men who destroyed our manor,' she began. 'I don't know where they came from.'

'Destroyed your manor?' Hildegard repeated.

'They rode into our vill and destroyed it the way they've destroyed your grange.'

'Did you hear them use any names?'

'They all called their leader "my Lord". He seemed to think he was the king because he said to our fathers when they objected, "Do as I say. You're nothing but bondmen and bondmen you'll remain!"'

Those were the words King Richard was reputed to have said when the rebels were hanged

47

at St Albans after the Great Revolt.

'And where did they come from, do you think?' Hildegard asked in a careful tone.

'They said they came from far away – and that they were loyal liegemen – unlike our fathers who...' Her voice dropped to a whisper, her words trailing away to nothing.

Hildegard wrapped her cloak round her despite the hot day. The girl was shivering violently. 'And then what happened?' she encouraged.

'They said they'd come to put matters right for the barons, then they took our fathers and uncles out of the fields and made them stand on the green and they pretended to have a trial.' She buried her face in the folds of her cloak and her shoulders shook.

'Go on, my pet,' Hildegard encouraged when her sobs abated a little.

With difficulty and with many hesitations, Maud whispered, 'After that they marched them down the lane away from the cottages and set the thatch on fire, and we thought they'd march them back again but one of the men rode back by himself and ... and he was laughing and he said, "They won't be rebels now!" And then he told us they'd been strung up – as food for crows–'

She stopped suddenly and Hildegard wrapped her cloak more closely about her.

But Maud had not finished her story yet. 'The other men came back. There were six of them.' The words seemed to stick in her throat again and she was unable to continue.

Eventually Hildegard was forced to ask, 'When the men came back, Maud, my pet, did they harm your mothers?'

Maud nodded. Her eyes moistened and then suddenly the dam broke and she burst into a flood of tears.

'And the rest of you?' Hildegard asked after a long time, when the child had cried her heart out. 'Did they harm you, Maud?'

She nodded then clung to Hildegard as if she would never let go. Eventually in a stifled voice she said, 'They killed my little brother. They cut him with their swords and killed him because he threw a stone at them to make them go away.'

'How old was your brother?'

'Five.'

Hildegard held the child and rocked her to and fro. It would be useless to show weakness when she was all the child had left.

When she could Hildegard rose to her feet, keeping a fold of her robe round Maud's shoulders. 'Thank you for telling me what happened. These men with their so-called lord must be caught and punished whoever they are.'

Maud was silent.

'Where exactly is your manor, my pet? Do you know its name?'

'It's near Pentleby.'

A long way from here, over beyond Doncaster. Gaunt's country.

Hildegard took her by the hand and together they climbed back up the bank. Petronilla, white-faced, was still waiting for them.

It was late now, the end of what should have been another perfect summer's day, with the sun descending in a ball of flame. It sent fingers of shadow across the meadow into the woods. Under the trees everything was reduced to darkness. An eerie silence pervaded the place now that the sheep had left the upper pasture. The fires had almost burnt themselves out and, standing in a mound of ash, only the blackened timbers of the house and barn remained with a faint glow from the dying embers.

When Hildegard and her two silent charges rejoined the others she told them they would leave as soon as they were ready. First, though, she had something to say.

The question uppermost in her mind was this. Why would a group of armed men pursue with such venom the daughter of a bonded labourer? It made no sense at all.

Chapter Four

Night fell. They were ready to leave.

After a quiet word with Maud, Hildegard briefly told everyone what had befallen her to turn her into a runaway. There was a stunned silence when she finished, then, one by one, the women gave the girl a hug. 'Now we know what we're facing we'll stand together,' Agnetha said for them all. 'They will not get away with it. You're safe with us.'

Before they set off Hildegard went back into the herb garden where the lovingly tended cures had been trampled into the dust. Now, in the blue haze of evening, she grubbed among the stems to find some of the leaves she might need. Stowing them safely in her scrip she returned to the others. 'Let's go,' she said.

So it was, under cover of darkness, the small community made its way along the ridge above the woods and out of the dale by a secret route, leaving the charred desolation of Deepdale behind. The hounds coursed through the trees on both sides as they stepped out. The two girls gripped each other's hands and all but trampled on Hildegard's heels in their eagerness not to be left behind, while the two nuns followed, Agnetha staunchly taking up the rear. They walked for some time in a wary silence. A half-moon slid little by little across the sky.

Eventually the rounded hills and sheltering dales of the North Riding lay behind them. Ahead came the flat land, ghostly under the vast sky of Holderness. The summer night had a silver quality. The faces of the women seemed luminous in the strange light. When they came to a fork in the path it was only faintly visible, a deceptive shadow in the undergrowth. One path dwindled in the direction of Swyne. The other disappeared into the west.

Hildegard prepared herself for what she was about to say. She knew there would be opposition.

'Let's stop here a moment.' She glanced round the group as they gathered. Their expressions were faintly visible in the gloaming. 'I want you four, Agnetha, Cecilia, Marianne and Petronilla, to go on to Swyne. You must tell the full story of

51

what's happened to the prioress. I'm going to go on to York with Maud and–'

'No!' To her surprise it was Maud who objected first. 'They'll put me in a prison! I won't go!' She turned as if to run off but Petronilla caught hold of her by the sleeve.

'Don't go running off again. You'll be putting yourself in danger, you goose. Listen to what Sister Hildegard has to say.' She held onto her and announced, 'No wonder she wears her hood up to hide from God. She's frightened He'll find her and punish her after what's happened.' She shook Maud by the arm. 'You'll be safe in York, goosey. And anyway, God isn't angry with you.'

'I hope she's not blaming herself for what those devils did,' said Marianne briskly. She went over and took Maud by the hand. 'I'm sure God doesn't blame you. Maud. You couldn't have done anything against armed men, my dear.' She gave her a little hug. 'Now, why don't you do as Sister Hildegard says? She'll put things right for you when you get to York.' The nun lifted her head and gave Hildegard an apologetic shrug as she met her eye and added, 'I know she'll do what she can.'

Agnetha spoke up. 'Of course you should go with Sister Hildegard, Maud. The sheriff must be told. These men have to be caught and punished. But,' she turned to Hildegard, 'it's a mad idea to go off by ourselves. I'm coming with you.'

'I'd like to come too,' Cecilia broke in.

'If it comes to it, so would I!' Marianne stepped forward.

'I can't give you permission to remain outside

the priory,' Hildegard pointed out. 'You'll be in trouble from Brother Alcuin if he hears you've been running about the countryside without his warrant–'

'I'm free to do what I like,' Agnetha interrupted. 'I haven't taken any vows yet. And I'd like to see anybody try and stop me coming with you. You included,' she added for good measure, giving Hildegard a strong glance.

Petronilla broke in. 'I'd like to go to York as well. If the prioress thought I was in danger at Swyne where the priory is unprotected from the ravages of men-at-arms, then I'd be safer at York, inside the walls where the bailiff's men will look after us.'

Hildegard frowned. What she said was true. 'But you, Cecilia,' she put a hand on her arm, 'I really believe you should go back to Swyne with Marianne. She'll need a companion on the way.'

'I'll do whatever everyone thinks best. I'm more than willing to defy the abbot's stand-in and come with you. Bless Brother Alcuin,' she added to soften her defiance.

Hildegard shook her head. 'You're courageous to make such an offer but you both have to live with the consequences. Don't make difficulties for yourselves. And someone needs to give a good account of events to the prioress.'

It was agreed. After an emotional farewell they started to move off in separate directions. Petronilla watched the two nuns set out on the track to Swyne, then turned to Hildegard. 'And I'm with you?'

She got a brief nod in reply. Why not? Hildegard thought. What the girl had just said about safety was probably true. Better to be inside the town walls where some sort of law prevailed than outside at the mercy of any armed horsemen who came along.

Accompanied by the two hounds, the four set off into the dark west, while behind them the two dressed in white headed towards Swyne and the thin line of expanding scarlet where the sun was beginning its ascent into another cloudless sky.

It was mid morning when they stopped in a glade in the woods to finish off some bread and cheese. Everything tasted of smoke. Because the weather was so hot, they all but drained a flask of ale with a broken stopper that Hildegard had carried carefully upright in a corner of her scrip ever since they set out. The path they were on led through thick woodland, well hidden from pursuers, but even so Petronilla was all for going on without delay. She fretted and fumed at the delay and jumped at the slightest sound. When a rabbit scuttled out of the undergrowth at her feet she gave a little scream. 'I won't feel safe until we're in among the crowds of the city,' she exclaimed with a dramatic shiver. 'Oh, Sister, I think we're done for!'

Agnetha rolled her eyes.

'No one has followed us.' Hildegard's tone was sharp. The silly girl was frightening Maud with her dramatics.

They walked on. Eventually Hildegard felt a tug on her sleeve. It was Petronilla again. 'Sister,' she began, 'may I ask something of a personal nature as we walk along?'

Despite her sombre mood Hildegard's lips puckered. 'I don't see why not.'

'It's this. May I ask, do you believe in angels?'

Hildegard frowned. 'It's an ancient and commonly held belief,' she replied cautiously.

Petronilla's eyes were fixed on hers. 'Some people believe that everyone has an angel to guard their body and soul,' she continued. 'And I'm told there are hierarchies of angels just as there are hierarchies of people.' She paused. 'I'm also told that archangels are the ones who carry out God's will and lesser angels exist to perform minor tasks for us in everyday life.'

'Yes, I've heard that too.' Hildegard was non-committal.

'But,' Petronilla went on importantly, 'as well as being helpers in a kindly way, angels also punish us. That's right, isn't it?'

'So some people say.' Wondering where this was leading, Hildegard would go no further than that.

Petronilla continued, 'Angels have work to do like everyone else in the world and when they see someone break the laws of compassion and respect they calmly and without any anger chastise the transgressor to help them become better people.'

'That's another common belief.' Hildegard led the way down a short incline between the trees with Petronilla, Maud and the two hounds jostling at her heels, but Petronilla caught up with her and began to trot by her side.

'Sometimes,' she continued, 'their punishment

55

is so harsh it takes the form of death, or so I'm told. After that the evildoer has to go down into hell where their impure soul is cleansed by the most horrible fires to make it ready to return to the world of humans. The hope is that it can live a better life than the one it forfeited. The angels,' she continued, as if having learnt the words by rote, 'are the true protectors of our souls. By their help we can attain the reward of everlasting joy in the heavenly paradise that awaits.'

When Hildegard made no comment she turned to Maud who was still following close behind and said, 'So you do see, don't you, my dear little Maud – there's no need to plan revenge on those violent men as I'm sure you would like to and as I most certainly would – because the angels will do it for you. That is their law. They punish evildoers. And no one can escape their terrible vengeance.'

Maud, her hood still up, walked on in silence.

At last they came out on a rise where the trees had been felled and the path led down into a wide dale with a river running through it. There were other signs of settlement: an enclosure, empty of kine, the distant barking of a dog, the scent of woodsmoke. Hildegard told them she guessed they were less than a mile from York, in a place called Two Mills Dale.

This was proved when they came across the first of the mills on the other side of a narrow causeway. It was now nothing more than a derelict hulk and was separated from the path they were on by a marsh meadow, incongruously bright for so melancholy a place, with kingcups, purple flag and bogwort among the bulrushes.

The mill had clearly been unused for many years, its roof partly caved in, the vanes rotted, broken paddles hanging askew, and the great wooden wheel itself looking as if it would never turn again. It hung half under the water, the surface of the millpond covered by a thick skin of duckweed.

Everyone seemed to feel ill at ease. Petronilla made little shuddering sounds, Maud increased her pace and even Agnetha looked warily across as if expecting something monstrous to emerge from the slime. Hildegard tried to allay their uneasiness with a story she had heard based on fact not fantasy.

Many years ago, she told them, the abbot of that time had built a new mill lower downstream. It was closer to the vills owned by the lord of the manor than this one. Soon the abbot's miller was in competition with the one employed by the manor lord. A dispute arose as to who was the best miller. Eventually the miller here had been put out of business. Now nobody even remembered his name. All anyone knew these days was the abbot's miller at Low Mill.

'An example of sharp practice if you ask me. I'm glad it wasn't one of our abbots who ruined his trade.' Agnetha cast a glance over her shoulder as they left the derelict mill behind.

Soon a pleasant and well-ordered domain came into view further on. It was a prosperous-looking sunlit mill house with seven geese in the yard, a thatch-haired child playing with a stick among a brood of contented hens and, from somewhere within the house, the sound of a woman singing. The regular clack-clack of the wheel as it creaked round and the pleasant and continuous splashing of water falling from the turning paddles added to the sweet harmony of the scene. For a moment Hildegard felt a twinge of longing for a life that could never be hers before quickly reminding herself that the longing to have what others have is a sin for good reason.

A short time after this they emerged from the woods and, at last, on the far side of a stretch of common land, they saw the great stone walls of York.

Chapter Five

The common was on a flood plain where the grass was still long despite the drought. Butter-cups and cowslips grew in profusion. Weeping willows sprouted on the riverside. Clustered right up against the city walls were the countless small encampments set up by the travellers arriving from different parts of the country to celebrate the feast of Corpus Christi and watch the mystery plays that would take place at the same time.

The group from Deepdale followed a well-worn track across this stretch of common land towards the town gate, but they were no more than half-way across when they noticed a small procession heading towards them. Every now and then the heads of the participants were visible between the reeds.

It was a band of children. They were singing a strange dirge in some made-up language and wore odd, flowing garments, bright patches of colour against the green of grass and tree. A boy of eleven or so led the way. Drawing closer they could see that his headgear was a makeshift crown of leaves and he carried a crook or sceptre of hazel tied with blue ribbons. One hand was held out before him displaying a dock leaf like a salver with something resting on it.

The children following were giving all their attention to this strange ceremony and they were almost level before they noticed Hildegard and the rest of them on the same path. The boy stopped and signalled to his followers to halt. The dirge dwindled into silence.

In an artificially deep voice the boy declaimed, 'Sisters, I am your lord archbishop. Bow down before the Host. In my hand I bear the body of Christ, and this holy servant,' he poked the child behind him with his crook, 'bears a monstrance containing a drop of the blood of our dear Lord Jesus.'

With a solemn expression the second child held up a beaker full of a brackish liquid.

'I suppose you're asking for alms?' asked Petronilla.

He shook his head. 'Only bow down.'

Hildegard bit her lip. Either she should chide the boy for sacrilege or she should play the role allotted. She couldn't bring herself to criticise such innocent piety. Nor could she bow before a leaf with what looked like a crust from yesterday's supper on it.

The dilemma was resolved when the boy-bishop bestowed a stately blessing on them all, then processed off followed by his little retinue. The children resumed their singing and disappeared into the long grass, the stalks closing behind them and leaving only a darkening to show where they had trodden them down.

Hildegard gazed after them. No doubts for them about the possibility of the magical transformation of bread into flesh, or pond water into the blood of Christ. The faith of little children was itself magical.

There was a trailing queue of people trying to get through Bootham Bar when they arrived at the north entrance in the city walls. Three or four severed heads stuck on pikes above the barbican gazed into the hidden depths of Galtres Forest.

Guards stood inside the barbican searching everybody for weapons. They were making a slow and thorough job of it. Men had their tunics stripped off and women were asked to lift their kirtles. When their turn came Hildegard gave the man a steely glance. 'Do I look as if I'm armed?' she asked. 'And what about these children and the lay sister – are they armed, do you imagine?'

'I'm only doing my job,' the guard grumbled, eyeing the eating knife Hildegard openly displayed in a sheath on her belt. With a sidelong glance at his companions he hurriedly waved them through.

'I'll go and see if I can stay at my cousin's over

60

near Walmgate,' Agnetha announced once they were inside the town. 'Let me know when you're settled in and if you want me to do anything to help. Where do you intend to stay?'

'We'll try St Clement's. The nuns there are always friendly to travellers from Swyne.'

They parted to go their separate ways.

Hildegard was surprised at the hordes of people pouring in for the festival. She hadn't expected to find the town so busy. Judging by their accents they came from all parts of the county and beyond. It was a far cry from Deepdale.

Here the streets were filled with pedlars and entertainers. Musicians played on every corner, some good, some painful to the ear, and working in among them were jugglers and magicians, fortune-tellers and pardoners, pilgrims visiting St William's shrine in the minster, itinerant healers and quacks, craft masters and apprentice boys in the distinctive colours of their guilds, as well as labourers out of bond, carriers, messengers, mendicant friars, servants, and merchants with their retinues. The town was bursting at the seams.

She bought the girls some hot pasties from a booth and then they made their way through the cacophony of sound to the nunnery on the other side of the river.

The Benedictine nun who watched the door was apologetic. 'I'm sorry, Sister. We haven't an inch of spare room. People started turning up in droves in the middle of last week. We're going to be full until the celebrations are over.' She gave a glance at the two girls standing on either side of

Hildegard. 'All I can suggest is that you try the Sisters of the Holy Wounds. They rarely open their doors to anyone, but I believe even they have decided to allow outsiders in for the duration of the feast.'

She explained how they could find their convent and before Hildegard turned to go she called after her, 'I'm not recommending them, you understand? But it's the only place where you're likely to find room to rest your heads just now.'

With thanks Hildegard led the way back down to the bank of the river. Following her instructions they stayed on the same side and walked on for a good distance while remaining within the walls. Apparently the convent was near the staithe where the barges discharged their cargo before returning to the Humber ports they serviced.

Before they reached the warehouses lining the quay, however, they came to a tall, windowless building with a large wooden crucified Christ dripping red paint set above a porch. There was a grille next to it. When Hildegard tapped on it a suspicious-looking nun peered through the bars.

'Greetings, Sister. We're travellers looking for accommodation–' Hildegard began.

Cold eyes sized her up, took in the two girls, then glared at the hounds. 'No animals.' The door on the other side of the grille snapped shut. Before they could turn away they heard bolts being worked loose and the big double doors ground open.

A crabbed nun appeared from the lodge, ringing a handbell. At its summons a shaven-headed man appeared from an inner recess. He wore the cheap woollen tunic of a convent servant. Hildegard was astonished to find a man within the precincts and wondered if he was a eunuch.

The nun indicated that her hounds should be left in the lodge and then she snapped, 'Follow Matthias. He'll show you to your accommodation.' She retreated to her lodge.

Without a word he led them up a narrow staircase into a stone corridor at the back of the building. Some way along he thrust open a door into a grim-looking dormitory crowded with chattering black-robed nuns. They fell silent when the strangers entered and, as one, turned their backs. As soon as Hildegard and the girls reached the end of the chamber a susurration of whispers started up behind them.

Matthias lifted a wooden beam from its socket and pushed open a further door. A small, square, stone chamber met their gaze. He stepped aside so they could enter.

Piled in a corner on the bare boards was a heap of straw-filled sacks. One small window high up near the rafters let in a trickle of light.

'Is this it?' Petronilla asked in astonishment. She remained in the doorway.

Matthias gave her a dark look and went out.

'I thought he was going to lock us in,' she giggled, coming into the middle of the cell to stand beside Hildegard. Maud stayed where she was.

'We'll make the best of it,' Hildegard told her in a firm voice. 'As soon as we've laid matters before the serjeant-at-law and heard from the prioress we'll be away from here. It shouldn't be more than a couple of nights at most. We can surely survive that!'

'I hope the prioress won't consider sending me back to my guardian.'

'She'll no doubt try to arrange a meeting for you both but she won't force you to leave the priory unless you choose to go. She'll have to wait for a reply from him, of course. Let's hope the courier finds him at home.'

Petronilla looked thoughtful.

After finding their way down to an equally forbidding refectory where they were grudgingly offered thin gruel slopped into wooden bowls, Hildegard settled the girls back in their quarters. Both of them seemed exhausted after their night walk. They dragged the straw pallets out and at once curled up ready to catch up on the sleep they had missed. Hildegard told them she was going into the town to find quarters for her hounds and to send a courier to Castle Hutton informing Lord Roger de Hutton of the destruction of his property. They were asleep almost before she finished speaking.

The first two errands were soon done. Her hounds looked mournful at being left behind in the town kennels but she was forced to harden her heart. Then a courier was dispatched to Castle Hutton. Next she made her way to the office of a serjeant-at-law known to the nuns of Swyne over many years of litigation. He worked from a warren of chambers off Petergate, attended by a couple of clerks. They were scratching away at a pile of documents as she was ushered in. There was a strong smell of sealing wax.

The serjeant listened without comment until she finished speaking. His frown had deepened when she told him about the attack on Deepdale, and his brow furrowed even more when she told him about Maud and her terrible experience at the hands of the same marauding men-at-arms.

'I have to tell you straight off there's little chance of bringing the malefactors to book if they're from outside our jurisdiction. It's beyond my remit.' He avoided her glance.

She understood at once. What he meant was that the men were probably maintained by Gaunt or some other wealthy magnate and it wouldn't be worth trying to get redress if that were the case.

He went on, 'It's best if you leave matters to the lord of the manor the little serf belongs to. It's not our concern what goes on there. He might not want to take the risk of making a complaint, of course.' Maud had either not known or would not tell the name of the landlord, merely saying that he rarely visited the place, leaving everything in the hands of his steward and a reeve, the latter being one of the murdered men.

When Hildegard made it known how unsatisfactory she found this response he agreed. 'The best I can do is send a man to make enquiries. But you can understand the difficulty, Sister. If these devils are maintained by somebody with power in Westminster, or even by one of his followers, it won't be worth your neck to try to get them to court. What was the name of the manor again?'

'Pentleby.'

'Never heard of it.'

'Nor me. It's said to be near Doncaster.'

The man folded his hands on top of his desk. 'The owner of your grange at Deepdale might think the same way about pursuing these fellows, regarding it as the safer option to let sleeping dogs lie, as it were. For all we know the attack might have been the result of a long-running dispute between local families, spilling over into our territory by ill luck.' He paused and frowned. 'You're sure it was the same bunch of malcontents who destroyed your grange?'

'They must be, they said they were looking for Maud.'

'So why on earth should they pursue a bonded maid unless she was one of their own?'

'Exactly my own question.'

'And what reason does the maid herself give?'

'She's still in a state of shock. She merely shakes her head.'

'Manor lords go to extremes when a bonded servant absconds. It's a loss of property. But we need names.' After a pause, he said, 'Whatever the reason for their actions it'll be down to Lord Roger de Hutton to deal with the havoc they've caused at Deepdale. It's his property.'

'I've already sent a messenger to Castle Hutton,' she told him. 'I just wondered if you'd heard anything that could identify them.'

He sighed. 'Too many fellas are being forced to live rough in the wildwood these days. They might be rebels. They might be anybody.' If he had heard rumours of a band on the prowl he was not admitting it.

'And about the runaway ward, Petronilla?' she asked.

'I'll send one of my men to make enquiries about this guardian she mentions, then we can look into her rights. I can't think straight off where it might be she claims to come from. Beyond Galtres, you say? I've not heard tell of any recent deaths out that way, not ones that would lead to a dispute about inheritance, any road. But don't worry. We'll get onto it. How old is she?'

'She claims to be seventeen.'

'Claims?' He raised his eyebrows. 'If she's not of age she'll remain the property of her guardian and he can do with her what he wills.'

'Even marry her against her inclinations.' Hildegard pursed her lips.

The serjeant nodded. 'We can understand, Sister, why these girls become runaways. Their wilfulness isn't always to blame.' He gave a sympathetic smile. 'I have a daughter of my own so I can understand it from both sides. She would certainly object if I was fool enough to insist she marry some old fella twice her age. We'll tread carefully and see how the land lies before we go barging in with both feet.'

Thanking him for this cold comfort, Hildegard took her leave.

She emerged onto the main thoroughfare deep in thought.

With nothing to do now but wait for events to fall into place – the prioress would surely send instructions as soon as Marianne and Cecilia told her what had occurred – she decided it was time to pay a visit to the chandler who had received delivery of their beeswax the previous week.

People filled the streets as busily as ever, but winding her way through the lanes she eventually found herself outside Master Stapylton's chandlery. It lay in one of the many craftsmen's yards off Petergate. She rapped on the door for admittance.

Chapter Six

After the disastrous events of the day before it was a relief to be standing in the well-ordered workshop where the chandler exercised his craft. His premises consisted of a comfortable two-story building – chandlery on the ground floor, living quarters above, wedged between a huddle of similar buildings not far from the minster gates.

The honey scent of beeswax swamped the air. It was heady after the unpleasant odour of burning timbers. Hildegard breathed in with a feeling of pleasure. On all sides of the workshop were graded candles hanging in rows, long, paired tapers, joined at the wick and fresh out of the vat, slung over wooden pegs along the walls to harden; thick stumps of what the Normans called *bougies* ranged on the trestles alongside squat altar candles covered in carving and destined for the guild churches.

'*I want them to have a beam of light,*' she read on one of them as she peered to read the careful lettering that spiralled round the stem.

Some candles were enormous, long and slender as flagpoles, and darkened to deep amber, richly honey-scented. Others were the colour and texture of toffee. Yet others were white and odourless, new wax, not left long in the honey.

Labels were attached to the groups. Bakers, she read. Coopers. Cordwainers. Glaziers. Lorimers. Guild candles ready to be carried by the members in procession on the eve of the vigil before the Feast of Corpus Christi.

At that moment the chandler came breezing into the workshop from an upper chamber, his arms outstretched in greeting, an apprentice at his heels.

'Sister! Well met! I didn't intend to keep you waiting. Do forgive me.' He was all smiles. 'Your beeswax has saved our lives, hasn't it, Stephen?' he exclaimed, cuffing his apprentice on the shoulder. 'I can't thank you enough for sending that consignment, Sister. If I'd failed to supply the guilds my name would have been mud.' He gave her a narrower glance. 'Let me offer you a beaker of wine while we talk business?'

Prepared for a hard bargain, but feeling that she had the upper hand given his desperate straits, Hildegard was glad of the chance to sit down for a moment before the bargaining began.

'You'll be staying for the pageant, then?' Master Stapylton asked as the boy returned with the promised wine.

'Not unless I'm suddenly given dispensation from my prioress. I'm here on another matter.'

He made a sad face. 'You're missing something remarkable. It'll be a good one this year. Lots of special effects. Everybody line perfect or I'll know the reason why! I'm sharing pageant-master duties with Master Danby of the Glaziers' Guild,' he explained with a certain amount of pride. 'In fact,' he added in a confidential tone, 'he'll be coming over himself to inspect my candles for his guild's church any time now. Maybe he'll whet your appetite and you'll find a reason to stay?'

'I wish I could but it's unlikely. At any rate, I'm pleased things are going smoothly for you.' She took a sip of what turned out to be an excellent Rhenish and probably came direct from the shipman with no intercession from the toll keeper. 'I heard you had problems last year with a few rowdies?' she continued in order to make conversation before they got down to business.

Master Stapylton frowned. 'With the feast falling on the anniversary of the Great Rebellion people were a bit edgy last summer. Some of 'em see Corpus Christi as a rallying point in the calendar. But memories are short and this year I believe everybody's set to enjoy themselves in the proper manner.' He chuckled. 'Of course, the archbishop has had his nose put out of joint as usual, but that's the only unpleasantness we've had so far!'

Hildegard raised her eyebrows to encourage him to go on.

'Too secular, not celebrating in the proper

manner! There was talk,' he continued, settling himself, 'to keep the church procession on the day itself, as now, and shift the pageant to the day afterwards, but we're resisting that with all our might. It just wouldn't be the same. It would take the shine off things, in our opinion.'

'I expect you're right. Maybe you can persuade Archbishop Neville to hold the procession the evening before, on the vigil of the feast?'

'That's been mooted but the Church isn't happy about that either. Nor are we. That's when the guilds hold a vigil in their own churches. It brings the members together. Good for our sense of fellowship. Good for the candle trade as well!'

'I expect the Church feels like you do about moving?'

'The truth is we'll just have to jog along in the old way, procession and pageant all ram-bang together. It shouldn't be a problem with a bit of goodwill on both sides.'

'I'm sorry I shan't be here to see it. I never have seen the pageant. It was not much of an event when I was a child.'

'It's all the thing now and quite a sight, what with the lighted torches just before dawn, the first wagon setting up outside Holy Trinity for *The Creation,* and all the rest coming down to the twelve stations round the town. Near on fifty guild wagons are taking part this time. Each with their own play to perform. Finishing at midnight with the greatest spectacle of all, *The Last Judgement.* Magnificent. And to set the seal on it the Host, under its golden canopy, emerges out of the minster in a blaze of light and processes round the streets. You can imagine what state the actors are in by the time it all comes to an end!'

'And the audience as well, I should imagine. Do they follow the wagons round or stay in one place to watch?'

'Some follow their own guilds. The wealthier merchants usually stay put in their stands. They don't want to be pushed about in all the hurly-burly, obviously. The mayor and his aldermen are having a stand erected near Common Hall up past Ouse Bridge.' He leant forward. 'There was talk of young King Richard putting in an appearance this year. We've heard nothing to confirm it, though.' He pulled a face. 'It might be all that trouble in April with the plot against his life that's put him off travelling up here. I heard he sobbed his heart out when he heard what they'd done to that Carmelite who tried to warn him of Gaunt's plotting.'

'Yes, I heard about that. It was a mysterious and terrible business all round. Quite heinous, whoever the perpetrators were.'

'Rumour has it that it was Gaunt's way of warning the king to do as he's told.' He sat back and gave an odd smile. 'Maybe it'll be Gaunt himself to grace us with his presence – if he dare show his face!' He broke off and rumbled somewhat in his throat. 'Well, no disrespect to the duke, of course.' A worried look crossed his face as if suddenly aware that his words might have fallen on the wrong ears.

Hildegard hastened to reassure him. 'They're trying to say that Duke John put down the rebellion in the north less brutally than Justice

Tresilian in the south.' There was a raised inflection in her tone to show that she understood this to be a mere rumour.

'That's what they tell us,' he agreed neutrally. He threw back the last of his wine. 'But this isn't what you're here for, Sister, and I'm keeping you from the rest of your business. As far as I'm concerned the pageant is an excuse to enjoy ourselves and celebrate the sharing of bread and wine.' He gave a jovial if forced smile and refilled their cups. 'Now, to the matter of a price for your beeswax.'

Hildegard was unsurprised by the views the chandler had carelessly revealed. After the Rising three years ago the rebels had been brutally punished, in Yorkshire as well as in the south. It wasn't just Chief Justice Tresilian who had presided over the bloody retribution – hanging and quartering the rebels when they were dragged before him – the Justiciars in the north had put down the rebels here with equal brutality, although individual killings had not been so assiduously recorded. Many people had simply disappeared.

As for the unfortunate Carmelite friar who, this April past, had warned King Richard of a plot against his life allegedly being hatched by the Duke of Lancaster, the king's uncle, John of Gaunt – he had suffered a hideous death as a reward for his warning. Abducted as he left the king's presence he had been tortured by his captors in an obscene way too terrible to speak of and the poor fellow had died several agonising days later as a result. His abductors were known but were too powerful to be brought to account.

Hildegard walked slowly back along the street. By the time she left, the glazier Master Stapylton had mentioned had not turned up, but they had concluded their business in a most amicable and mutually profitable manner.

Despite the troubles he had touched on, York seemed a cheerful place, with a palpable air of excitement in the streets due to the forthcoming celebrations. There was little sign of violence. The suspicion that there would be keenly felt absences, however, was inescapable. Husbands, sons and others had disappeared without trace after the rebellion. Now, three years on, although their places were filled by a town full of visitors, a private sense of loss must be felt by many.

Even though the situation was bleak, Hildegard took some comfort from the business with the chandler. It meant that something had been salvaged from the terrible destruction at Deepdale. She had gold. They might even have enough to start again. Managing to carve a path through the crowds she chanced to find herself at the top of a busy street called Stonegate. There was a small church nearby. Dedicated to St Helen, patron saint of the Glaziers' Guild, its doors were invitingly open. The scent of incense wafted out into the street. Aware that she had missed all the offices of the day since fleeing Deepdale, she was about to enter to offer a prayer to St Helen when a man appeared in the doorway, blocking her entrance.

Evidently he had not noticed her because he

was calling back over his shoulder as he came out. 'Hurry up, Jankin, we don't have all day. De Hutton's steward will be fretting and sending out search parties for us.'

The next moment he turned and stepped forward into the sunlight straight into her path. 'Sister! My apologies,' he exclaimed with a deep flourish. 'I beseech your forgiveness. I didn't see you there. Do come inside.' He stepped back to allow her to enter.

From the doorway she could see the inside of the church ablaze with sunlight pouring in through the stained glass windows. A scatter of jewel-bright colours filled the nave. When she stepped inside and lifted her head she noticed a small square of coloured glass depicting a shield above the inscription: *da nobis tuam lucem domine*. Give us your light, O Lord. It was the glaziers' motto.

The man who had made way for her was still standing at the door and she turned to him. 'Forgive me, master, but I couldn't fail to overhear you mention Lord Roger's steward just now. Am I to understand he's in York at present?'

'Indeed he is. I'm to provide some glass for him. Or rather, for Lord Roger de Hutton's chantry.'

'His chantry?' A look of alarm crossed her face. 'I trust Lady Melisen and her baby are–?'

The glazier gave a reassuring chuckle. 'Thriving, both of 'em. She was in my workshop not a week since, looking at the *vidimus*. No, it's not for the baby Lord de Hutton wants prayers said.' He peered into her face. 'You're acquainted with the steward from Castle Hutton, are you?'

He was clearly impressed when she nodded.

'He's an old friend,' she told him, not going into details. 'I would be honoured if you would give him my greetings when you see him...'

'Better than that,' replied the glazier. 'Come along with me now and tell him yourself. My workshop is just a few steps along the street here.'

He was a genial-looking fellow, expensively dressed in a summer cloak lined with taffeta, the badge of his guild displayed on one shoulder, a silk turban on his head. A little on the stout side, somewhat red-faced, with a coarse-looking beard sprinkled with grey, fastidiously clipped, he now inclined his head. 'Forgive me, Sister. We don't stand on ceremony in this town of ours. Maybe you need permission to mix so freely with us poor sinners?'

'I make up my own mind what I do.' Seeing his startled expression she added, 'Within the Rule, of course. And nothing would please me more than to have a few words with you and the lord steward.'

Now would be a chance to get Ulf by himself and explain what had happened to Lord Roger's property. If she could tell him the full story it might help soften the blow when Roger learnt of it.

'But this chantry?' she continued as they went outside after she had made a hasty offering. 'Is it for the repose of his own soul that Lord Roger's going to such expense?' It was the first she had heard of any such thing. Brother Thomas hadn't breathed a word.

'Sadly no. It's for his father, Earl Robert. He

died this Candlemas past.'

'I'm sorry to hear that. The news hadn't reached us.' She frowned. She knew Roger had been fond of his father, even though the old man, in his nineties, an extraordinary age, had rarely left his castle on the coast up beyond Hartlepool for the last twenty years. To have a chantry built expressed the depth of Roger's sorrow. But it showed the depth of her sequestration in the wilds that no word of it had reached her.

They walked along the street a little way and eventually entered a short alley leading into a yard. They came to a stop outside a house with a glaziers' sign above the door: two crossed grozing irons on a blue ground. They had been followed from the church by a lad with rumpled hair whom Hildegard took to be the master's apprentice. When she saw him in a proper light she judged him to be about twenty; nearing the end, then, of his apprenticeship, with only a year or two to go.

The glazier followed her glance. 'My apprentice, young Jankin,' he confirmed. 'And I'm Master Edric Danby,' he introduced himself, adding proudly, 'Guildmaster.'

A townsman of some standing, then.

'I'm delighted to have a chance to talk to you. We sisters are somewhat starved for news. I didn't realise what an excitement the Corpus Christi pageant was going to be. The crowds are already impressive–'

'And that's Sister Hildegard's voice and quite impressive itself!' called a man's voice from close by. Ulf, Lord Roger's steward, appeared in the doorway of the house, his head bent to avoid hitting it on the lintel. 'What the devil are you doing out of Deepdale?' he demanded with a grin.

'Selling beeswax to Master Stapylton,' she told him, avoiding any mention of the disaster that had really brought her to town until she could talk to him in private. 'But Master Danby has just told me Roger's father died?'

Ulf turned his mouth down. 'Poor old fella. But he had a good run as they say. Roger's cut up, of course, even though he now gets the title.'

As if to make up for being ignored the master glazier made a sweeping gesture with one arm. 'I'd deem it a privilege if you stepped inside, Sister. You may better catch up on events over a mug of wine.'

'And you can cast your eye over the picture Lady Melisen wants the master here to turn into a window,' added Ulf. There was a strange gleam in his eyes which caused Hildegard to guess that something was going on. As Ulf didn't elucidate she prepared herself for the unexpected.

The apprentice followed them inside.

Ulf hasn't changed much, she was thinking as they took their places around a table in the window overlooking the yard.

It had been a year since they had last met and he was still the same affable fellow she had known all her life. Tall and broad-shouldered with an easy loose-limbed way of moving, even as a boy he had the look of somebody who could take care of themselves in any situation. It wasn't surprising he had become Lord Roger's right-hand man. The son of Earl de Hutton's chief

78

forester, he had risen to the rank of steward by sheer ability. The only thing different about him was his forever untidy shoulder-length hair. Bleached by the sun more than ever, it accentuated his tanned complexion and enhanced the ice-blue sparkle of his eyes.

At present he was striding around Master Danby's workshop, poking into everything with the greatest interest. 'So this is the crucible where you work your magic!' he declaimed, straightening and spreading his arms to include the entire workshop. Danby puffed with pride. Ulf peered into some clay pots containing coloured powders ranged along the window sill. 'And this is?' He lifted one of them up.

'Pot metal,' explained Danby. 'We buy in sheets of coloured glass from the Rhineland but paint on it what we wish. That's where the real skill lies – the magic, if you like,' he added with a chuckle.

Ulf lifted the pot to his nose, then replaced it on the long trestle that ran the length of the room. Content in his domain, a man at ease, Danby picked it up and replaced it on the window sill. An orderly man as well as content, Hildegard observed.

Now the master sent his apprentice to call up a flask of wine from someone called Dorelia in a back room, then turned to his guests.

There was already one man present. He had gone unnoticed at first but when Danby introduced him as his brother Baldwin, also a glazier, he stepped forward a pace from out of the shadows in a corner of the workshop and bowed his head to Hildegard. The brother was tall where

Edric Danby was short, and he was thin as if deprived of sustenance, while his elder brother was well covered, no doubt from the contentment of dining well. Baldwin's hair was clipped close to his skull and he wore his capuchon pushed down round his shoulders in artful folds. A large jewel on a silver chain was displayed in the opening of his tunic. Hildegard looked at it twice. If it had been real it would have been worth a small fortune.

Baldwin was eyeing the visitors as if they were interlopers preventing him from doing business. Hildegard noticed an empty beaker of wine in his hand. It showed he had been enjoying his brother's hospitality for some time while he waited.

Ulf had evidently only just arrived. He was peering along the racks of glass and commenting on the colours.

'Those blue tablets of glass are from France,' Danby told him, happy to explain. 'We mostly use glass from around Cologne as they seem to have good conditions for making it and it's easier to get it by sea and upriver rather than carting it the length of England from France. And there's the trouble with the French as well. Makes supplies unreliable.' He slid a small tablet from the rack and held it up to the light. 'Myself, I prefer the yellowish lustre of this Rhenish glass.' He handed the translucent tablet to Ulf with an air of pride.

The apprentice, face beaming at something that must have happened in the back kitchen, returned with a jug of wine and without being told poured a generous amount into four beakers as well as his own, refilled the one held out by his master's brother, then went to sit on a stool next to a partly whitewashed workbench.

There was a pot on the bench with several sticks of charcoal and a few brushes of different sizes sticking out of it. A variety of other containers were set in an orderly fashion on a shelf at head level. The apprentice took one of them down. It was a receptacle for the offcuts of glass that were of no further use and he selected a few pieces, put them in the mortar and began to grind them with the pestle.

Baldwin spoke up. 'Master Talcot wants to borrow yon journeyman of yours to draw the face of God.' He gave a somewhat contemptuous glance towards an inner chamber.

The apprentice's head was bent over his task, tousled hair in disarray with the vigour of his movements, but when he heard what Baldwin said he looked up with a laugh, brushed a hand across his face and said, 'That Master Talcot and them barkers! His apprentice told me what he wanted – but I ask you, how's God going to be heard if he's wearing a mask?'

'Aye, well that was his theme,' Baldwin countered, 'for what it's to do with you, Jankin. He was in here shortly before you lot came back,' he addressed Danby. '"Can we borrow that there apprentice of your brother's?" says he. I says, "What do you want with that grinning young ape for?" "Not him," he says, "that otheren that draws like an angel." The daft bugger. "He'll have your guts," says I, "that's no apprentice. Proper

81

journeyman he is and he'll cost you." He went off then but said he'll be back.'

Master Danby inclined his head towards the open door and called out to someone in the adjoining workshop. 'Hear that, Gilbert? Get your sen through here and let's have a proper look at you.'

A young man appeared in the doorway of the inner chamber. He walked with a limp, his right leg taking little weight, and Hildegard saw that it was twisted from the knee down, a fact which he tried to conceal with a cloak slung over one shoulder. Apart from that he was what the girls would deem handsome, being broad-shouldered and well proportioned, with a smooth, creamy complexion and good bones.

His hair was most remarkable. It was the colour of flax. Held smoothly back from his brow by a tie of leather it swung forward level with his shoulders as he released it. Fine and straight and smooth, it shone like gold leaf.

His eyes were pale, silver-grey like November rain, and as translucent as the grisaille glass in the great north window of the minster. They swept the group with a bemused glint. 'Have I copped it, master?' he asked in a soft, foreign-sounding burr.

Danby cuffed him affectionately on the shoulder. 'Nay, lad. It's the Guild of Barkers. Master wants to borrow your skills as they've got none of their own. The small price of a king's ransom came up, eh, Baldwin?'

The brother shifted, eyeing everyone as if expecting a knife in his ribs. 'That's the long and the short of it.'

'What do you say, lad?' Danby gave Gilbert an encouraging glance.

He didn't even think about it but said, 'Aye, why not? But only if I get a cut of this ransom you're talking about. What's to do?'

'You'll have to go along and find out,' replied Danby.

'They want the face of God on one of their masks and mebbe put in an angel face or two on a couple of others. Lucifer. Second angel... You'll be good at that,' he added with an edge.

Gilbert ignored him. It was clear, however, that he was flattered to be asked and eager too, no doubt, to try his hand at something other than glass painting.

'You get along as soon as you like,' Danby told him. 'I'm off to Stapylton's soon to get the candles before he sells 'em off to some other devil.'

He turned to Jankin. 'Did you tell mistress to come through?'

'I'll go and remind her.' He jumped up with alacrity and went out.

Danby and Ulf were well into a discussion over the *vidimus* – the full-scale drawing the steward had come to see on behalf of Lady Melisen and Lord Roger – and they were just about to go through into the inner workshop to have a look at it when Jankin returned. He was followed by a young woman. She was about nineteen. Wearing a green gown.

'Mistress Danby,' he announced.

Her beauty made the room fall silent.

83

Chapter Seven

Even Edric Danby, who must have laid eyes on his wife a thousand times, seemed momentarily lost for words. Then he stepped forward and in a proud voice announced, 'My wife, Mistress Dorelia Danby.'

With a smile that seemed convincingly unaware of the charged atmosphere, she glanced round, murmuring, 'Guests, Edric? How pleasant.'

He ushered her to a seat by the kiln with as much gentleness as if she were made of the same glass he usually handled. 'You'll take a drink while I show the lord steward what we've drawn up so far?'

'Thank you, master,' she replied as by rote. She sat demurely by and sipped her wine, her wide violet eyes trailing equally over the nun and the assembly of men.

Almost at once Baldwin muttered something about having to be off, threw back his drink, and slipped from the workshop without another word. Jankin picked up his pestle again and Gilbert said something about going on down to have a word with Master Talcot before he got too drunk to make sense. He lingered, however, when he noticed Hildegard's attention turn to some small pieces of vellum on a nearby shelf.

The master had referred to the *vidimus* – *Let us see*. But the drawings that had caught her eye were small preparatory sketches made with what looked like silverpoint. Danby was eager to point out that they were the prototypes for the full-scale drawing. The one on top showed the Virgin crowned in splendour, a subject apparently chosen by Melisen. Hildegard smiled. No unpleasant scenes of torture or spiritual suffering for Roger's young wife.

Danby placed the drawing on the trestle. The details had not been filled in and the face of the Virgin was a mere oval.

He spread the others out one by one.

Some were plainly border patterns, stylised oak leaves, a few shields, interlaced flowers, and two figures which must surely be the donors. Roger was recognisable from the rich garments he was wearing, his broad shoulders, horse-rider's legs, Norman beard exactly replicating their model.

Ulf stayed the master's hand for a moment. 'Whose work is this?'

Master Danby gestured towards Gilbert. 'That young devil's,' he said.

Ulf was grinning. 'A most wicked likeness, brother!'

Gilbert stared humbly at the floor.

The figure representing Melisen was a rough outline of a woman with long hair and it was this that the two men began to discuss. 'He'll draw her from life, of course,' said Danby. 'It's what she's asked for. But be sure to tell Lord Roger that I'm only doing as requested. It's not my preference. That's not coming into it.'

'You won't take the blame for anything. Don't worry on that score. Otherwise, no problems?'

85

The master chuckled. 'None whatsoever. Tell him I'm honoured by his choice.'

Ulf replaced the sketches on the trestle. 'I don't know whether you know this but you should.' He lowered his voice. 'Your brother asked for a cut of the action. He even sent somebody to the Hutton stand we're erecting to plead his case.'

'He did what?' The master looked put out. 'That was somewhat forward of him.'

'I told Lord Roger so. He said he'd prefer the organ grinder to the fool.'

'I'll not pass that comment on,' replied Danby with a rueful smile. 'Baldwin's working away a lot, somewhere over in the West Riding, and maybe he's hoping to spend more time back home. He wouldn't mean anything spiteful by trying to muscle in, I'm sure.' Despite his defence of his brother he was clearly upset. His wife looked on without comment. The apprentice continued to pound the shards of glass into powder with a faraway expression on his face.

'Whatever the case,' Ulf continued, 'my lord is very well pleased with what he's seen of your work so far.' He raised his stoup and clashed it with that of his host. Danby, smiling, looked, even so, somewhat wounded by his brother's apparent disloyalty.

Hildegard left when Ulf did and they came to a stop on the corner of the street before parting. 'That journeyman really has a skill out of the ordinary,' she commented. 'Danby's a lucky man.'

'He is. Gilbert would be setting up on his own but for the fact that he's a foreigner. He'll find it difficult here, even with his master's support.'

'Where's he from?'

'Some way down south, midlands somewhere. He appeared six months ago.' He gave her a sidelong glance.

'Oh,' she replied, taking in the possible implication that Gilbert had been outlawed in another shire.

'Yes,' he confirmed. 'No doubt Danby suspects what he's taken on as well.'

'I believe the master's a man who runs his life according to where his heart leads him,' she observed. The burden of having to admit to what had happened at Deepdale made her attempt at a smile falter.

Ulf, aware of every nuance of her expression, bent his head. 'There's something wrong?'

It was then, omitting nothing, she told him about the destruction of the grange.

He was enraged by the time she finished. 'Why didn't you tell me straight away?'

'You were at the workshop on business. I'm telling you now.'

'So who the hell were they?' He ran a hand through his hair in bewilderment.

And so she told him about the poisoned gift of two runaways the prioress had sent from Swyne. He smiled wryly at that description but was clearly furious by what had happened. 'You might have been slaughtered.' He gripped her by the forearm and seemed too overcome to say much more.

'I sent a messenger to Roger at Castle Hutton,' she told him.

'He'll have a wasted journey, then. Roger's already left. He and Lady Melisen are establishing themselves for the duration of the feast at a place called Naburn Manor a few miles downriver. I'll let Roger know what's been going on when I get back there later today. He's going to be incandescent.'

She told him everything she knew, both what Maud had told her and what she had observed herself during the attack. 'Their horses were good ones. He was most likely a knight, the other two his henchmen. He wore a silver emblem on a chain. Not Gaunt's chain of 'esses' but something else. I can't place it.'

Ulf listened carefully and after a few concerned questions about her well-being and a warning to be careful, told her he was going up Micklegate to inspect the stand Roger was having built where he, Lady Melisen and their guests could watch the entire pageant in comfort.

He was still flushed with anger, however, and his parting words were, 'Whoever did this to you and your sisters will wish they'd never been born.'

'I would *so* love to see the mystery plays,' sighed Petronilla next morning as they shook out their straw pallets and tidied up the sleeping chamber. She gave Hildegard a hopeful glance.

The nun shook her head. 'Are you hoping to stay in York with the Sisters of the Holy Wounds even longer?'

Petronilla frowned. 'Heaven forfend. Last night was the worst I've ever spent. I do believe I have flea bites on every inch of my body.'

'I told you to rub yourself in pennyroyal,' Hildegard remarked. 'We'll find something to soothe your bites while we're in town. But what *are* your hopes for the future – now you've eluded your wicked guardian?'

Petronilla rolled her eyes but made no other reply.

It was true what she said about their lodgings, thought Hildegard, and yet they had no choice. Until word came from Swyne they would have to stay here. She sighed with impatience. Waiting on other people to make decisions, or for a change of fortune, was not her nature. Inwardly she fumed at being trapped in York when all she wanted was to face up to the problem of Deepdale. She was damned if she was going to accept its destruction with the equanimity of a sheep. She was ready to fight back.

Crossing herself briefly at the thought of damnation she vowed that if the place could not be restored to its former state she would look elsewhere for suitable land. Deepdale, or somewhere like it, would rise again.

More immediately, Petronilla's guardian had to be contacted. The prioress would understand that. But would she understand the urgency? It wasn't the prioress who was trapped in a broiling city, her senses assaulted by the sights and sounds and stench of so many bodies squashed into one small place under a burning sun. It was festive all right, with all the flags and bunting and the atmosphere of excited expectation at the forthcoming processions, but after the silence of the moors it struck Hildegard as the backdrop to hell. At peace in her priory, surrounded by the familiar fields and woodlands, the prioress would scarcely realise the need for decisiveness nor would she understand Hildegard's impatience at being forced to wait on others.

She felt a qualm of guilt. The prioress's continual reproof was of Hildegard's impatience. She gave another sigh and finished with the pallet by giving it a final savage shake.

Arrangements would have to be made for Maud too, she was thinking as they made their way through the whispering nuns in their gloomy dormitory. Now orphaned the poor little thing was homeless on top of everything else. Not only would the murderers of her family have to be hunted down and brought to justice, she herself would have to be found a safe haven. If it turned out that she had no living kin the sisters would probably want to take her in even if they had to pay to buy her freedom from her overlord.

Wondering how best to cope with the frustration of doing nothing until the situation changed, Hildegard decided to take it as an opportunity to visit the famous shrine of St William here in York Minster. It might afford some solace to them all, she said, when she put the idea to her charges. Petronilla, at least, was enthusiastic.

'I'd adore to see it!' she cried. 'It's the most famous shrine in England. How I've longed to make pilgrimage there. Shall we have to wear special garments and carry palm leaves?' she asked excitedly.

Hildegard could already see she was devising a

fetching outfit in which to make her appearance as a pilgrim.

'Probably it's more devout to turn up as we are,' she replied, careful not to deflate her enthusiasm.

It was one of the most famous shrines in England, equalled perhaps only by the one to St Thomas a Becket down in Canterbury, and it attracted pilgrims from all over the British Isles and from even further afield. Before they set out Hildegard warned the girls that at a time like this, with visitors flooding into the city for the feast, it would probably be seething with folk and they should be prepared to have a long wait to get inside. Petronilla was undeterred. Despite her vanity and rather shallow nature her quick delight in the smallest incident softened Hildegard's heart.

Now the child skipped along as soon as they were free of the convent precincts. It was plain to all of them that they were not welcome there. It seemed it was only their silver the convent wanted. Gladly they set off to the shrine. Even Maud, slipping her hand into Hildegard's, pushed back her hood a little and lightened her step.

The minster itself was easy to find. It was visible as they made their way through a warren of small backstreets. Pinnacled and romantic, it soared above the roofs of the houses. There had been a church on the same site since before the Normans invaded, since before Danelaw, and even before the Saxon kings ruled in the north and, Hildegard told them, some people believed there had been a holy place here even before the time of the Romans, who called the town Eboracum and made it an outpost of the empire.

Awed, they joined the slowly moving queue in the yard waiting to enter through the great doors. By the time they managed to get inside both girls were plainly tired, but even so they stopped in wonder on the threshold.

Pale stone columns rose to an immense height as narrow and gracefully unfolding as ancient trees in a forest. The roof was delicately vaulted and ribbed with gold bosses emphasising its long length. Great windows of coloured glass, set within a lace-like tracery of stone, held the lustre of gems. Like Petronilla and Maud, the many visitors, dwarfed by the splendour of such height and breadth, gazed upwards in open-mouthed admiration at the work of the anonymous master masons who had conceived the idea of building such an edifice.

'It must be bigger than the king's palace!' whispered Petronilla.

Even Maud, clutching her hood to keep it in place, had raised her glance to stare upwards.

A choir of canons and boy-choristers were practising for the forthcoming Mass deep within the recesses of the nave. It sounded like the singing of angels. Despite this, Maud, after that one swift glance at the soaring roof, barely gave another glance at anything except the floor, merely following at Hildegard's heels like someone both deaf and blind. Petronilla, on the other hand, was so entranced she almost forgot to talk until, drifting alongside Hildegard with the pilgrims towards the entrance to the candlelit shrine, she tugged on the nun's sleeve and whispered, 'Sister, I've seen a most beautiful man. He's like an angel himself. See?' She pointed to one side. 'Over there near that pillar. I thought it was me he was looking at – but to my chagrin I realise it's you.'

Chapter Eight

Hildegard glanced over. A figure wrapped in a grey cloak was leaning against one of the pillars in the new nave. It was Master Danby's journeyman, Gilbert. His hair was unloosed. It shone like pearl in the filtered light. He bowed his head when he saw Hildegard glance over and she replied in like manner. Then he returned to a study of the Bell window, gazing up at the bright-yellow bell pattern with his translucent grey eyes as if nothing else existed.

Hildegard had to explain to Petronilla who he was. The girl could not take her eyes off him.

After a long wait in a queue that snaked all the way along the nave they eventually reached the steps leading down into the small stone crypt. It was jostling with pilgrims. Many were vying for a place underneath the shrine in the niche made for that purpose and there was a constant din of prayers being offered, along with the shrieks and moans of those suffering in physical and spiritual torment.

Hildegard felt shaken by such anguish and stood a little to one side out of the crush with Maud clinging to her sleeve. The place was dark and hot and reeked of sweat and unwashed garments. The billowing clouds of incense did little to sweeten the air. Undaunted, Petronilla inspected the entire place, slipping through the press until she reached the shrine, eventually returning to where the other two were waiting. Then they lit candles for St William and at last re-emerged into the fresher air above ground.

'He's still here,' observed Petronilla in a tone of voice that made Hildegard wonder what she had been praying for at the shrine. Sure enough, though, it was Gilbert, visible through a gap in the crowd.

He had gone to stand below the Five Sisters window this time. The vast expanse of silvery figured glass allowed a clear, northern light to fall over those who walked beneath it. It dwarfed them, and the colours of their clothes were reduced to a subtle mingling of browns, greys and russets.

How appropriate that he should be looking at the Five Sisters, Hildegard thought. The same wash of silvery light entering through the patterns of grey glass had been brought to mind when she first saw him. He was gazing up with rapt attention as before, but this time did not notice when they walked by. She wondered if he was waiting for someone.

Petronilla skewed her head until he must have looked like nothing more than a grey shape between the slender stone pillars.

They stepped outside into the blazing heat of another stifling hot June day. There was not a breath of air. Despite this Maud's hood was still up. Petronilla donned her hat and tilted the brim.

Hildegard pulled on her own wide-brimmed straw. 'I propose we go out along the river where it's cooler,' she suggested. 'If we walk by the postern down near St Mary's Abbey we'll avoid the crowds pouring in through the barbican, as well as the sight of all those severed heads being pestered by crows on Bootham Bar.' Everyone had carefully avoided mentioning the sight as they came in.

'Thank the Lord,' Petronilla commented. 'You agree, don't you, goosey?'

Maud gave a brief nod from beneath her hood.

The meadows outside the walls were even more crowded with encampments than when they had arrived. Fires had been lit and the smell of cooking wafted towards them as they approached. With Maud walking a few paces ahead Hildegard glanced down at Petronilla, and deeming it a good opportunity casually asked, 'And how was it that you and Maud turned up together at Deepdale?'

'The prioress sent us,' Petronilla replied, somewhat evasively.

'I know that already.' Hildegard was patient. 'But I wonder how it is you were together?'

There was a pause. Then Petronilla's eyes brightened. 'Oh, this is a story, Sister, listen! It was like this. I just happened to be walking along a road – having run away from my wicked guardian – when I saw a small figure ahead of me. She looked just like she does now except that her cloak was more ragged. That russet one she has on was given to her by the nuns at Swyne. They were so kind to us–'

'Well that's their job,' Hildegard broke in. 'They delight in being kind. But you say you just happened to see her walking ahead of you?'

'There's more to it. It so happened there was a little yard by the road with hens running around, and as we passed by one of them got off its nest and went to peck at some corn...'

Hildegard stifled a sigh. This was clearly going to be a long story and she wondered if it was going to lead anywhere after all.

'Well, in a flash,' Petronilla continued blithely, 'the little figure – who at that time I didn't know as Maud – stopped in its tracks, then suddenly darted to the nest and picked up the egg, hid it under the cloak, then hurried on. At that moment a woman burst out of the house, screaming about thieves taking her eggs and how she was going to call the constable and she stood in the road, shouting after Maud, who, thank heavens, took no notice but simply increased her pace. I thought the woman was going to raise hand and horn against her so I went up to her and said, "I'm astonished at all this fuss, mistress. It'll look bad for you if you go blaming that stranger up the road when it was a fox who took your egg. I saw it with my own eyes." I know it was a lie, Sister, and I will confess it, but it seemed unfair to shout after a poor wretch of a

96

child for no more than an egg.'

'So what happened next?'

'The woman gave me the blackest look. "Did you see a fox?" she demanded. So I had to tell another lie but I don't regret it. "He ran away towards those barns," I said. "Good gracious me!" the woman exclaimed. "That's where my chicks are kept," and she went running off. I caught up with Maud and was quite surprised to find it was a girl. I said, "You nearly got yourself caught there. I hope that egg is worth it." But she just kept her head down, so I said, "Let's walk along together as we are both alone," and she didn't object. So that's how we came to travel together.'

'And how is it you finished up at the priory?'

'We joined a band of beggar children. I know it's low to beg but we were hungry and they seemed to know all kinds of tricks to get people to give them scraps, but after a while we tired of their roughness, and when I saw some men working in a field I asked them whose domain it was and they said it belonged to the prioress of Swyne, so I said, "That's where we're going. How far is it?" and the labourer told me and so we both went there.'

'Lucky for Maud you took pity on her,' Hildegard remarked.

'It was. She could have finished up in the stocks.'

It had been a long, hot day. The girls looked exhausted by the time Hildegard conducted them back to the convent of the Holy Wounds.

The nuns there, as was their duty, kept strictly to the offices of the day and didn't bother about the comfort of their guests with their tolling bells and vociferous chanting. They were giving voice in the chapel again when the porteress admitted them, so Hildegard took the girls up to their small chamber, telling them, 'I may have to go out again. I know this waiting is making us all impatient but we will hear something soon and then we'll leave. I'm going to have another word with the lawman and when you've both rested a little you might ask the nuns if there are any small chores you can do to help.'

She couldn't resist giving them both a hug before she went out. Doused thoroughly in pennyroyal they were sprawled asleep on their straw pallets almost before she was through the door.

Justice had to be done on Maud's behalf. Hildegard was determined to do what she could. Surely the lord of Pentleby manor, like Lord Roger, would object to his property being destroyed and his villeins murdered. He would demand redress. The men would be apprehended. Witnesses would have to be called. It would all take time. She was prepared, however, to pursue the matter to the bitter end. They could not be allowed to go unpunished.

Then there was Petronilla's guardian to be contacted, whether the child wanted to speak to him or not. Reluctantly she had named a merchant in Knaresborough.

Hopefully Hildegard climbed the narrow stairs to the serjeant-at-law's chambers. Again, however,

he had nothing useful to tell her. Secretly Hildegard doubted whether he had sent anyone to
investigate but she daren't annoy him by suggesting so. It would not be top of his list now the town
was full of strangers, with many out to cause
trouble, and with the feast day imminent there was
even less chance that the necessary procedures
would be followed with any particular haste.

Her mind full of worries, she left the warren of
rooms, came out onto the street and began to
walk back towards the bridge. At first she noticed
nothing amiss. A crowd of people – men, women
and children – were running on ahead up the
street in a sort of loose pack. They were shouting
something but were too far away for their words
to be audible. A few others were starting to come
out of their shops to see what was happening.
Several ran on to join the rest.

Hildegard increased her pace. The mob ran out
onto Stonegate and when she rounded the corner
she saw a group of onlookers at the entrance to
one of the yards. They were craning their necks to
peer down the passage.

Clearly something was up. Realising it was the
yard where the chandler, Master Stapylton, had
his premises, she increased her pace until she
reached the edge of the crowd. A constable was
already beating onlookers back with a stick
urging them to move along. 'Nothing to see. It's
all over. Go to your homes now. Come on, shift
yourselves!' People scattered before his blows
and then reformed behind his back. Two women
evidently just back from market, judging by the
produce sticking out of their panniers, were

standing nearby. One of them gave the nun a shake of the head. 'St Florian's been busy, Sister.'

'Why, what's happened?' She was puzzled. Florian was supposed to put out fires.

'Fuss over nothing,' said the second woman with a sniff.

Hildegard frowned. 'But it looks like trouble, mistress. Look at the crowd. And isn't that smoke?'

'Indeed it is.'

A wisp of blue smoke hung between the tenements. 'There's been a fire in one of them workshops,' the other woman explained.

Hildegard was uncomfortably reminded of the fire at Deepdale. 'I trust no one's been hurt?'

'Apparently not. Lucky for folks with property in the yard there's a well there with water still in it. By the look of things they've got the better of the flames. Nothing to do with Florian in my reckoning!' She gave a nod to her friend, bid Hildegard the time of day, and moved on.

A man standing nearby had been listening in. He gave an unfriendly chuckle. 'Nearly had Stapylton's candles up in flames, it did.'

Hildegard turned to him. 'Was it at Master Stapylton's workshop, then?'

'It was.'

'At least the fire seems to be out,' she replied, annoyed by his tone.

'It's a miracle, as you folk might say. First a big whoosh of flame like an explosion, then the timbers are set alight. If they hadn't got to it straight away all them houses would have gone up in smoke. Nobody would have got out alive.'

'These things happen,' murmured Hildegard, appalled at the picture he conjured up.

'Aye,' he grunted with pleasure, 'especially with the day that's coming up.'

She gave him a sharp glance. 'What do you mean?'

He tapped the side of his nose like a conspirator. 'Corpus Christi? Think on, Sister, think on! The third year after Master Tyler's death, come feast day?'

'Are you suggesting it was arson?'

'Am I?'

'But what's it got to do with the chandler's?' she asked.

He gave her a sudden, wary look and dragged a smile onto his face. 'Puts a damper on the candle show round town if there are no candles for their Eucharist procession. Damper? Get it?' With that he wandered off, chuckling at his own feeble joke.

Hildegard frowned after him. It was difficult to know which side he favoured from a tone of such slanted venom. Could it be true, though? Had somebody fired the chandlery as a sign of protest? If so, they had surely chosen the wrong man. Stapylton had seemed to favour the rebels.

Three years ago there had been rioting in all the main towns of the north, just as in the south.

It was true that the workshops of those in the candle trade had been set on fire in London because of their believed support for the holy sacraments. To supply the church was trade, however, and not necessarily an indication of a craftsman's allegiance.

In the Ridings the rebels, mostly apprentices and small merchants, adopting King Richard's emblem of the white hart, saw Wycliffe and the church reformers as their allies. Both sides wanted an end to what they saw as the superstition and priestly ritual used to bolster the power of the Church. The chandlers were in some respects the innocent victims of the rioting that followed.

An explosion in a chandlery, unless it was an accident, suggested that 'the hurling time' was not forgotten here in York.

Hidden away in the grange at Deepdale for the last year with nothing more urgent on her mind than the growing of crops and the general welfare of her nuns, Hildegard felt out of touch. She found it difficult to gauge the mood of the town. Its air of seething excitement might be entirely innocent, arising from the imminent Corpus Christi feast day. It might, however, conceal a violent discontent.

The alarm now over, people were beginning to drift away from the entrance to the yard and she found herself being carried with them towards a busy stretch of the street called 'Pavement'. Canvas booths were being set up by an army of traders in readiness for the festivities. Banners fluttered above the heads of the onlookers. A gaudy huckster or two was already pacing the makeshift boards, playing to the crowd.

She found herself drifting close to a platform in the middle of the row. Standing on it was a man dressed as a mage. In full spate, his patter was attracting a large and noisy crowd.

He certainly looks the part, she thought, as she paused to listen. Black hair, clearly false, bushed out from under a spangled hat, and he wore a flowing cloak stitched with silver stars that glittered with every movement of his arms. He was making large claims for a greyish powder contained in the glass phial he held aloft. Necks craned. Apparently it was a potion to restore manhood that could not fail.

Hildegard lingered on the fringes of the crowd to hear what outrage he would come out with next. Two middle-aged men in front were discussing the possible effects of the powder and urging each other to make a trial purchase.

The mage noted their interest. 'I despise money,' he announced. There were jeers, which he ignored. 'There are many things worth more, my friends. Health, for one! The golden sun in the morning, for another. The patter of...' he paused and let the audience fill in the pause before adding, 'rain on leaves. And love!' he continued swiftly. 'Love! Where would we be without it? This,' he waved the phial about, 'will give you love. Buy it now. Give it a try. I urge you. It's worth a thousand crowns but I can let you have it for half that – no! For one-fifteenth!'

There were guffaws from the crowd at this reference to the hated poll tax. The mage – cat's eyes, a long nose, sallow cheeks and a liar's lips – gave a complicit smile. He lowered his voice. 'Let me tell you a little secret, my friends.'

Everyone leant closer.

'The cardinals of Rome have paid ten thousand crowns for this same substance.' He displayed the phial again. 'The nobility of France paid *ten times* that amount. And all the seigneurs of Spain have dipped into their coffers of gold and silver and offered up their entire fortunes–'

'If they've paid you so much, why are you wearing them old things on your feet?' demanded a voice at the front.

Everyone craned to see the mage's boots. It was true they were worn down but, like his cloak, they were sprinkled with silver stars that glittered when he moved.

'I'll tell you why, my friend,' said the mage, 'because I give away what I earn–'

'In that case, give us the love potion!' demanded the same wag.

'But like any man...' continued the mage imperturbably, 'I have to feed my body and pay my way. Therefore ... what do I ask of you? What little do I ask? I'll tell you. I ask only two groats!' He shook the phial so they could see the powder more clearly. 'Two groats!'

There was sceptical muttering from his audience.

He went on. 'By the greatest good fortune I have a friend who is a famous traveller. My friend – a scholar, by the way – found this powder in the ruins of Troy. He had it sent to me by a secret courier. This friend also sent a little of it to John of Gaunt and Mistress Swynford – and you've all seen the results there!'

Laughter followed. Everyone knew Gaunt had lost count of the children he had fathered, in wedlock and out, some with his known mistress, Katherine Swynford, others as a result of many other liaisons.

'I'll have some of that!' shouted a grey-haired fellow, pushing his way forward in a welter of cheers and ribald comments.

'Two groats only! Who can't afford that?' The mage reached into one of his sleeves and drew forth an identical phial, and on receiving a couple of coins which slipped at once into the pouch chained to his belt he bestowed the phial on the eager purchaser.

Several hands reached out now the ice was broken and he did brisk business for some time, never ceasing his praise of the stuff he was marketing and the great good fortune of those who were now in possession of it.

'Ten days!' he declaimed, 'you must remain celibate for ten days to give the potion chance to work its charm.'

Ten days. thought Hildegard. The mage would be long gone by then and unlikely to be called to account when his powder failed to deliver.

With a wry smile she was about to walk on when she noticed a familiar figure in the crowd. It was the master glazier's brother. Baldwin.

His face was as black as thunder. His two companions wore similar expressions as if the mage had personally insulted them. She wondered what it could be about. Surely they couldn't be taking him seriously? She saw them begin to mutter among themselves and throw violent glances his way. Maybe they have already tried the love potion, thought Hildegard, and discovered that it does not work for them.

As she moved away she noticed the mage

glance into the crowd and catch sight of the men. He was an expert actor. Maybe few others had noticed the slight stiffening of his gestures as he handed another phial to a customer. But straight away he raised his hands to address his audience.

'And now, my dear friends, for something you have never witnessed before. May I request a volunteer from the audience?... Anyone?'

One and all fell silent.

'A lad capable of holding up a velvet curtain? Is there one strong enough in York or are all your men weaklings?'

A youth at the front half scrambled and was half pushed by his companions onto the stage to defend the honour of his city. He stood there, looking back at the audience with a dumb expression like a sheep to the slaughter.

The mage's eyes were sharp as he gazed as if randomly over the crowd but Hildegard thought he took especial notice of Baldwin and his companions. They were unarmed as was the law within the walls. Even so.

She watched him raise his hands for silence, making the silver spangles glitter in the sunlight.

'I shall now endeavour to do a most dangerous act. If it should go wrong, I am a dead man.'

Baldwin narrowed his glance with contempt.

'I shall, with all the arts I have acquired in Outremer, make myself become as incorporeal as the very air itself!'

There were catcalls. The mage ignored them. He first positioned the box centre stage with a curtain held out, then, after repositioning him several times as if the merest inch was vital he

106

took a small copper dish from among the paraphernalia in a bag at his feet, put a candle underneath it, and set light to the wick.

The flame burnt almost invisibly in the bright sunlight. All eyes were upon it. The boy who had been asked to hold up a piece of cheap purple cloth was craning to see over the top of it with as much interest as everyone else. The tension increased. No one knew what to expect. Someone gave a nervous laugh. The flame flickered but remained alight.

The mage, too, had fallen silent and shut his eyes. He seemed to have fallen into a trance. Suddenly there was a spurt of fire from the copper dish.

Thick black smoke funnelled into the air and spread rapidly among the crowd. People at the front started to cough. There was a scramble to get away from the stage.

When the smoke cleared the mage had gone.

Chapter Nine

The boy was still standing there with the purple curtain held in front of him, but in a moment Baldwin had clambered onto the stage and pushed him to one side.

A gasp went up from those who were not too blinded by the smoke to see. Contrary to what they expected there was no mage hiding behind it. Baldwin yanked aside the canvas flap at the back of the stage and jumped down. He could be heard cursing as he fell among some barrels. By now his cronies were barging onto the stage as well. There were confused murmurs from the crowd.

From her position on the edge it was easy for Hildegard to slip between the booths. She came out into a passage between the back of the row and some tenements in time to see Baldwin and his men searching with baffled expressions among a miscellany of rubbish. Of the mage there was no sign. There was little space among the barrels and sacks for a man to hide himself.

Some way further down, a cart was being un-loaded by a brawny bare-headed fellow in a wool-len tunic. Hildegard heard him give a derisory laugh when one of the group asked if a man in a spangled cloak had been seen running his way. The driver of the cart, a grey-bearded old man with an old sack over his shoulders, jiggled the reins of the stock pony between the shafts as if impatient to be on his way.

Baldwin went up to him. Hildegard could hear him demanding to know whether anyone had come out of one of the booths. The old fellow, like his companion, shook his head.

She saw him give a bored glance over Baldwin's shoulder. The latter took this as a hint, told his companions and they set off in pursuit.

Hildegard did not understand what their quarrel with the mage was about but she feared for his safety should they find him. The carter clicked his horse into action and it began to amble towards her. As it passed she caught a glimpse of the toe of the carter's boot from under his cloak. Content, she headed off down the street.

Agnetha had found temporary lodging with her cousin and his wife. They lived in a two-storey cottage on the other side of town. When Hildegard crossed the bridge and turned onto the street where the convent was located, she saw the lay sister step out ahead of her from where she had evidently been waiting.

They greeted each other warmly but then Agnetha gave a grimace. 'These sisters here wouldn't unlock the door for me. No visitors, they said.'

'Did they tell you I'd gone into the town?'

Agnetha shook her head. 'Merely snapped their grille shut as if I carried the plague.'

'Yes, they are rather brusque. But what's wrong? You look worried.'

'I am.' She had gone back to wearing the clothes she had worn when Hildegard had first set eyes on her, laying down the law over heriot tax to the abbot and his officials at Meaux. On her head was a white kerchief knotted at the back of her neck and she had adopted a plain kirtle of rough unbleached cotton, with a housewife's apron tied over it.

Hildegard looked her up and down.

'I know.' Agnetha ran an apologetic hand over her skirts. 'Listen. It's not how it looks. I've not given up on my intention to take the veil. You know me better than that, Hildegard. I'm not so light of purpose.'

'So what's happening? Can you talk here?' They were standing in the shade of the porch. Hildegard glanced round. They were alone. The street had a few passers-by at the far end. But to be certain they were not overheard she gestured to Agnetha to follow her and they both moved away from the door and began to stroll towards the quay side.

'I've been talking to my cousin and his wife,' the lay sister began. 'It's on their advice I've adopted my dairywoman's garb. Listen, Hildegard.' She clutched her by the arm. 'The way things are, the monastics are going to get caught in the crossfire.'

'What crossfire?'

Agnetha looked uncomfortable. 'You know how the rebels targeted the abbeys? It's not just lawyers they hate.'

'Rebels? You mean during the Great Revolt?'

Agnetha nodded.

'But that was three years ago...'

'Yes–' She broke off.

'And here in York they didn't attack St Mary's Abbey nor the nunnery of St Clement's. And the Holy Wounds convent is built like a fortress as you've seen for yourself – and anyway,' she bit her lip, 'surely all that's over?'

'Those first two places are run by Benedictines. Everybody knows St Mary's came to a compromise with the town over their financial disputes by the time the rebellion broke out. And anyway,' Agnetha went on, 'they have Gaunt's protection. They'll be safe if it starts up again...'

'So? Why are you looking so worried?'

110

'I'm just listening to what my cousin says. It's dangerous, Hildegard. You have no protection here.'

'So on that basis I should change my white habit for a black one and go in disguise?'

'I'm only saying be careful. He says there's something dangerous brewing.'

'What sort of thing?'

Agnetha shook her head. 'He couldn't say. There are rumours. I thought you should be warned.'

'And that's why you've come over here, to warn me against being a Cistercian?' Hildegard drew herself up. She was shocked. Agnetha was one of the most level-headed people she knew. That cousin must have turned her head with his fears.

Now Agnetha gripped Hildegard by the arm. 'I'm not saying this lightly. My cousin's a guild member and hears everything.'

Hildegard remembered the fire at Master Stapylton's. She asked Agnetha if she had heard about it.

She nodded. 'They're saying it was arson. That confirms what I'm saying, doesn't it?' Her grip tightened for a moment before she let go. 'Look, I must get back. I've promised to watch the children in return for my bed and board. Trust me, Hildegard. I am not reneging on my promise. I just know I'm safer this way. Please. I beg you. Watch your step.'

With a last urgent glance, she turned and hurried off, merging with the other goodwives and burgesses crossing by at the end of the street. As soon as she left a man stepped out from the

111

porch of the convent and gazed after her. Then he turned and giving Hildegard a glance went back inside the building. It was the servant Matthias.

Agnetha's warning was troubling. Hildegard went up to the convent entrance, was stopped by the locked door as before, and waited impatiently until the porteress pushed open her peephole to see who was there. After a pause, locks were scraped back and Hildegard stepped out of the heat into the icy gloom of the convent. Matthias was nowhere to be seen.

The porteress poked her head out of her cubbyhole. 'Missive in my office,' she announced without preamble.

Emerging long enough to heave the bolts back across the doors again she scurried into her cell and returned with something in her hand. She made no attempt to hide her interest in its contents as she handed it over, and she continued to hover as Hildegard inspected the seal.

With an abrupt thank you she pushed the letter into her sleeve. The last thing she was going to do was open it in front of prying eyes. The contents would be round the convent in no time. Leaving the porteress with her curiosity unsatisfied she hurried into the cloister to find a corner where she could open it unobserved.

The seal was that of the prioress. It was the letter from Swyne she had been waiting for. Cecilia and Marianne must have arrived safely and told her what had befallen the grange at Deepdale. The prioress could move fast when she had to.

Desperately hoping that she was being recalled to the priory and that there would be welcome instructions regarding the two runaways, she prised the seal away and opened out a single piece of vellum. It was much scraped, having clearly been used many times over, but it now bore a clear message in the prioress's familiar style.

She had written:

Sister, greetings. Unfortunate news regarding Deepdale. You will find a lesson can be learnt from such events. Meanwhile, remain in York with our guests until enquiries yield results. Soon something shall be brought to you. Take it to our mutual friend. Do not under any circumstance leave it with him. Allow only sight of it, as requested. Understand me.

The angular swoop of a signature and the familiar seal pressed into the green wax confirmed the missive's authenticity.

It took no more than a moment to understand what was being given into her care. Last year she had been sent on an errand to Tuscany to bring back the famous Cross of Constantine at the wish of His Grace the Archbishop of York, Alexander Neville. Hildegard had given it as instructed to the prioress. She, however, for some reason of her own, had been reluctant to hand it over to the archbishop. Hildegard surmised that it was because it was thought to be so powerful – possession of it was seen to confer on the owner more authority than that of the Holy Roman emperor and the pope combined.

113

Hildegard had experienced at first hand to what lengths the unscrupulous would go to obtain the cross.

In Italy the Gran Contessa's ambition to rule over the wealthy city state of Florence had led her to risk her immortal soul in pursuit of it. She had seen it as a means of gaining the earthly powers she craved. Hildegard had been abducted and almost lost her life in a plot to steal it. Escaping, however, and surviving many other dangers, she had eventually brought it back home to England where it had since remained in secret custody at Swyne.

Now it was to be brought here to York. She would be its custodian yet again.

She shuddered at the thought of it. If there had been a way of circumventing the prioress's orders she would have welcomed it. But she had to obey.

Puzzling over the matter, she couldn't imagine why it had to be taken to the archbishop himself. He could easily have gone to Swyne to have a look at it while on one of his visitations at nearby Meaux. Clearly there was more to the story than she was being told.

Suddenly remembering Brother Thomas's promise to escort her if ever she should need him again, she made her way to the upper floor of the convent where there was a small chamber that served as a scriptorium. After writing a short note, she signed it, pressed her own seal to the hot wax, then went down to the domestic quarters to find a messenger from among the many servants working there.

The maze of kitchens and storerooms was

confusing. Eventually, spying a reliable-looking boy loitering near the buttery, she offered him a penny with the promise of further reward if he took the letter to the courier and returned promptly with a receipt. He sped off with alacrity.

Then she joined everyone in the chapel for the last office of the day.

Unfortunate news indeed, she thought with some bitterness as she closed her eyes and pondered the prioress's instructions.

It wasn't the disappointment of finding they were not being recalled to Swyne that kept Hildegard awake that night. Nor was it the fleas nor the discomfort of the straw pallet on which they were forced to lie. It wasn't the singing of the nuns at the nightly office, either. She could have joined them.

It was something else. Something more personal for which she could find no resolution.

She tossed and turned, afraid lest her rustling should disturb the girls. Next morning she rose without waking them and set off for the minster.

Already thronged with visitors from outside the town it was a sanctuary of beauty and tranquillity after the punishing austerity of the nunnery. It embodied what she longed for most: peace – peace in the realm, of course, but peace in her own heart as well.

The catastrophe at Deepdale, as she well knew, was not the source of her unrest. It was something that had started long before that event. She knelt in front of the altar in a side chapel away from the sound of passing visitors and bowed her head. *Let my tongue cleave to the roof of my mouth if I do not remember thee*. Forgive me, oh Lord, she prayed. Forgive this sinful misdirecting of your words.

It had been in a place like this, the minster at Beverley, where a truth had been revealed to her; it offered a choice between two paths. According to orthodox belief one led heavenwards, the other to eternal damnation in the fires of hell.

Recently his absence had afflicted her with a deeper melancholy. Time had changed nothing. The path they both believed would lead to hell opened as invitingly as before.

Not that she had a choice whether to take that path. He was on pilgrimage. Might never return. Or if returning, might be changed beyond knowing, cleansed of his lustful folly as she should be cleansed of hers.

A year at Deepdale, however, had done nothing to make her forget him. Some days the battle was easier, some days she was overwhelmed with longing. Today, for some reason she could not understand, the sanctuary of his presence was all she desired.

Once he had felt the same. *'My soul be damned,'* he had said.

Impatiently she rose to her feet. If it was not Hubert de Courcy she desired, would it be some other man?

Finding her prayers to be useless, she walked savagely down the long nave towards the west doors, but hesitated, reluctant to go out into the streets of the town. She ran her fingers over the leather bag hanging from her belt. It contained a

116

gift he had sent her. A gift that meant that she possessed something of him no matter how far away he was.

Agnetha knew she had risked her life to enter the burning grange to retrieve it.

Six months ago, in the dead of winter, a messenger had arrived at Deepdale with it.

Hoar frost on the bare branches. Ice in the water butt. A sky so low with unshed snow it seemed to touch the tops of the hills enclosing the grange in its hidden valley. Sheep bleated in the fold. Thin cries of newborn lambs. Chilblains and sleepless nights. Winter, hard as it is in the north. Then the messenger appeared.

He stood at the kitchen door and refused to come in, merely giving her a muttered, 'From the abbot,' to inform her of the provenance of the parcel he thrust towards her. After he left she had unwrapped it and gazed at it in wonder, caught first by the fact of the gift and second by the beauty of the little book. It was a missal. She had turned the pages and read the words.

Later she wrapped it in the strip of embroidered silk that had belonged to Hubert's Knight Templar great-uncle. She remembered how it had been given to her anonymously last year and how she had held it out, intending to return it as soon as she knew who owned it, but he had refused to take it back. His hand had enfolded her own, the silk held close within her palm. *'Keep it,'* he urged. *'Take it as a pledge of everything in my heart.'*

When she eventually forced herself out through the great west doors into the minster yard it was already teeming with the worldly comings and goings of a throng of visitors. She took a deep breath and set out.

Another hot day looked likely. The sun was again beating down out of a cloudless sky. The wells would be further depleted More ruined crops, she thought. More deaths.

She crossed the river by Ouse Bridge where St William was reputed to have saved the lives of the people who fell in when the bridge collapsed as they swarmed to greet him. A story, she judged, with no truth in it, but it was a kind one. At least St William had been strong enough to keep his vows.

As she climbed the steep rise of Micklegate towards the church of the Holy Trinity at the French priory, she had the idea of trying to walk off the turmoil of longing and confusion, but she noticed one of the convent servants, the one they called Matthias, unmistakable with that shaven head, trailing along behind her.

He was an overweight, somewhat odd-looking fellow.

She did not know what had made her turn her head to look back but as soon as he noticed that she had seen him he sloped off onto a side street. As unfriendly as the rest of them, she thought. The Benedictine nun who had suggested the convent had warned her that the Sisters of the Holy Wounds disliked outsiders. Of course, it was nonsense to imagine he had been following her.

When she reached the priory at the top of Micklegate Hill a team of labourers were building a scaffolding across the length of the facade of their church of the Holy Trinity. Surmising that it must be intended as the first station for the pageant, she started to cross over to have a look. A sturdy construction, with a wide platform where benches were being installed, it seemed elaborate enough for someone of importance.

The crowds were denser than ever just here. Micklegate Bar was one of the major gateways and there was a constant stream of people entering the city through the Bar as well as folk going about their everyday business within the walls. Combined with the constant teams of pack animals taking produce to the outlying neighbourhoods, it was difficult to find a way forward.

A group of burgesses were strolling over from one of the merchants' houses on the other side of the street. Yet, as she threaded her way through the crowds she noticed that this expensively attired group was having no difficulty at all. As soon as they approached people stepped out of their way, doffed their caps, and made deferential little bows, while a servant with a mace sauntered in front wearing a smug smile as he effortlessly carved a path for his masters.

To her astonishment, Hildegard recognised Ulf in the middle of this group.

As far as she could make out he was carrying out an inspection of the stand. Then she remembered what he had told her at Danby's workshop.

Dear Ulf, she thought now, her heart softening. She had known him almost all her life. They had played as children in the bailey at Castle Hutton, gone tadpoling in spring, built snowmen in winter and searched for beech nuts among the autumn leaves. It was Ulf who had taught her how to use a bow and arrow and wield a knife in self-defence.

Now it was apparent he had become a major figure in Lord Roger de Hutton's household. She watched him make some comment to a mild-looking fellow wearing a chain of office.

Seeing that he was busy she would have turned away then, but for the fact that a couple of constables were beginning to round up a little gang of beggar children close by. The constables had the intention of putting the gang outside the gates but the children apparently had other ideas and refused to go.

A hollow-cheeked man with a flea-bitten hood looked on without emotion. He might have been their master, keeping out of things, or he might have merely been an onlooker like herself.

Meanwhile the protesting children were beaten roughly towards the Bar. There was nothing Hildegard could do but call out to the constables to treat them more kindly.

Ulf heard this exchange and it sent him over to add his protests, but his presence made little difference. The children were forcibly herded through the postern and thrown outside the city walls.

'We're well shut of them,' said a passer-by. 'We don't pay our taxes for nothing, bloody little scavengers.'

Hildegard was about to give the stranger a homily on charity when Ulf caught sight of her and came over.

'Hildegard! I didn't realise it was you!'

'Sir Ulf,' she responded with a rueful glance after the children. 'Your support was welcome but it seems there's little to be done with so many people swarming into town.'

'It's a new city ordinance. The constables are only doing their job, albeit with more vigour than necessary.' The steward's expression was worried as he bent his head close to her own. 'I've been thinking about you, Hildegard. Have there been any developments?'

She told him that the serjeant-at-arms had had nothing new to tell her when she last saw him. 'I noticed you inspecting the scaffolding just now. Who's it being built for?'

'Roger and his guests.' He went over and addressing one of the men with him said, 'My lord arrives later this morning. Can you ensure the carpenters make those adjustments?'

'No problem, sir. Lord de Hutton will find nothing on which to censure them.' Bowing he moved off with his men.

Ulf turned back to Hildegard. 'That's Mayor Simon de Quixlay with some of his aldermen. Roger's going to station himself at the number one spot all day so it had better be right in every blessed detail or my head's at risk.' His eyes flashed with humour but he immediately became serious again. 'So is there nothing new to tell me?'

'Aren't events at Deepdale enough of a novelty to see you through the week?' she grimaced.

His blue eyes clouded. 'Roger's already sent men over to find this manor near Pentleby and another posse have gone to Deepdale to see what we can save. You still don't remember seeing any badges or livery?'

She shook her head. 'They made sure they weren't wearing any.'

'Roger went crazy when I told him. He sees it as a personal insult. If the fools had known it was his property they'd have kept well away.'

'They were determined to find Maud. I don't think even Roger could have put them off.'

Ulf looked puzzled. 'Is she betrothed to one of them, or what? It doesn't make sense. All that trouble for a runaway serf.'

'Betrothal was the last thing on their minds.'

Ulf shook his head. 'Has she said anything else?'

'Only what I told you.' She had confided that the men had raped the women and the other young girls like Maud. 'The poor child is still rigid with shock. The last thing to do is to rush her. She needs time to recover. Only then will she be able to unburden herself and tell us the full story.'

'You believe there's more?'

Hildegard bit her lip. 'I pray not but she'll need to talk when the time's right.'

'So what's your plan now – are you going back to Swyne?'

She shook her head. 'I've got instructions to stay here.'

Surprised, he exclaimed, 'You've already heard from her?' He meant the prioress, as Hildegard understood at once.

She nodded. 'Her instructions arrived just before compline yesterday.'

'She doesn't let the grass grow, does she? Did she tell you when she wants you to escort the girls back?'

'She doesn't want them back just yet. If at all. Petronilla's guardian may arrive and insist on taking her home with him. It's his right. And given what happened at Deepdale those murderers would presumably think nothing of trying to snatch Maud from the priory. She's safer here. They wouldn't stop at slitting everybody's throats either, given the chance. We had a lucky escape, thanks to Dunstan's quick wits. The prioress is right if she thinks they're both safer in the town than at Swyne.'

Whether Ulf suspected there was another reason keeping her here or not, he did not pursue the topic but instead told her about Roger and Melisen's plans. Apparently they had already arrived at the manor in Naburn further down-river where they intended to lodge throughout the festivities.

'We have the matter of the chantry window to discuss with Danby as well as the pageant to endure.' He pulled a face. 'I'd prefer a joust myself but we can't choose what we do in Corpus Christi week, can we? A crowd of guests have been invited and Roger's keen to put in an appearance at the pageant. He's heard that someone of great eminence may be present.'

'You don't mean King Richard?'

'That's one of the rumours but we've heard nothing to confirm it – to my mind that discounts the presence of our young king.' He raised his eyebrows.

She understood at once. 'Heavens! A stand-in? Let's hope you're wrong and *he* doesn't put in an appearance. Master Stapylton hinted as much. I've got the impression the town won't tolerate it. On the anniversary of Tyler's murder? He'd be mad to show his face.'

'And we all know Gaunt isn't mad, except with ambition.' He gave a grim smile. 'So what makes you say the town won't put up with it?'

'A little fire that flared up.'

'I heard about that. Was it arson? That's the rumour. It's being blamed on the White Hart lads. If you hear anything to find the–'

'I'll tell you. You know I will.'

Changing the subject he mentioned that Lady Melisen would be delighted to have her opinion of the designs for the glass if Hildegard could spare time to come by Danby's workshop after midday. Then he mentioned again that Roger was in a rage at what had happened at Deepdale, gave a swift bow and was called away to deal with further matters concerning the erection of the scaffolding.

So the Duke of Lancaster was expected. That would not go down well. Agnetha's warning took on an added force. If the man had an iota of diplomacy he would keep well away. And so would his son, Henry of Derby, the one they called Bolingbroke. The presence of anyone from the House of Lancaster could act as a touchpaper to a, literally, flammable situation.

In the meantime all Hildegard could do was wait for a reply to the note she had sent Brother

Thomas at Meaux and for the arrival of the messengers with their unwanted burden from Swyne. Calculations told her that the latter, travelling more slowly than the messenger bringing the prioress's original missive, would be unlikely to arrive before evening. Thomas, if he was able to escort her as he had suggested, and coming a shorter distance, might even precede them.

The child running errands for the Sisters of the Holy Wounds to whom she had entrusted her note to Thomas was lurking outside the entrance when she returned. He jumped forward as if he had been waiting for some time and stood with his bare feet pressed firmly together, his back as straight as a stick, and told her, lispingly, through a gap in his front teeth, that he had delivered her message to the couriers as she had directed. 'My gracious lady,' he added for good measure.

He had been lucky enough to catch a courier just before he left for Beverley, he told her with pride. From there it was no more than four or five miles further on to the abbey. She was pleased with him and told him so. It meant her message could already have reached Meaux. She gave the little lad the extra she had promised for his pains and as he scampered away she decided to have a word with one of the cloistered sisters about his bare feet.

With Agnetha's warning of trouble on her mind she went up to the sleeping chamber where she had left her few belongings. There was no sign of the girls. They must be helping the nuns in return for our keep, she decided.

All their belongings smelt of smoke. She bundled a few garments under one arm and went down into the inner yard. No one had bothered her by so much as an unfriendly glance since she arrived in York, except here in the convent, but that was not to say that there was nothing simmering under the surface. If she was going to be picked out as a Cistercian at least her garments would be clean. She went over to the spring.

Mumbled prayers and a snatch of singing came through the open door of the chapel to prove the place hadn't been abandoned. A strong smell of incense wafted outside. A dry tree stuck out its sparsely leafed spikes in one corner. The sun's heat was intense.

She dipped the few garments into the cold water, first a voluminous white linen overgown, then the cotton shift that went under it, and finally a gorget. The light fabric ballooned up until the water soaked into it and dragged it underneath where it swirled in diaphanous clouds of white linen. It wouldn't take long for them to dry in this heat, she was thinking, as she gave each garment a good scrubbing, squeezed them out, then pegged them on the line slung across the yard.

The nuns did not want for water as their convent was built over a spring. It spouted pleasingly from the mouth of a wyvern into a deep stone trough.

She went back to sink her arms in the water after she'd finished hanging everything out. It swept, cool and clean, up to her elbows before she reluctantly withdrew them. Not bothering to dry them she pulled down her sleeves so they were covered, went to the door of the chapel, noticed the girls standing side by side near the front and decided on a sudden impulse to accept Ulf's invitation to meet at the glazier's workshop.

It was a year since she had seen Roger and Melisen de Hutton.

Chapter Ten

Hildegard had already guessed that the network of yards and snickets that lay behind the row of cottages on the riverbank just a short walk from the convent was where the stews were located. Now, stepping out from the porch into the sunlight, she saw a Dominican friar sidling out of a gap between two houses up ahead.

When he noticed her his expression changed to one that might have been mistaken for holiness. 'Ah, greetings my dear Sister, bless you, to be sure.' He spoke in such a fawning manner she thought for a moment he was actually going to ask her for alms. But it transpired that he merely wanted to lend a semblance of respectability to himself in case anybody had noticed him lurking in the vicinity of the brothels. Now he began to stroll along beside her as if she might be thought to condone his lechery.

While the bands of child beggars were swept outside the walls by civic ordinance, like so much garbage, the mendicant Orders had a licence to beg and were welcomed in – indeed, made especially welcome not just by the brothel-keepers but, as many knew, by the bored wives of wealthy merchants.

The Dominican's white habit looked much like their own, but Hildegard resented the fact that he assumed they shared the same point of view. She decided to test him.

When there was a pause in his monologue she threw in a casual remark. 'I see the constables are doing their job of putting the gangs of beggar children outside the walls.'

He pulled a face expressing approval. 'Indeed. Mayor de Quixlay, courting popularity among the poor as usual, wanted to make some dispensation for them over the festivities. He was voted down to our intense relief.'

'The competition would have been unfair,' she remarked, wondering whether he would hear the irony in her tone. He didn't.

'Indeed,' he replied. 'We must all uphold the law.'

Especially when it works in your favour, she thought. They reached the bridge. Hildegard made some excuse to get away and they parted. As she crossed the street into Conyngsgate she thought, nothing will change in this realm until the mendicants set their affairs in order. It was most unlikely. In the meantime all the Orders were tainted by the same accusations of greed and hypocrisy.

A handful of servants wearing the de Hutton

livery of a *lion d'or* rampant on a ground gules were lounging around in Danby's yard when she reached the glazier's workshop.

'Is your lord within?' she asked of them generally.

A spry young fellow nodded and jumped forward to sweep open the door for her. She entered to the murmur of voices.

The workshop was crowded. Hildegard had to peer over the tops of heads to catch sight of Lord Roger.

A man with his back to the door was blocking the little passageway leading from the yard. He wore a light sleeveless tunic over a cambric shirt bunched in under a thick leather belt and was bareheaded. When he moved aside to let her in she noted again the jewel glinting on a chain round his neck. This was the third time she had seen Master Baldwin.

He gave the man standing next to him a nudge. Edric Danby turned and seeing who had arrived, greeted Hildegard with a beam of pleasure.

He wore an orange turban on his head, despite the hot weather, but his dark-blue surcoat was of a light linen suitable for such intense heat. Even so he looked as if he was about to expire. His face was filmed with sweat and he wiped the back of his hand across it before he spoke. 'You're most welcome, Sister. The lord steward told us he'd invited you along and Lady de Hutton was just saying she hoped you'd come by and offer your opinion. It seems we've reached stalemate.'

Roger himself came forward and gripped her by the arm. 'Bad business, this attack on Deepdale, Hildegard. Praise the Lord none of you were harmed. We'll bring those devils to book, don't you worry. I'll have them tracked to hell and back. It's all in hand.' He released her arm.

Lady Melisen stepped forward in a scented cloud of lavender. 'It's shameful, Sister. All your hard work gone for nothing. But now I need your support against another set of dreadful men!'

Gilbert, with a stick of charcoal in one hand and his hair loose, had a smile on his face. Jankin was attending to the filling of the wine cups, and two pages in de Hutton livery were leaning against a workbench with bemused expressions as if they'd never seen anything like it. Clearly these were not included in Melisen's sweeping description.

'There they are!' she announced, indicating her husband, the glazier himself, and the steward. 'Just listen to them! You won't believe your ears!'

'Oh now, my Lady, I'm sure we can reach some accommodation with your wishes that won't run counter to those of Lord de Hutton.' Master Danby spoke in the tones of somebody who wants to make peace at any cost.

His words brought forth a sarcastic laugh from a dark-haired woman standing next to Baldwin whom Hildegard had not immediately noticed. Evidently she was Baldwin's wife, judging by the way she was resting one hand on his sleeve. Her fingers and wrists were weighted with gauds and baubles and her dark hair was coiled in a crispinette kept in place by an embroidered padded roll. With a narrow smile she was taking obvious pleasure in Master Danby's discomfort.

The glazier introduced the sarcastic woman as his sister-in-law, Mistress Julitta. She bestowed on the nun a perfunctory nod. Standing in the background was the master's young wife, Dorelia, her violet eyes vacant as she gazed off into space in a world of her own. The discussion resumed and Hildegard observed everyone in silence.

Julitta was a plain woman. She looked more so next to Dorelia's luminous beauty, yet there was something hard about her that did not yield precedence to anyone. Hildegard concluded that she was the sort of woman who would go to any lengths to please a man and to whom experience had taught the most effective method of doing so. All this in a flash. I'm being unfair, she thought.

It was certainly the case, however, that in such close juxtaposition, Dorelia looked even more ethereal, her features devoid of expression, her strangely empty eyes, though beautiful, never resting on anyone for more than a moment. As the matter of the glass was discussed, Hildegard silently pondered a question suitable for one of Melisen's elevated supper party discussions: which is the more dangerous – stupidity or cunning? She glanced from Dorelia to Julitta and could not make up her mind.

What puzzled Hildegard was the undercurrent of hostility emanating from Baldwin's wife.

Gilbert was watching everyone in silence. It was difficult to guess what he was thinking. His pale eyes reminded her again of the grisaille glass in the minster. He has her measure, she realised, as his glance rested briefly on Julitta's hard features.

As affable as usual, and happily unaware of any undercurrent, Master Danby invited them all to try to resolve the issue of the glass by going through to the inner workshop where they could have another look at the sketches he and his journeyman had put together.

He led the way to the inner sanctum where there was a long trestle in the middle of the room with a little stack of vellum pieces on it. 'As you know, anything can be changed at this stage. We only aim to please.' He gestured towards his journeyman. 'Gilbert has been working up a few changes but we can change things again. As soon as we get it right we can proceed with the *vidimus*.' He punched his journeyman on the shoulder. 'Go ahead, Gilbert. Show 'em what we've knocked together.'

They all positioned themselves around the trestle and Gilbert picked up one of the pieces of vellum from the top of the pile. It was small, no more than five inches square and done in pen and ink.

'Are we all agreed on this one?' Danby asked.

Roger gave a brief nod. 'We saw that last time. I liked it then and I like it now. It's good. The Queen of Heaven. Very good. I said so before.'

'Except that she still has no face,' objected Melisen. 'I trust you will give her a face when it's drawn to scale? I don't want a simple blur of light. I want – and so does my Lord,' she added hastily in deference to the fact that he was footing the bill, 'we expect definite features to make her human.'

132

'Human. I'll make a note of that.' Gilbert put it to one side. It was difficult to tell what mood he was in. Had that been a note of irony? He turned the drawing over and showed them the reverse. 'My lady?' He held it in front of Melisen so she could have a better look.

'And this one we like as well. The angels on either side. You've added more detail to their wings. That's really quite wonderful. And the baby is so charming. Yes, we love that.'

'And these little roundels,' added Roger, 'the ones with my coat of arms on them and the ones with the flower. They're good.'

'This little fox is very sweet,' commented Melisen, fingering the smaller sheets with the border drawings on them.

Gilbert took it from her and pushed it out of sight.

'That's his sign,' said Danby. 'Gilbert, the little fox.' He smiled with innocent good humour at anybody who met his eye.

'Is this a drawing of some sleeves?' Melisen had found another small drawing and held it up. 'Look at the folds. You can almost feel the softness of the silk. I take it they were silk?'

Gilbert made no reply.

'You seem to be in agreement on most of it,' Hildegard remarked. 'Where's the problem?'

'It's in the figures of the two donors,' said Roger, turning his back to glare at the wall. He was plainly irritated but unwilling to let off steam in his usual manner in front of strangers.

'I saw the drawing of you when I was here with Ulf before. It looked very fine.' She gave Gilbert a smile as she knew he was responsible for it.

Roger turned back with a sigh. 'It's what Melisen has in mind for the depiction of herself that's causing the problem.'

'You simply don't understand,' Melisen scolded. She turned to Hildegard. 'If Lady de Clare can do it, why can't I?'

Hildegard's lips parted in astonishment.

Melisen continued, 'I want myself depicted exactly as I am. Gilbert is quite willing to attempt the drawing.'

Roger gave the journeyman a baleful glance. 'I'm sure he is.'

Gilbert was unabashed. He took the collection of smaller drawings from Melisen and put them back tidily on the trestle. 'If I may make a suggestion, my Lord, why not allow Sister Hildegard to be present while I do the drawing of Lady Melisen?' He gave Hildegard a glance. 'That way my master will have no qualms about anything indecorous taking place and, my Lord, I trust you will feel the same way?'

'It's what'll be going through your mind while you draw my wife babe-naked that worries me!' snarled Roger.

Lady de Clare, it was well known, had been drawn as Eve in the Garden of Eden with only her famously long hair covering her modesty.

'Oh, sweeting,' cried Melisen, putting her hand on Roger's sleeve. 'I'm sure Gilbert has never had an impure thought in his life. You'd be willing to be present, wouldn't you, Sister?'

'Would you?' demanded Roger.

To Hildegard it seemed he had already bowed

to Melisen's desire. She knew him. He was making a meal of his objections now, but it was really all over. He had given in, proving that his fifth wife could twist him round her little finger. Astonishing, thought Hildegard.

In order to ease his defeat she said, 'I've heard about the glass depicting Lady de Clare.' She turned to Melisen. 'I assume this is the one you're referring to?'

Melisen nodded.

'I admit I haven't seen it myself but I'm told it's a most reverential depiction, and if everything is holy under God as we are told, then I see nothing wrong with the naked human form as such. It'll stand as a memorial to youth and beauty. Any husband would be proud to sponsor such a theme. And, as Lady Melisen has pointed out, there is a precedent for a donor to appear unclothed. And the figure will be small, no doubt. And if you want your chantry to be celebrated, Roger, this will do it...' She tailed off feeling that she had overdone things.

Roger gave her a stony glance. 'So I'm to relish having a pack of strangers gawping at my naked wife in return for a few prayers?'

'I'll draw her in profile,' suggested Gilbert, as if that would help. He received an even stonier look.

Hildegard had one more idea. 'Why not let her wear a close-fitting garment like the one Eve wears in the pageant?'

Melisen clapped her hands. 'I knew she'd solve it! What do you say, My Lord? You can't possibly object to that!'

After an involved discussion about the quota of

135

truth to illusion in the glazier's art, it was agreed. She could wear the Eve suit and still appear with her natural youth and beauty – as if unadorned.

Danby wiped his brow. He was plainly delighted that the commission was now firmly in the bag and invited everyone to return to the larger workshop where they would be more comfortable and could tie up any other loose ends while they finished their wine. When they went through Gilbert remained at his bench. Hildegard lingered. 'Will that be satisfactory from your point of view?'

He gave her that bright smile she had seen before when his eyes seemed to shoot sparks of silver. 'It won't affect my drawing – although I can't believe Lady Melisen will be satisfied to do as they tell her–' He broke off with a laugh. So he had got her measure too. Proving it, he added, 'I might draw in the lines of an imaginary Eve suit just to tease her.'

'She would probably take a hammer to the glass in that case!'

'Indeed, I pray she will, should I be so dishonest!'

'It won't put you off to have an audience?'

'Nothing puts me off drawing. Let's just keep my master and Lord Roger happy.'

'Agreed. So when do we start?'

'Let's go through and find out.'

She was slow to follow. 'Gilbert, is Fox really your name?' she asked.

He shook his head.

'I thought not. I heard your master refer to you as Gilbert of Leicester.'

He lowered his head so that his hair fell in a silver veil over his face. He began to move things about on his workbench to no purpose.

'I suppose you must know Lutterworth if you're from that part of the world?' she continued, genuinely interested.

He didn't lift his head. 'Everybody knows that place.'

'Did you ever hear Wycliffe preach?'

'We all did. You couldn't avoid it.'

'I've heard he's quite brilliant?'

'That's what they say.'

She turned to go, then remembered how they had got into this conversation. She turned back. 'So why did you choose a fox for your sign?' She was smiling, imagining it must be something to do with having a pet cub as a child.

Instead of responding he gazed at his workbench in silence. His eyelids quivered. When he eventually looked at her his glance was as hard as steel. 'You should know the answer to that one, Sister.'

He stepped back with a small bow to allow her to pass, then followed after, limping and trying to conceal his deformity under the fall of his summer cloak.

Roger would probably have objected to Melisen being drawn naked by anyone but the fact that Gilbert was young and good-looking despite his crooked leg must have made matters worse. While they all stood out in the street waiting for the horses to be brought up, Hildegard tried to smooth ruffled feathers. She said to Ulf, 'Tell

137

Roger he shouldn't be too bothered about this drawing. It's only for one morning. It isn't as if Gilbert's going to be drawing her every day.'

Ulf agreed. 'Fuss over nothing. It's a mistake for men to marry women so much younger than themselves. Melisen's only a year older than his daughter. Naturally he's jealous when there's a handsome young fellow on the scene. Master Danby's just the same.'

'I hadn't noticed Danby was jealous of anybody.'

Ulf considered the matter. 'You're right. He's too much the other way. I meant the age difference. Old men and women half their age? Danby's maybe too complacent.'

'With regard to the journeyman you mean?'

'Who knows? Although I imagine Gilbert has far too much common sense than to put his livelihood in jeopardy. It was an odd atmosphere in there, though, if that's what you're hinting. Was it to do with Lady Melisen's request or was something else going on?'

'It's probably the usual jealousies. I imagine Mistress Julitta can't be happy about a child like Dorelia taking precedence over her – just because she happens to have snared a guildmaster. She doesn't seem the type to be happy in second place. Baldwin seems to be under her thumb, though. Did you see how she never let him away from her side? He's a different man when he's with his fellows.' She told Ulf what had happened at the booth when the mage did his disappearing act.

'She's probably wise to keep him on a short

138

leash if he's liable to go on the rampage,' he replied. 'Still, it's Danby I feel sorry for. He's a decent type. I hope the new wife isn't making a fool of him. Since he remarried he doesn't seem to know whether he's coming or going.'

'Is Dorelia his second wife?'

'His first died a year ago. There's a little daughter somewhere around. I believe he's on the square. He certainly saved Simon de Quixlay's bacon.'

'What do you mean?'

While the horses of Roger's large retinue were being brought up the street by the grooms he explained.

'You were in your hermitage while all this was going on. It began with a quarrel between two aldermen, John de Gisburne and a fellow called John Langton. They started arguing the toss over who should be mayor. Gisburne was disliked because of his allegiance. Everybody believes it gives him an unfair advantage. He has his fingers in a lot of pies and he'd been commissioned to supply an Oxford college with lead–'

'Lucrative stuff, then.'

He nodded. 'He's not short of a penny or two but there've been murmurs – the provenance of his lead, for instance. That's never been proved and he point-blank refuses to appear before his guildmaster to explain himself. There've been other things as well, making it look as if he sets himself above the law.'

Ulf peered over the heads of the grooms until he saw his own squire leading his horse in the crowd. 'It's not only guild business, Hildegard,' he said hurriedly as the horse was brought up. 'The year before the Great Rebellion down in London a group of citizens broke into the Guildhall here in York and forced Gisburne out of office. They persuaded Simon de Quixlay to stand as mayor instead. It was a bit of a riot. The Justiciar had to step in and twenty of the rioters were sent to London and imprisoned in the Tower.'

'The Tower?' she asked in astonishment. 'As bad as that?'

'It got worse. Some supporters followed them down and holed up in a place called Tottenham Manor and they finished up in the Tower as well. The whole pack of 'em were eventually released, five months before the Rising. Of course, they came straight back and elected Simon de Quixlay all over again. It's old history,' he told her, taking the reins from his servant.

'I heard nothing. It must have been when I was living as a recluse.'

He nodded. 'Grieving for Hugh.'

She brushed that aside. 'You said Danby saved Quixlay. What happened there?'

'The rebellion in London happened.'

'What do you mean?'

'Within days riots broke out up here as well and the walls and gates of the Dominican priory were smashed, along with damage to St Leonard's, the friary and a few other places. That same day de Quixlay summoned the bailiffs and the commons to the Guildhall. He insisted on a new ordinance imposing a fine of forty pounds on anybody who tried to transfer any plea made for alleged crimes inside the city walls to the court of King's Bench down in London.'

'Which must be what Gisburne did – to get his enemies put in the Tower?'

'That's exactly it. But de Quixlay was adamant. He said if anybody commits a crime here then we'll be the ones to try them, not some foreigners down south.'

'And Danby?'

'He made a speech in support and swayed everybody against Gisburne's faction. But that wasn't the end of it. In the July following the London riots Gisburne and his gang got hold of the keys of Bootham Bar and broke into the city. Then they rode round trying to persuade men into their own livery–'

'Persuade?'

'Most strongly.' He grimaced.

The de Hutton retinue was preparing to move off.

Ulf swung hurriedly into the saddle. 'They even broke a fellow's legs for refusing to join them. Gisburne was bound over to keep the peace – and he hasn't held office since.'

'So he's given up on being mayor?'

Ulf glanced down with a grimace. 'Let's hope so. We've had enough of him. There is talk he's now going to build a chantry that'll outdo the one Roger's planning.'

She put out a hand to detain his horse as the retinue began to move off. 'Apart from Danby,' she asked, 'who are Simon de Quixlay's supporters?'

'Most of the guildsmen as it happens. Danby

carries a lot of weight with them. Not just with glaziers, but with the masons, carpenters and mercers as well. All those who want a quiet life so they can get on and make a profit! But de Quixlay's a popular fellow in his own right. He got the butchers on side by backing them when they objected to "schameltoll". It was an unfair toll, he said, and he gave it short shrift.'

The horses were creating a great commotion of jingling bridles, stamping hooves and general kerfuffle as they started to take the de Hutton retinue back down the street. But Hildegard had one more question. She walked along beside Ulf as he allowed his mount to join the cavalcade. 'Ulf, do you know if Gisburne has anything to do with the Duke of Lancaster? Is that his unpopular allegiance?'

'Funny you should ask that,' Ulf replied. Leaning down from the saddle he said quietly, 'Gisburne has recently been given the lease on a couple of manors up by Knaresborough way.'

Knaresborough Castle and the land around, as she well knew, belonged to Duke John of Lancaster.

He gave her a lopsided grin. 'Civic quarrels, Sister. Nothing to do with us! Be thankful you missed it all!' He waved his riding whip in a salute and urged his horse after the others.

The head of the cavalcade had reached the end of the street when Ulf turned and called out, 'Come to Naburn Manor, Hildegard. We have a Tuscan chef!'

Then, with great tumult, they were gone.

Hildegard frowned as the street fell quiet. Put

two ambitious people in contention, she thought, and you have the seeds of war. This Gisburne sounded like bad news with his powerful connections. De Quixlay's strength seemed to lie in his popularity with the people. She remembered John of Gaunt and how he was hated, and how by contrast young King Richard was so beloved. Maybe the mood of the town was not as she had first imagined.

After she took her leave of the glazier with his silent wife and began to walk back along Stonegate, her thoughts strayed to foxes.

Gilbert's reply to her question had been ambiguous to say the least.

What did he mean, she should know the answer to that one?

Chapter Eleven

The scriptorium was empty again. Sometime after compline, when the only lights were the candles at the ends of the corridors and the one she carried, Hildegard went inside and fumbled around on one of the desks for the writing tools. She took up a sharpened quill from a box, dipped the point into the inkwell, swirled it around and began to write.

After the usual flowery greeting required when addressing an archbishop she wrote as briefly as she could:

143

I beseech Your Grace to grant me the great honour of an audience at your earliest opportunity on behalf of my prioress at Swyne. I await Your Grace's reply at the convent of the Holy Wounds in York.

She left it at that after the usual valedictory flourish. He would guess at once what it concerned.

Running the chalk over it, she folded it twice, melted some wax over a small flame to seal it and that night placed it under her head while she slept.

As soon as she heard the bell for prime, she went to find the small boy who had been helpful last time. He was still barefoot.

'Are you not to have any shoes, then, young master?' she asked.

Blushing and wiping sleep out of his eyes he nodded. 'The sister says when she has the time she'll make sure I get some.'

'When she has the time?'

'Her being busy and whatnot.'

'I see. Well, in the meantime, while you're waiting, you may save enough pennies to purchase your own shoes. Here's another message for you to take to the courier if you will and tuppence to go with it.'

He took the letter, and the two pennies, bowed, and ran off.

Busy, she scoffed. Busy praying. Well that wouldn't put shoes on the child's feet. She decided she had better ask in the town for a reliable patten-maker.

Almost as soon as he left she was called down to the lodge by one of the novices. 'Visitors outside the porch,' she informed her, adding, with a suspicious look from beneath her veil, 'Two *men*.'

'Thank you, my dear Sister,' Hildegard replied more grandly than usual. So they were here already. She hurried down the corridor while trying to betray as little haste as possible.

Two men she recognised as *conversi* from Swyne stood just outside the convent doors. They were grinning broadly. They were not allowed to set foot inside, they told her. 'Not so much as the toe of one boot on the edge of a tile,' one of them added. She smiled. They were the last ones to wreak havoc among a gaggle of nuns. They carried something in a sack.

'Produce from Swyne,' one of them announced with a wink when he saw her glance alight on it.

'Thank my lady prioress, if you will. Tell her I shall make sure it reaches its destination.'

They had ridden through the night. She offered them something to break their fast but they refused, saying they had to get back. They left with cheerful waves. They seemed to like it when they thought the prioress was up to something.

Hildegard took the sack along to the scriptorium, as it seemed to be the most unfrequented corner in the whole place. It was tied at the neck by a piece of rope and inside was a softer wrapping. Not wishing to remove the whole thing from its cover in case somebody should unexpectedly come in she merely pulled it to one side.

For centuries the cross had been kept in a magnificent, jewelled reliquary, locked by means of a delicate gold key. She shuddered, remembering what had happened to the key. The reliquary was probably still in the possession of the Gran Contessa of Florence who had sent her man Escrick Fitzjohn to steal it from the custodian. Unluckily for her, a sacristan, its guardian, had removed the cross beforehand in order to keep it safe from thieves.

Now the cross was rehoused in a flat wooden box of English oak that looked new and, she supposed, had been made at Swyne. When she had brought the cross back from Tuscany she had had to hide it in among her clothes and carry it the whole way in a bag on her shoulder like any old souvenir from a pilgrim's travels.

She took the box to the narrow window where there was a better light and peered inside. It was just as she remembered, a rough piece of wood, crusted with age. It looked like nothing.

On the back would be the inscription that proved it to be the cross the Emperor Constantine had kept by his side for his own private devotions after his conversion, the cross he had carried into battle when he had defeated his enemies at the Milvian Bridge near Rome, a cross associated with miracles.

A cross, furthermore, that was believed to bestow untold worldly power on its owner.

She ran her fingers underneath until she felt the shallow indentations she remembered. When she turned the cross over she read the inscription: *in hoc signo vinces*. In this sign you shall conquer.

A velvet cloth, the colour of blood, lined the box.

Satisfied that all was in order she rewrapped the entire thing and thought for a moment about the best place to hide it until the archbishop sent word for her to bring it to him. There was nowhere she could be certain it might remain undiscovered. She decided to keep it by her side at all times. It would fit inside her leather travel bag as it had done before.

Brother Thomas arrived later that morning. He too, like the *conversi*, had an expectant air and was clearly pleased to get out of the abbey on what must have seemed like an adventure.

'I came over as soon as I could. I hope I'm not too late. What's it all about?' he asked, pacing the lane outside the nunnery, having suffered a similar rejection by the porteress as the *conversi*.

'I have instructions to take a certain object to the archbishop to let him have a look at it,' she told him as she paced by his side. 'Don't ask me why, I can't tell you. But that's what the prioress has asked me to do. And she gave a special warning that I must on no account leave it with him. I thought it best to have a witness to what goes on.'

'It sounds special, then, this object. Is it a relic of some sort?'

She looked into his honest face and decided to tell him the truth. 'It's the Cross of Constantine.'

A look of awe passed over his face and he quickly crossed himself. 'So you really did bring it back from Tuscany? The cloister was buzzing with rumours about that. One of the archbishop's men started the story. We thought he was spinning a yarn to impress us.'

'He was telling the truth.' She told him briefly of the appalling events that had taken place.

'I can see why you feel you need an escort,' he said. 'Although any meeting with Alexander Neville is best done with an ally beside you.'

'I've already asked for an audience. I'm waiting to hear from him. Meanwhile,' she made an apologetic face, 'I've committed myself to act as chaperone this morning to Lady Melisen while she poses for the donor drawing for Roger's chantry glass. I said I would be free, not expecting you and the messengers from Swyne to appear so speedily.'

He smiled. 'You know how it is when you get the fever to be out and about. I grabbed the opportunity to come over at once. As we can't do anything until you hear from His Grace don't worry about leaving me alone in the wicked city. I have one or two errands I can do around here. We have our own Corpus Christi celebrations to organise at Meaux and I promised to pick up some extra candles for the sacristan.'

'Are you getting them from Master Stapylton?' she asked.

He said he was.

'Then you need to know there was a fire in his workshop. They say no one was hurt but would you ask after him for me? There were so many people around afterwards I didn't like to pester him myself.'

He nodded. His hair was untidier than usual, she noticed, and he had a week's stubble on his chin, giving him a rakish look. In a capuchon and houpelande instead of his white habit he would not look out of place in a tavern playing dice. She smiled. This was an unexpected view of the young monk. He was usually correct to a fault. He must be in want of the austere guidance of his abbot, she decided with a secret smile.

He gave an apologetic shrug now and said, 'I'd better not keep turning up here, you know. Those nuns are already looking askance at you. Why don't we meet at St Peter's later this afternoon? If the archbishop has replied by then you can tell me what he says in private and we can discuss how we're going to get out there. I suppose he's at Bishopthorpe and not Cawood?'

'I sent my message to his palace at Bishopthorpe. If he's elsewhere it'll no doubt follow on until it reaches him.'

'Just so I'm certain I have a bed for the night I'll go along to the Franciscans and see if they can offer me something.'

Repeating their agreement to meet up again at the minster, as St Peter's was usually called, they separated. Hildegard set off at once to Stonegate. She was wondering who that loose-tongued servant of Archbishop Neville's was, the one who had started the rumour about the cross.

'Lady Melisen hasn't arrived yet,' announced Jankin, the glazier's apprentice, when the serving lad showed her in. He offered her a seat by the window.

'Ale or wine?' he asked.

'As it's so hot today I'd better have ale,' she replied. She was glad she had changed into her

149

crisp, clean habit. It was her summer one but even so she felt her head swimming in the heat of the workshop. The kiln, she noticed, was alight.

Dorelia was sitting quietly in a corner with some embroidery on her lap. She was wearing a pale-green shift with diaphanous silk sleeves overprinted in a darker shade. They were in the new fashion and fell in graceful folds to the floor. She didn't raise her head even when Jankin came back with the ale. He handed Hildegard a stoup, then refilled Dorelia's clay beaker without being asked.

'Master won't be long.' He darted a glance at Dorelia, then went over to his workbench and pulled out a stool. His tight breeches strained over his thighs as he stretched out his legs. 'Too stifling to work in this weather,' he said, generally.

Hildegard murmured an agreement. It was certainly overheated in here. She wondered why the kiln was burning. She supposed it was for some work in hand.

Moments passed.

Nobody spoke.

A bee flew in through the window and buzzed once round the workshop before flying out again. Dorelia rose to her feet and stretched in a languid sort of way as if she had been sitting too long. The lace of her bodice was loose. Flapping the edge of one sleeve she fanned her burning cheeks.

Jankin's glance flickered and fell.

Eventually she leant across the apprentice to try to reach a pair of scissors lying on the bench on his other side. Her sleeve brushed the back of his neck and he gave a sudden smile like a contented cat and moved so that it brushed him again.

Something familiar about the pattern of her sleeves drew Hildegard's attention. Then she recalled where she had seen it before. It was the same pattern Gilbert had drawn so beautifully on one of the little squares of vellum he was making into a book.

Then Danby walked in and the strange mood was broken.

He was sweating.

'Another scorcher!' he announced as if perhaps they hadn't noticed. 'That kiln's the last thing to get close to in weather like this. I'm firing some pieces for a window in the minster nave,' he explained to Hildegard after the usual greetings.

'And you can't trust us to get the timing right,' Jankin chipped in with a grin.

'Wouldn't trust you as far as I could throw you.' Danby punched him genially on the shoulder. 'It's the third firing,' he told Hildegard. 'I don't want my silver stain ruining.' He looked pleased with the world as he usually did, despite his words, adding, 'This is going to show 'em what we can do.' He rubbed his hands with relish.

'I suppose the secret of how you get such colours lies in the firing?' She took a sip of ale.

'Every craft has its secrets and I'm hanging onto mine. But I can tell you this. St Peter's is going to have the best glass in the country.'

'Is Gilbert ready to set about this drawing?' Hildegard asked him.

'He is. You can go through if you like. He should be in there at his bench, the quiet little sod.'

She could see he was itching to get on with his work. Jankin had picked up some lead calmes and began to shape them in a half-hearted manner round a piece of glass. Taking her ale with her, Hildegard went on into the inner workshop.

Gilbert was there after all, working quietly, his head bent over some vellum as he made a rapid sketch in pen and ink. At the sound of someone entering he cupped his hand round his drawing and darted a glance.

She went over. 'It seems we have to wait for your model to appear,' she greeted. 'I hope your time isn't being wasted?'

He put down his quill and whipped the leather thong off his hair to allow the sheet of silver to fall to his shoulders. His eyelids quivered. Even his lashes were silver, like flecks of foil.

'Time is never wasted,' he replied.

Hildegard walked over to the open window. It gave onto a private yard where there was a line of washing drying to a crisp in the sun. When she turned back Gilbert had selected a piece of charcoal and it was a different sketch he was working on now.

'Your master tells me he's firing some glass. It must be hard work on a day like this. Wouldn't it be cooler by night?'

'He won't work by night. The guild forbids it.'

'Honest then, and in this weather!'

'My master's honest in all weathers.' He darted a glance from beneath his bright lashes. Then, as if he imagined he was being unwelcoming, he told her a little about the minster window they were working on. 'It's The Last Judgement. Usually goes in the West window. But they're planning something really big to go in there. At present there's some indecision about where to put ours. Master's hoping it'll persuade them to give him the commission for the big one.'

'It's an important undertaking, then?'

'If they're impressed enough it should see the master out. Unless he lives to be a hundred and ten.' He paused. 'As we pray he does.'

'I've often wondered how you decide what to put in – at least when your donor doesn't have such strong ideas as Lady Melisen about her husband's chantry window.'

'It's fairly standard if it's for the Church. Scenes from the Old Testament, called the "type", and parallel scenes from the New Testament, called the "antitype". You pair things, like.'

'I've heard of that. You mean like Jonah living in the belly of the whale for three days, then coming out alive, and Christ dead in his tomb for three days before being resurrected?'

He lifted his head. His eyes were piercing. 'Everything has its parallel. Like a forewarning of what's going to happen. It gives symmetry to our understanding of the Book.'

Hildegard hadn't expected a conversation veering towards the theological. She said, 'Your windows aren't called the Bible of the Poor for nothing, then. In fact you're writing the Bible in glass just as Wycliffe is writing it in English.'

His expression was sharp. Sharp and suspicious.

'I'm sorry – I didn't mean to offend you by comparing you to Wycliffe,' she said hurriedly, unsure what he thought to the preacher's ideas. 'I happen to be in favour of having the Bible written in a language people can understand. Latin's all very well but to most people it's just hocus-pocus.'

He laughed. 'Is that the orthodox Cistercian view these days?'

'If it's not, it should be.'

'What about what Wycliffe says about the Eucharist?' he asked, as sharp as a knife.

She gave him a careful glance. Over the water in the rest of Europe people were being burnt alive at the stake as heretics because they refused to accept the turning of wine into blood as more than a symbol. There were no miracles, said Wycliffe, only superstition and an ignorance as to the true causes of things.

'I can understand his arguments,' said Hildegard. 'His logic seems without fault. Unfortunately he doesn't write with much clarity. It might take somebody else to put his ideas forward in a way people can grasp. His argument seems to rest on a subtle point in our theory of knowledge. It's difficult enough to understand without being couched in cumbersome phrases.'

'I've found it slippery enough myself when I've–' He broke off, as if having said too much.

'As you told me yesterday,' she continued, 'it must have been difficult to avoid hearing him preach, especially if you lived in his part of the world.' That let him off the hook.

There was no blame in listening to a preacher, especially if he was standing outside your church door as you left after Mass. She had no intention

154

of trapping him into admitting to what was deemed heretical – although she couldn't vouch for his intention towards herself.

Why that question about the Eucharist? she wondered. The Inquisition saw it as a test of orthodoxy. The wrong answer in the wrong place could send you to a hideous death.

It was a strange conversation to be having with a glazier. They had stumbled into it and now they looked at each other with equal wariness.

It was true nobody was being burnt at the stake for holding such views, not here in England, but there were those not yet in power who wanted to follow the example set in Germany and France and rid the world of heretics. Freedom of speech was abhorrent to them. Wycliffe's preachers were travelling the country in russet robes and carrying few possessions because they had been hounded out of Oxford for questioning the pope's interpretation of the Eucharist. Many of them had been thrown into prison, although as far as she knew they were all out now.

It was a quagmire, however. Bread. Wine. They remained just that in Wycliffe's view. When the priest raised the Host and offered the chalice no miracle took place. It was a symbol only, if of another truth.

Gaunt and Archbishop Courtenay had bribed Wycliffe's supporters with gifts of rich livings and browbeaten those who held to their views by threats of prison. It had silenced many of them. Wycliffe himself, old and tired, had withdrawn to an obscure manor near Lutterworth in the midlands where he could write undisturbed.

Suddenly voices were audible in the yard. It sounded like Melisen and her retinue.

Gilbert began to shuffle his drawings out of sight.

Hildegard had spotted something, though. 'This one…' She placed her hand on his arm as he was about to push it underneath with the rest. 'What is it?' She could see what it looked like. It was a fox wearing a triple crown preaching to a herd of geese. It was what it meant that interested her.

'Master told you the fox is my sign. I'm just playing around with a few ideas,' he replied. He avoided her glance.

'Is it for a window?'

'What sort of window?' He gave a harsh laugh. His expression hardened. When she didn't reply he said, 'You mean a Lollard window? Is that what you're suggesting, Sister?'

She watched him put the drawing out of sight. It might well be a design for a Lollard window if she had guessed right about something. She decided to take a risk.

'I was thinking about what you replied when I asked you why you'd chosen a fox for your sign. You said: I should know. It puzzled me. I couldn't see why I, in particular, should know. Then I happened to remember that commentary on one of the psalms made by Bernard of Clairvaux, the founder of my Order. It mentions foxes, and he writes at length about what the fox stands for. He meant something very specific.'

Gilbert had allowed his hair to fall over his eyes again and she had no idea what effect her words

156

were having, whether she had got it right or whether he was merely letting her talk.

There was noise from the other workshop and Lady Melisen's voice was heard, greeting Master Danby and giving orders to her retinue at the same time.

Hurriedly Hildegard said, 'It made me wonder if you'd read Bernard's commentary or heard it mentioned and decided for that reason that it would make a good symbol to use?'

She continued, 'If you have read it you'll know he was referring to heretics. More than that, he was saying that if they won't change their views they should be exterminated.' Gilbert's sign could be a simple reference to the psalm – or it could be a play on Bernard's idea of foxes and heretics. It was something that could turn a stained glass window into a rebel shout of defiance.

Or stand as an affirmation of orthodoxy – with all the punishing horror that implied.

Type and antitype.

Before Melisen entered Gilbert muttered, 'So you picked up on that reference? I can see I shall have to watch my step.' His lips tightened. 'Or you yours?'

Chapter Twelve

Thomas had stabled his horse with the town hostler and when Hildegard met him in the minster as arranged, she had to explain that she would have to hire a horse as she had arrived on foot from Deepdale. 'The alternative is to go by river,' she suggested.

'Let's do that. We'll be less conspicuous.' He glanced at the leather satchel she carried over her shoulder. 'Have you got it there?'

She nodded.

'So when do we leave?'

The archbishop's letter requesting her to attend him had been waiting at the nunnery when she returned from the drawing session at Master Danby's. It offered her an audience that evening after vespers.

'We have time to kill,' she said. 'What would you like to do?'

'Let's sit awhile in a niche somewhere and you can tell me about the calamity at Deepdale and what you intend to do about it, and then you can amuse me with your account of this drawing session you've just attended.'

The minster was busy with the usual activities and nobody was bothered by the two Cistercians sitting together under one of the windows. The sun slanted through, casting a bright light over the faces of those who passed, and picked out the colours of their garments, the reds, the blues, the yellows, making them like the jewel hues of the glass itself.

'Lady Melisen must have wished she had never insisted on being drawn from life,' she told him, avoiding the topic of the devastated grange. 'There can be nothing more tedious for the sitter. Gilbert is so painstaking he wouldn't allow her to move at all until he was satisfied. Of course, we were forbidden to make a sound. It seemed to go on endlessly, the thin scratching of his pen, Gilbert's glares at the shuffle of my feet as I changed position or got up and walked around the workshop, Melisen staring rigidly at the wall just as he had positioned her. She had her hair down,' she added. 'It's very long. It covered her like a cloak and there was no need for a suit. And besides it was so stifling hot in there–' She broke off. 'Perhaps I've told you enough! Anyway, it was a terrible penance, for me as well as for Melisen. Gilbert gave me the blackest look when I went over to see some of his drawings.' She frowned. 'You might be interested in the conversation I had with him before Melisen arrived.'

'What was that about? Craft and illusion again?'

'Not entirely, although...' she grimaced, 'I suppose there is a connection. No, it was more subversive, you might even say heretical, than that.' Briefly she told him what Gilbert had said, omitting his unexpected warning.

'Our founder offers many challenges,' Thomas replied carefully when she finished. 'I see it as a failing that he didn't counter Abelard's arguments when he had the chance. It has left us with

159

the suspicion that he was unable to do so. But you're uneasy about Gilbert?'

'He's surprisingly well read for a journey-man...'

'Linking him with the rebels, then, who pride themselves on their knowledge of the scriptures?'

She nodded. 'Maybe. At any rate he knew what Bernard meant by the foxes.'

'Maybe he's been listening to marketplace preachers?'

'That's what I thought. It makes me wonder if it has any bearing on what Agnetha hinted – about trouble brewing?'

Thomas looked thoughtful. 'Stapylton told me something interesting while I was haggling over the price of candles. He said he didn't think the fire in his workshop was accidental.'

When it was time to leave they hired a boat at King's Staithe. The archbishop's palace was a little way downriver. Thomas rowed and they passed the watergate and the inlet to the king's fish ponds. Soon both banks became more wooded until the spire of St Oswald's was visible against the summer sky and a huddle of houses on the waterfront showed they were just off Fulford. The village was swiftly left behind and they were soon floating between thick woodland again.

It was a calm night. The only sound apart from the soft dip of the oars was an occasional screech of an owl or the plop of a rat as it slipped into the water. Shortly before the river began its long meander through open countryside they came suddenly on the blazing lights of the palace on the opposite bank.

Thomas manoeuvred the bows towards the shore. In a moment they felt the boat bump against a wooden landing stage. He tied a line to a post and even before he finished a couple of guards appeared with flares held above their heads. There was a rattle of arms as they marched up.

'Who comes?' grunted one of them.

'Sister Hildegard and Brother Thomas of Meaux.'

The guard held his flare close to Thomas's face, noted the white habit, and demanded, 'On what business?'

Hildegard stepped forward. 'Private business with His Grace. He expects us.'

The man seemed satisfied with this and told them to follow. He led them up a long avenue towards a lighted gatehouse. Under the flickering cressets within, a few guards were playing dice and barely looked up when they entered. A page was sent to announce them and a few minutes later they were being shown inside the palace.

'This is lavish,' whispered Thomas in her ear. His mouth was slightly open at the amount of gilding in the small chamber where they were asked to wait.

Hildegard had been here before. 'This is only the anteroom. Wait until you see his audience chamber.'

An armoured door was flung open and they were ushered through.

Thomas gasped.

At the far end was the archbishop's throne. It seemed to be fashioned entirely of gold. Two large brass stands, taller than an average man, stood on either side of it, bearing thick beeswax candles. The air was heavy with the scent of honey. Archbishop Neville himself was standing at a table hewn from Purbeck marble illuminated by a chandelier of Venetian glass, each facet glittering with the light of many candles. Beyond the light the chamber was in darkness.

The archbishop beckoned them to step closer. Hildegard felt constrained to bend her knee and she heard Thomas drop to his own.

'Up, up. Who's this?' Neville demanded of Hildegard.

'Brother Thomas, a monk from the Abbey of Meaux, and my escort.'

'Very wise. Now, your prioress...' Neville paused heavily for a moment, his pouched red face turned to her, 'wishes you to return the cross after it has been verified.'

'I have promised to do that.'

'I know better than to thwart her.' He smiled in a way that did not reach his eyes, which were blue and calculating.

He called to one of several servants standing by unseen in the shadows. 'You can all go to your beds.' The servants filed out. There was a further movement and a man stepped into the pool of light. Hildegard's eyes widened.

About twenty or maybe even younger he was a sturdy, muscular, swaggering sort of fellow. But for his bejewelled and gold-embroidered surcoat and the expensive-looking sword dangling from the studded belt on his hips, she might have taken him for a man-at-arms. He was shorter than she was but made up for it in confidence.

Now he looked the two monastics up and down and, she noticed, checked Thomas with a practised glance for any concealed weaponry. The archbishop did not introduce him. Hildegard surmised that he was a military commander from the south; he was certainly not one of the northern magnates, the Duke of Northumberland, whom she had seen many times, nor his firebrand son, Lord Harry, and yet there was something about the way he spoke to Neville – as if the archbishop was his vassal and he the overlord.

Thomas seemed stunned into immobility.

'Let's see it, then,' said the stranger. He flicked his fingers to bring her closer and indicated the table.

She unslung the leather bag from her shoulder and placed it on the table in the pool of light. When the simple oak box was withdrawn from its cloth cover the stranger frowned. No doubt he had been expecting a jewelled reliquary as costly as his own encrusted garments.

'I was forced to bring it back from Tuscany without its usual container,' she explained.

'I've told him that,' said Neville somewhat testily. He reached forward and lifted the lid.

Both men crowded round and Hildegard withdrew a little to give them chance to have a proper look.

The expression on the stranger's face was hard to decipher. Finally he turned away, scratching his neck. 'It doesn't look much.'

'I warned you not to expect the heavens to open and let forth the sound of trumpets,' murmured the archbishop.

The stranger's eyes flashed. 'So you did, Neville, so you did.'

The archbishop lifted the cross out of its scarlet bed and held it up. There was a strange reverence in his gesture. He seemed moved by knowledge of its history. 'The Donation of Constantine,' he breathed. Then he gave a sharp glance at his guest. 'If you doubt what it is there's an inscription on the back.'

As if satisfied with his brief communion with what was for him a most holy relic, he handed it over. The young man's stubby fingers, scarred, Hildegard noticed, as if in the joust or in some swordplay, probed along the underside of the cross, turning it over and peering at the inscription. He translated with a smile. 'In this you will conquer.' He lifted his head, 'Or might we prefer to say: with this I am victorious?'

The archbishop cleared his throat and glanced at the two Cistercians. Thomas had made himself almost invisible.

Slouching, the stranger pushed it back to Neville and then gave Hildegard a narrow look. 'So how much will she accept?'

Neville gave an exclamation. 'My Lord–'

'I haven't time, Neville. Let's get to the point…'

The archbishop turned away to conceal his exasperation.

Hildegard said, 'It's not for sale.'

The small eyes blistered into her own and

became even smaller. 'I asked how much.' He put his head on one side.

Hildegard tried to explain why it could not be sold. 'When it was agreed to allow me to bring it back to England, it was done so on the understanding that it would be given into our temporary stewardship, to be returned when the canons of Santi Apostoli requested.'

The stranger gave a curse. 'Don't play with me, Sister.'

Hildegard turned to Archbishop Neville. 'Your Grace, I understand you are on good terms with my prioress. I myself cannot enter into negotiations but perhaps you could approach her directly?' She knew the answer would be no, whatever this conceited, battle-scarred young devil thought.

Neville met her eye and she noticed a brief expression of gratitude. Turning to his guest he said, 'That sounds acceptable. I have promised to return it but I'm sure, if we keep our word, we shall more easily attain our desire.'

The man looked uncertain. It seemed he was about to force the issue but then he gave a sudden sound of capitulation. 'I haven't long,' he growled. 'Start negotiations and be quick about it.'

Neville inclined his head. The cross was rewrapped and Hildegard walked from the chamber in astonishment that they had got their way

As they left the building she whispered to Thomas, 'She will never agree.'

'Let's get out of here,' he replied. 'I can't believe my eyes.'

He took the bag with the cross inside and they

walked briskly through the gatehouse, where the game of dice was progressing, and out onto the avenue. When they were out of earshot he asked, 'You know who that was, don't you?'

He stopped and looked down at her. In the pale starlight she could see his expression. It was dazed. 'That was Lord Derby,' he whispered. 'Henry Bolingbroke.' And just in case she still didn't understand he added, 'John of Gaunt's eldest son. King Richard's cousin.'

Chapter Thirteen

They continued between the trees and were soon out of range of the light from the flares. Their eyes were dazzled, both by the sumptuousness of the glittering palace of the archbishop, and by the inner dazzle and confusion aroused by the presence of King Richard's rival, Bolingbroke.

'I saw him down in Westminster,' Thomas explained in a hushed voice, 'and again in Lincoln not so long ago. It was him all right.'

'What on earth's Neville up to, brokering the sale of a cross he knows he has no right to?' The prioress, although sceptical of human intention, seemed to have a practical regard for the archbishop. She would be speechless.

'I can't imagine what he's up to. Your guess is as good as mine.' Thomas hefted the bag awkwardly under his arm.

Everything was quiet. The river lay ahead of

166

them, shining like a sheet of black silk beyond the trees. As they approached the bank, the water could be heard gurgling under the wooden struts of the landing stage. It was dark now. There was no moon.

Thomas went on ahead, probably with the intention of handing Hildegard down into the boat, when he turned as if to say something, then gave a sudden shout. To Hildegard's astonishment he pitched forward and vanished into the darkness. She heard a thump as he hit the ground. Then hell seemed to break loose as several hooded figures burst from behind the trees, and she found herself grasped roughly with a knife at her throat, while both arms were trussed behind her.

She kicked out at her attacker but there was nothing she could do. Expecting a blade in her ribs she was surprised to find herself being dragged down the bank towards the water. Fearing that they were going to try and drown her she began to struggle even more wildly, but she was pushed into the boat and heard her assailants scrambling back up the bank side.

There was the further sound of scuffling and Thomas, she assumed it was he, landed in the boat nearly capsizing it. He made no movement and she feared he was dead.

Managing to shake the hood from her face she was just in time to see a shadow fumbling with the boat. The next moment it was given a good push, sending it floating out into midstream. The current caught it and they began to drift down-river away from the palace.

'Thomas?' she whispered. 'Is that you?'

To her relief a groan came from somewhere out of the darkness.

'Are you hurt?'

'My head,' he groaned. 'I saw stars. Where are we?'

She could hear him struggle to sit up. His hands appeared to be free because she saw them grasp the gunnels beside her.

'Untie me, can you?'

'Did they hurt you?' he asked as he pulled at the rope binding her wrists.

'Mostly my feelings,' she replied. Her hands were released and she began to rub her wrists. Suddenly she looked at him in horror. 'Have you still got the cross?'

The boat lurched as he felt feverishly around in the bottom of the boat. Then, in a dead voice, he said, 'They've stolen it.'

There was no point in bewailing their loss. Looking back at the riverbank they could see and hear no sign of their assailants. They had melted away as smoothly as they had emerged, at one with the black night.

'We have several choices,' said Hildegard rapidly, pulling herself together. 'Either we get back to shore and try to follow them with the help of the guards. Or we return to York and rouse the constables. Or...' she hesitated.

'Or?' he prompted.

'Or we go on downstream to Naburn Manor.'

He gave a start. 'Lord Roger de Hutton? Do you think he might help? What can he do?'

'I don't know. I just feel it's the wisest course. I'm not sure I trust the palace guards.'

'There's only one problem with any of that,' Thomas commented.

'What's that?'

'They've taken the oars as well.'

The fire was banked high until it was roaring up the chimney in a sheet of flame and everybody had to keep standing up to move the benches back in case their clothes caught light.

Hildegard and Thomas sat swathed in woollen blankets on stools right in front of it. They were still shivering, more from shock than from the fact that they had had to swim from halfway across the river when the boat drifted past Naburn Manor. Someone now thought to place jugs of mulled wine beside them.

'So just run through this again,' said Roger, sweating in the heat despite the ties of his nightshirt being undone to the waist, revealing a mat of glistening ginger hair. There was no standing on ceremony since the two wet and shaking monastics had emerged from the river and come dripping up from the gatehouse with a guard of half a dozen armed men. Even Melisen was wearing just a long blue silk overgown and probably nothing underneath. The entire household had been roused from its slumbers. A crowd of servants still hung about the doorway in their nightshirts.

'There were six or seven of them. They just burst out of the woods,' Thomas repeated. 'We had no warning whatsoever. It's all my fault. I was carrying the box with the cross in it. "The Donation of Constantine", he said! You know

169

what that means.'

'What does it mean?' asked Roger irritably.

'Oh, sweeting...' Melisen interjected. 'It's the pope's right to hold power over kings. The king of England is the pope's vassal just as you're the vassal of the king. Obviously most of the kings of Europe object. Especially with two popes claiming precedence.'

'Oh, that,' scoffed Roger. 'What's Neville worried about? Neither pope's intending to show his face here, are they?'

Melisen ignored Roger and assessed the newcomers. 'Aren't you both warm enough yet? This fire's likely to set the whole manor alight.'

'Damp it down,' ordered Ulf, nodding to one of the servants crammed in the doorway. 'And then get out of it. The show's over.'

'Why don't we ask our guest to look at poor Brother Thomas's head wound?' suggested Melisen, giving the monk a sympathetic glance as he made a slight groan. 'This strange fellow turned up at our gates yesterday and so charmed us with his wit he earned bed and board for himself. He claims to be an expert in the healing arts.'

'Yes. Bring him forth!' ordered Roger, regardless of the hour. 'But I still don't understand.' He turned to Hildegard. 'How couldn't you get any sort of glimpse of these ruffians? Didn't they wear livery?'

She shook her head. 'It was too dark to see anything.'

'Any ideas who they were?'

'Doesn't it seem obvious?' She felt bitter. She had already told them about the mysterious stranger who wanted to buy the cross. Thomas had repeated that he knew who it was and would lay down his life if he was wrong. Now she gave Roger a bleak glance. 'I should have known he wouldn't be thwarted. The son of Gaunt? Hah!'

'If Bolingbroke's got his hands on it you'll never get it back,' Roger told her.

'We have to,' she exclaimed. 'He'll use it to usurp the throne. It'll be a sign to everybody that he has the divine recommendation of Constantine. You don't realise how seriously people take these signs and symbols—'

'Only when it suits them,' he interrupted irritably.

'He's probably the so-called "eminent personage" who's to share our stand at the pageant,' Melisen commented.

'I won't be able to look him in the eye.' Roger glowered and shifted his chair further back from the fire. He seemed to have taken it for granted they would not be accusing a royal prince of theft. 'Damp it down,' he growled, with a gesture towards the fire. 'Do as my steward tells you.' A boy crouching among the ashes threw some more sods on it. The heat gradually abated.

'It's the middle of the night,' somebody remarked, as if they had only just realised.

'You're right. We'll think more clearly after a good sleep.' Roger got up and gave a professional examination of Thomas's head. As a veteran of the French wars he was used to wounds and bloodshed. 'He'll live,' he commented. 'But you might as well get that fellow to have a look. Hildegard's in no fit state to tend the wounds of others.'

She had an emerging bruise over her right eye from being thrown into the bottom of the boat.

'He didn't have much to say that was any use,' Thomas remarked when Roger and Melisen retired.

Ulf quirked one eyebrow. 'Never underestimate my lord. He'll cook something up in that devious brain of his. He'll have riders scouring the country on the other side of the river in a trice.'

'I thought I heard a boat put out.' Hildegard went to the window that was patched with hundreds of small mullions. It was half open and let in the night air.

The river was visible between the trees more as an absence than anything else. She and Thomas were lodged in the guest wing where there were several vacant and spacious chambers for them to choose from. The guests at Naburn, Roger and his large retinue, had taken over the master suite, and the lord of Naburn himself, one of Roger's tenants, had been relegated to the chambers over the gatehouse. Other guests were yet to arrive.

She turned. 'Whose land is that on the other side of the river?'

Ulf was tight-lipped. 'It belongs to Lord Malbas.' He didn't need to say more. The name had come up often enough in the past. He and Roger were often in dispute over boundaries as Malbas claimed land adjacent to Roger de Hutton's territory in the north.

'Would he be likely to shelter the thieves?' she asked.

'Not if he knew they came from Bolingbroke.

172

He might be a litigious devil but he and Roger share some affinity. He'll have his men out of their beds as soon as he knows what's happened, don't you worry.'

'Then all we can do is wait for morning,' she said.

But just then the door opened. Someone entered. He looked surprisingly familiar. Hildegard watched as he came on into the room and, spying Thomas, went straight over to him. 'So you're the fellow they say has a wound?' He ran sensitive fingers over Thomas's head. 'It's just the one blow,' he murmured. 'Looks clean. What did they use? A piece of wood?'

'Felt like half of Filey Brigg,' muttered Thomas.

'You're from that way on, are you?' asked the newcomer. His accent slipped from that of the southern counties into a hint of Yorkshire. Hildegard knew where she had last seen him. He had looked somewhat different then. The spangled cloak and giveaway boots had been exchanged for a more sober houpelande and night boots.

When he had recommended a painkilling unguent she would probably have recommended herself if she'd been asked, he turned, about to leave the chamber, and it was then she spoke up. 'I see you managed to escape Master Baldwin's attentions at the booths the other morning, sir?'

The stranger came to a swift halt. He turned. 'Sister?'

'I saw you on York Pavement selling a love potion. Your magic was sufficient to make you vanish into thin air, much to the chagrin of certain men whom I suspect you already knew.'

He came over to her. 'You witnessed all that, did you?'

She nodded.

'I'd never seen them before in my life. It was most unexpected. Luckily I can think on my feet, otherwise I guess I wouldn't be standing here now.'

'They seemed to know you well enough.'

'And it was a Master Baldwin, you say?'

'He's a glazier,' she told him.

'Baldwin.' He looked thoughtful. 'If it's not too late, Sister, I'd appreciate further conversation?'

'I feel refreshed from my swim in the river,' she told him. 'What is it you want to know?'

'I want to know about this fellow, this glazier. Is he working here in York?'

'His brother is Edric Danby, master glazier and guildmaster of York.'

'Means nothing to me. Anyone else in the household?'

'Mistress Julitta, Baldwin's wife...'

He shook his head.

'And his brother-in-law's wife, Dorelia, and a couple of–'

'Dorelia?' He looked stunned. He went over to the window seat and dropped down onto it like a puppet with cut strings. After a pause he said, 'I thought I saw her in the crowd when I was assembling my equipment for the show, and yes, she was accompanied by a fellow in an orange turban and one other fellow. I took no notice of them but looked only at her, remembering how I had once known her in Wakefield and yet not quite able to believe my eyes. She didn't notice

174

me, of course, and was too soon swallowed up in the crowd, and I thought that was the end of the matter, that I had been mistaken...' His face had turned dark. 'But married? To a guildsman? And here – in York?'

'Is there something wrong?'

He looked bemused. 'Only that she was betrothed to a handsome young devil without any fortune of his own when I knew her. I'm surprised she gave him up, especially after inheriting her uncle's fortune. They could have been comfortable together.'

'They must be two different people,' said Hildegard. 'This one is poor. According to gossip she arrived without a dowry and practically with nothing but the clothes she stood up in.'

'Is that so?' He frowned. 'And I am attacked by men I know nothing of – for what? Glancing at a beautiful woman?' He got up. A skinny man, skeletal almost without the swirling folds of his mage's cloak, he moved towards the door. 'Dorelia,' he murmured half to himself. 'A beauty beyond compare. Once seen, as they say, never forgotten. I was not mistaken.' He turned with his hand on the latch. 'Thank you, Sister. There's more to this than meets the eye.'

He left.

Hildegard's mind was in turmoil. Intriguing though the mage's response had been, it was to the loss of the Cross of Constantine that her thoughts returned again and again through what remained of the night.

The theft had been so well organised, so

quickly executed after they left the archbishop, that it was difficult to believe that Bolingbroke could have organised it with such speed. He would scarcely have had time to issue the orders to his men. And would he stoop to common theft to get what he desired? Yet it had to be him. There was nobody else who could make use of a talisman with such a potent reputation.

A hard, cold rage had slowly crept over her. She couldn't believe she was so stupid as to lose the cross – not after everything she had suffered in Tuscany to get hold of it last year. It was as if she had already forgotten the lengths people will go to achieve their ambition – as if she thought things would be different here in England. She was a total fool – it was humiliating, enraging, and also, she was forced to admit, it was frightening. If the Gran Contessa could commit those heinous crimes of which she was guilty in order to grab the cross to enable her to rule a city, the depths to which someone might descend in order to gain the Crown of England could lead them to the very mouth of hell itself.

This might only be the start. But she would not let them win – wherever they were. She could not let them win.

All this she said as she paced the floor in front of the three men. Roger wore a ferocious scowl and was pulling at his red beard. 'The last thing I want is that bastard Gaunt putting either himself or his son on the throne,' he growled. 'What do the rebels say? "We want no king called John." I second that.'

Ulf was gazing out of the window, his eyes like ice. His fingers played up and down the hilt of his sword as if he couldn't wait to use it.

Brother Thomas had his hands folded and his head lowered as if he was meditating. In fact, he was, but not on any religious theme. He looked up after Roger spoke. 'I think you're right. Bolingbroke must be behind it. We should report the theft to Archbishop Neville and let him deal with it. It happened within the purlieus of his palace. That makes it a Church matter and canon law must be applied.'

'Tell Neville his guest's a thieving bastard?' Roger threw his head back in a mirthless laugh. 'He'd deny it to hell and back. He's clearly in on the whole thing.'

'Oh now, surely...' Thomas remonstrated.

Ulf turned from the window. His voice was cold. 'The men are just about to beach the boat. Let's see what Lord Malbas has to tell us.'

Roger's tenant, a mild, middle-aged knight with a rather bossy, buxom wife, had already descended from his gatehouse by the time Roger had led the rest of them down the stairs and across the yard. They all went together to the landing stage where four of Roger's men were alighting along with a couple of strangers in the Malbas livery – a red water bouget on a white ground. They saluted Roger and nodded pleasantly in the direction of his steward.

'No go, My Lord. They must have got clean away along the bank back towards York.'

The leader of the two men they had brought

over stepped forward. 'He's right. We've had men out most of the night keeping a lookout for sheep rustlers our side of the river. We lost near twenty or so night before last.'

'Haven't you got them down to the summer feeding ground yet?' asked Roger, looking smug.

The man lowered his head.

'Still, that's neither here nor there. Could a gang of ruffians have slipped through your cordon?'

'Only with a dozen arrows in their backs.'

'My thanks to your lord,' Roger replied after he took this in.

'He has a further message, My Lord, which is why he thought fit to send us over.'

'And?'

'He offers any help you require in bringing them to justice. He says he's sick and tired of divisions. It simply allows the villeins to run riot.'

'Thank him. I may yet call on him. Meanwhile go and get yourselves something to eat and drink.' Having sent them off he turned to his own men. 'Is he on the level?'

They nodded. 'We caught them sitting out in the fields with lighted torches. They're really in trouble for letting their sheep be stolen. Malbas is dancing with rage, they said.'

'Silly fool should have got his flocks down by now. Anyway, where does that leave us?' He turned to Ulf. 'What would you do if you'd just committed a robbery in the grounds of the archbishop's palace?'

'I'd either get back inside the palace where I'd come from and put my feet up. Or,' he went on,

'I'd try to get out on the road to my ultimate destination. That's if,' he added, 'I was somebody who'd like to possess a sacred relic.'

'Is that what this is about?' asked one of Roger's men. 'What's it reckoned to be worth?'

'More than the entire wealth of Rome,' replied Roger, shortly. 'Why do you ask? Do you want to put in an offer?'

'I was just wondering,' the man muttered.

'Wonder about who's got it. That'd be more use. Do you know?'

'If I did, My Lord, I'd be out after him and then be coming back asking for a goodly ransom.'

'There's no way anybody could have got out onto the York road,' another of Roger's men remarked. 'They've set guards at intervals all the way back towards the city walls because of all them folk pouring in for the feast. The only way you'd get out of the archbishop's park is along the riverbank. It's thick woodland there and you'd have to ferret through. I used to play in there as a lad,' he added, to give value to his opinion.

Ulf looked at Roger and said, 'I'll give instructions for a search party to go over and have a scout round. They might pick up a trail. You,' he turned to the man who had just spoken, 'get some of the lads together. And you lot,' he nodded to the others, 'get back in that boat and row alongside as they search the woods. You never know, they may just flush someone out and force them into the water. If they do, drown 'em.' He turned but swiftly turned back. 'Make sure you get hold of the relic first.'

That seemed the best that could be done. It

was agreed that it would be foolish to go to Alexander Neville at this stage, just in case he was more deeply involved than Thomas wanted to believe. They decided to keep matters to themselves until they had a clue as to what and whom they were dealing with.

Hildegard and Thomas prepared to leave for York. 'I must inform the prioress what has happened. Doubtless she'll want me to remain here until the thieves are discovered.' She did not relish the thought of the response she would get when the prioress heard of the theft. To lose the cross! Excommunication would be uppermost in the prioress's mind. Penance for a thousand days the most lenient.

With fixed expressions they prepared to leave.

It was another scorching day. Even now, in early morning, the sun smote down like molten brass. Hildegard did not envy the men ordered to scour the woods in their heavy mail shirts and basinets.

They rode for some way along the track in the direction of Fulford. Their horses were kicking up clouds of dust all the way. Thomas had his hood held over the lower part of his face with one hand. Hildegard had unpinned her gorget, fresh after its second laundering in as many days, and repinned it to cover most of her face, arranging the tip of her kerchief to shield her eyes.

One or two labourers were working in the distance, moving like snails in the heat haze shimmering on the horizon. One of them leant wearily on his hoe to watch them pass.

After they had gone some way she turned to look back down the lane. There was no mistake. A rider on a dusty-looking palfrey was keeping his distance but undoubtedly following them. When they came to the junction that linked the Selby road with York, she and Thomas turned left and continued towards the city by way of Fulford Cross. She swivelled again and this time noticed that the rider had lengthened the distance between them as if reluctant to draw attention to himself. When they had turned, he had turned as well.

They reached the Cross. Women sat outside their cottage doors, dazed by the heat, their spindles lying unused in their laps. A few dogs were sprawled, panting, in the shade of a wall. Children played at the village spring, the water they splashed sinking quickly into the ground, drying at once. When they were through the village she asked Thomas to cast a discreet glance over his shoulder. 'Is that rider still following us?' she asked.

After a moment Thomas said, 'There is a rider. Who is it?'

'At this distance it's difficult to tell. He's making every attempt not to get too close.'

'Maybe he's simply on the same route as us.'

'If that's the case where did he come from? There's only the one road leading in and out from Naburn Manor. If he comes from there, why doesn't he catch up and ride along with us?'

'We'll keep an eye on him,' vowed Thomas.

Chapter Fourteen

The forbidding sight of the nunnery of the Holy Wounds was visible from the end of the lane. Hildegard guessed she would have to go on bended knee to the mother superior to beg another few nights' board. Thomas had returned to his lodgings with the Franciscans and the horses had been left at the town stables. The rider, if he had been following them, had disappeared as soon as they came within sight of the city walls.

The first person to greet Hildegard when she was admitted into the lodge was Petronilla. She had her sleeves rolled and her small hands were red raw. She gripped Hildegard by the sleeve and whispered urgently, 'I was hoping you'd come back and rescue us, Sister. We can't stay here.'

'Why, what's the matter?' She led the girl into a corner off the main corridor.

'These sisters are not like those at Swyne,' Petronilla told her in a distressed whisper. 'They expect me to scrub floors, morning, noon and night. My knees ache with crouching on stone floors and scrubbing, and look at my hands!' She held them out.

'They do look sore. Perhaps I have some ointment for them.'

'I can put up with the pain for a while but when will it end? Do you see this corridor?'

Hildegard glanced down the long length of

gleaming terracotta tiles where they stretched from the porteress's lodge to the far end wall of the nunnery. She knew they turned at right angles for another stretch and then again, to form an enclosing passage to the whole building.

'I,' announced Petronilla, 'have scrubbed this entire corridor for two days. And frankly, Sister, I've had enough. And that's not all,' she went on. 'In fact, that's the least of it. What's really outrageous is what they're doing to poor Maud.'

Hildegard's eyes sharpened. 'What are they doing?'

'They're only trying to turn her into a martyr saint, that's all.'

'What on earth do you mean?'

'Come with me. I'll show you.'

She led Hildegard on tiptoe into the inner courtyard and crossed to the door of the chapel. 'Now, don't make a sound,' she whispered. Cautiously she pulled open the door and stepped inside. Hildegard followed.

At first it took time for her eyes to get used to the gloom. When they did so she peered in astonishment. Someone was lying face down in front of the altar. There was a muffled sound as if she was either crying or repeating in a rapid undertone an endless series of Hail Marys.

Petronilla glanced up at Hildegard. 'What do you think to that?'

'Is that Maud? But what has she done?'

'Nobody will say. But what can she have done? Come on, I'll get her to show you something.' Petronilla walked noisily down the aisle. 'Maud, get to your feet. There's someone to see you.'

Maud took no notice. She was barefoot, the soles of her feet black with dirt. Her hood covered her head and she lay face down on the stone pavers below the altar step.

'Maud?' Hildegard knelt beside her. The child had her arms outstretched as if reaching for something she had no hope of attaining. 'Maud, it's me, Sister Hildegard.' She put a hand on her arm with the intention of turning her over but the girl flinched away. 'How long has she been in here?' she asked over her shoulder to Petronilla.

'Since yesterday. No food, no drink and the sisters coming in every now and then and praising her for her devotion.'

'Did they tell her to do this?'

'Who knows? They don't talk to me. I'm a child of the Devil, apparently. Scrubbing floors is supposed to make me good.'

Hildegard reached out and touched the back of Maud's hands. Her skin was like ice. 'You must get up, now, my dear. You've done enough. Let me help you.'

She took hold of her by the shoulders and Maud rolled over, turning her tear-stained face upwards. She was deathly pale. Her eyes were glazed with misery. But it wasn't that that startled Hildegard into an exclamation of disbelief. It was the series of knife wounds covering the insides of both her arms. They were deep cuts, freshly made, the blood bubbling where the incisions opened as she moved.

Underneath her was a knife, still bloody. As she opened her palms she revealed two deep crosses etched into the soft flesh.

'Do the sisters know about this?' Hildegard demanded.

'Of course they do. They encourage her. They say, "How devout you are, Maud, you'll be a saint one day. St Maud," they keep saying. They stand round her with candles and sing while she cuts herself.'

Petronilla knelt down beside Hildegard and shook Maud gently by the shoulder. 'Come with us, you goose, please, I beg of you. We're going to get away from here. Let Sister Hildegard help you. She's closer to being a saint than any of these horrible women.'

Maud was unresisting when they sat her up and she leant back against Hildegard as if she had no idea what she was doing, nor the strength to help herself.

'I can't leave,' she whispered when Hildegard tried to encourage her to her feet. 'Let me be. I have to stay. I'm evil and have to finish my penance or I'll go to hell.' Tears began to roll down her cheeks. Her blood-soaked palms curled helplessly in her lap.

Petronilla clasped her by the wrists and her own eyes filled with tears. 'Of course you're not evil, you silly goose. Who told you that? Some mad old women who should know better. Isn't that right, Sister?'

'I know Maud is a good child. She has done enough praying for imaginary sins. Come on, let's see if you can rise to your feet.'

'I'm bad!' Maud cried out. 'You don't know! I have to stay! God will strike me down for my great sin! I shall suffer in hell-flames for eternity.

185

Please, let me be!' She struggled but was too weak to put up much resistance.

'There is a way of assuaging all sin,' replied Hildegard more calmly than she felt. 'And that is, as you well know, to make a full and honest confession to a priest. Have you done that?'

Maud shook her head. 'There is no priest who would hear me. And if he did he'd put me in prison and I should rot in hell just the same.'

'There is a priest I know who will hear your confession and never think of putting you in prison. I'm going to take you to him if you'll permit me?'

Maud didn't answer but she didn't resist when they helped her to her feet. She had been lying on the floor so long she could only move stiffly like someone stricken in years and the wounds on her wrists started weeping blood again.

'And you did this to yourself?' asked Hildegard lifting her wrists to have a proper look at them. Maud nodded.

'I shall bathe them for you and then we'll leave.' She knew the girl had no possessions she could take with her other than the small bundle she always carried. She turned to Petronilla. 'Is there anything you need to fetch before we go?'

'Nothing.' Petronilla began to cry. She held her head erect, however, as if the tears belonged to someone else and she kept pace with Hildegard and Maud in their slow and painful progress towards the open door of the chapel.

They were halfway across the yard near the fountain when a loud voice demanded, 'And where might you three think you're going?'

186

Hildegard lifted her head and saw a figure in black standing in the doorway between them and the lodge. Without replying she led the wounded child forward until they were at the foot of the steps. She felt Petronilla clutching tightly onto her robe. The black-gowned nun didn't move from the doorway and they were forced to a standstill.

'I'm taking this poor child to an apothecary,' Hildegard said in a firm voice. 'As you can see she has several deep cuts which need urgent attention.' She raised Maud's hands palm upwards to display the bloody incisions.

'Nonsense! They're only wounds of the flesh. They're as nothing to the wounds of Christ. She is merely making amends for her sins.'

'And what sins would a child have committed that cannot be pardoned without inflicting this barbaric penance?' asked Hildegard.

'Child? She's fourteen years old or so we're told. Let me remind you, Sister, I am the superior of this nunnery,' the nun proclaimed. 'And I will not relinquish souls given into my keeping.'

'I'm unaware of anyone placing her in your keeping for more than a few nights' lodging,' Hildegard replied with contempt. 'Nor am I aware that anyone asked for her to be turned into a martyr. I'm appalled that you can treat a child in this cruel manner.' She tried to move past the nun but she refused to give up her position in the doorway. A large iron cross rested on her bosom and some well-used wooden beads swung from her thick leather belt.

'Get your hands off that child,' she snapped.

187

'She belongs to us now.' Her lip curled. She turned her head and shouted to the porteress. 'Fetch Sister Michael!' The porteress scurried out of the lodge at once and ran in a fluster of skirts to do as she was ordered.

Hildegard was thinking rapidly, but apart from physically pushing the woman out of the way she could see no polite resolution to the problem. She said, 'I feel strongly about being kept a prisoner here, Mother. You have no jurisdiction in my Order. I ask you most humbly to allow us to pass.'

The nun gave her a contemptuous glance and refused a reply. At that moment a heavily built figure appeared at the far end of the corridor. 'Hurry!' screamed the mother superior over her shoulder, all control gone in an instant. 'They're abducting our saint! Help! Help!'

The newcomer trundled towards them, the porteress and several other black-robed figures trailing in her wake. Sister Michael replaced her superior in the doorway with folded arms.

Hildegard stepped back a pace. 'I'm astonished you should seek to threaten us. This is an outrage.'

As she spoke she began to push Petronilla towards the door under cover of her cloak. The porteress was still puffing along the corridor with the other nuns. The way to the street was momentarily clear if only Petronilla would realise this in time. All she had to do was evade Sister Michael and the mother superior.

Gripping Maud tightly by the back of her cloak Hildegard urged her forward and Petronilla, to

188

her relief, slipped between the nun's heavy skirts and the wall, dodged the outstretched arms of the mother superior and hurled herself at the main doors. While she was tugging at the bolts Hildegard stepped forward and banged her forehead hard into Sister Michael's face who, arms still folded across her chest, lurched backwards with a grunt of pain.

It was the opportunity to allow Hildegard to propel Maud through the gap that opened up and push the mother superior back hard against the wall as the bolts slid fully open and the key was turned. Then all three burst through the great doors and out into the street.

Without pausing to see whether the nuns would pursue them into what was for them forbidden territory, they sped like lightning towards the town. Hildegard realised she was almost carrying Maud by the scruff of her gown and when they reached the first corner and turned into it she released her grip. Bending down so she could look into her face, she asked, 'Tell me the truth, Maud, do you want to go back there or come with us?'

Maud began to sob, and throwing her arms round Hildegard's neck, cried, 'Don't let them kill me. I don't want to die. Please, please don't let them kill me!'

It was one of Hildegard's advantages that she had resources of her own as well as recent payment from the sale of beeswax. She took both girls into the nearest inn, bathed Maud's wounds in the running water from the pump in the yard, then ordered as much food and drink as they wanted, digging into her scrip for the coins.

Surprisingly, no one had followed them. That didn't mean to say someone wouldn't be delegated to step outside the nunnery walls and attempt to take Maud back at some time. But for now they were safe. Nobody would try to snatch a young girl from inside a crowded eating house under the very noses of a crowd of townsfolk.

'The nuns may have been misguided and cruel,' said Hildegard when both girls were each settled with a pie covered in thick gravy, 'but I'm sure they would never have killed you.'

Maud shook her head. 'Not them. The others,' she said, her head down.

'What others?' asked Hildegard.

'That knight and his men-at-arms.' She burst into tears.

Hildegard put an arm round her and gave her a hug. 'What makes you think they'd try a thing like that?'

Maud merely shook her head and tried to scrub away her tears.

'I don't think that gravy's going to taste very nice with your salt tears in it,' Hildegard said after a moment. She offered the girl a corner of her sleeve. 'Wipe your face with this. Everything is going to be all right.'

Petronilla said, 'I told you Sister Hildegard would help us when she came back.'

At that moment a man came up to them. He was tall and stoop-shouldered with a few red whiskers on his chin and a dusty green hood pulled well down over his face. He slid onto the

190

bench next to Petronilla and leant across the table. 'Sister Hildegard?'

Startled, she looked up. 'Who wants to know?'

'Master Theophilus.' He glanced right and left and leant even closer. 'You don't recognise me, do you?'

She stared hard at his face, then gave a puzzled frown. 'It's you? In disguise?'

He nodded. 'Keep your voice down. I followed you all the way from Naburn Manor because I didn't want to talk in front of the monk. The fewer people who know about this the better.'

'What do you want?'

'Just the name of the place where I can find the young woman we talked about. I've been thinking about that name you mentioned. The man,' he said with a quick glance at the two girls to see if they were listening. 'I need your discretion.'

'Can you tell me what it's about?'

'Not here. But yes, I will tell you. It should interest you.'

'As you can see I have my hands full at present.'

'I understand. I saw you haring down the street just now as if the hounds of hell were after you.' A smile split his face. 'You can tell me your story in exchange for mine.'

'I have to get these two girls to a place of safety,' she told him. 'I doubt whether I can find lodging in the town. It's fuller than ever with the pageant only days away so it may take some time. I need to hear your story before I give you the information you want.' He could glean Dorelia's whereabouts by asking around the town taverns, she was thinking.

As if he had read her mind he said, 'Fair enough. I like your caution. Of course, I could go to an alehouse and make enquiries. The only reason I don't want to do that is it might make the situation worse if it gets out that I have an interest. Let's meet later when you've dealt with your other business.'

'At the minster, then, around vespers,' she said quickly. She would take the girls to Thomas at the friary and ask him to convey them speedily to Naburn Manor. They would be safe under the protection of Lord Roger and Lady Melisen.

Master Theophilus offered to accompany the three of them through the town. He walked tall and protectively beside them and Hildegard was glad of his presence even though there was no sign of anyone in pursuit. He left them near the friary with an encouraging nod. 'Till vespers, then.' He was soon swallowed up in the crowd.

The town was busier by the hour. Now there were frequent groups of craftsmen dressed in the costumes they would be wearing during the mystery plays threading their way through the crowds on their way to and from rehearsals. A young man in a white shift wearing a bent-wire halo with a dove fixed to the top greeted her by name and she did a double take before realising it was Jankin as the Archangel Gabriel.

'I've not turned into a spicer,' he called back over his shoulder, indicating the crowd of apprentices who accompanied him. 'I'm borrowed because of my good looks!' He was whisked off by the laughing group, all of them wearing an assortment of bizarre costumes.

192

Thomas was astonished when they turned up at the friary. Briefly she explained what had happened. He bent his head and said kindly to Maud, 'I'll certainly hear your confession, my lady, if you so wish. I'm ready to listen whenever you're ready.'

He got a nod of agreement in response and straightened. To Hildegard he said, 'I'll take them to Naburn after that. Maybe while I'm there I'll hear the latest from Lord Roger about the theft of the cross.'

Maud touched him on his sleeve. 'Shall it be here in the chapel?'

He nodded. 'If you so wish.' With a brief acknowledgement to Hildegard he led the way into the pilgrim chapel at the friary gates. They went in after him and sat against the back wall to wait out of earshot.

Maud's confession took longer than Hildegard had expected. They could glimpse her bowed head as she talked in privacy at the far end of the building in a little arched alcove.

Hildegard's thoughts strayed to the theft of the cross. Word had still not been sent to Swyne admitting its loss. Secretly she hoped it would be found before she had to own up to its theft. There were no suspects apart from Bolingbroke. If he had it they would have to wrest it from his clutches at all costs. The problem would be how to do so.

She recalled the archbishop's man whom Thomas had mentioned as having set in motion the rumour of its return to England and wondered if he had anything to do with it. Loose-tongued might equal other weaknesses, such as common assault and larceny.

Suddenly the two figures rose to their feet and Maud followed Thomas with bowed head down the nave towards them. Instead of an air of relief at being released from her burden, Maud seemed as stricken as before. Thomas was white-faced. Hildegard went to meet them.

'If you're ready I'll take them both on to Naburn Manor,' he said.

She gave him a quizzical glance. 'Very well.' She reached into her scrip. 'Let me give you enough to pay for the horses.' He made a gesture of refusal but she ignored it. 'I'm grateful for your help, Thomas.' She knew he could say nothing of Maud's confession but she was puzzled by the look on his face. 'Is everything now settled?'

He shook his head. 'Such evil to exist in mankind is hard to stomach.' He shepherded them all towards the doors, then said in a lowered voice to Hildegard, 'The poor little soul. I'll return as soon as I've spoken to Lady Melisen. There's a need to treat Maud with the utmost gentleness.'

'She's already told us what happened.'

He was grim-faced. 'There's more. Much more.'

Chapter Fifteen

Alone again, Hildegard set about finding somewhere to stay for the night. Everywhere was full. She was offered a space in a reeking, shared chamber above a butcher's shop in the Shambles and said she would think about it. Meanwhile she found herself in Stonegate and, remembering the rambling building where Master Danby lived and had his workshop, made her way there. At least he might know of someone with space to offer.

There was no Jankin to answer the door this time. Dorelia answered it herself, looking flustered, and when Hildegard commented on Jankin's absence she said carelessly, 'He's up on Pageant Green, I expect. Making a hash of his lines.' Her violet eyes were briefly animated and then she looked down again as if having done wrong to show a little spirit.

She opened the door wider. 'Come in, do. Master's at one of his meetings but he won't be long.' She added a little shyly, 'I'll be glad of somebody to talk to.'

'Don't you get much opportunity?' asked Hildegard lightly as she followed the girl into the front workshop. 'What about Mistress Julitta?'

'Oh, you know, she does try to rule the roost, and anyway, they're all a bit...' The girl gave a shrug and a sudden smile that was like a flash of summer lightning, adding, 'They're older than me.'

'You're not from round here, are you?' Hildegard asked when she didn't continue. They were sitting comfortably with a beaker of wine apiece near the open window in the front workshop by the time she replied.

'I'm from down Wakefield way, me.'

Hildegard looked suitably astonished. 'Heavens, this is a long way from home. Don't you miss your kin?'

The wide eyes showed no emotion. 'I ain't got none to speak of, not now. I ain't got nothing. My Uncle Jed was the last one that died. Master Danby's all I have now.'

'So how did you and the master happen to meet, living so far apart?' Hildegard asked, not having to feign interest.

Dorelia's bottom lip puckered. 'It were by means of his brother,' she said after a slight pause. 'Master Baldwin.'

'That was lucky,' Hildegard replied. 'But it must have been just as lucky to meet him as Master Edric?'

'Aye, if you can call that luck!' Her eyes flashed. Then she seemed to remember herself and lowered her head to fiddle with a piece of lace on her sleeve, mumbling, 'I was certainly at my wit's end when he happened along.'

'Was this in Wakefield?'

'Aye.'

'What was he doing down there?'

'Working.'

'It's a long way to travel to do a bit of glazing.'

There was another slight pause. 'He was just working out that way,' she repeated.

Hildegard let it go. She would find out what Master Baldwin had been doing over in Wakefield when he brought his brother together with a girl half his age. There was the handsome swain to be considered, as well as the uncle's bequest.

Remembering her meeting with Theophilus when the bell for vespers began to toll, she quickly told Dorelia why she had called round. Before she had finished the girl was shaking her head.

'We have no room. It looks big here but it's mostly workshop space. There's an attic and that's it. But I know who has room and it's only a short step from here.' She got up eagerly. 'Let me give her a call.'

She slipped out into the yard through a side door, gesturing for Hildegard to follow. Passing the door to the inner workshop Hildegard noticed Gilbert inside. He was standing over the trestle with a large brush in his hands, whistling to himself and whitewashing the surface with broad loving strokes.

Dorelia was knocking on the window of a cottage across the yard when she went outside and explained, 'She's a widow woman and I know full well she has an empty chamber where her son used to be.'

It was as she said. The widow was delighted at the prospect of having a nun stay with her. 'The usual roustabouts that come to town at this time wouldn't do for me. But I'd willingly let it to you, Sister.'

'I'd be happy to pay you a good price,' Hildegard told her. 'It might be for several nights.'

'Stay as long as you wish,' Widow Roberts replied.

Hildegard made a down payment to show she was serious and then excused herself. 'I have something to attend to in the town,' she told them. 'But I'll be back this evening.'

There was no sign of Theophilus when she stepped inside the echoing vault of the minster. It was crowded at this time of day, most people making for the chapel where the service for vespers would be held, others, sightseers and the usual sprinkling of pilgrims, a few law men waiting for business, but no mage, red-whiskered or not, and she was just about to turn round and go back outside in case he had decided to wait there when she felt someone fall into step beside her.

'Heavens! You startled me. It seems you can appear as well as disappear at will!'

He chuckled, 'Just one of the professional skills of a mage.' He had a teasing look. 'So, Sister, shall we find a private corner or keep walking?'

'Let's walk.' They went outside and began a slow circuit round the minster yard. It was still hot in the late sunshine but they kept to the shadow of the north side. 'I'm sorry I'm so late,' she began, 'but I may have some news for you.' She told him how she had just left Dorelia. 'She told me straight away she was from Wakefield.'

'I knew it. There's no way I could ever forget that face, even though it's a couple of years since

I last saw her. I knew her uncle,' he explained.

'She mentioned an uncle.'

'Jed?'

She nodded.

'We made a pledge to help one another,' he paused, 'as one does.'

She gave him a covert glance. 'As members of the same brotherhood?'

He ignored that and instead pointed to the passers-by. 'I've had a pleasant wait,' he told her. 'Studying the book of life.' The crowds were perambulating in the shade afforded by the minster and his sharp glance flickered over them. 'It's most instructive, watching the skittle-sharpers and the thimbleriggers. Those of that ilk. For sheer professionalism watch that pardoner over there. See him?' She followed his glance. 'He was here when I arrived, already filling his money-pouch. Look, he's found another mark!'

They watched.

The pardoner, an attractive fellow in a smart capuchon folded Turkish style on his head, had approached a young and pretty woman carrying a shopping basket. He said something to her in passing. It was obvious it was a compliment from the way she fluttered in response and turned to look back at him.

'First he flatters her,' observed Theophilus. 'Now look, he walks on but he draws her back with some other light comment to which she feels obliged to reply. She pretends she's about to walk away but he's not having that. Watch, see what he does.'

The pardoner briefly rested his hand on the woman's shoulder.

'He'll be in her bed next!' the mage chuckled.

The young woman was shaking her head and just then a portly red-faced fellow somewhere near forty came puffing up.

'The husband. And not pleased,' observed Theophilus, narrowing his cat's eyes. 'But what can he do?'

The pardoner said something to the husband. Theophilus gave another chuckle. 'The cheek of it! He's getting him on his own side! Watch this.'

The pardoner said something to make the husband laugh while at the same time handing the wife one of his pardons. Then he put his hand on the husband's arm, man to man, and they walked off, leaving the wife holding the pardon.

'She's trying to work out which of her sins it'll wipe from the slate,' the mage decided. 'And look, he must be telling the husband a dirty joke. Look at his face! Maybe he's guessed one of his little sins. See, the fella's already digging into his money bag to pay for the sale to his wife ... and now he's buying another for himself! Two strikes in one!' Theophilus glanced at Hildegard. 'It's good to watch a cozener at work. I told you he was a master! We can always learn from observation, don't you agree?'

Hildegard was amazed at the mage's open admiration of such deceit and decided she could not trust him. All she said was, 'I'm surprised they can sell pardons in the street. Why are people still being hoodwinked into paying?'

'They want to be hoodwinked,' he said at once.

'They long for it. That's why they like magic and falling in love and talk of miracles. It turns them into children – full of helpless wonder, with no responsibility for their own destiny.' He gave her a feline glance. 'Isn't that the case with all belief, Sister? Aren't we encouraged in it? Making us feel helpless in the face of the Almighty? Isn't it then the priests can step in and take over? For a price,' he slyly added.

'It's a view,' she replied, taken aback by his cynicism.

'And you...' he murmured. He didn't bat an eyelid. 'He will return to you. And soon. Believe me.'

'He?' She felt her colour rise before she could stop it.

'Your earthly love.'

They walked on. Hildegard could not trust herself to speak.

They reached the end of their circuit. Only then could she say anything. Her tone was somewhat frosty. 'Now Dorelia's identity is confirmed, I trust you'll use the knowledge for good.'

'I'll not let the matter drop. Trust me.'

Trust him? That will be the last thing I do, she thought. That little speech about the pardoner had been a neat ploy that would make most people forget a question about brotherhood. Why would he want to avoid answering? That was the interesting part.

She was about to take her leave when he offered her a seat on the stone parapet that ran along the wall on one side of the yard.

'One thing before you leave, Sister. If there's

201

anything I can do about that earlier matter with the two girls and their escape – the whole town's buzzing with it, by the way, as I expect you realise? – then let me know.'

She shook her head. 'That's in hand now.' She wondered what he thought he could do.

'But there is something else.' He bent his head closer and she could smell the oil he wore. It was resinous, foreign, and she couldn't name it.

'What else?' she smiled.

'I couldn't help hearing talk of a theft when I was at Naburn Manor.'

'There is a difficulty.' She might as well admit it. 'The suspect has every advantage over us.'

'It would be no difficulty for me to get inside the palace to try to pick up a little information. I would do that for you. I'm still in your debt – because of what you told me about Dorelia.'

'I doubt whether anyone could get inside there and get out again without documents in triplicate!'

'May I try? There will be no danger to your own involvement. As I know nothing of the theft if they apprehended me – unlikely, believe me – I would be unable to tell them anything even under duress.'

She laughed. 'I look forward to your report in that case!'

After she had told him where to find Dorelia and where she herself could be contacted should he have news of the theft – said jokingly, because it was only a boast – they parted, she to the friary to leave a message of her whereabouts for Thomas, and the mage off on some secret mission of his own.

Of course, there was no possibility of anyone getting inside the archbishop's palace. It was well guarded because of the crowds still pouring into the city and spilling out into a disorganised rabble over the fields and meadows outside the walls.

It was also said that Archbishop Neville had massively increased his guard since the Rising. Afraid of losing his head to a rebel sword, he had even sought refuge for a time in the castle at Scarborough. As reward for his treacherous slaying of Wat Tyler, Ralph Standish had immediately been made constable of the castle as well as being knighted at Smithfield with Mayor Walworth and the other murderers. The archbishop had presumably used the occasion to cement their alliance. But whatever the truth of the matter, the mage would find it impossible to get inside the palace now.

She reached the friary and hesitated. As for that remark about her earthly love – it had shaken her, coming at her like a bolt out of the dark, but it wasn't much of a shot. The mage probably assumed that every woman had a lover, particularly nuns, such was their reputation these days and such his cynicism. She had changed colour before recovering her composure. That would have confirmed what was no more than a lucky guess.

His skill wasn't in magic, she decided now, it was in the power of his observation.

Perhaps, though, there was a kind of magic in that.

A band of pipes and tabors struck up at the end of the street. Following behind it was an excited gaggle of children in fancy costume. Evidently they were cherubim for they all carried wings furled neatly under their arms. A couple of devils stalked along beside them, quipping with the passers-by and making teasing feints into the crowd. They disappeared into one of the guild houses nearby. A water-seller was doing a brisk trade and the shopfronts were still down to allow the merchants to profit from the influx of visitors.

Hildegard lingered on the way back to Widow Roberts' house beside a belt-maker and wondered about making a purchase. Although early evening it was still hot, and the press of people in the narrow street made it hotter still. She fingered one or two belts, but wasn't in the mood for haggling. A crowd was gathered round someone further up the street, so she put the matter of a new belt behind her and allowed herself to be swept along.

They were gathered round a man standing on a wooden crate so he could look round the ring of people that formed his audience. His russet gown and bare feet if not his scholarly tones made it clear what he was. He was one of the free preachers, a Lollard.

He was disparaging a belief in the sacraments in a calm and measured voice.

'Who are these pope-appointed churchmen?' he was asking. 'I can tell you – they are the very men who grind the poor underfoot. They preach poverty and live like kings. Preach humility and

204

have the arrogance of emperors. Preach truth and practise deceit. Do they expect us to believe in miracles against all the laws of rational thought? Yes, they do. And if we point out their errors they hound us from our homes, throw us into prison and burn our books.'

There was a buzz of agreement and one or two muttered objections and Hildegard noticed a woman cross herself and walk hurriedly away, but for the most part he had his audience in the palm of his hand.

She was about to settle to listen to what more he would say on the subject of rational discourse when her head jerked up at the sound of an explosion.

As the reverberations died away a terrific ball of fire erupted from the direction of the booths at the top of the street. The crowd was equally dense up there. Even so, after the initial shock, an uncanny silence descended. Everything seemed frozen in time except for a single scream that went on and on as if it would never end. The sound brought the scene into motion. As one, the crowd scattered. Some, like Hildegard, ran towards the fire. Others fought to get away from it. The scream continued at the same unearthly pitch.

In the middle of all this a man emerged from the thick of the crowd with his clothes ablaze. There was more scuffling to get out of his way. Women cried out. Men cursed and shouted instructions. Someone, however, stepped forward and threw the burning figure to the ground and with his bare hands and the force of his body weight managed to stifle the flames. From the direction of the booths the scream that had seemed endless came to a stop.

Hildegard was halfway up the street by now. A panicked crowd was rushing towards her. She flattened herself against a shopfront to let them pass, then set off at a run until she came to the scene of the fire.

Flames were billowing from one booth to the next. Vendors feverishly pulled their goods out of harm's way. Apples, pears, quinces, cheese, fabrics, embroideries, leatherware, pewters, pots, metal goods, all were being dragged out of the burning booths. A man selling fowl in cages tossed them one by one with their squawking contents onto the cobbles.

Hildegard ran up to a couple of men dragging a blackened body from the wreckage of the booths. 'Is there anyone else in there?'

'Fuck knows. There was a shoot of flame, then the awnings caught fire,' one of them replied.

She knelt beside the man who had been dragged out. His face was blackened with smoke. He clutched Hildegard's sleeve. 'My wife's in there–' He started coughing, overcome by the smoke that was still pouring from the booth where, it appeared, he had been selling fabrics. Bales of burning cloth plumed acrid smoke into the air.

She ran towards the booth. It was the first one in the row and must have been the one that had gone up in a ball of flame and, as with any instant flare, had died as quickly, but not before it had set alight the rolls of cloth inside. Now, as well, it

206

was the smoke billowing out in a suffocating pall that made it difficult to approach the source of the fire.

A line of people were already handing buckets of water from a nearby house. There were complaints about the dry well in the square and a confused moment when nobody knew what to do with the emptied buckets. Then another source was found and the human chain quickly re-formed. The need to cope with fire among the clustered buildings within the city walls had instilled the habit of cooperation in the town-dwellers.

Inside the first booth among the wreckage of her merchandise lay the body of a woman. It was only recognisable as such by the embroidered slippers she wore. Hildegard knelt beside her. It might have been her death cry that had continued in such prolonged anguish. A constable came to kneel at her side.

After a moment he said, 'Come away, Sister. There's nowt we can do for her.' He offered her his hand to help her to her feet. 'Her man's in a bad way. Will you go with him to St Leonard's?'

It was nearly three hours later when Hildegard eventually left the hospital. It was dark now. She paced from under the archway and walked along the bank of the river towards her lodgings. The monks running the place had attended to the man's burnt skin with speed and efficiency, but when it was clear there was nothing more anyone could do but to assuage his pain she came away.

Widow Roberts was standing outside her door when she turned into the glazier's yard.

'Come in,' she said. 'I heard what happened.'

Hildegard sank down onto a chair in the comfortable kitchen and allowed the widow to bring her a drink and a slab of bread and cheese. She felt exhausted although she had done very little. It was the sight of the charred body of the young woman that affected her most. One minute she had been selling fabrics to the holiday crowd and the next she was dying in that ghastly way.

'What made the booth burst into flames like that?' she wondered aloud.

Widow Roberts came to sit at the table with her. 'They say it came out of nothing. It's Holy Fire. To warn us of the approach of the Antichrist. The beginning of the End Days.'

What was unarguable was – it was the second such explosion in as many days.

Chapter Sixteen

'I heard about it on my way back through Fulford. They were all talking of nothing else. Some people are already leaving the city. They say it's not worth celebrating Corpus Christi if they're going to burn for it. There's a perverse logic to their reasoning. I'm just relieved to see you're unharmed.'

'And the girls, Thomas?' Hildegard asked him.

'Melisen has taken them both under her wing.' Thomas was sitting in the widow's chair by the window later that night, the widow already having gone up to bed.

It was a warm night. The casement was open to let in some cool air. Out in the streets normal life continued unchanged. Revellers could be heard with the occasional sudden run of footsteps as the constables gave chase. Curfew was impossible to maintain at a time like this. The whole town was jittery. Extra constables had joined the watch. Mayor de Quixlay had acted at once. A proclamation had already been read out at several strategic points in the streets, announcing that information leading to the arrest of those who had caused the explosions would be rewarded.

There was little doubt in the civic mind at least that it was by human agency that the mercer's booth had been set on fire. The general view was that fabric just didn't explode of its own accord. Apocalypse or not.

'And now for that other matter.' Thomas leant forward, keeping his voice low. 'Lord Roger's men scoured the woodland all the way to the city walls and found no one. What they did find was evidence of horses having been tethered among the trees not far from the palace walls and a passage they had forced along the riverbank through the undergrowth.'

'Are they sure about that?'

Thomas nodded. 'That man of Sir Ulf's was positive. He's something of a woodsman and claimed the path had been forced only hours before.'

'It may mean nothing more than poachers,' she pointed out. 'It doesn't necessarily let Bolingbroke off the hook.'

209

'And then there's this.' He delved into his scrip and produced a small, dull object and handed it to her.

She thought it was a belt buckle at first but then realised after a closer look that it was a pilgrim badge. At least, it was like the badges made from pewter or lead peddled to the pilgrims at the shrines. They were mass-produced in moulds and usually showed a variety of images associated with the particular saint of the shrine – the three arrows crossed through a crown for Saint Edmund martyr, or the wheel of St Catherine, for instance.

This one, however, was in the shape of a hart with a small chain round its neck. The sign worn by King Richard's followers. She turned it over in her fingers.

'It could have been dropped by anybody,' she said after a pause. 'A lot of people wear them. It's not a crime. It's a sign of loyalty. Somebody might have been living rough along that stretch of woodland.'

'Nobody would be so foolish as to live outside the law so close to its remit.'

'So what do you think?'

'The evidence of riders forcing a path away from the palace could suggest that Bolingbroke may not be involved. And this, if dropped by one of the riders, might mean another allegiance entirely.'

She knew what he was getting at. 'If,' she repeated. 'If.'

She turned the badge over again. There was nothing else to observe, not even a thread of cloth to show what sort of garment it might have been torn from.

'Many people wear these,' she remarked at last, handing it back. 'King Richard's supporters, sometimes the rebels who fled to the countryside after the Rising, of course, but let's suppose there were recent horsemen in the woods and let's suppose they stole the cross. Let's also suppose the Company of the White Hart are responsible – heaven knows, they're rife around here – but then ask yourself: how would they know about the cross and, aware of its existence, the question remains – why would they go to the bother of stealing it?'

'For the same reason Bolingbroke might want it. To seal the validity of a claim on the Crown.'

'But this is Richard's sign and he already wears the crown.'

'To possess the cross would strengthen his hold.' Thomas looked certain. 'We all know he's threatened by Gaunt – by prophecies warning that he'll lose his crown – that Gaunt has a better claim. Many are beginning to mutter that there's something in it. A sign to appeal to the superstitious would swing the people more firmly in Richard's favour.'

'You see the king's popularity on the wane?'

'Don't you?'

'I was somewhat out of touch in Deepdale. Even so, it's true I've heard grumbling against him since I got to town. Some sounds like justifiable criticism of the broken promises after Smithfield. But he is the rightful king – to claim otherwise is treason. Gaunt knows that.'

211

'But does his son accept it?'

'Back to Bolingbroke.' She sighed, then added, 'It's unlikely that the White Hart would steal the cross when the king could simply demand to have it handed over.'

'Good point. But would your prioress comply – even if the request came from the king himself?'

It was late. The sky was streaked with lurid purple even though sunrise was still a few hours away. Thomas stood up. It was clear talking would get them no further at present. 'I'd better be getting along. These speculations are leading us into a quagmire of confusion And I mustn't miss matins.' His expression was sombre. 'Have they any suspicions about who would set the booths on fire?'

She shook her head. 'Only rumours. The general view is that it's somebody who wants to spoil the festivities, but if that's the aim it's failed Apart from those few who were queuing to leave soon afterwards, everybody else is standing firm.'

'"They're not going to frighten us off with a bit of fire" – yes, I've heard that line.'

Thomas went to the door with a solemn good-night. As he crossed the yard Hildegard thought she saw the door to Master Danby's workshop snick shut. There were no lights on over there. She went back into the kitchen and stood to one side of the window but everything remained in darkness. Assuming the events of the past few days were getting the better of her nerves she closed the shutters over the kitchen window and made her way at last to bed.

The Feast of Corpus Christi was three days off.

Time enough for the murderer to continue his random acts of arson if he chose.

The gates swung back with a bang to release the heat and roar of the raging furnace within; it was the mouth of hell, tongues of flame licking towards her, pulling her into the devouring heart of the fire. The banging came again. A voice called.

'Sister? Are you awake? Quickly!'

Hildegard sat up in confusion. Her glance flew round the unfamiliar chamber and it was a moment before she remembered where she was.

The widow's voice came again. 'There's someone to see you.'

Scrambling from under the thin sheet she pulled her habit over her nightshift, tied the belt in a firm knot and went to the door. When she opened it the widow was standing at the bottom of the stairs wringing her hands. 'For you, Sister. It's the constables.'

Turning back she pulled on her boots and returned to the stairs. Standing below were two men armed with staves. They wore the blazon of the City of York. They looked up as she appeared. 'Sister Hildegard of Meaux?'

'Not exactly,' she corrected as she made her way down the stairs. 'I'm of the priory at Swyne.'

'Near enough,' one of the constables said. 'We want you to come with us to the Common Hall.'

'Why? What's happened.'

'It's to do with yesterday's fire,' the second one told her. 'Other than that you'll have to come along to find out in person.'

With a constable on either side of her Hildegard was escorted into the yard. She had a hazy impression of a group of people watching from outside the glazier's workshop, Gilbert's blond hair bright in the hot sun, Danby's orange turban. It seemed it was already mid morning. She must have slept like the dead last night.

The men marched her one in front and one behind down the short alley into Stonegate and then proceeded to carve a way through the already busy streets towards the river. The Common Hall was where the mayor and aldermen had their council meetings and held hearings for those taken on suspicion.

When they entered it was bustling with activity. The mild-looking man she had seen only the other day inspecting the pageant scaffold with Ulf was standing at the far end on a dais surrounded by several officials. She was led to the bottom of the steps and he broke off what he was saying and came to the edge. 'Is this the one?' he asked the constables.

'It is, sir.'

Simon de Quixlay looked her up and down. 'I'm told you were one of the first on the scene at yesterday's fire?'

'I was.'

'We'd like a serjeant-at-arms to ask you a few questions.' He nodded to a man standing at a writing desk nearby. 'The clerk will take down your statement. Carry on,' he said to the two constables. Job done they went off. A serjeant-at-arms beckoned her over.

'Well now, Sister,' he said in confiding tones.

'Would you care to help us clarify events?' Without waiting for her assent he went straight on. 'Maybe you'll enlighten me as to how you came to be on the scene?'

'I was walking up towards the booths when one of them burst into flames. I ran up to see if there was anything I could do to help.'

'Walking up, you say?'

She nodded. 'Past the shops.'

He looked interested. 'And then you ran towards the fire? That's a strange thing to do, isn't it? To run towards a fire? Surely it was obvious you were running towards danger? Most people would run the other way if they had any sense.'

'I don't know about other people,' she replied, irked by his tone. 'I only thought to run towards it.'

'To see if you could help,' he repeated.

Again she nodded.

'And where exactly did you run from?'

'I told you, from the street.'

He gave a chuckle that was meant to sound affable but his eyes were like gimlets. 'From the street. So some way away, then?'

She agreed it was some way.

'And exactly where in the street were you when you saw the flames?'

She took a breath. 'I was standing close to where the preacher was giving his talk.'

'Ah, the preacher. This would be one of Wycliffe's followers?'

'It sounded like it.'

His eyes narrowed. 'And you have witnesses, do you? I mean, you would have been noticed in such a crowd.'

'I doubt it. Why should I be? There was a great press of people round him. I was just one among many.'

'A Cistercian, though,' he pointed out. 'We don't get many Cistercians listening to barefoot preachers, do we?'

'I have no idea of the figures involved. It would need a proper survey before I could answer that.'

He leant forward. 'I can assure you, Sister, we believe there's nothing wrong with listening to preachers in this town. We encourage it. I can even assure you that the preacher would have his licence from Mayor de Quixlay. There is nothing wrong in listening to a licensed preacher. Not for us.'

'I'm glad of it. He was making sense.'

The serjeant looked sceptical that she should hold a view like that but he turned briskly to the clerk. 'Did anybody mention seeing her in the street?'

The clerk referred to his notes and then shook his head.

The serjeant quirked an eyebrow at her.

She responded with a comment that she had been looking at leather belts at a stall further down and that maybe the vendor would remember her. 'Unless I then sprinted up the street through the crowds to reach the booth to set it alight, as you seem to be suggesting, I could not have reached it any earlier than I did. More's the pity,' she added, 'as then I might have been able to prevent it happening in the first place.' How? she thought. How could anybody have prevented it? Unless they had prior notice.

The clerk was scribbling furiously. He handed a note to a messenger standing by who in turn hurried off down the hall and handed it to the chief constable. From there it would presumably pass down the line until the vendor himself was hauled in to vouch for her, or not.

'You're at present lodging at the widow Tabitha Roberts' house in Danby's yard?' asked the serjeant, abruptly.

'That's right.'

'If you decide to change your abode you'll let us know. My gratitude for your help.'

She was surprised he was allowing her to go without asking what she had seen when she arrived at the booth. As she turned away a man came up to her. It was the one who had thrown himself on the burning stallholder and helped drag the second one from the booth. He walked along beside her to the doors.

'I was the one told them you appeared from down the street. They're only doing their job,' he said. 'That poor devil they took to St Leonard's is still in a bad way. I thought I'd take a walk over there. Would you come with me?'

They went out into the street under the cold eyes of the chief constable. It was a short distance along the path between the wall of St Mary's Abbey and the river. While they walked the stranger said, 'I was wondering if you managed to notice anything I might have missed, given that you were one of the first on the scene and didn't seem blinded by panic. The recollection of most of the bystanders is muddled because of their

217

fear and their haste in trying to get away.'

'I saw very little. The sound of the explosion followed by a whoosh of flame drew my glance. Then I saw the crowd scatter. Then that man emerged with his clothes and hair alight. And then you...' she gave him a swift glance. 'That was a quick and courageous thing to do.' He was thickset, built like a blacksmith, yet he walked with the sort of physical confidence that might come from time spent in the wars.

He didn't enlighten her. 'I was in the right place at the right time. His lucky star was shining. But what I want to know is how it seemed to you – the way the fireball exploded. I didn't really notice much after seeing that, being otherwise engaged.'

'It seemed to set the awnings alight and that's what caused the real damage. I don't think it was such a big explosion. It was where it came from that did most harm. By the look of things the poor woman who died had been unrolling a bale of cloth for a customer. The flames must have run along her arm when the cloth caught fire and set light to her kirtle. Meanwhile the awning over the booth was ablaze and must have descended like a hand of flame over her head. She didn't have a chance.'

'And which direction did it come from in your opinion, the explosion?' His eyes were sharp as he looked into her face.

'From that little puppet tent next door. It was on the end of the row of booths next to the mercer's booth.'

'Are you sure?'

'No, but that's what it looked like in the confusion of the moment.'

'You know they went over the place with a fine-tooth comb and found something odd?'

She shook her head. 'What was it?'

'A metal dish. When they asked the puppet man what it was, he said he'd never seen it before in his life.' The man stopped at the gates of St Leonard's. 'I've changed my mind about coming in. Sorry if I've dragged you away from your business.'

With nothing more than a raised hand in farewell he slipped away along the riverbank towards the town.

Hildegard enquired at the lodge after the man who had been brought in from the fire. The porter looked sorrowful. 'He's hanging on to life by a thread, that's the best we can say. The poor fellow's delirious.'

'I know your brothers are doing everything possible. Does he know his wife has died?'

The porter nodded. 'He's been sent quite mad with grief over her death, screaming imprecations against a crocodile, can you believe. He was conscious through the night and was begging to see her. We had to tell him the truth.'

There was an argument going on in the yard when she returned to her lodgings. It was fairly one-sided. Baldwin and his wife Julitta were haranguing Edric who was looking at them in a bewildered fashion as if he didn't know them. Jankin was hanging out of the window and

Gilbert stood in the doorway to the workshop with his hands by his sides.

Danby rubbed a hand over his bald head. He had taken off the turban and was holding it in both hands, clearly undecided about something, his glance now and then returning to his brother.

They all fell silent when Hildegard entered the yard. With a brief greeting she went over to the door of the widow's house and let herself in. Widow Roberts was standing in the kitchen. It was obvious she had been listening in to the argument in the yard and what she heard had distressed her.

'It's that Julitta, she causes dissension everywhere she goes.' She gave Hildegard a worried glance. 'Baldwin is all for having them run out of town and she's urging him on.'

'Who's that?'

'Anybody who sympathises with the rebels.' Widow Roberts went to the window and looked out. 'He's claiming the rebels are setting the fires to scare people away from celebrating Corpus Christi. Edric's resisting. He knows they wouldn't do any such thing.' She gave Hildegard a swift glance. 'I don't mind who knows I'm saying this.'

'It's all right with me. But what can Master Danby do about it?'

'He's on good terms with the mayor. Baldwin imagines a word from Edric and the whole gang of apprentices will be swept out of town. And then what? To live as outlaws for the rest of their days?' She glanced out of the window again. 'They're still arguing with him, poor fellow. Edric is such a peace-loving man. He doesn't deserve

220

those two.' She turned. 'Baldwin was jealous when they elected his brother as guildmaster. Mistress Julitta's just as bad. They make a good pair. She can never resist a dig at poor Edric, and Dorelia's no use to him, she's just a child. All she knows about is playing and buying new ribbons. I don't know where it's going to end.'

'Have the brothers always been like this?' Hildegard asked.

The widow nodded. 'Everybody's always liked Edric. He was a good boy and now he's a good man. Baldwin's been jealous since he was knee-high. It's not Edric's fault if folk take to him. If Baldwin would put himself out to be pleasant they'd like him as well. He just doesn't see it. He'd have to admit he was in the wrong. And that wouldn't do. That wife eggs him on in his folly. I think she gets her pleasure from watching them at each other's throats. Anyway, Sister, you don't want to involve yourself in all this. I'm a neighbour and I can't help hearing them row. Can I get you anything?'

'Do you have a supply of water here?'

'I do.' She went to a wooden container on the side, lifting the lid and dipping a metal cup inside. 'There now. Fresh spring water. We're lucky we have the well.' She sat down and watched Hildegard drink. 'I trust your business with the constables was no cause for alarm?'

'They just wanted to know what I'd seen yesterday.'

The widow nodded. 'I heard you were one of the first on the scene. Who'd have thought the puppet would go up? He's going round trying to convince everybody it wasn't his fault. Not that anybody's blaming him but I suppose he feels bad, knowing it started there. It was empty, he says. He never leaves the puppets in there when he's not using it in case of theft. They're precious, those dolls of his.'

Hildegard stretched out her legs. The ties of her boots, she noticed now, were criss-crossed unevenly, she had donned them in such haste when the constables arrived. She bent to retie them.

News travelled fast in this town but the widow didn't seem to know yet about the copper dish found in the puppet tent. Time would no doubt rectify matters. In the meantime it made no sense.

Chapter Seventeen

Hildegard offered to do a few chores, although, in truth, there was little that needed to be done in the widow's small, spotless home. She lived, neat and tidy, in the tranquillity of her widowhood and barely left a trace of herself.

After sweeping an already clean chamber, and with the problem of the missing cross nagging at her without respite, Hildegard told widow Roberts she was going round the corner to St Helen's church to sit in quiet contemplation for a while.

In a few minutes she had found a place against the back wall just inside the doorway.

Grey pillars down the short nave. Yellow sunlight. Incense. A glint of gold on the altar. Light in many colours spattering the tiled floor.

She closed her eyes. It was as cool as spring water in here. The day was the hottest yet. It multiplied the flies attracted to the street by the food stalls. They flew in through the open door before being attracted back to the heat and the smell of sizzling meats outside. Gradually the silence took over.

She sat for some time. When she eventually opened her eyes there were as many unanswered questions as when she had closed them.

The place had been filling up. She gave the newcomers a cursory glance. Some rich apparel was on show.

A couple standing off to one side of the altar at the front were particularly well turned out. They did not greet anyone but stood as strangers, the woman stern-faced, wearing a white wimple, a large silver brooch pinning it tightly under her chin. Her escort was soberly dressed but the quality of his garments could not be disguised. Grey silk of the best. An undertunic of deep purple, its sleeves slashed to reveal a crimson lining. The woman was also dressed in grey with an embroidered overmantle in a pale, light weave suitable for hot weather.

The rest of the congregation looked plain beside them, although, if they were members of the Glaziers' Guild, they would be comfortably off these days. The man gave the woman beside him a quick glance, then, noticing that her eyes were closed, turned and cast a look over the people standing in the nave. Then he turned and gave his full attention to the priest.

Hildegard shifted her attention to the stained glass in the East window glowing with blue, gold and scarlet. The priest stepped into the flood of coloured light and began to intone the liturgy in rapid Latin. An altar boy swung a heavy censer whose fumes had the unfortunate effect of reminding Hildegard of the smoke billowing from the remains of the booth the previous afternoon. She forced herself to think of life as something eternal and to consider what the priest intended with his large claims about the truth.

There was no one from Master Danby's workshop present.

Unable to give the ritual proper attention she got up and slipped outside, leaving the drone of Latin and the scent of incense with a feeling of relief.

Brother Thomas was at that moment walking along the street. 'I was coming to find you. Widow Roberts said you'd gone to St Helen's.' His sharp eyes examined her expression. 'Are you all right?'

She shrugged. 'I couldn't sit there, knowing that that poor man is probably dying in St Leonard's. That Maud is still suffering. Those armed men are still at large. And that the cross is missing and we're nowhere near finding who stole it.' She gave him a close look. 'How's your head? I forgot to ask in all the turmoil yesterday.'

'It's not so bad. Your bruise seems to have gone down.'

'Arnica. I needed it after hitting that Sister Michael in the face.'

They walked across the road to the place where

the booths were once again doing brisk business as if nothing had happened. They were without awnings now and the stock was somewhat charred, but there were plenty of buyers jostling to make their purchases at a discount. The place where the fire had broken out had been cleared and now a woman stood there, offering fortunes for a groat.

'She's got her predictions wrong. She should have been here yesterday morning,' Thomas said with a grimace. Just then a scuffle broke out. The first they knew about it was when there were angry shouts and a few encouraging cheers from a group of men standing nearby.

The crowd scattered to make room, then quickly reformed around two apprentices. Thomas went over and Hildegard followed. When they reached the group they saw two lads squaring up to each other. It was no brief skirmish but was turning into a vicious bare-knuckle fight. Both had bloody noses already and the crowd began to cheer every time one of them landed a punch.

Thomas shouldered his way through the onlookers and dragged both boys apart by the scruff of their necks. 'Pack it in. Admit your differences and shake hands on it like gentlemen.'

He was tall, strong, and spoke with an urgent authority that made both boys fall silent in surprise. 'Come on, now.' He shook them both. 'I haven't all day.'

One of the boys broke free. With blood streaming down his face he gave the monk a glare. 'I will never, ever shake that traitor by the hand!' With that he pushed his way through the crowd and ran off.

Thwarted of entertainment, the onlookers began to disperse.

'You don't need to ask what that was about,' one of the idlers said to Thomas. 'Drunken brawling. That's what. It's them apprentices. They can't take their drink these days.'

'To be fair,' said Thomas, 'they seemed sober enough. Just drunk on a difference of opinion.'

The boy who remained snuffled through his bloody nose and slunk away without looking back. The crowd had melted as quickly as it had formed. Thomas rubbed his hands on his sleeves. 'What were we saying?'

Hildegard gave him a soft smile. Hubert would have done exactly the same as that. She touched his arm. 'We weren't saying anything. Come and have a beaker of wine at Widow Roberts'. That is, if you youngsters can hold your drink.'

'It's like this,' she began in an undertone when they were sitting in the shade of the eaves outside the house with a beaker each of Rhenish, 'whoever stole the cross may not understand its true significance. They may be willing to settle for a ransom.'

Thomas looked unconvinced.

'First we need to find out if it really is something to do with the Company of the White Hart, although what their purpose could be I have no idea.'

'And if, on the other hand, the thief is Bolingbroke?'

'We're done for.' She gave a wry laugh. 'Let's try one avenue at a time. We need to talk to the rebels.'

Thomas gasped. 'What, talk to them here in the town?'

She shook her head. 'No. To the ones living outside.'

'Outside the law, you mean?' He looked astonished.

'There must be someone who can put us in touch with them.'

She could see Gilbert in the workshop across the yard. He had finished whitewashing the surface of the large trestle and now appeared to be marking a drawing out on it. He was absorbed in his work.

Thomas idly followed her glance, then his jaw dropped. 'You mean the journeyman? Are you serious? Do you think he's a sympathiser?'

'It's a risk I'm willing to take.'

Thomas had asked what she would say to Gilbert and she had told him that she would think of something. She had to do it when she was sure he was going to be alone. Danby, as a guildmaster, couldn't be expected to condone anything illegal, but Gilbert would consort with other journeymen and apprentices and must be aware of the avenues by which they could be contacted.

Danby went indoors just before Thomas left for nones and had been inside ever since. She could see him talking to Gilbert, their heads close together as they discussed something.

Before he left, Thomas had said, 'These friars

227

are rare boys. You wouldn't believe some of the tricks they get up to. Pity they don't know anything useful.' Then he said, 'Do you want me to come back later?'

She told him she would come out to meet him at the friary after she had spoken to Gilbert. She didn't know how long it would take to find an opportunity.

Now it was evening. Widow Roberts had cooked a tasty pie, and with one eye on the workshop, Hildegard had eaten it quickly and later rinsed their bowls out, then offered to fill the water bucket at the well.

While she was outside she saw Danby and Dorelia come out and sit on the bench against their wall to catch the last rays of the sun. It was pleasant now the heat had gone out of it.

After a casual exchange or two, Hildegard went back into the house. To add to her impatience they went on sitting outside until it was twilight. Gilbert could be seen in the workshop by the light of a tallow and continued to work until Danby went in and ticked him off. The candle went out.

Danby came outside with a cresset which he placed in a bracket on the wall. He put his arms round Dorelia's waist. She leant back against him but her eyes were wide open. They eventually went indoors. After a moment a candle illuminated an upper chamber with a diffuse golden glow.

Gilbert came to the door of the workshop and stretched. Baldwin stumbled back, evidently from the tavern, and went inside his own house at the top of the yard. As soon as she was sure Gilbert was alone Hildegard hurried out.

'If you please, a word in private.'

He glanced at her with surprise.

In a voice kept low so as not to be overheard, she said, 'We were talking about certain things the other day concerning the White Hart brotherhood. Everybody knows some of them have to live outside the law due to circumstances beyond their control. I would like to talk with them. I believe they may be able to help me.'

Gilbert gave her a long stare. His pale eyes seemed transparent as if they could be seen straight through like a window, but whatever lay in the inner chamber beyond he now kept hidden.

Before he could reply there was a commotion from the direction of the street and a figure strode into the yard followed by a little page. It was the man in grey silk she had noticed in St Helen's.

'Master about?' he demanded of Gilbert without any preamble.

'In 'is bed.' Gilbert, it seemed, could be equally curt.

'I bet he is, the lucky devil. I'd be in my bed if I had a wife like that!' He swept across the yard with the page running to keep up. 'What about Baldwin? He about?' he called over his shoulder.

Gilbert shrugged. He knew he was because he had just seen him come in from the tavern.

The newcomer banged on Baldwin's door. 'It's Gisburne!' he shouted. 'Open up!'

A shutter flew open. 'Oh, it's you, John. Come

inside,' said Julitta's voice, all syrupy and welcoming.

'That's Gisburne?' asked Hildegard in astonishment.

Gilbert nodded. 'Know him?'

'I do not. Nor would I like to from what I've heard. Didn't he try to intimidate Mayor de Quixlay's supporters with threats of violence a few years back?'

Gilbert made no reply.

After Gisburne had entered the house she stared for a moment at the closed door. Baldwin's argument with Danby earlier that day had taken on a different hue. She moved closer to Gilbert so that she could not be overheard. 'About what I asked just now. Can you help?'

He shook his head. 'What do you imagine I can do?' He turned abruptly and went back inside.

So had she got him wrong? It was late now and with no other plan in mind she made her way upstairs to bed. She had not been in it more than a moment or two when she heard Gisburne making his way noisily across the yard again in the direction of the street.

After that everything fell silent. Later came the distant sound of a bell. It was the deep bass bell from the minster, the sound enlarging then decaying and moving into silence. As the last reverberations faded she heard something else. It was the groan of a door being opened in stealth.

On bare feet she hurried to the window. It was the door opposite. Danby's bald head gleamed briefly in the suddenly quenched light of a candle before he pulled up his hood. He was quickly followed by Gilbert, bright hair visible until he covered his too. Together the men crept out of the yard towards the street.

As soon as they reached the passage the door to Baldwin's house opened and a figure slipped out. It wasn't Julitta. It was Baldwin again. He moved carefully across the yard in the steps of his brother and the journeyman.

Hildegard dragged on her boots and ran lightly down the stairs. She had noticed a dark cloak hanging on the back of the kitchen door and now she pulled it on over her white shift and hastened out into the night. When she reached the corner of the alley she glanced quickly both ways, caught sight of the dark figure of Baldwin and followed after. Further up she could see the two others, and beyond them three or four constables carrying flares.

Danby stopped to have a word with them. In the silence of the shuttered street his words carried clearly. 'All quiet, lads?'

They made some comment, wished him good-night and continued up the street, checking doors and peering into crannies as they went.

Danby and his journeyman turned off in the direction of the bridge. Baldwin slipped out of the shadow of a doorway, muttered a 'God be wi' ye' to the constables from under his hood and followed them. He made no attempt to catch up. Instead he kept close to the walls of the buildings with his head down. It was obvious he did not want them to know he was trailing them.

They crossed the bridge. The two ahead paused for a moment on the other side as if conferring, then they turned left along the lane that led towards the convent of the Holy Wounds. Hildegard felt her throat constrict. The last thing she wanted was to be noticed by anyone from there. To her relief the two men turned almost at once onto a side street.

Baldwin was still shadowing them. He too disappeared into the street. Hildegard hurried to catch up.

When she turned the corner she realised they were heading into the stews. It looked as if Master Danby and his journeyman had merely come out to spend a few hours among the whores. She had to admit she was surprised. It made Danby's vaunted adoration of his young wife look like a sham. And as for Gilbert, well, he was young, probably unable to find a girl of his own anyway, and yet she felt oddly disappointed to think that their night excursion had come to nothing more than this.

They were still plodding on, however, Baldwin slipping after them like a wraith. She saw them reach an intersection where the crossing lane led into a warren of lighted alleys with many girls standing round open doors, waiting for trade. Hildegard pulled the hood of the dark cloak further over her face and crossed the street.

Danby and Gilbert were now walking up the slope on the other side, right past the lines of girls. The road ran up parallel with Micklegate and followed the same incline towards the city walls. Gilbert, she noticed, was limping more than ever and Danby kept slowing his pace so as not to be seen walking ahead.

Baldwin reached the intersection. As he did so one of the women standing in a doorway called to someone over her shoulder. A man appeared behind her. He came out onto the street and called out, 'You after your money already, Baldwin?'

'Not tonight.' Baldwin was curt and clearly annoyed. 'Get away now. Get back inside.'

He went on up the hill. Hildegard was aware of interested glances as she approached but she kept her head down and walked on as if with some independent purpose of her own. Danby and Gilbert were going along more slowly as the hill began to tax their energies. Baldwin slowed to match his pace to theirs.

Eventually they came out at the top near the wall of the French priory. There was an open space next to the walls with one or two trees dotted around and several wooden structures, unlit, and apparently deserted. Staying out of sight, Hildegard waited to see what would happen next.

Danby cast a brief glance round about but failed to notice Baldwin who had retreated behind a tree. He didn't give a single glance into the deep shadow of the building where Hildegard was standing. Without a word he pushed open a door into what looked like a storage shed and stepped inside. Gilbert followed.

After a moment Baldwin emerged from behind the tree and stood looking up at the building. It remained in darkness. After a few moments and with a muttered oath he turned and walked hurriedly away.

When she was sure he wasn't coming back Hildegard went over to the door and tried to peer through the gaps in the planks but there was no light inside and she could see nothing but unbroken darkness within.

She pushed the door. It was unlocked. Wondering if she was being foolhardy she pressed her shoulder against it and cautiously pushed it open. Still nothing.

She slipped inside. It took a moment to get used to the darkness. A single splinter of light from the floor above sifted through the gloom enough to show that she was in the store where the pageant wagons were kept. Lurid shapes leapt into sight, scenery, stage equipment, ropes and pulleys strung from the beams as hoists. They loomed on all sides with a mysterious menace, half alive in the darkness.

To one side she could make out some wooden stairs leading up to a trapdoor. It was from the upper floor that the faint murmur of voices came. It must be a pageant meeting, she hazarded.

But then why had Baldwin bothered to go to the trouble of shadowing his brother like that? It was obvious he expected to discover something else, as she herself had.

She moved deeper into the warehouse. There was nothing here to give rise to suspicion. Sinister as it looked at first glance it was really only a collection of paper sets and gaudy effects. There were flames painted on a screen, laughably unrealistic when she looked closer. The more she stared, however, the more they seemed to take on a mysterious power of their own.

She was about to turn and feel her way back towards the door when the trapdoor was suddenly lifted, letting down a powerful beam of light beneath it. She froze, concealed behind the painted canvas. A man's legs appeared followed by the edge of a cloak and the rest of a thickset body. He was saying something to the men in the room above as he descended. He was quickly followed by Danby, and after him, Gilbert, awkwardly swinging his lame leg and refusing help. The three of them stood at the bottom of the ladder waiting for a fourth man to descend.

Hildegard kept quite still behind the scenery and held her breath.

They weren't discussing pageant matters. That was obvious. The first man was trying to convince Danby of something.

'He won't,' he was saying, 'he won't do it. I'll wager you half a noble if he does.'

Wedged in among the canvas flames she made sure she had a view of the ladder, then waited with pounding heart. They were looking up impatiently to the roof space and the first man called up. A deep voice responded.

'Patience, fellow. I need to make sure I've got everything.' Then a foot in a worn leather boot felt around for the top rung of the ladder and the man began a cautious descent.

When he stood firmly on the ground with the others he gave a laugh. 'You forget, I'm not used to physical activity like you lads.'

Hildegard gaped. At first she thought it was the preacher she had seen yesterday in Stonegate before the fire broke out in the booths.

235

Her glance sharpened when he pushed back his hood. In the fall of light from above, she saw fine-boned, saintly looking features, but instead of a tonsure like the preacher she had seen yesterday, his hair was thick and dark and fell untidily to his shoulders.

Yet he wore the russet gown of a Wycliffe man.

The others were treating him with an attitude bordering on deference. The first to descend the ladder now claimed the privilege of carrying his bag and heaved the strap over his shoulders.

Danby put a comradely hand on the preacher's arm as if to reassure him and Hildegard heard him distinctly when he said, 'The silly young devil should have asked her what she was after–'

'I didn't know how,' Gilbert broke in. 'I thought it best to keep my trap shut.'

'He did well,' the preacher said. 'You have my gratitude. Let's go.' For all his bookish looks the man was decisive. The others were quick to follow his lead. They went towards the door.

If Simon de Quixlay welcomes the barefoot preachers, against the will of the Duke of Lancaster but by the will of his own citizens, Hildegard was thinking, why is there need for such secrecy with regard to this one?

There could be only one answer. He was one of those on the run from Archbishop Courtenay of Canterbury, the chief prelate of all England, the man sworn to exterminate them from every corner of the realm. There was a price on his head.

Pope Urban, for once in agreement with the antipope in Avignon, had demanded that the dissidents be silenced. King Richard had said he would see to it. Yet he had done nothing to obey the pope's edict.

The archbishop, however, had made it his personal mission to pursue those who refused to recant. They had been thrown out of Oxford, forbidden to teach anywhere else and then tried for heresy in the episcopal court. If they still failed to recant their so-called heresies they were thrown into jail.

One or two escaped this fate as soon as they saw which way the wind was blowing and settled in a prosperous little fenland port on the river Cam and pretended to concern themselves with innocent matters. Others, more committed to the cause of free speech perhaps, travelled the country speaking their minds.

This man must be one of these.

The four figures slipped from the building. Hildegard prayed they would not lock the door from the other side. To her relief she heard them walk briskly away, leaving it unlocked. The building descended into silence. She waited for as long as she dare, then hurried over. The door opened easily and she let herself out.

The men had gone.

She headed towards the main street. About to make her way openly back down Micklegate rather than retrace her steps through the stews, she had gone only as far as the church of the Holy Trinity where the pageant stand was being erected when a man stepped from out in front of her.

He didn't speak, but before she could move he grabbed her by the arms and swivelled her round. Next thing she felt the cold blade of a dagger at her throat.

Her first thought was that it must be Baldwin, unrecognisable with his hood over his face. But her assailant was bigger, beefier, and he gave off a stale smell, like rancid beeswax. She could feel his broad chest against her back as he held her with a force that allowed no escape.

'One move and you're dead meat,' he grunted.

He began to push her round the side of the church, forcing her underneath the scaffolding and in amongst the trees in the churchyard.

Chapter Eighteen

The bailiff's men at Micklegate Bar were still letting a few stragglers in through the night gate. It meant that the street was not entirely deserted. In fact, as Hildegard first approached, she had been aware of a noisy group of players descending the steps from the chamber above the gatehouse where they had probably been rehearsing.

Remembering this now and praying that they were still within earshot, she stamped hard on her assailant's foot, and when his grasp momentarily slackened she managed to slip down, away from the immediate danger of the knife blade. His surprise lasted long enough to give her time to throw herself in under the wooden scaffolding outside the building. Her assailant lunged after her with a furious roar, but she dodged into the maze of posts and, being thinner than he was, managed to squeeze into a narrow gap between two supports and run out onto the street.

She erupted into the middle of the group of players. They scattered with cries of surprise followed by rapturous greetings when they took in the fact that she was a woman and in distress.

'May I join you, my lords?' Hildegard cried, throwing a glance over her shoulder.

They must have caught sight of her assailant even though he had retreated at once into the shadow of the church wall, and clearly taking it to be a domestic tiff, one of them gave a deep flourish and said, 'Knight errant at your service, my lady!' He raised his voice. 'Yours to command! Beware ye who mean this damsel harm!'

His friends cheered. They were dressed as cardinals, in wide-brimmed hats, red robes, the figure at their head wearing a triple crown in the guise of a pope. Instead of carrying a sceptre, however, he wielded a quart flagon.

He offered it now with the words, 'Lady, pray join us and partake of the wine of life.'

Jovial, not at all menacing, they insisted on escorting her to safety, chaffing each other, laughing and declaiming the lines of their play, the noise bringing curses from the upper windows of houses lining the street. This roused them to a tempest of shushing, loud enough to wake everybody else within a hundred yards. Hildegard was carried along with this jovial mob over the bridge and on into the safety of the town. Her assailant was nowhere to be seen.

They reached Pavement and straggled to a halt.

239

One of her escorts knelt at her feet. 'And this is where we part in sorrow, to meet again upon the morrow! Goodnight, fair friend!'

The pope kissed the backs of both her hands. 'Good night, dear lady!' he declaimed.

'See you on the green, you pious pontiff!' One of them waved goodbye and took his leave. A general scene of hugging and bowing followed and they began to disperse in ones and twos to different quarters of the town.

'Which play are you in?' asked the pope as he kissed the backs of her hands again for good measure.

Realising that they had mistaken her habit for pageant garb she thought quickly for a play that might have a nun in it and replied, *The Last Judgement.*'

He roared with laughter. 'Then I'll see you in hell, dear lady.'

The street rang for some time with their farewell cries.

Hildegard was escorted to the corner of Stonegate by a couple of cardinals and, whispering her thanks, slipped quickly into the glazier's yard and on into the house. She was shaking. Saved by the pope and a school of cardinals, she thought. Thomas would never believe it.

'I think he was that big, slow, stupid brute who does all the heavy work for the Sisters of the Holy Wounds. I got a good glimpse of his face in the light from the cressets when the cardinals arrived.'

'Do you think it was by chance he saw you?'

240

Thomas asked now.

The monk had turned up that morning with a worried look on his face that had vanished as soon as he set eyes on her. Now they were sitting outside in the yard. It was another scorcher.

'I have a feeling he's been watching me.' She told him about other occasions when he had appeared as if from nowhere.

'On the other hand,' she said, considering the matter, 'it might have been chance. Maybe he thought he could take the opportunity to try to force me into telling him where Maud is. I had to go a little way down the lane towards the convent and he could have seen me then, near the stews,' she added. She remembered coming across the Dominican in the same locality and thought, not for the first time, how a religious calling seemed to make little difference to the way some men behaved.

'I was worried when you didn't appear last night. You said you would but I convinced myself you simply hadn't had an opportunity to speak to the journeyman.'

I would never not turn up once I'd said I would,' she told him. 'But I'm puzzled. Why would Matthias attack me? What would he hope to gain? Or did that mother superior of theirs put him up to it? She surely can't think she'll get Maud back by abducting me?'

'If she does she certainly doesn't know you,' said Thomas.

'Anyway, even Matthias won't be stupid enough to try anything on in broad daylight. In future I'll take extra care at night. It was probably just bad luck that our paths crossed.'

Privately she wondered how Matthias had known it was her when she had worn her hood up. She felt a moment's disquiet at the thought that he might have been watching the yard that night and followed her just as she had followed the others. It hadn't occurred to her to look behind her. By now it was common knowledge that she was staying in Danby's yard.

Keeping her fear to herself she said, 'This morning something had arrived by the time I came down.' She pushed a piece of paper across to him. 'It was under the door. Widow Roberts was still in bed. I didn't sleep much and was up first.'

It was a note. Thomas read it with a furrowed brow. 'So they have something to tell you. And they're going to send somebody to take you to a meeting as you requested.' He turned the scrap of vellum over. It was blank. He held it up. 'From the rebels? But anybody could have written it. It's unsigned. Are you going to accept?'

'Having come this far it would be irrational to refuse.'

'Then I'm coming with you.'

The morning had started hot again and as the day progressed the temperature shot up. There was talk of water from the town wells being rationed. They sat in the shade of the overhanging roof, wearing straw hats, fanning themselves with rhubarb leaves from Danby's vegetable plot, and sipping beakers of well water laced with wine. Widow Roberts remained indoors, singing

242

as she went about her chores and eventually coming outside with a basket saying she was off to market.

After she left the yard fell silent.

Gilbert could be seen inside the inner workshop. He appeared to be marking out the *vidimus* on the whitewashed table. Edric went in and out. They heard the murmur of voices. Then the master was seen at an upstairs window and there was a flash of white as Dorelia briefly appeared. When Edric came down again he was smiling and his shirt was awry.

Gilbert, hair tied back like a pirate, was still bending silently over his work. Neither he nor Danby gave a single glance across the yard.

Jankin came whistling outside to fetch water and made some comment about the weather as he let the bucket down. After he wound it to the top again he staggered back inside with it. The splashes on the paved yard dried instantly.

Of Baldwin there was no sign. The shutters of the house at the top of the yard remained closed, maybe to keep out the heat. The crowds along Stonegate could be heard shuffling past the end of the passage in a constant slow stream. A hurdy-gurdy struck up in the middle distance. A few accompanying voices were heard. Mainly it was just the soporific sound of the crowds passing by as softly irregular as waves breaking on a distant shore. A bell began a slow toll from a nearby tower.

Hildegard daren't set foot outside the yard in case she missed the promised messenger. It was a charade, not mentioning anything to Danby. Was

243

she supposed to pretend that she didn't know how the message had reached her? She said this to Thomas. With sweat trickling down his forehead he recommended patience.

'We are told you wish to meet us. We may have information of interest to you. A guide will be sent to fetch you.'

That's what the message said. It had been written in a graceful hand.

Apologising, Thomas went off to Lady Mass. He returned, reeking of incense, straight afterwards.

And then, sometime before sext with the sun at its height, when they had retreated to the cool of Widow Robert's kitchen, a figure boldly entered the yard and began pacing about, looking at the cottages as if unsure which one to approach first. Hildegard went outside and Thomas followed.

'Yes?' she asked.

The man came towards her. He looked like a cleric, but after seeing the actor-cardinals on the previous night and the town filling with fantastical figures as most of the members of the forty-eight guilds plied in ever increasing frequency to their rehearsals, she was unwilling to take him at face value. As well as the vestments of a chantry priest he wore a wide-brimmed straw hat, obscuring his face.

He was fishing something out of his leather bag as he approached. 'I said I would do it!' He held out a piece of parchment with a green wax seal on it.

She took it. 'What's this?'

Looking over her shoulder Thomas said in an

244

awed voice, 'It's the seal of the Archbishop of York!'

'I would have brought you the seal itself but I thought this would suffice. I deemed it the best way of showing I had kept my word.'

'Theophilus?' Hildegard peered at the messenger.

He touched the brim of his hat. 'Greetings, Sister. Now,' he went on briskly, 'do you have a drink to offer me? It's a long walk from Bishopthorpe Palace.'

They sat in the cool of the kitchen drinking watered wine.

'It was like this,' said the mage. 'When I managed to get inside the palace last night there was a great feast. Some important personage...?' He cocked a glance.

'We know,' said Hildegard quickly.

'While that was going on I had a good look round in every chamber.'

'But how did you get inside?'

'Ask not of the mage,' he reproved. 'Suffice to say I made no forced entry but was invited in with as much ceremony as if I'd been a visiting prelate.' He chuckled. 'Which as far as they were concerned, I was. However, that's not the point of the story. I kept my ears and eyes open as I said. I drew a blank. No mention of any theft in any quarter. Unless they're unwontedly loyal, they're as innocent as newborn babes.'

'Discretion is probably one of their strengths,' muttered Thomas.

'I can tell you, they were as loose-tongued as

anybody else in their master's absence. I adopted the dress of a retainer, at one point, the better to hear the truth.' His eyes gleamed at the memory. 'I can tell you emphatically – they know no more than I do of any theft!'

'We can guess the truth, then, can't we?' Thomas said. He avoided looking across the yard towards Danby's workshop.

'But,' continued the mage, 'I did hear talk of a sum of money. I heard of an offer to purchase something of great value from your priory at Swyne, Sister. Something worth more gold than any Lombardy banker has ever dreamt of. I heard talk of local matters, too. I heard a name. I saw guests. And I heard the old king's minstrel play.' His cat's eyes alighted on Hildegard.

'Master Gyles?' she asked quickly.

'Ah,' said the mage, 'I thought you'd know him.'

'I have met him,' Hildegard replied cautiously.

The king's minstrel, Master Pierrekyn Gyles, had retired from court and come to live as a corrodian in York. He had passed on information to supporters of John of Gaunt last year as she had discovered almost too late. She suspected that his usefulness as the eyes and ears of Duke John was the reason he had been granted a corrodiary at St Mary's Abbey by the King's Council – which, of course, was headed by Gaunt himself. St Mary's, in fact, was an establishment that owed much of its wealth to Gaunt's generosity. A well-placed spy in York would always be useful to a man like the duke.

But Pierrekyn Gyles, though! A guest at

Bishopthorpe Palace! A dangerous man. She shivered. 'He's an exceptional musician,' was all she said.

'As he would have to be in order to be employed by the royal court,' said Theophilus carelessly. He got up. 'The name Gisburne came up.'

He went to the door and looked out. The yard was empty.

When he returned he said, 'I would question the loyalty of everyone you meet. It is not always apparent who to trust in these walled towns, where antagonisms run deeper than one would imagine.'

He lowered his voice. 'There's schism in the ranks of the brotherhood. Much discontent with King Richard's behaviour since the Rising. Going back on his word as he did after Smithfield is seen as unkingly and not worth the allegiance of good men.'

He lowered his voice still further. 'He's seen as a betrayer of his people. It has led some to a desire to follow a preacher instead, one of those who has lately been hounded from Oxford by Archbishop Courtenay.'

'Do you have a name?' asked Hildegard.

'It's a barefoot preacher by the name of Magister Will Thorpe. He's been outlawed for his beliefs and, so my informant told me, has fled north. Whether the Archbishop of Canterbury is acting on Gaunt's orders or merely carrying out Pope Urban's recent edict to root out heretics is open to question. Master Gyles,' he tapped the side of his nose to indicate that this was confidential, 'is of the opinion that certain members in the rebel faction want to break their traditional links with clerics of all kinds – and ally themselves with a temporal lord.'

'Which one?' asked Hildegard at once.

'That, dear Sister, is open to conjecture. It seems to me,' he said in a sombre tone, 'that the wish in some quarters is to involve King Robert of Scotland.'

'Traitors to their own country!' exclaimed Thomas. 'They surely can't be serious?'

'You're talking of treason,' added Hildegard. So it wasn't the French, then. It was nothing to do with the Abbey of Meaux.

'Maybe loyalty has diminished so far in importance,' said the mage, 'that only personal profit remains? But tell me, Sister,' his tone lightened, 'is my debt settled?'

'I never thought of you as being in my debt.'

He bowed, happening to glance out of the window. Then he replaced his straw hat and turned briskly towards the yard and left.

Hildegard gazed after him in astonishment. 'No farewell? Did I offend him?'

The monk rose and went over to the window. Hildegard joined him. They watched the mage, so-called, with face concealed under the brim of his hat, striding off down the passage that led into the street. Baldwin was standing outside Danby's window, gazing after him with a puzzled frown.

He may have been lurking out there for a while, thought Hildegard, noticing a stoup of ale in his hand.

248

As soon as Theophilus was out of sight, Baldwin made his way into Danby's house and went straight into the back workshop. They could see him through the window at Gilbert's shoulder, where the journeyman was continuing to mark out the scale drawing of Roger's chantry window. Baldwin's lips were moving but his words were inaudible across the yard.

Still no messenger turned up. Thomas went off to the next office of the day and returned. Meanwhile, Gilbert came out with a hunk of bread and cheese and gnawed his way through it. Baldwin had disappeared into his own cottage. Hildegard wondered when he did any work. Jankin had been mixing colours in several little pots which he stood in a row on the sill, and the master himself had been busy writing up what looked like accounts at a table in front of the open shutters in the front workshop. It was like a beehive, buzzing with industry.

Apart from that brief appearance at an upstairs window, Danby had been working all morning without a break. He came outside now and sat down next to Gilbert on the bench. Jankin disappeared and was doubtless busy in the back room where the cook and the kitchen lad lived.

Hildegard went to stand on the doorstep, fanning herself with her straw hat and wondering just how much any of them had noticed or heard. 'Another fine day, master,' she called across.

Danby waved to her. 'Join us, Sister.' Evidently he didn't realise Brother Thomas was in the house with her. He made room for her on the

249

bench. 'You can tell Lord Roger we're making progress with his glass,' he told her. 'Gilbert here has nearly finished measuring out the final drawing. No doubt we'll be seeing him round here to have a look at it before the pageant makes passage through town impossible.'

'His steward is keeping an eye on the castle at the first station,' she told him. The stands were called 'castles' locally.

'So he mentioned,' Darby replied. 'I'll send somebody up there later on.'

The heat seemed to make everyone drowsy and the master fell silent. Someone had caused that cryptic note to be written. It could only be him and Gilbert.

The latter made no sign of acknowledgement when she sat down but was staring into space as if seeing something at a distance. Edric gave him a nudge. 'Stop work, you young devil. I can hear your brain whirring. Take a break.' He turned to Hildegard. 'He'd work all day and all night if I let him.'

Gilbert's eyelids flickered and then he turned his gaze briefly on his master's face. 'Work is in the gift of the Lord,' he said. 'We should honour it.'

It sounded like a pious quotation but in the light of dissenter opinion it could have been a criticism of bonded labour. Without further comment he stuffed the last of his bread into his mouth, brushed the crumbs from his tunic and went back inside.

Edric shook his head. 'He'll work himself into the ground.' No remark of any significance followed.

Hildegard's thoughts roamed without purpose over the information the mage had passed on until they snagged on the question of whether Archbishop Neville had sent a messenger to the prioress at Swyne, putting Bolingbroke's wishes before her. According to Theophilus there was a rumour that 'a precious object' was for sale, and although wild estimates of its possible value seemed to have been made, none of them had come anywhere near it's true worth.

Edric eventually rose to his feet, saying, 'Come and have a look at what we've done so far.'

It was cooler inside the workshop. The windows ran along the north wall letting in a constant, grey light. The pleasant temperature made it easier to understand why Gilbert was content to remain at work. The other reason was obvious – it was his joy in what he did.

The full-scale drawing was impressive. It was designed in several sections, three roundels at the top, the long expanse of the main image of the Virgin and child with the sun's rays behind them, and along the bottom edge the figures of the two donors, one on each side, and between them a small scene she had not seen before. Gilbert was just marking it out. There was not much detail. He had drawn the outlines of a few shapes, one a figure stretched out on a bier or maybe a bed, another one seeming to hover above and a third inside an arch, presumably meant to represent a doorway. Underneath was a roundel that over-lapped the frame, neither in the scene nor outside it. It was blank.

'What happens next?' she asked.

'We finish cutting the glass to size, lay it in place – see the colours marked on each segment? And then comes the clever part.'

'What's that?'

'Painting in the detail on the coloured glass.' He looked pleased at the prospect of starting on it.

Gilbert lifted his head and gave them both a silvery glance. 'Maybe this time he'll let me get my hands on one or two sections myself, eh, master?'

Edric put his thumbs in his jerkin and looked delighted at the mettle of his journeyman. 'All in good time,' he said, but it was clear he was agreeable and Gilbert nodded, looking well pleased with things himself.

Hildegard roamed impatiently about the yard. Widow Roberts made a brief appearance and then went out again. Having lived in the town all her life she had many friends nearby.

Thomas was sitting in the kitchen reading a well-thumbed breviary when she went back in. It made her remember her missal, the one she had saved from the Deepdale fire. Although she carried it with her she hadn't opened it since they arrived. It struck her how matter-of-fact was Thomas's belief. It was a fundamental part of his identity. To have such certainty amazed her. She had felt the same when confronted by Sister Marianne's unquestioning faith.

Now he closed the book and looked up. 'Maybe they'll wait until nightfall?' he suggested. 'Why don't we take a stroll? You're on tenterhooks.'

'Just to the end of the street and back,' she agreed. 'We don't want to miss them.'

Thomas slipped his breviary into his sleeve. Donning her straw hat she followed him outside.

The sun was merciless. When they left the shadow of the little alleyway it struck them with its full force. The smell of the crowd mingled with the wafted aroma from an open brazier on the corner where a man was frying fritters and selling them as fast as he could produce them. A mixture of scents from the apothecaries sweetened the sour smell of too many sweating people pressed together in one place. The explosions had made only a slight difference. The streets were crowded. Everybody seemed determined to make the most of the festivities to come.

'I ought to go to the kennels and look in on my hounds,' she said. 'I've neglected them shamefully. I'll take them with us when we go.' She felt Thomas's sleeve brush the back of her hand. 'We're not going to get far in this crowd,' she added.

A voice whispered. 'You'll get as far as you want to go, Sister. Follow me.' With a start she glanced aside at the unfamiliar voice. A stranger held her sleeve. 'I've got a horse waiting for you. I'm told you wish to speak to someone?'

'Now?'

He gazed at her without answering. She glanced over her shoulder. Thomas was right behind her.

Without another word the man slid into the crowd. He wore a leather hat and had a wide belt slung over one shoulder like a peddler, and his

253

dun-coloured jerkin merged in with what everyone else was wearing. She hurried to keep up in
case she lost sight of him, trusting that Thomas
would follow.

Chapter Nineteen

The stranger led them away from the main thoroughfare and into Goodramgate and out towards
Monk Bar, the east entrance into the city. There
was a handful of guards at the postern and they
checked them, though with little interest, probably at this time of day glad to see people leaving
rather than arriving to jam-pack the town even
more.

Outside the walls, a little way into the Jewish
quarter, their guide came to a stop. A couple of
horses were hitched to a rail with a lad standing
by. The man tossed him a coin.

Turning to Hildegard he said, 'Let's go.' He
held a stirrup for her but she ignored it and
mounted in the usual way.

They were short-legged ponies, tough and
hardy enough to travel long distances without
effort. To her surprise he mounted the second
one and took up the reins as if about to set off.

'What about the brother?' she asked.

'I have no instructions to take a monk with me.'

Before she could object he brought his whip
hard down on the rump of her pony and it leapt
forward from standing into a full gallop. Her hat

fell off. The second pony raced alongside and she could tell that they were used to trying to best each other. The animal's mouth was hard. Hauling on the reins did no good. The spirit of competition invaded its being.

A snatched glance back through the cloud of dust they were kicking up showed a blur of people where Thomas was standing. For a moment she thought of slipping from the saddle and throwing herself clear, but only for a moment. The urgency of the mission drove her on.

They rode at speed until they reached the woodland, and the guide hurled his mount through the trees onto a snaking path that contrary to her expectations seemed to take them back alongside the walls, although, of course, these were not visible.

The sun was an indication that they were now riding in a more northerly direction. They rode for some time. The man did not let up. He kept glancing back to make sure she was following. Eventually, when she was beginning to wonder if he was lost, he slowed and allowed her to draw alongside.

'We wait here until nightfall,' he told her. He got down and set about gathering a few sticks. She sat on a fallen tree and watched.

He came back and threw the branches into some sort of mound, then bent to set the spark from his tinderbox to it. Going to the saddlebags he brought out a tin mug and sprinkled some herbs into it. He set it over the flames. When it was hot he drank from it, then offered her some.

Throat dry with the amount of dust their horses had kicked up she swallowed it gratefully enough. It was mint.

'Who are we going to meet?' she asked.

He shook his head.

'Don't you know?' she asked in a provoking tone.

'I do. And you'll find out for yourself in good time.' He finished the rest of the boiled water and kicked the fire to pieces.

It was dark in the woods. A slash of blue sky was visible between the treetops but they were in the wildwood, maybe even on the edge of the royal chase, and the light was filtered at best. They walked their horses for a while, and only when the sky started to turn mauve did her guide remount his pony. This time he led at a more leisurely pace, ducking under branches, forcing a way through the undergrowth with a certainty that made Hildegard sceptical. They were lost. They must be. And yet he moved with confidence, as if the way was secretly marked.

It was nightfall when they came to a rise that took them above the tops of the trees. There was a good view over the surrounding woodland. No landmarks broke the dark sway of beeches in full leaf. Not a prick of light shone anywhere. The only illumination was from the glimmer of the summer sky.

They continued on their way.

Some way ahead chalk cliffs no higher than the height of an average man appeared out of the gloom. Her escort set off between them through a gap that appeared as they approached, and then he continued down a long slope that curved away at the bottom. The smell of woodsmoke floated faintly on the night air.

As they turned the corner of the cliff Hildegard felt a shudder of alarm.

In the middle of a natural bowl hollowed out of the chalk was an encampment. Hidden like this it might have existed for some time. It certainly looked well established. There was only one way in, or out, that she could see. Beside a wicket across the approach was a line of horses tethered to a rail. There must have been thirty or forty she guessed. Visible in the light of a few flares many men were moving about attending to their chores.

In the middle of the camp blazed a large fire with a hind slung between poles over the flames. That's one thing at least the king's sheriff would have their heads for, she thought.

A man came out of the shadows to take her pony as she dismounted. Someone else indicated that she should follow and, leaving her guide who melted at once into the background, she found herself being led towards a makeshift awning on the other side of the fire. Several men were sitting on rough-hewn logs in its shelter.

One of them, a big, red-haired fellow who seemed to he in charge, indicated that she should come forward into the light. 'I'm told you wanted to speak to us?' he invited. 'Do you have information for us?'

'No. I'm here because I believe you have information for me.'

'It's a roundabout way to have your doubts

257

resolved, Sister. Did you not think to ask a priest?' There were a few chuckles.

'My main reason for wanting to meet you is because I believe you stole something from me.'

There was a ripple of interest. The leader pulled at his beard. 'I've been accused many times of stealing from women, both in the day and in the night, but I usually find that they themselves give willingly and regard it as no theft. And now you're complaining?'

There was open laughter. Hildegard bit back a retort. It would be prudent to see how things lay before saying too much. All she said was, 'The object stolen was a cross.'

'What would I be doing with a cross? Do I look like a pope?'

'The cross was stolen from my keeping three nights ago in the grounds of the archbishop's palace. I wish to negotiate for its return.'

'Ah, another deal on the table,' he said to his companions. 'Valuable objects, crosses, it seems. Is it gold, set with jewels?'

'I'm sure you know it's nothing more than a piece of wood. It has only a symbolic value.'

'Symbolic!' one of the men hissed. 'The whole system's symbolic – of the common man's bondage! How many angels can dance on the head of a pin, Sister?'

'I have no opinion on angels or their ability to dance,' she replied, lifting her chin.

As she did so she recognised one of the men sitting under the awning. It was the scholarly-looking fellow she had glimpsed in the pageant warehouse. If she had wanted evidence that Gilbert and his master were involved with the dissenters, here it was. He was sitting on a tree stump, a little apart from the others, a quizzical smile on his face.

When she caught his glance he spoke up. 'Are you one of these monastics who claim to expound the word according to the truth of allegory?'

'I believe Hugo of St Victor does so, and Walter Hilton, and one or two others of that kind.'

'But not you?' He looked genuinely interested at her reference to some of those who assumed that only the priesthood could understand the Bible. Hugo was a theologian popular in Paris for many years and he was often quoted by those who wanted to seem fashionable as well as orthodox.

'I believe most things should be explained as straightforwardly as possible,' she said after a pause. 'Nobody should be prevented from finding the truth. Expert knowledge is often used to keep the people in their place. If a person can read, then they can read the truth and should be allowed to do so.'

'She could fit in well here,' he observed, his dark eyes turning to the red-haired fellow.

'Let's get to the point. This cross – if we have it, and I'm not saying we have – is being offered to the highest bidder.'

'My bid is my right to it. There can be none higher. I was the one who brought it back across the Alps.'

'A fair right. But it's not for us to make decisions without consulting every man. We don't organise ourselves in the old way, with a leader

259

dictating to the rest. I'll put your request to my brothers. We'll see what they have to say. You may leave.' He nodded to one of the men standing by who stepped forward with alacrity and attempted to grip her by the arm.

'Just a moment.' She brushed his hand aside. 'I've come a long way. Is that all you're going to say? I wonder if you realise the importance this relic has for certain factions?'

The chief spokesman lifted his head. 'For your faction, Sister?' He raised his eyebrows in an invitation to admit who had sent her. When she failed to reply he asked, 'Maybe you can match its importance with gold?'

'I doubt whether anyone could raise enough to equal its imagined value.'

'In that case I offer my gratitude for taking the trouble to speak to us.'

Before she could protest further she was being escorted away whether she liked it or not. The firm grip of the man delegated to show her towards the horses did not slacken, but before they reached them the man she took to be Will Thorpe walked up. He was followed by a lad carrying the same heavy bag she had noticed before.

'I was on the point of leaving when you arrived,' he explained. 'Let's ride together.' With a grunt of indifference the saddler unroped two horses, then looked along the line until he found a small pony for the boy. When they were on the move the bookish fellow said, 'I'm heading up to Durham. I can guide you through the woods as far as the highway where you'll find a clear road back to York.'

They rode out of the camp. She felt uneasy. There was something going on beyond what the leader had told her. The situation made no sense. When they were away from the camp and riding through woodland she turned to her companion. 'They treat you with respect, magister.'

'Respect for learning isn't quite extinguished,' he said, adding, 'despite Archbishop Courtenay and Pope Urban's efforts.' She saw him turn to her in the pale moonlight that filtered through the trees and there was a flash of a smile out of the darkness. 'I trust you find my words neither treasonable nor heretical?'

'I'm not a justiciar nor a pope. You're only saying what many people think. At least we can still think freely.'

'Though plain and forthright speaking is becoming somewhat restricted by our law-makers? We live in sad times.' He rode on beside her, the boy taking up the rear on a little prancing pony with white socks.

It was difficult to carry on a conversation while trying to find a way through such dense wood-land. The stranger pointed out the occasional blaze cut into the bark of a tree which, if she had not been looking for it, she would have taken as natural, but they were waymarks, he explained, and made the path easier to follow.

Soon they reached the king's highway. They rode from under the trees and came to a halt on the wide verge where the brushwood had been cut back by order of the king to assist travellers against surprise attack by outlaws.

'I go north now.' The magister pointed up the

road with his riding whip. When he turned he was looking serious. 'There are differences of opinion in the brotherhood as you might have noticed – but I trust I've been able to shepherd the flock back to its true purpose.'

He hesitated, then told her, 'They have the cross, of course. And there are those who wish to sell it to the king of Scotland in return for arms.'

'That was the rumour,' she admitted.

He leant forward. 'Do not despair. There are others who want to trade it for gold in order to pay the scriveners to write their pamphlets.'

'That's no help to me.'

'There's a trader,' he peered at her through the darkness. 'You may have heard of him. He's called Robert Acclom and sails out of Scarborough.'

'Trader, you call him? He's one of the most notorious pirates sailing the northern ocean.'

'I believe it. Whatever the case, he's bringing arms up the coast in the next few days to sell to the Scots. I don't need to tell you with what desire some rebels regard the weapons of war. It leads them to madness. They hope to do a deal with Acclom and cut out the Scots as well as their own brothers of the White Hart, but I fear Acclom will not give up one iota of his trade with King Robert. It's steady trade and far too lucrative for a man like him to relinquish.'

'But you're saying they hope to sell the cross to him?'

He gazed sadly into her eyes. 'Sister, unlike us, they are ignorant of the power of ideas. They do not see that ideas last when iron has turned to rust.'

He lifted his whip in farewell and with the words 'God assist you in the true way' urged his horse on. She watched them both, the man she assumed was the outlawed theologian and the silent boy carrying his bag of books. After they vanished into the night she turned her horse's head in the opposite direction and set off towards York.

After less than a mile she slowed and eventually pulled to a complete halt. Magister Thorpe and his boy were long gone. Bright moonlight shed its reflected rays all around. It was like daylight but for its ghostly hue. Every stick and stone was visible – as was the highway curving away to York – and the road leading back to the rebel camp.

With a sense of the inevitable, she turned her horse's head towards the north. She made sure she kept within the fringe of trees where the cleared ground stopped. Now she knew how to decipher the path she could find her way through the woods to the camp. The cross was there. She could not allow it to be bartered for arms.

With no clear idea how she was going to get it back she continued towards the junction where she had turned onto the highway with the magister. Apart from the sound of her horse moving through the dry grass nothing stirred. The woods were cloaked in silence. She reached the turn-off. Where the grass had been flattened by their horses' hooves as they stopped to talk it shone like silver, a clear sign of their presence.

She set off into the trees. The moonlight cast leaf patterns over the scene. Something flickered and caught her eye. When she looked more squarely there was nothing to see but the trunks of the silver birches gleaming out of the darkness.

Chapter Twenty

She left her horse among the bushes and crawled out onto the chalk cliff overlooking the encampment. The fire where the hind had been roasting was now a heap of embers. In its glow she could see the men directly beneath her vantage point. Sprawled at their ease they were tearing chunks off the remains of the carcass of venison while a flagon of liquor was passed from hand to hand.

Someone began to sing. One by one the others joined in.

Firelight shone on the men's faces, gilding them with its glow, beautifying the harshness of individual features, softening mouths, the curve of a nose, furrows on a forehead, emphasising the individuality of men brought together by a common belief.

The song they sang was a lament for a land of lost content. One that had probably never existed in the entire history of the world. Somehow it expressed the heartfelt longing for something beyond the careworn existence that was their lot.

Hildegard's thoughts strayed to a particular pilgrim in Outremer, the Abbot of Meaux, and her yearning to see him return to his own far country brought tears to her eyes. Other songs followed and the words floated into the night, clear then faint, with a sound like the heartbeat of humanity. One she recognised as a rebel anthem of great fame. The men's voices rang out with the strength of their common aim:

'–And on that purpose yet we stand–
whoever does us wrong–
in whate'er place it fall–
he does against us all!'

And then came a rousing chorus. Despite its final triumphal shout, she heard something defeated and grieving in its cadences. The desire for freedom moved her. But it seemed so hopeless. The dark forces ranged against these landless, masterless men were too strong, too brutal, too cunning for such innocent hopes.

She must have drifted off to sleep, the pangs of hunger briefly forgotten under the lulling of their voices, because something brought her swimming back into the present with a jolt. It was the rustle of a creature going about its nocturnal chores. Nothing more than the sound of a twig breaking. She wriggled forward to peer over the edge of the cliff.

The men were sitting round the dying embers of the fire but they were mostly silent now. Most rested their heads on their saddlebags and slept.

The red-haired spokesman she had met earlier was discussing something in a low voice, elbows on knees, head thrust forward, talking to someone she was sure had not been present before. Red-beard might imagine he's not their chief, she thought, watching him now, but his natural authority would make him the man others would look to for leadership whether he wanted them to or not. The other fellow was a blusterer, trying to hold his own.

A disturbance over by the row of horses occurred. New arrivals, she saw, as several figures dismounted. Then her eyes widened.

Escorted by a posse of armed men were Brother Thomas and Master Danby.

She wanted to cry out, but instead held her breath and watched as they were urged forward. An argument was going on. A couple of guards searched the two men for weapons. She saw Thomas protest when his knife was taken from him.

'It's got something written on it!' exclaimed the man who had wrenched it from Thomas's belt. His voice floated up clearly to her hiding place. 'Is it Latin?' He showed it to the man next to him.

'That's Latin all right,' came the reply.

Thomas held out his hand. 'My father gave it to me shortly before he died. May I have it back?'

The first man laughed. 'Cheek! You think we want this in our gizzards?'

'I'm a monk. I don't kill people.'

'Not on a crusade, then?'

'Why worry – unless you consider yourself Saracen?'

For that he got a punch in the stomach, but it went no further as the leader said something in a harsh voice, and the man who had hit Thomas made a mumbled remark and turned away. Red-beard addressed the man sitting beside him.

'Keep a better control over your men, brother. We like to treat our guests with courtesy. Tell him to hand the knife back – unless he aspires to be a common thief.'

The knife was returned to Thomas who slipped it into his belt with a nod of thanks.

'Where's the nun?' asked Danby, stepping forward and brushing his captor aside. 'We were told she was here.'

'She must be nearly back at York by now. She left in the company of the magister some time ago.'

'We didn't see her.'

'She must have hitched herself to the magister and gone on to Durham with him, then. You know what these celibates are like.'

A few guffaws followed from those round the fire until one of the rebels objected to having the magister's name brought into disrepute.

At that moment Hildegard heard a whisper in her ear. 'Time to go down and join them, eh?' When she turned there was a blade brushing her cheek. 'Come on.' The man moved back with the knife held flat in front of him, its edge towards her. 'Get up nice and slowly.'

Wanting nothing more, in the circumstances, than to be standing alongside Thomas and Danby, she obeyed without demur.

'So you couldn't bear to be parted from us, lady?' Red-beard sounded genial enough but the man sitting next to him rose to his feet.

'What the hell is this?' he demanded. 'Who are

267

all these people? First a monk, then a stinking burgess, now a bloody nun!'

'Calm yourself, brother. The burgess is an associate of Mayor de Quixlay and therefore our good friend.'

'De Quixlay?' Despite his tone the man sat down again. He glared balefully round the group.

Hildegard noticed now that he was accompanied by a number of men, ruffians with a particular livery, difficult to decipher, something greenish on a white ground. He wiped the back of his hand under his nose and asked, 'Are they going to sit in on what we're discussing? Because if that's the case you can forget it.'

'No,' replied Red-beard. 'Unless brother Danby has some message to convey and is here because of more than curiosity about the nun, he and his companions are going to turn right round and go straight back to York. As for the sister–'

'Slit her throat and have done with it,' the other grunted.

'No! That wasn't the agreement!' Danby stepped forward and was hurriedly restrained.

'Indeed it wasn't,' Red-beard replied calmly. 'We'll take her with us as nothing to the contrary was discussed.'

'What?' Hildegard herself moved forward but this time no one attempted to stop her. 'Where are you going? Why should I come with you?'

'Why? Because you'll be persuaded. Otherwise a little force may have to be used. You're our hostage now, having returned of your own free will.'

Hildegard looked into the man's eyes. Despite

his genial tones their expression was implacable. He had left the question of their destination unanswered.

Rising to his feet he ordered the fire to be put out. 'And see these two safely to the highway. Make sure they leave. Everybody else to horse. We have some night riding to do.'

Two men took Hildegard by the arms. 'Shall we rope her, master?'

Briefly glancing over his shoulder, Red-beard gave a laugh. 'I don't think we need show such discourtesy, do you?' He moved off in a group of his closest confederates and Hildegard saw Thomas and Danby hustled away.

As they went Danby shouted to her. 'I didn't plan this, Sister. He promised you'd come to no harm.'

'Nor shall I,' she reassured him. 'I trust him.'

With swords coercing them there was little either Danby or Thomas could do but leave as they were ordered.

Soon the sound of hooves could be heard drumming away up the track out of the camp.

Dawn. A sense of the sea. Not the smell of salt in the nostrils, impossible when salt has no odour, but that crystalline sense of windswept ocean, the sound of surf, the mew of seabirds in an expanse of sky.

For what had remained of the previous night Hildegard and the rebels had ridden with forced speed and only now the cavalcade began to slow with an awareness of a new sense of place.

They had crossed moorland, desolate in all

269

directions, the rise and fall of heather-covered hills lacking any sign of habitation.

The last summit brought this shock of the sea and a vision of pink-edged clouds with the sun rising from the deeps. Its light was reflected in a bloody path across the waves. Everything became drenched in colour as the sun rose higher. It was evanescent. Apocalyptic. Rays of light struck rainbows through the damp manes of the horses.

Moving towards and against the transplendent light, the riders milled about on the cliff top. They looked now crimson, now black in silhouette.

The master of the rebels, still nameless, turned in the glowing shine like a red flame, his face like fire, his wild hair blazing from underneath his leather casque.

A few quiet orders caused a camp to be organised. The horses were hobbled. The men settled to pottage and hunks of bread, cross-legged on the promontory, unexhausted, destination attained.

Hildegard sat away from them and watched.

A lieutenant had carried a sack across his saddle all the way through the night. She saw him lift it down and carry it under his arm when he went to join the others at the fire.

The leader came to her where she was sitting apart. 'I trust that was not too arduous for you, Sister?'

'I'm used to riding,' she replied shortly.

'No doubt you're wondering about your purpose here?'

She looked up at him.

'I can tell you now.' He sat beside her on the ground. 'We have an assignation with a representative of the Earl of Douglas who in turn, of course, represents King Robert of Scotland. In exchange for this lump of wood which he, like you, values so highly, he is willing to give us gold. You know what that means? We can go on publishing our notices, maintaining a life outside the law, disseminating the truth, furthering the cause of freedom. We'll wait here until we see the Scottish ship coming into the port below.'

Rising to his feet he beckoned and she followed him to a ledge of iron stone lower down the cliff.

Several hundred feet below was a hamlet on a curve between the headlands. A swift-flowing beck carved a channel from off the moors and drained into a natural harbour. On both sides of the bay, houses clung to the strata of red rock. They seemed hewn from rock themselves. The sea licked at the foreshore and broke in fangs of surf against the cliffs at the entrance to this haven.

'How long do we wait?' she asked.

'For as long as necessary.'

'And then I can go?'

'After you've witnessed the exchange. Your presence legitimises our transaction.'

'You trust me not to object?'

'Objection would be foolish. As you already know, there's a faction here who would slit your throat from sheer pleasure and a hatred of religion.'

She gazed down at the small fishing village in its hollow. No help could be expected from that quarter.

271

She nodded and climbed back to the top of the cliff.

The day passed uneasily. The two sides of the same cause eyed each other with suspicion and kept to themselves. One group listened to readings from a well-thumbed missal, the other played dice and drank.

The tide had been at its height when they arrived, the surface of the water covered with small sailing boats, but it began to recede soon afterwards, sending the boats and their full nets to shore. A cog appeared and stood off in the bay for a while and then sailed on. The ebb revealed a shelf of level rock, like the floor of a palace, but lethal enough to rip the bottom out of the strongest ship.

Unseen by day, the moon pulled the tide to extremes, making it run foaming up the side of the red cliffs, high above the green mark of weed, and then forcing it back far out over the scaur to lay bare its deceptive fissures and lethal outcrops of ironstone.

Hildegard sat in a hollow on a shelf of rock lower down the cliff, out of sight of the men. Most of them seemed to have forgotten she was present and she was unmolested. This was where Red-beard found her again. He sat down. They looked out over the sea in silence.

Eventually she asked, 'So you consider it better to work outside the law to further your aims?'

'When the laws are bad there's no choice. Besides, the law itself sets me outside its limits now it's used me.'

'Used?'

'I was in France,' he said shortly, as if that was explanation enough.

'My husband was in the French wars as well,' she said. 'He didn't return.'

'Many didn't. Our militia were luckier, though, than the poor devils slaughtered at Roosebeke by the Duke of Burgundy.'

'I was in Flanders shortly after that battle. Bruges was filled with beggars, war-wounded, men who would never work again, those on the brink of death.'

'It was that that made me decide to do my best with what was left of my days.'

'And this is it?'

He looked her full in the face. 'The best I can do.'

Eventually he got up to go. 'Tide's on the turn.'

Shortly after midday a delegation from the village climbed by a cliff path to the camp. Evidently they knew what was afoot.

'Go-betweens,' the lieutenant said, nodding. 'They control the waterfront.'

Red-beard welcomed them, accepted their offerings of fish with goodwill. Commenting in an aside on their ragged clothing and bare feet, he offered what bread and ale they had to spare.

The two groups sat down together.

Three groups, thought Hildegard, with a glance at the men in the obscure livery who, she had been told, would slit her throat for pleasure.

A disagreement became apparent, although not pursued very far. It was a variation on what the magister had told her – whether to cut out the Earl of Douglas and offer the cross to the fishermen in return for armaments they claimed to possess. No mention was made of offering it to Douglas for arms instead of gold.

There was some scepticism about the reality of the fishermen's arms until a shipwreck was mentioned. Several weeks ago, a cargo destined for Scotland owned by the pirate Robert Acclom had come aground on the scaur below. The fishermen let it be known they wanted to make the most of their good fortune.

They were willing to hand over the arms to their countrymen instead of risking slaughter by selling them on to their original customers, the Scots. In return they would be happy to accept something of similar value they had heard about which they could use for barter at a future date. With whom they envisaged this barter taking place they did not specify.

'I see no wreck,' someone commented after a brief examination of the coast from the height of the clifftop.

'That's because we need firewood as much as you do,' came the reply. A few knowing glances followed. 'Do you want to come down and see what we've got? It's mostly this sort of stuff.'

With a flourish that made everybody step back, the spokesman produced a sword from under his rags. It was best Rhineland steel. Any professional man-at-arms could see that. Hildegard observed the fishermen from a position on the fringe of the group. They had a shrewd, hard look and, despite their ragged appearance, bore themselves with arrogance towards the landsmen. She would not want to cross any of them.

Red-beard took the sword and weighed it in his hands like a man who knew what he was doing. 'We travel in peace, brothers, otherwise we might be tempted. It's gold we need so we can publish our beliefs, not steel. The Earl of Douglas has promised gold.' He handed the sword back. 'You'll easily find a purchaser in these times. Be sure of it.'

'The Duke of Northumberland will offer for arms at any time,' somebody suggested.

'God knows, he needs them,' somebody else added.

'Let's hope he has enough gold for your needs,' said the lieutenant. He still had the sack close beside him.

The day passed. Again the tide rose. Red-beard came to sit beside Hildegard in her niche out of sight of the others beneath the rim of the cliff.

'After seeing what happened after Tyler was murdered and the king reneged on his promise to set the bondsmen free, I realised we would always be defeated by the trickery of our rulers,' he began. 'They'll never give anything up. Sharing power is something they don't understand. Our only chance is to make ourselves strong. I asked myself: what's stronger than the sword? There's only one answer: the word.'

Hildegard nodded. It's what the magister had said.

'One day,' he continued, 'I'll have a little cottage and a plot of land where I can grow cabbages and beans. One day maybe there'll be a wife, a son, a little daughter.' He gave a bitter smile. 'Yes, all that – on the day the world grows honest and justice prevails.'

The sea was changing from dark blue to the colour of wine. The land itself was gradually being drained of light. A shape, too big and constant to be a wave, was spotted near the headland. Flares from the village suddenly appeared. They streamed along the dark edge of the shore, lighting the way across the scaur. An answering blink of light came from the vessel.

It was at that moment that hell broke loose.

Everyone on the cliff top was engulfed in a chaos of glinting steel. The men in the obscure livery set about slicing the throats of as many men as they could lay hands on. The true brothers of the White Hart retaliated. From out of the hillside swarmed a further band of cutthroats, ragged, many barefoot, narrow gutting knives working as lethally as the broadswords carried by the rebels.

Hildegard made herself invisible in the rocks on the cliff side but she saw the lieutenant stumble from out of the fray with the sack. She called out but her voice was lost in the clash of steel on bone and the sickening howls of slaughter.

The lieutenant lurched towards the edge of the cliff and then his glance fell on her where she crouched in horror among the rocks.

'Forgive the theft. Take it back. Destroy it–' He fell at her feet in a pool of blood.

She tugged the sack containing the cross from

276

under his body and backed away with it. Her eyes dilated as she gazed on the butchery, men falling, no guessing who was fighting whom. She saw the red-bearded leader lay about him with his sword and she saw many men fall under it.

Next minute she watched as a thrust of a blade from the thick of the battle pierced him as he raised his arm to strike again. He turned, still wielding his sword against his attacker, and retreated to where the body of his lieutenant was lying.

Hildegard called out. 'Here, you're hurt, let me help.'

He lurched towards her, a black shape against the setting sun, his voice hoarse. 'It is a mortal wound, lady. There is no help. These are my last moments.'

He stumbled over the rocks and she stretched out her arms to take the weight of his fall. He rested there in her arms, his breath snatching at the air as if it had turned thin, while above, among the shadows in the lift and hollows of the cliff, the slaughter continued.

Between gasps he tried to speak. She had to bend her head close to his lips to catch the words. 'The cross...' he rasped. 'I saw him give it ... take it ... destroy it ... too much discord ... civil war ... if Gaunt has it we are finished...'

'I'll take it—'

He clutched her by the arm. 'Don't betray me. Give me your promise?'

'I will not let Gaunt have it. Never. As long as I breathe.'

His eyes closed and a wisp of a song came from

between his lips. *"And on that purpose yet we stand–"'* his dying grip slackened, *"whoever does us wrong – contrives against us ..."* we will be free, lady ... every man, every woman ... one day...'

Struggling to raise himself to his knees, his left hand clutching the front of his hauberk, he crawled towards the edge of the cliff. 'Let me see the sea!' He reached out for her arm.

'I don't even know your name to pray for you,' Hildegard whispered, helping him as best she could.

'No name,' he slurred. 'No prayers. Nothing but this!' He gazed out across the rolling waves as if there was something glorious to be seen on the horizon.

Then his hand fell away from his wounds allowing his intestines to slither to the ground. Blood gushed from his mouth.

He fell.

Hildegard brushed a trembling hand across his face when he was still. His skin was hot as if he still lived. She closed his eyes. Behind her the clash of arms continued as the combatants pressed on down the cliff path towards the village. Fading.

She sat on unnoticed.

Eventually it ended. Hildegard retrieved the sack from where it had fallen. Drawing the reliquary from inside, she prised the lid off and lifted the cross from its red velvet bed. Then she went to the brink of the cliff.

The cross felt light in her hands. It was only a piece of worm-eaten wood. And yet it caused violence and death because of the things people believed about it. It divided people. It spread darkness instead of light.

She imagined hurling it out as far as she could over the sea. She saw the long arc of descent as it vanished for ever in the thundering surf.

Already a line of fisherfolk were making their way up the cliff path to claim their dead and plunder the foreigners. A handful of rebels, much cut and bloodied, attended to their own. She saw them take the corpses down to the shore. They toiled back up, collected a few horses and left soon afterwards. Hildegard remained in the hollow of rock as night pulled its cloak over sea and land.

Later there were lights on the beach where a flotilla of rafts could be seen lit by flares. Many hands pushed the rafts one by one from off the shore in a confusion of fire and surf. They floated out beyond the line. Black shapes bearing their burden of dead on the ocean.

The next moment flames rose up. The burning pyres drifted slowly on the receding tide. They seemed to rest on nothing. Floating in a void between Earth and heaven. Hildegard watched with moving lips until the last flame was extinguished by the waves. Now it was over.

Now it was.

A horse was running loose. She called it. And began the long melancholy ride back across the moors to York.

Chapter Twenty-One

The sun was beating down out of a molten sky. Nothing new there. It seemed the hot weather would never end. It might easily be the beginning of the Apocalypse as many believed.

Master Edric Danby was sitting outside his workshop on his usual bench against the wall. At first sight it was a scene of normal domesticity. His shirt was undone, however, and his bald head shone unprotected in the glare of the sun. He was mumbling something to himself and paid no heed when Hildegard, hot, dishevelled, weeping within herself, arrived back after her ride across the moors.

A spilt flagon lay on the ground beside the glazier, the liquor evaporating in the heat.

At that moment the widow Tabitha Roberts came out of her house carrying a cup. She didn't notice Hildegard at the entrance to the yard. 'Drink this posset, Edric, do, for the love of God.'

'What ails the master?' Hildegard asked, stepping forward.

Tabitha turned in surprise. 'Thank the Lord you've returned. Maybe you can talk sense into him.' She tried to force the cup to his lips.

With a roar Danby dashed it to one side. 'Posset, woman? Do you think that's going to mend me?' He thrust his head into both hands and began to sob. His whole body heaved.

The widow turned away. 'I'm at my wits' end with him. I've had enough.'

Gilbert appeared in the doorway. His face was as pale as usual, his bright hair pulled back in its ponytail, his grey eyes wary.

The widow wiped her hands on her apron and with a last glare went inside her own house.

'Gilbert?' Hildegard went over.

'He's been like this since he got back. Drinking and howling–'

'But why?' She felt frightened. 'Is Brother Thomas harmed?'

Gilbert shook his head. 'He'll be back here straight after prime. It's Dorelia. She's vanished.'

'What do you mean?'

Gilbert went back inside the workshop and, astonished, she saw him bend his head over his work as if nothing else mattered.

Danby looked up, then recognition dawned and when she went over he reached out to grip her by the sleeve. 'Not a ghost, then, but safe. Thank St Benet and all the heavenly host. We couldn't believe our eyes when we saw you brought into camp t'other night. Then having to leave you – I can't tell you how it wrenched us to the soul – and then, like a judgement, to come back to this...' His chest heaved again.

'What's happened to Dorelia?' she asked.

'Absconded. With that apprentice of mine! I'd no idea–' He lapsed into incoherence again, repeating, 'I'd no idea – right under my nose – how could I not notice? How could she...? Didn't she mean anything she said? Lies, all lies. Her look when she said those soft words ... looking

281

me in the eyes and brazenly lying to me... Oh God, help me!'

Hildegard sat down next to him and let him rant.

She was in this position when Ulf strode into the yard with a jangle of spurs.

He checked in astonishment when he saw her, then hurried forward. 'Struth, Hildegard! Am I glad to see you. I couldn't believe they'd left you behind. Call themselves men! I only found out yesterday morning when I came down to look at the glass. When Roger heard he came down himself to give them a bollocking. He sent a search party to look for you and found the camp, but everybody had left by then. He's got men scouring the forest for you. I'd better go and tell him you're back. Brother Thomas is doing nothing but praying.' He shot a swift glance at Danby. 'And I see the master's in the same state.'

'Can you tell me what's happened? I'm not getting much sense from him apart from the fact that his wife has run off with his apprentice. Is it true?'

Ulf nodded. 'He says they'd gone when he arrived back next day after that night ride to meet the rebels. He's been sitting like that ever since by the look of him.'

'But where have they gone to? Did they leave a message with anyone?'

Ulf shook his head. 'Took their chance while they could. They'll be lying low somewhere, pretending to be man and wife.'

He jerked his head and Hildegard paced beside him to the end of the yard out of Danby's earshot. When she looked back he was sagging against the wall, his eyes shut, tears trickling down his cheeks into his beard.

'Poor devil,' Hildegard remarked, 'he's in a state of shock at present. I expect he'll be raging shortly. He's already thrown Tabitha's cup of posset to the ground. She's gone off in a huff.'

'She's done as much as a neighbour can but he won't he helped. Dorelia and Jankin though?' He shook his head. 'Coupla dark horses. Danby says he had no inkling.'

'Surely somebody must have known what they were planning?'

'Baldwin says he's been asking questions of everybody they know. So far he's drawn a blank. It's obvious they've been working out how to do it for some time, to cover their tracks so well.'

She glanced down the yard to where Danby was now rocking backwards and forwards with his head in his hands. 'Poor man. But it could be worse.'

'What do you mean?'

'The rebels,' she blurted. 'They were ambushed. Both the leader and his lieutenant are dead. As well as most of their men.'

Ulf gazed at her in horror. 'Ambushed?'

She nodded.

He took her by the arm. 'What's all this about? Is it to do with the stolen cross?'

She nodded. 'That badge you found suggested that the men of the White Hart Company were the ones who had stolen it – so I hinted to Gilbert that I'd like to meet them. He and Danby fixed up a meeting–'

'So they said. And then they left you to your fate...' he intoned, his expression grim.

'They had no choice,' she quickly pointed out. 'There were twenty or thirty armed men and just the two of them, with only Thomas's small eating knife between them. Don't be angry with them. They did the sensible thing by coming back as quickly as possible and raising the alarm.'

'I suppose so,' he admitted, clearly finding such behaviour beyond his understanding.

She told him quickly what had happened after Danby and Thomas had been escorted back onto the road to York.

She could see he was horrified. With a forced humour he said, 'The world must have gone mad. All this for a relic. Next you'll be saying these rumours about Sacred Fire are true. These are the end days all right! Step forth the Antichrist!' He looked searchingly into her face. 'So where's the cross now?'

She touched the strap of her leather bag and his eyes widened.

'Can I see it?'

'Later. It's caused so much bloodshed I feel I never want to set eyes on it again. The leader of the rebels wanted me to throw it into the sea so that no one would use it against King Richard. I couldn't do that. It was loaned to me on the understanding that it would eventually be returned to its guardians in Florence.'

'Even so–'

'It was an earlier promise,' she explained, 'stronger and made in clarity of mind.'

Ulf seemed to accept this. 'So it was the Com-

284

pany of the White Hart who stole it, as you suspected.'

'They were wrong to do it and it was wrong that men in their own brotherhood betrayed them. Both sides were slaughtered without discrimination–'

'But those locals, the fishermen – whose side were they on?'

'Nobody's but their own by the look of it. They must have thought they'd get the cross in return for handing over the arms they'd looted from Acclom's wrecked ship. But something odd happened. A light appeared from a ship in the bay. That's when the fighting started. It looked like a signal. If it was it was a trap that caught everyone in it.' She gripped the steward by the arm. 'So many died, Ulf. There were no winners. But I promised the rebel friend of Magister Thorpe that I would not allow the cross to fall into the hands of Gaunt.'

'So they stuck to their resolve even in death: *we want no king called John.*' His lips tightened with emotion. 'You have to hand it to them for tenacity.'

Hildegard was beginning to tremble as the scenes of slaughter danced before her eyes. Ulf saw how shaken she looked and put a hand on her shoulder. For a moment they stood without moving. She was aware of the warmth of his fingers through the fabric of her thin summer habit. He was reassuringly alive. She placed her hand over his and cupped in its vitality, drawing strength from it.

After a moment their hands slipped apart and they began to walk slowly back to where Danby was sitting while she explained in greater detail what had happened after the glazier and Thomas had left the encampment. Danby, she noticed, lifted his head to listen when he heard her mention the White Hart Brotherhood.

'The issue seems to boil down to a split between them,' she explained. 'The original faction were trying to live according to their ideals, no one person set above another, respect for learning, freedom, truth–'

'Friends of the White Hart boys offered safe houses to the clerks from Oxford,' Danby contributed. 'Those who refused to recant over this Corpus Christi business. They were all outlawed for it.'

'Men like Will Thorpe?' she asked, remembering her escort on the way through the woods.

'A good, brave fellow,' muttered Danby, wiping his eyes.

'Him and others,' Ulf agreed.

'There's Aston, Swinderby, Herford, Purefoy, the list goes on,' Danby told them. 'Outlawed, the lot of 'em, by that bastard at Canterbury, Archbishop Courtenay. Herford's even gone to Rome to argue the issue with the pope, daft devil. He'll get no joy there.' Danby closed his eyes again, lifted the flagon to his lips and emptied it.

'The splinter group were more interested in arming themselves with weapons the fishermen had scavenged from a ship destined for the Scottish king,' she told them.

'Bastards,' Danby muttered. 'That's not what the Rising was about.'

'I expect Acclom's involved.' Ulf frowned.

'You mean that shipman running vessels out of Scarborough?' Danby opened his eyes.

'Piracy's his usual trade.' Ulf gave a scowl. 'But he carries anything for anyone.'

'They said he lost a ship a few weeks ago on the scaur.'

'It'd be carrying arms, then,' said Ulf.

She nodded. 'So they said.'

'Those fisherfolk live by looting. Acclom wouldn't be pleased if they'd laid hands on his cargo. He probably set up the ambush to get it back – or to teach the looters a lesson they won't forget.' He looked thoughtful. 'We can only speculate but it seems to me he must have had an ally in the brotherhood to start the fighting off.'

'And you believe the signal came from one of Acclom's ships?' Hildegard asked.

'Don't you?'

'Maybe,' she said slowly. 'The light was failing and it was too far off to see its ensign. The true rebels were hoping to sell the cross for gold. They had no belief in its power. For them the only value it had was its agreed equivalent in coin. The bunch of outlaws they took into their midst preferred to sell it to the fishermen for the arms they scavenged from the shipwreck. That was the nub of the dispute. And the fishermen were after the cross because they could use it for barter.'

'Cross?' Danby lifted his head.

'That's what this is all about,' she explained. 'It was stolen from me a few nights ago by the White Hart rebels. That's why I wanted to meet them. They thought it could be used to raise money so they could go on publishing their tracts.'

'It must have been worth a fair penny or two,' he grunted. 'Made of gold, was it?'

'It was only worth what it was believed to be worth. To most people it was just a piece of old wood. Ancient, though, if the stories are true, and deserving of reverence for that reason at least.'

Someone came into the yard just then. It was Agnetha.

The dairywoman carried a basket over her arm containing fresh cobs of wastel baked by her sister-in-law, a baxter of the guild as she explained now. Her expression was worried. Addressing Hildegard she said, 'I called at the nunnery of the Holy Wounds as I hadn't heard anything from you for a few days, but they were enraged when I mentioned your name and spoke of you as a she-devil. I left as soon as I could get away. The girls are safe, I take it?'

Hildegard noticed the tone of reproach in her voice. 'They are safe and well now.'

'I was worried. How long have you been here?' Her tone was cool.

'Just a few days. I should have let you know. But I had to leave York suddenly. I've just got back–'

'I can see that.' Agnetha gave her travel-stained appearance an up-and-down look. Hildegard outlined relevant events as briefly as possible with regard to the girls. She told the dairywoman about Maud's confession, that although Thomas had been unable to say much, whatever the girl had admitted had shaken the young monk to the core.

Agnetha's mood softened. 'The main thing is you're safe, Sister. And the girls are safe too.'

288

Ulf said he had to bring Roger up to date. His page and two men-at-arms who had been lounging in the entrance to the yard followed briskly after him as he strode off.

Agnetha produced an earthenware pot from the bottom of the basket. Tabitha, her good humour restored, welcomed her into her kitchen. The pottage was doled out. Danby, offered some through the window, merely waved his hand and gave a heavy sigh as if food was poison to him.

With Agnetha and Tabitha treating her like an invalid, Hildegard finished her portion as soon as she could, then made an excuse to go upstairs. She wasn't used to having anyone try to look after her.

As soon as she gained the privacy of her room she startled herself by bursting into tears. She sobbed in silence, both arms gripped round her chest to stifle the sound. Outside she could hear Danby howling again. It brought her quickly to her senses. Death might have laid a brutal hand over those honest men with their small demand for justice – but there was nothing to be gained by giving in to grief.

She removed her stained clothing, sponged herself down with a little water from the pitcher, then changed into fresh garments. When she went downstairs again she was as composed as ever.

The chandler, Master Stapylton, was in the yard when she returned. She went out to greet him, followed by Agnetha. Gilbert was standing in the doorway of the workshop. Danby must have gone inside, because Gilbert called, 'Stapylton's here, master.'

Danby's voice came from within. 'Tell him I'm not in the mood for visitors.'

But Stapylton was already pushing his way inside. The two women followed. When they entered, Stapylton was bending over Danby saying, 'Come on, mate, brace up. Let's get you straightened out.'

Danby was sitting next to the cold kiln in Dorelia's chair and allowed Stapylton to set his garments straight and even fasten the ties of his shirt, but after a moment he pushed him away. 'Leave that. It doesn't matter. Nothing matters now. The White Hart lads have taken a beating. That's your concern. Not me and my stupid faith in women.'

'You can't blame all women for the actions of one.'

'Nor all men for the actions of some,' added Hildegard. She addressed Stapylton, telling him briefly what had happened, and concluding, 'So you knew about their encampment as well, master?'

'We all knew they were out there somewhere. Though nobody knew exactly where. They kept it a secret for fear of losing their heads. It was a bad law that put them outside the walls. We couldn't change it but we could soften its blows. They speak for us.'

'Aye,' broke in Danby, 'we owe them a debt.'

'But while we talk free speech, safe in our houses, they live it out in the wilderness. Lived,' Stapylton corrected. His eyes filled. 'I can't believe it. Were many slaughtered?'

When Hildegard told him her estimate he shook his head. 'It's all a confusion. I don't know what to make of it.' A look of alarm crossed his face. 'I could lose everything talking like this if Gisburne gets back in power. I assume I'm among friends?'

He glanced nervously about the workshop.

Hildegard nodded, and could not be doubted now. Agnetha stood beside her. Gilbert continued to work quietly at the bench without lifting his head.

Danby gave a snuffle and searched for a rag. He wiped his face. 'You're with friends, Will, you know that.'

'I know nothing – I thought I was with friends t'other day when my workshop nearly went up in flames.' His eyes fixed on the back of Gilbert's head.

Danby heaved himself to his feet. 'Show our guests some hospitality, Gilbert. There's still a dreg of Rhenish left, I hope.' He pushed them all outside. 'I want to be alone.'

Gilbert brought another bench out after he distributed the wine and sat down on it to take a break. His silvery gaze flickered over them all but he was as silent as ever. Agnetha looked at Stapylton. 'Your fire must have caused enough damage, master, but it could have been worse. My cousin told me about it.'

'Who's that, then?' His glance sharpened.

'Jack Enderby.'

With a look of relief he gave a nod. 'He's a good

lad, Jack.' He cocked his head. 'You're not that cousin of his who faced out the abbot at Meaux over heriot tax, are you?'

'That's me.'

'By! You're a one all right! That was sticking your neck out!'

'It was really Sister Hildegard who persuaded the abbot to give in,' Agnetha said.

'He agreed straight away,' Hildegard said quickly. 'He has a genuine sense of justice.' She felt a blush coming and turned hurriedly to Stapylton. 'Have you found out how the fire started?'

'It wasn't Holy Fire, that's for sure. There was a dish of wax left over a flame. None of my lads would do a thing like that. It's about the first thing I teach 'em when they start their apprenticeship. Everybody knows melted wax'll catch fire if it overheats. No warning. Just puff! Up in flames. It's that what must have caught some rags left hanging above. And that's another thing. Who put them there?' He scowled. 'It was deliberate.'

'So the stage was set, as it were?'

He nodded.

'And if it was as you describe, the fire would have started after the fire-raiser left?'

'He could have been long gone,' he agreed.

'But who would know how to do a thing like that?'

'Anybody can set a fire,' Stapylton scoffed. 'It doesn't take brains, only a nasty turn of mind. There'd been folk in and out all morning but definitely nobody there when I went out mid morning. Nobody could have got in after I left,

292

unless it was a magician able to walk through walls. I locked my door that day,' he explained, 'because of all the stock I had in there.'

'So who'd been in and out the rest of the time?' asked Agnetha, getting straight to the point.

'Everybody. It'd be easier to say who hadn't been in.' He suddenly jerked his head up and looked full at Gilbert. When the journeyman returned his stare he dropped his glance and muttered, 'Customers. Anybody buying candles for their altars.'

'I called that morning,' Gilbert announced in his soft, foreign burr, as if to pre-empt something.

They all turned to stare.

Stapylton's voice had a strange absence of warmth. 'He comes along with his master but stays below because of his...' He gestured towards Gilbert's twisted limb. 'I remember you were down there by yourself for some time,' he challenged.

'I was.' Gilbert stared at him as if daring him to put his suspicion into words.

'And then there was the puppet tent fire...' Hildegard remarked, to deflate the tension between the two men. Her glance shifted from one to the other. She would get to the bottom of this. It was no good accusing Gilbert in public and even Stapylton seemed to realise the folly of that. It would be denied – unless there was proof. And anyway, what possible reason could the journeyman have for trying to fire the chandler's premises? Stapylton was being ridiculous.

He was staring into his flagon with a bitter expression.

'People were thick around all the booths that day,' Hildegard continued. 'The whole town was jam-packed. There was that crowd round the preacher. Stonegate was simply swarming with folk.'

The booth that was set on fire was close to the glaziers' church too. The masters and their apprentices were in and out all day, praying to their saint, Helen. Glancing at Gilbert she decided not to mention this fact. Indeed, it might not be the same person who set both fires. 'As an attempt to spoil the pageant,' she said, 'it hasn't worked.'

'How could it?' Stapylton looked up. He was scathing. 'People aren't so lily-livered they'll stop doing what they want because of a little frightener.'

'Anybody with half a brain would guess that,' said Agnetha. 'There must be something else behind it.'

'Such as?' Stapylton narrowed his eyes.

'I've no idea.'

Baldwin and his wife came into the yard from out of the street.

Mistress Julitta was wearing an expensive-looking silk overmantle with an embroidered border in multicoloured thread, with the ubiquitous beads and bangles jangling on her wrists and on her bosom.

She swept straight through into the workshop, ignoring everybody and saying brusquely, 'Where is he?' Then they heard her say, 'Sort yourself out, Edric. You know she was no good. You're well rid of her.' There was a muffled reply and Julitta reappeared, saying over her shoulder, 'You try my patience, you really do.'

A glance passed between her and her husband. Baldwin turned away. His wife had brought two beakers out with her and now helped herself to wine from the jug. She handed Baldwin his and went to sit a little distance away, as if unwilling to mix with the rest of them.

Stapylton had fallen silent and after a few moments he, too, went inside. Hildegard saw him put a hand on Danby's shoulder and bend his head. Through the open window she heard him say, 'Listen, old son, will you pull yourself together and come over to see me in the morning?'

When Danby looked up Stapylton turned, aware that his words were audible through the open casement. 'Just something about that stock I told you about. Yes?'

Danby barely gave him a glance. 'I'm not ready for visiting folk.'

Stapylton clapped him on the back. 'Think about it.' He came outside and raised his hand before heading for the alley.

Gilbert got up and limped beside him. He said, 'I'll bring him over.'

Stapylton nodded without meeting his eye and went out.

If Baldwin had noticed the frost in the air he pretended not to and was already pouring his brother another mug of wine. He took it inside. They heard him say, 'Get that down you, you sot wit. They're never worth it. Any Jack'll tell you that.' He came outside again but made no further comment.

Danby appeared a moment later with the

295

beaker in his hand. His tone was bitter. 'I rue the day you brought her here, Baldwin, and that's the truth.' He threw the drink back in one gulp, then held his beaker out again. Baldwin refilled it without speaking.

Gilbert's glance washed over everyone and came to rest on his master and then on the drink in his hand.

Without a word he went inside, appearing a moment later in the back workshop where the trestle with the half-finished *vidimus* was waiting. Hildegard saw him pull back his bright hair in its leather tie as he resumed his work.

Chapter Twenty-Two

When Brother Thomas turned up after Mass he was contrite as well as relieved to find Hildegard unharmed.

'I didn't know what to do, whether to trust the brotherhood to keep their word to do you no harm while we fetched help, or lay about me with my knife. The only comfort was Danby. He seemed to have confidence in them. And, indeed, here you are, safe and sound.' Despite his words he looked shamefaced.

'There was nothing you could have done, Thomas. If you'd resisted, for sure you'd have finished up with a sword through your ribs and that wouldn't have done any of us any good.'

She led him into the privacy of the kitchen and

told him what had transpired after he left. As she came to the scene of slaughter that ended things she had to keep a tight hold on her feelings.

When she finished she managed a bemused glance. 'I'm wondering how the White Hart men found out about the cross. I remember you told me that one of the archbishop's retainers had been talking about it at Meaux…?'

'It was a rumour that was set going during one of Neville's visitations. I've no idea who started it.'

Her thoughts flew to Bishopthorpe and the mage's mention of the old king's minstrel, Pierrekyn Gyles. Ever since she had heard his name she had felt uneasy. 'What if,' she said now, 'having heard the rumour that the cross existed, Master Gyles passed on this information to Bolingbroke? We know he's maintained by Gaunt, making it likely he'll want to keep in the good books of his master's son.'

'Go on,' said Thomas.

'Gyles would know how useful the Cross of Constantine could be in furthering Gaunt's ambitions for the House of Lancaster–'

'But we know now it wasn't Bolingbroke who stole it from us…'

'Do we?'

'I thought we did. It was the White Hart fellows….'

'But what if someone tipped them off?'

He stared at her.

'What if,' she went on, 'it was Bolingbroke who made sure they were informed – and they did exactly what he expected them to do?'

'You mean he tricked them into stealing it?'

'More than that. He could have set up an ambush when they came to trade it on. Maybe the rebels who turned up later at the camp were really working for Bolingbroke? Then he would have ordered one of his followers to retrieve the cross in the confusion of the fight–'

'And the theft would not be traced back to him...' Thomas looked thoughtful but then he frowned. 'So why didn't his man do that?'

She shook her head. 'Maybe the battle was fiercer than anticipated. Those fishermen with their gutting knives were deadly and may have been unexpected contenders. Maybe Bolingbroke's man was himself killed?'

Thomas pondered the matter. 'I grant you, it makes sense to see the whole thing as a set-up. A plot to destroy a cell of outlaws – and a chance to snatch a valuable relic at the same time.'

'If Bolingbroke was informed of the existence of the cross some time ago,' Hildegard continued thoughtfully, 'it might have been long enough to have devised a second plan should his first, more direct approach – to buy it from us – fail.'

'There is a flaw,' Thomas sighed. 'Remember what the mage told you? He was emphatic that nobody at the palace knew anything about a theft.'

'Why should they?'

'Surely there would have been a whisper. You know what servants are like.'

'We only have the mage's view – for what it's worth.' She recalled her first impression, his lips, made for deceit, and his cat's eyes that gave

298

nothing away except extreme amusement at the folly and hypocrisy of mankind. A shiver ran up her spine. It was he himself who had advised her to trust no one.

Thomas noticed her shiver and moved closer. 'What is it?'

'If Bolingbroke is involved, where does he imagine the cross is now?'

Thomas failed to follow this idea through to its conclusion and thus missed what really troubled her. He grimaced nevertheless. 'They'll be running round like headless chickens trying to find it.'

After he left she wrote a brief, factual account to the prioress, without mentioning the specific subject of her missive. If it should fall into anybody's hands other than the prioress it would appear to concern a consignment of provisions for the priory kitchens.

Waiting for a response would be like waiting for an axe to fall.

Ulf returned. When he entered the kitchen he was forced to stoop under the low ceiling. The widow tactfully withdrew to another part of the house.

'Roger's at the first station inspecting the stand they've built for him and his guests,' he told Hildegard. 'He's delighted at being able to call off the search for you and he's now switched his efforts back to finding out who destroyed Deepdale. He sends you this.' He held out a brace of pheasant.

Hildegard took them and for a moment stood with the birds dangling from her hand before hurriedly telling him of her fear, that by now it would be common knowledge that she had been to the rebel camp.

Danby had told Stapylton. Stapylton would have told other guild members. They would have spoken about it in front of their servants. The servants would have spread the story of her involvement far and wide about the town.

Then there was the fact that one or two rebels had survived the massacre. They would be wondering what had happened to the cross. They knew it had a value. When the coast was clear they might return to look for it and, failing, would extend their search elsewhere.

She herself would be one of the leading suspects in its disappearance. Whoever wanted it badly enough would come looking for it. For her.

'But it's not the rebels I fear so much,' she told him. 'They're unlikely to risk entering the city themselves. It's...' she hesitated.

Ulf understood at once without the name being voiced.

He paced the kitchen floor. 'Back to your former suspect? You believe it was him who staged the theft at Bishopthorpe?'

'I don't know what to think. We'll find out soon enough, though, won't we? They'll come looking.'

'You can't stay here. The walls of York won't protect you. There's no protection whatsoever.' He went to the window as if expecting Bolingbroke's men-at-arms to come thundering into the yard.

When he turned back he said, 'You'd be safer at the manor, Hildegard. Come back with me.'

She shook her head. 'And stay in hiding with the cross? For how long? I'll have to get back to Swyne sometime.'

She put the birds on the slab and watched the blood dribble from their beaks. 'Everything is mere supposition, Ulf,' she said at last. 'We don't know if he – Bolingbroke – is involved.'

'If it wasn't Acclom's ship you saw in the bay, then it was someone else with sufficient wealth to commission a ship. In my opinion it leaves only one contender. We know how ambitious the Lancasters are. Even the rebels recognise the use of the cross as a symbol of power. That's a fact Bolingbroke would never ignore.'

She sat down on the bench and rested her elbows on the table with her head in her hands. 'I can't think straight. It could have been Earl Douglas, couldn't it? The Scottish connection.'

'Then how did the rebels get wind of it if not through Bolingbroke?'

'I don't know. I'm still shocked and can't think straight. I've never been so close to men butchering each other in cold blood like that, Ulf. It's the most barbaric thing I've ever seen.' She gave him a stricken glance. 'It's what my husband used to do as a knight-at-arms. No wonder he would never talk about it. The blood, the hacked limbs, the wounded flesh – men dying in agony with the exultant shouts of their killers in their ears.'

He put his hand on her shoulder. She could feel the warmth, the life of him, through her linen

301

shift again. It was more than she could bear. Tears slid silently down her cheeks. She dashed them away.

'It was the look on the leader's face as his guts spilt out...' she whispered when she managed to speak. 'His awareness that it was all over. I felt such compassion for him but there was nothing I could do. Not one thing. The rest of it was horrific. An atrocity. No standards of civilised feeling. No humanity. Broken skulls. Brains revealed, still pulsing. The sound of swords grinding through bone. The horror. And for what? To stop a group of people with no real power thinking and speaking the truth as they see it?'

Another thought surfaced, based on something Hubert de Courcy had told her during that strange, revelatory night of vigil in Beverley Minster last year.

He confessed that he had been a knight in the service of a French duke before he became a monk. 'I have killed men,' he had told her. She saw his face in her imagination now. The horror in his eyes. *I have killed men.*

She lifted her head. 'I can't make sense of it at present, Ulf. To hear stories of battle is one thing. Chivalry. The glory of it. All the glitter and romance. But to witness it is different. It's brutal. I can never feel the same again.'

He looked down at her in consternation.

'Go now, if you will.' She touched the back of his hand. 'I need to think about it. Don't worry about me. No one will come looking for the cross here. I'm sure the rebels – the one or two who survived – have more pressing concerns on their minds just now. They won't risk showing themselves in York. Whoever was pulling the strings probably wanted only to exterminate a cell of the brotherhood. Constantine's Cross was merely the lure to that end.'

When he saw she was determined to stay where she was, he reluctantly took his leave.

After he left, for once the yard was empty. It seemed to pulse with heat, the sun a small, burning disc in a cloudless sky.

Agnetha and Thomas had gone back to their duties earlier and the widow was out visiting in the town somewhere. Baldwin and Julitta were inside their house with the shutters across.

Even Edric had retreated indoors to the coolth of the workshop and could be seen sprawling there, half-cut, in Dorelia's chair next to the cold kiln, another flagon of wine at his feet. Gilbert, at work on the *vidimus*, was visible as a patch of silvery light in the window of the otherwise shadowless grey of the workshop.

She had reassured Ulf that the surviving rebels would have more pressing matters on their minds than the cross. Now she was alone with her fears she was not so sure. And there was Bolingbroke to consider.

She recalled that flash of light from the vessel in the bay. There had been no ensign. It was a ship that could have belonged to anyone, to any fleet. It was a fact, however, that no one had made much of a search for the cross in the aftermath of that surprise attack.

The few survivors had given only a cursory inspection of the battle scene. Once they had

303

dealt with their dead they had set off by way of the carters' track over the moor. She had seen them leave. It suggested that they were taking the same long route back to the camp.

And yet, according to Roger, they had not returned there. He and his men had met no one on the road from York, and when, following Danby's instructions, they had found the camp, it had been deserted.

The surviving rebels had probably turned north, maybe hiding out in the woods again, maybe even making for Durham where they might expect to find a safe house in the wake of the magister.

Hildegard was familiar with the moors. She had crossed back to York by the narrow trail that was used by travellers unencumbered by carts. The moorland eventually gave way to the vast tract of royal forest known as Pickering Vale. There was a well-fortified castle on a rise in the middle of it. It commanded a view over the forest for the purpose of keeping the king's deer safe from poachers. She had avoided it. It belonged to John of Gaunt.

It occurred to her that any survivors with an affinity with Gaunt's son would probably make for Pickering Castle. There they were sure to find food, shelter and a change of horses.

She was convinced no one had followed her by the less well-known route she had taken.

If, however, Bolingbroke's men were in fact looking for the cross, they might now turn their attention to the place where information could be more easily picked up.

To the nearest town of any consequence.

To York.

Ulf was right. There was no protection here.

The town stables were situated down Walmgate and conveniently next to them were the kennels. As soon as she appeared in the yard the kennel-man hurried up to Hildegard with a look of relief. 'Am I glad to see you, Sister. We had a bit of trouble early on–'

'What, with my hounds?' she demanded in astonishment.

One of the kennel lads stood grinning nearby. 'Not their fault, Sister,' he broke in. 'They're fine characters.'

His master gave him a scowl. 'You speak when you're spoken to. Nobody wants your opinion.'

The lad didn't wipe the grin off his face but he kept his mouth shut to allow his master to tell Hildegard what had happened. 'Some visitors came roaring in here this morning asking about hiring a brace of hounds to help 'em fetch back an absconding servant, and your two animals were out in the yard being exercised by that grin-ning young devil, and they nearly had his arm off, trying to get at 'em. I can't be having my customers frightened off by undisciplined ani-mals–'

'I've come to take them anyway,' she told him, not wasting time by trying to defend them. 'I never intended for them to be here for so long. Can we settle up now?'

'Gladly.' He cuffed the grinning lad on the head as he passed him on the way into his office. It was a lean-to shed on the side of the kennel compound. When, business done, Hildegard came out, the lad was still there.

'So you got on all right with my hounds, did you?'

He nodded. 'Sorry to see them leave, Sister.' He eyed them both as if they were old friends and they returned the look with kindness.

Hildegard pondered the three for a moment. 'Mm, well...' She couldn't think of any particular use she could make of his enthusiasm. 'These fellows they took exception to, what were they like?'

'Usual swaggering types with big money-pouches, Sister. One had a hawk on his arm.'

'Maybe it was the hawk my hounds didn't like?'

He pushed his hands in the pockets of a rather grubby tunic and, evidently unconvinced, kicked a stone. 'Mebbe.'

'What would your master say if I asked to hire you to help with these beasts for a few days?'

He looked up with shining eyes and demanded eagerly, 'Might you think of asking him, then, to find out?'

One of the swarm of children who ran about the town, he was unkempt, skinny with lack of regular meals, and destined to a life of servitude. That was the best he could expect. The worst was to lose his work and have to beg, with all the unpleasant consequences that would entail.

His master's eyes gleamed as he pocketed his fee and willingly gave him leave to go. The lad himself almost danced along as he accompanied Hildegard and the hounds back to Stonegate.

306

Danby was surprisingly coherent when she appeared at his door with a request. 'Plenty of room in that back kitchen of mine for a little 'un. Let him curl up on a pile of straw with my kitchen lad.' He eyed the hounds. 'They'll look after you. Is that the idea?'

'I thought they would be no problem out here in the yard,' she told him.

He nodded. 'Take the lad through if you like. See if it suits.'

To Hildegard's surprise the workshop opened out into a substantial living chamber with a brick-arched fireplace at one end. An old woman was bent over a cooking pot and a small boy was chopping something on a wooden board close by. Straw bedding jutted from an alcove near the fire. Through the window was a parched-looking garden enclosed on all sides by the backs of other houses.

'This all right for you, young Kit?' she asked her new kennel lad.

'Better'n what master has.' He went over to the small boy, slipped out his knife from his belt, and without being asked, started to help him with the chores.

'I'll call you when I need you.'

The old woman hadn't looked up once.

Danby beckoned when she came out. He led the way to the inner workshop and invited her inside. For once Gilbert was not at his bench. He closed the door.

'I went over to Stapylton while you were gone. It sounded urgent, what he had to tell me.'

'Yes?'

'He thinks Gilbert set fire to his workshop.'

Hildegard frowned. 'I thought that was the way his thoughts were wending. What would make him think that?'

Danby was grim. 'Gilbert was there, down below by himself, while we were talking guild business t'other morning. Then we leave. Then the fire starts.'

'But why would he want to set the place on fire? Does he have a grudge against Stapylton?'

'I can't see why he should. No, it's more than that. At least, this is Stapylton's thinking.'

Danby seemed to be finding it difficult to get things straight in his mind and he went over to the bench and gazed down for a moment at Gilbert's meticulous and graceful drawings. His expression was sad and the words seemed to be forced from him.

'I told Stapylton that we're all on the same side. Gilbert wouldn't cause malicious damage. I told him that and do you know what he said? He said: "These young hotheads, who knows what they won't do in the name of the cause? They see us as old has-beens, waiting patiently for a change that will never come. We're on the same side as far as our hopes go – but they're impatient with our methods. The have no faith in us."'

Danby gave her a bleak glance. 'So, after that, it's in my mind that Gilbert might be willing to put lives on the line in the mistaken belief it's going to further our aims.'

'Lives?'

Danby nodded. 'Anybody's – and maybe even his own.'

Hildegard went to the window.

Her hounds were lying in the shade next to a bowl of water. Duchess had her head between her paws and her ears over her eyes and Bermonda was sitting upright as if on guard. They took it in turns. First one, then the other, in the manner of wolves. The sun was beating down without mercy. There was no breeze at all. She decided she would take them to the river to allow them to cool down. While this was running through her mind, her thoughts were going over what Danby had just told her.

When she turned round he was touching the edge of the whitewashed trestle marked out with Gilbert's drawing. He wore an expression of such deep sadness her heart turned over.

When he felt her watching him his head jerked up. 'It's a powerful thing when it happens. When it happens twice in as many days it can break a man.' He touched the region of his heart.

'Betrayal is difficult to live with. But don't lose faith just yet. Gilbert may have no thought of violence,' she told him. 'This is only the master chandler's guesswork.'

'What do we do? Wait and see? Let more folk be burnt to death?' He gave her a swift glance. 'You don't know, do you?'

'What?'

'That market trader they dragged free. He died yesterday. Still raving about crocodiles, they say.'

Hildegard felt a pang of grief. She had almost forgotten him in the sequence of events that had taken place since she had last seen him at St Leonard's. 'I think I know why he was talking about crocodiles. It was because he knew the fire was started in the puppet tent. You know there's a crocodile in one of those little plays?'

Danby nodded. 'That's it, is it? He was trying to warn us. Meanwhile, I worry. Where is Gilbert now? Is he setting another explosion somewhere where he'll kill and maim many more? Does he imagine he's going to persuade folks to his views that way?'

'Did he say where he was going?'

'He sits in the minster, he tells me, looking at glass. "Learning from the ancestors", he calls it.'

'I saw him there the other day.'

'Aye, the other day. But who does he meet there? Some fellow conspirator? And what's more to the point, where is he now?'

'I'll go along to the minster and have a look. Even if he sees me he'll have no reason to suspect I'm looking for him.'

Danby's eyes brightened for a moment. 'It would set my mind at rest, Sister. If I go chasing along there he'll know there's a reason and maybe it'll put him on his guard.'

Hildegard called her hounds. Duchess stood up and shook herself. Bermonda stretched her forepaws along the ground. Then they followed her obediently out of the yard. From now on she would go nowhere without their protection.

Chapter Twenty-Three

The great metal studded doors stood open. It was as busy here as in every other part of town. Strangers stood goggle-eyed in the nave. The soaring pillars drew exclamations of astonishment from those who had never been here before. They stood gazing up, lost in its grandeur, easy prey for pickpockets.

A few craftsmen from other districts discussed the manner in which the columns must have been built and the possibility of them toppling to the ground should God so decree. A child hid itself underneath its mother's mantle and peeped upwards with bedazzled eyes.

Hildegard was used to the place. Even so, when she glanced up she felt her spirits soar just as the columns soared. It was magnificent work. It made Gilbert's visits here understandable. The glass within the slender windows dazzled with brilliant hues, shedding patterns of glowing ruby, sapphire and emerald over the flagstones and scattering the upturned, awestruck faces of the visitors with jewelled light.

A hurried glance, however, showed no sign of Gilbert sitting in front of the windows nor anywhere else within the building.

Heart sinking a little she walked slowly between the pillars with her hounds at her heels. She reached the end near the high altar, then turned back. No one with that striking shade of hair was standing in front of the grisaille glass in the north transept. No one was sitting under the bell window nor anywhere else. She let herself out through the south door.

The streets were full of angels.

All shapes and sizes, young and old, they paraded in giggling bevies of a dozen or more, white robes trailing or hitched under glittering belts, wings folded or flaunted with pride and great inconvenience to everyday mortals making their way round the town. Hildegard circumvented these gorgeous obstructions until she reached the yard leading into Danby's workshop.

There she hesitated.

More bad news might set off his drinking again. She saw the tablet of glass in his hand. Its cutting edge. Its dagger-like point. Its stain as dark as blood.

She decided to hold off for a while. Give him chance to strengthen again. There was still a chance that Gilbert was on some innocent errand, that she had missed him in the packed crowds.

She poked her head into the yard, caught a glimpse of Danby working alone in the workshop, confirming that Gilbert hadn't returned by a different route. Then, without being seen, she went back into the street.

She would set about finding him and if she couldn't find him, she would do what she had intended to do earlier. She would take her hounds for a bathe in the river before they expired in the heat.

Gilbert had vanished, just like Jankin and Dorelia. And yet, like them, his presence seemed everywhere. She looked in several churches where she knew there was good glass, but there was no sign of him. Praying that Danby and Stapylton were wrong in their suspicions she eventually headed towards the river with the feeling that she had done as much as she could.

It was as crowded on the bank of the Ouse near Lendal as elsewhere in town. The heat had sent droves of people into the water. She strolled along, looking for a quiet spot where she could release the hounds, passing St Leonard's, going out further to where the meadows began with their hundreds of small encampments. Evidently people were still pouring in for the festival, and even in the stifling heat cooking fires were being stoked. Billows of woodsmoke drifted at the foot of the walls.

Managing to find a shelving slope on the riverbank that was less crowded she released the hounds from their chains. Duchess plunged into the water at once and began to swim strongly into midstream. Bermonda ran in and out at the water's edge, daring herself to go little by little into ever deeper water until finally she launched herself in with delighted little yips.

A crowd of children were playing nearby and she watched them enviously, dogs and children, wishing she could go for a swim herself. One of the boys was wading out to his waist, reaching for something floating on the water. It was a flotilla of white feathers and it made Hildegard imagine the miller upstream wringing the neck of one of his geese for his Corpus Christi dinner table.

The boy splashed back to his companions with a shout of triumph, holding one of the feathers aloft. The others circled and tried to snatch it away but he ran, laughing, up the bank to store it in a little cache of treasures in the grass.

Duchess swam back to shore and gave Hildegard the shower she desired. Laughing, she shook the water from her kirtle. Bermonda came up and did the same. She sat on the bank and spread the skirt of her habit to dry.

It was a rare moment of peace after the horrors of recent events and, tired out after the hard ride over the moors, she allowed her eyelids to close. Little by little the tension of fear began to drain from her limbs. From far off came the shouts of children at play, and deeper and closer than that was the lulling murmur of conversation from around the campfires.

Gradually the sound of distant singing detached itself from the rest. High and clear, it became louder as the singers approached. Stirring from her slumbers Hildegard imagined it must be a company of pageant players coming up from the meadows where rehearsals were sometimes held. After a moment or two she recognised it as the little dirge the children had been singing when she had arrived in York with Maud and Petronilla, an age ago.

She opened her eyes and saw the same little group approaching along the riverbank. This time the boy-bishop was leading a girl of about eight by the hand.

They walked with great ceremony through the grass and drew to a halt not far off. The boy-bishop was intoning some gobbledygook as before and waving a hand in an approximation of a blessing, but suddenly the girl threw herself to the ground and started screaming and writhing in what was a passable imitation of someone in religious ecstasy. It reminded Hildegard of a particular novice during her own training.

The child continued to writhe and sob. After a while it became alarming. The others were standing around, eyeing her with some curiosity, forgetting their parts in the charade.

When the girl didn't get up, Hildegard went over.

'She's gone crazy in the head,' one of the boys said when he saw her. 'Ever since she saw the Virgin in a bush.'

'She says she saw the Virgin, does she?'

A small girl slipped her hand into Hildegard's. 'I'm frightened of her. She does this all the time, Sister.'

'Let her be,' said the boy-bishop. 'She's got to let the devils out.'

'Who told you there were devils in her?' asked Hildegard.

'She did. She says Our Lady came to her in angel meadows and told her to set the devils free or she would go to hell and burn for ever.'

'I doubt whether Our Lady would say a thing like that to a child,' observed Hildegard.

Suddenly the girl stood up and pointed across the meadow and in a terrified voice cried, 'See!

315

The angel of the Lord! See his fiery sword! He comes to bring punishment to those who don't repent! Praise the Virgin and all her angels! Repent! Repent!' Then she fell forward again, clawing at the ground, burying her face in the hot grass, and sobbing as if in genuine terror.

Hildegard went over. She knelt down. 'Dear child, get up. You are forgiven.'

The girl lifted her head and seeing that Hildegard was a nun flung herself into her arms, sobbing. 'I saw her, Sister. She came to me in the meadow and asked me to help her. And she was covered in the blood of the Devil. And she screamed in agony. I saw her. But I refused her. I was in fear for myself. She is our Holy Mother, the Virgin, Queen of Heaven. The Mother of God. I have to speak though they rip out my tongue! Save me!' Then she cried out, her terror so convincing it sent shivers up Hildegard's spine. Suddenly the girl sprang away and ran a few steps with one arm flung out. 'See! There she comes again in her robes of glory! Save me, blessed mother!' She fell to her knees.

All the children turned but the only thing that met their gaze was the softly blowing meadow grass, rippling in a gentle breeze that ran far along the riverbank towards the woods. The children, nonetheless, started to run screaming in all directions. The more the girl intoned and pointed, the more they allowed themselves the luxury of panic.

Hildegard stepped forward. 'I think that's enough, all of you. There is nothing there. This child needs to be taken home now.' Her matter-

316

of-fact tones brought some order to their hysteria and she asked, 'Can any of you tell me where she lives?'

'She doesn't have a home,' one of the girls said in an important voice, breaking off her hysterical cries in mid flow. 'She's staying with an aunty.'

'Then let's take her there.'

One by one the little troop came to accept the idea of a grown-up taking charge and they followed randomly through the meadow towards a row of cottages on the edge of the open land in the shelter of the city walls.

When the child appeared, accompanied by a nun, a harassed-looking woman came rushing out of one of the houses. 'Has she been causing trouble again, Sister? I am sorry. I can't say how much I regret it, putting you to all this inconvenience, having to bring her back. I don't know what to do with her.'

'She seems troubled by something she's seen.'

'All nonsense. What can she have seen that others haven't? She's causing a disturbance because she's having to stay with me. She will not settle.'

'Has something happened to her mother?' asked Hildegard.

'Died this year past so she's been sent to me. Poor little morsel, pushed from pillar to post. Who wouldn't invent a vision or two, eh?'

The woman picked the child up in her arms and held her tight. 'Come in now, Lucy, do. It's all over. We love you fondly. And we'll always keep you safe.'

Several of the group peeled off into the house

and Hildegard realised that the woman already had a large brood of her own. She felt sorry for her, but there was little she could do to sort out another family's domestic arrangements.

As the woman followed the children she turned briefly at the door. 'It's the old story. Her dad's been beguiled by the witchcraft of another woman.'

The boy-bishop stood by. 'We'll go back into Angel Meadows, Sister, and see if we can catch sight of the Virgin ourselves. Maybe we can offer a prayer and she'll take the devils out and make Lucy happy again.'

He gathered the remnants of his little troop. They struck up their dirge-like hymn once more as they wound solemnly through the camps.

And then she saw him. Gilbert. She had scarcely left the row of houses when she glimpsed his bright hair.

He was sitting on the bank of the river with his back against a tree, a pad of some sort on his knees and a drawing instrument in his hand. As she approached she saw he was making a sketch of the people sitting close by. She went up to him as it seemed the natural thing to do. Her hounds followed.

'Taking advantage of a break in work?' she called. He didn't show any surprise at seeing her. His expression could only be described as innocent.

'May I have a look?'

He held up a page of drawings. Somehow he had managed to catch the exact look of the family sitting nearby underneath the tree. Mother, father, a toddler and a babe in arms. Without distortion he revealed them in all their pride and poverty. She looked at it with admiration. 'You draw like an angel, Gilbert. Are you going to give this to them?'

He shook his head. 'It's for my pattern book. They'll maybe see themselves in a church window one of these days. The Holy Family. Flight into Egypt.'

'So you're working, even in this hot weather?'

'I always work.' He showed her the book. Its pages were protected by two boards of wood, the whole thing held together by leather straps. He turned over the page he was working on and on the other side, the wool side of the vellum, was a drawing of herself with Duchess and Bermonda beside her. So that's how he saw her. She gave him a quick glance.

'When did you draw this?'

'Earlier on. I saw you walk past and go to sit near the river.'

'You've been watching me?'

'I'm not the only one.' He turned to the next page. There was a drawing of a man with familiar brutal features. He was unmistakable. It was the servant from the convent of the Holy Wounds, Matthias, the one she suspected had held a knife to her throat a few nights ago.

She gave a hurried glance over her shoulder.

'It's all right. He made himself scarce when those children turned up. Do you know him?'

'He works for the nuns. He's a sort of handy-man.'

'Is it something to do with those two girls you brought with you?'

She agreed it was. 'How did you know about them?'

Gilbert smiled. 'Everybody knows you snatched them free. You made yourself popular. He's gone anyway. Time for vespers, I expect.' His lip curled in disdain. He closed up his pattern book and put it carefully inside a leather bag on the grass beside him and then gave her a careful look. 'If you wait here long enough you'll see someone else of interest.'

'Who?' she asked.

He shook his head. 'Wait and see.'

Chapter Twenty-Four

The representatives of the Holy Family had packed up and left by now and Gilbert and Hildegard were alone under the oak tree.

The sun had fallen like a ball of fire to the distant edge of the cleared land on the other side of the river. Its light was slanted, sending long fingers of shadow across the meadow. The little campfires stood out brightly as pinpricks of light and their brightness made the shadows seem deeper.

It was still light enough to recognise someone at several paces. And yet, under their tree, in the shadow of its spreading branches weighted with summer leaf, they were probably hidden well unless someone came right up to them and walked in to where they sat.

'What is this about, Gilbert?' she asked. Danby's suspicions were uppermost in her thoughts.

He shrugged. 'I don't know. See what you make of it. I haven't made sense of it myself yet.'

'Is it something to do with your master?'

He nodded. 'Actions always have consequences. He will discover this soon enough. His sorrow is not ended yet.' He put a sudden hand on her arm to stop her reply. 'See?' he breathed. 'Look there, along the path. He's on time.'

Hildegard peered in the direction he was pointing and drew in a breath. She was mystified by Gilbert's air of secrecy. 'But it's Baldwin.'

'Every night for three nights he has walked along this path in the same direction. If you watch you'll see he goes along the river to the woods.'

'And then?'

'I haven't had the courage to follow him.'

'He's going for a walk. Taking the evening air. That's all.'

'Is he?'

'Why should you think otherwise?'

Baldwin – it was definitely him – was approaching along the path and Gilbert lowered his voice to a whisper. 'You don't know what happened just before Dorelia disappeared. I was there the night the master was out searching for you.' His face was a pale oval in the twilight. It was turned towards her. His eyes were dark hollows reflecting no light. It was like looking into a void. 'I was

321

there all the time,' he whispered. 'They don't know what I heard. They assume my leg makes me deaf as well. Or stupid.'

'I'm sure they–'

'Don't waste your breath with your compassion. It's unwanted. Just know that I was there unheeded all that night.'

'And?'

'There was a visitor.'

'To your master's workshop?'

'Indeed.'

'He must get many visitors. He's a well-known guildsman–'

Baldwin was now level with them. Gilbert put a warning hand on her arm and they waited in silence until he walked past. The glazier carried on along the riverbank just as Gilbert had predicted.

'This was a visitor the master would not have welcomed,' he continued in an undertone. 'It was John Gisburne.'

'What did he want?'

'Dorelia.'

'What do you mean?'

'He must have thought, "If Master Baldwin can sell Dorelia to his own brother he can certainly sell her to me."'

Hildegard could not believe what he was saying. 'Did he go into the house?'

'Of course he did. Baldwin let him in. Dorelia was alone. The old cook of the master's is as deaf as a post and the two little servants would be asleep. There was nobody else there, apart from me, whom they discounted, and Jankin, whose presence they rather objected to until Baldwin suggested he go out in the town with a wad of money. He was reluctant to do that. He's fond of Dorelia. He knew what they were up to. But he went. He went all right.'

Gilbert rubbed a hand over his brow. Without thinking he unloosed his hair and it fell in a flood of light to his shoulders. As if he knew it could be seen in the darkness he pulled up his hood to conceal it. 'Gisburne,' he said, 'left towards dawn.'

'You didn't do anything?'

'With Gisburne's armed thugs standing guard all night? I did think of causing a diversion but I couldn't get out. They locked the door of the small workshop where I sleep, maybe not realising anybody was in there. I weighed up the chances of getting my throat slit if I shouted to be let out and decided against. Besides, I didn't know how amenable Dorelia was – she'd taken Baldwin's money before.'

'What do you mean by that?'

He gave a disparaging laugh. 'I forget you're a nun. My apologies, Sister. I hope I haven't shocked you–'

As he had said to her earlier, she now said to him, 'Don't waste your breath. Do you mean Baldwin sold her to other men?'

'He sold her to his brother. Other men have come into the picture. It's been difficult for them. The master hates to let her out of his sight he's so besotted. But Baldwin has found ways of keeping him occupied while he turns a profit for himself.'

'Are you serious about this?'

His silence was affirmation enough.

'How can you go on living there?' Hildegard frowned into the darkness.

He paused. 'The very question I ask myself – a thousand times a day.'

It was dark now, or at least as dark as it ever gets in midsummer. Baldwin had disappeared into the woods. The trees on the distant boundary of the meadow were like a smudge of charcoal.

'The thing is ... the thing is,' he continued, 'I fear something worse might happen if I leave. At least, that *was* my fear.' He paused again. 'Now my fear is it's too late to think like that.'

'Too late?'

'I fear the worst has already happened.'

'Gilbert, you must tell me everything. What is the worst – that Dorelia and Jankin absconded?'

He gave a raw laugh. 'He was mad enough to do it but I doubt whether it would have occurred to him. And certainly Dorelia wasn't going to swap a golden goose for a mere apprentice. I haven't put all the pieces together yet but I'm convinced they didn't abscond.'

He got up. His limp seemed more pronounced for a moment and he pretended to have found necessary some minor adjustment to his leather bag. It gave him chance to balance himself on the rough ground before hoisting the bag over his shoulder and setting off towards the path.

'Wait!' she called. 'What is there out there in the woods?'

'Trees.' He turned to look back. 'And then it comes out in Two Mills Dale.'

Baldwin must be going to visit the miller at Low Mill, she decided. The fact that he had procured a wife for his brother meant little. Girls were bought and sold for their dowries every day. The question of Dorelia's alleged fortune, however, remained unanswered and, she realised, the doubt already voiced by Theophilus echoed what Gilbert seemed to be hinting.

Dorelia had been bought and sold at least once.

Remembering the pimp in the stews the other night and what he had shouted to Baldwin made her pause. *'Have you come for your money already, Baldwin?'* the man had called out. What had that been about? Payment for some glazing work the man had done? Or something else?

Uncertainly, she peered into the darkness towards the woods. If there was an innocent explanation she would have a hard time explaining her presence should she turn up at the mill – and if there was something going on she could do nothing about it by herself. She would have to fetch help. She followed Gilbert in the direction of the town and when they reached the busy streets she put a hand on his arm. 'What is the worst you fear?'

He shook his head. 'I can't say.'

Her grip tightened. 'Can't or won't?'

'Can't.'

'Did you see Dorelia again, after that night?'

He nodded. 'After I heard Gisburne leave I called out to her to unlock the door. At first she didn't seem to hear me so I started to bang on it. That brought her down and she took the latch off. "What are you doing locked in?" she asked. I said, "Ask your customer." She didn't like that. I think she believed nobody else knew. I just walked past her. I couldn't be bothered with her. I went for a walk.'

'Where to?'

He looked startled. 'Just through the town. Nowhere special. It was early. The vendors were getting their stalls ready for another day. I just walked about the streets.'

'When did you get back?'

'Late. It was after noon. I heard that big bell in the minster tolling the midday. It was after that. I had nowhere else to go. When I came in the master had already returned. Dorelia had gone. The master assumed she was out somewhere watching the jongleurs. He clung to the belief that she would come back until it started to get dark. Then it came over him. The truth. That she had left him and Jankin was also missing, therefore – they must have left together.'

'Did they take anything with them?'

'That's the strange thing. Jankin's sleeping chamber was cleared out, floor swept, nothing left but his bed. Or so the master said. I don't go up there. The stairs,' he explained. 'But Dorelia hadn't taken a thing. The master came to the landing outside their chamber and just stood there with one of her gowns in his hands and said, "She left this behind." It was a green brocade he had given her and really liked her in.'

'How do you explain the fact that she didn't take anything?'

'I told you, all the pieces aren't in place yet.'

'But she and Jankin had been lovers for–'

'It'd been going on for weeks. I don't know how they got away with it. Jankin liked sailing close to the wind – a kiss behind the master's back, a hand touching her breasts moments before the master walked into the workshop. Jankin was a devil that way. Dorelia encouraged him. They thought it a great joke to make a fool of the master.'

'Do you believe she's gone back to Wakefield?'

'Why should she? She had no one there.'

'What about her betrothed?'

'Her what?'

'Didn't you know?'

His expression changed and his eyes narrowed.

'I wonder if Danby knew?' She watched him closely, trying to make out what that change of expression meant.

'He wouldn't mention it to me even if he did,' said Gilbert after a pause. 'There was never a word about anybody else, not in Wakefield nor anywhere.'

And if no mention of the betrothed, then presumably no mention of the inheritance.

Gilbert innocently confirmed this when he said, 'She was the penniless waif, alone in the wicked world, and the master saw himself as the knight on the white charger riding to her rescue.'

'But I thought you said Baldwin sold her to him? That spoils the picture somewhat.'

'Master handed over a large sum of money – to pay a marriage broker Baldwin claimed to know.' His lip curled. 'I think it was Baldwin himself, pulling a fast one. He likes money, as does Mistress Julitta. You may have noticed.'

'You think very little of Baldwin.'

'You'd think little of him if you knew him.'

She shrugged. 'Maybe.'

'You have realised how he gets his money?' asked Gilbert in a bland tone.

They were at the end of the alley, near the yard, and he lowered his voice. 'The master isn't the only one who forks out for a little personal comfort. Go and ask around the stews. Then you'll find out all you need to know about Master Baldwin and his wife and what service they provide.' He made as if to walk off but she put a hand on his sleeve.

'What do you mean?'

Gilbert's face was expressionless. 'He brings girls over from the West Riding to York where nobody knows them.'

'Girls?'

'Girls who have no family to protect them. Girls whose fathers sell them because they can't afford to keep them. Girls sacrificed to save their families from starvation. He sets them to work in different houses and rakes off a profit from them all.'

She looked at him in horror.

'Dorelia was probably one of them but he offered her a more respectable fate. At least on the surface.'

'How do you know this?'

'Ask around if you don't believe me.'

I will, she thought. 'What about Danby?'

'What about him?'

'Does he know about the others?'

He shook his head. 'Loyalty rates high with the

master. He won't hear a word against his brother.'

What he had told her could be checked, even by a nun, she thought grimly. Indeed, Danby himself could have checked it if he had heard the rumours – which surely he must have. She couldn't believe it was something against which he would turn a blind eye. If there was an iota of truth in Gilbert's suspicions she would certainly find out.

Before they went on into the yard she said, 'So do you think Dorelia and Jankin are together?'

He didn't reply.

'You were the last person to see Dorelia,' she reminded.

'The last one?' He looked confused, then admitted, 'Yes, I suppose I must have been one of the last.'

Her question went unanswered.

She watched him go to the door. He claimed he was putting the pieces into place. That's what she was trying to do herself. What she could not tell was whether they were using the same pieces and whether, when it was completed, they would see the same picture.

Danby had asked her to check up on Gilbert for a very different reason. If he was a fire-raiser it was an activity that seemed to have taken second place to his interest in Baldwin and his master's wife.

And the whereabouts of Dorelia and Jankin remained a mystery.

Danby was visible inside his workshop. He was

sitting in the gloaming staring into space. When Gilbert appeared in the light of the cresset in the yard his jaw dropped and then his eyes lit up. He rose to his feet and strode outside with arms outstretched, clearly assuming it was a good sign to see his journeyman accompanied home by Hildegard. He raised his eyebrows at her.

'We met down by the river,' she responded. 'Gilbert was doing a few sketches for his pattern book.'

'Is that all?' Relief seemed to flood visibly through him.

She nodded. Now Gilbert would tell of his suspicions.

Instead, however, he simply made as if to push past into the workshop. Danby was not to be moved aside yet, however. His fondness for the journeyman was clear in the look of relief with which he had welcomed him back, but he couldn't let the matter go without showing displeasure. The journeyman had been absent from the workshop without permission. Danby stood firmly in the doorway.

'So, have you got a good account of yourself?' he began.

Gilbert shrugged and did not look him in the eye. If he hoped that was the end of it he was mistaken.

'Where the hell have you been?' Danby poked him hard in the chest.

Gilbert kept his head down.

Danby pushed him again so that he stumbled backwards. 'Skiving off? Come on, cock, explain yourself!' He pushed him a third time. 'You've

330

never been drawing in the dark. I want to know every last movement you've made today.'

Gilbert made another attempt to push past him.

Danby barred the way. 'You're due a hefty fine, d'you know that? Skiving off. I'm going to make sure you pay every penny.' He folded his arms. 'Explain yourself, and this had better be good.'

Gilbert's eyes were washed empty when he looked up. 'I'm not your bloody apprentice, Danby. I'm a journeyman. I work when I choose.'

'So why did you *choose* to leave that glass half finished – *sir?*' he added sarcastically.

'I had the idea that as the workshop seemed closed for the day I'd make myself scarce until you were sober enough to give me your instructions.'

Danby took a step back. He seemed halted less by his words than by the contempt in his employee's voice. He reddened. 'You fuckin' impudent young devil!' He raised his fist as if to strike him.

Gilbert was blank-faced and didn't budge. 'Strike me, master. I'm not made of glass. I won't break. It's my leg not my fists that's the problem. I can defend myself!'

Danby suddenly dropped his fist, and putting his face in his hands rocked back and forth on his heels muttering, 'No, no, no, what the hell am I doing? What am I thinking of? Have I lost my senses?'

He raised his head, his face showing the strain he was under. 'Punch you? Punch *you*, Gilbert?' he exclaimed. 'Never! Never in this world. The

Lord strike *me* down if I do. But you're right to despise me. You have right on your side and I can't deny it. I'm incapable of running my own workshop. You're right. I am not fit. And I'm shamed by it. That I should let myself carry on like this! What a show I'm making of myself! What a bloody show!'

He stepped aside. 'Come on, come on in, come in. Have confidence, lad. It's all over. Come inside, do.'

Gilbert, keeping a wary eye on Danby, limped towards the threshold.

Danby let him through. 'While I was sitting here I was doing some hard thinking. And everything is changed. I've seen the light. Believe me, son, everything's different!' He led the way into the workshop. 'I'll put my hand on my heart. I'm myself again. You'll explain to me in your own good time. Now let's get on.'

'Get on?'

'We've time to make up. We have glass to finish.'

'Working?'

'What else?'

'Working outside the hours?'

'I'm not guildmaster for nowt. If I say we work by candlelight, we work. I'll square it with the other members should they dare to call me to account.'

Without saying another word, Gilbert went to the peg and took down his leather apron. As he tied it on he gave Danby a careful look, but his master was already lighting candles and soon the workshop was awash with light.

Danby went to the rack and selected a sheet of

coloured glass to place over the drawing. He laid it carefully on the trestle. Then he went to the stove and began to light it. He took the metal rod used for marking out the glass and placed it in the coals. Hildegard, having been forgotten, hovered in the doorway. Danby took the rod from the coals when it was red-hot and began to follow the line of the drawing under the glass. When he finished he spat on the hot glass, tapped it and broke it to shape in one deft movement. His skill was beautiful to watch.

Gilbert handed him the grozing iron. 'What about Mistress Dorelia?'

Danby's hand didn't falter as he trimmed the edges of the glass. 'Never heard of her.' He paused, then straightened. 'May they rot in hell, the both of 'em.'

He bent over his work again. 'I thought you could try your hand at the silver stain on the Virgin's hair tomorrow,' he murmured. 'It's time you got your chance. You'll do a grand job.' He lifted his head. 'The person you mentioned is not here and if she showed her face I would not have her back for all the gold in Westminster. Now let's get this job finished, lad. It's behind time.'

Next morning, Danby and Gilbert were up shortly after dawn, busy again in the workshop. Sleepless, Hildegard had heard one of them go to the well and had crawled out of bed to see who it was. Gilbert. Carrying a bucket of water back inside.

After they had got down to work the previous evening Hildegard had walked up to Micklegate with her two hounds in the hope of having a word with Ulf. He would know whether it was worth taking Gilbert's remarks about Baldwin seriously. But she was told he was out of town. She left a message and, doubtful about raising an alarm based entirely on hearsay, decided to wait until he came back before doing anything else.

After all, Dorelia and Jankin could be anywhere, in another town setting up as man and wife in a place where nobody knew them. After her experience at the hands of Gisburne, nothing was more understandable than that Dorelia, accompanied by her true love, should run away as far as possible.

As for Baldwin, what he did, alas, was not against the law.

Just before eight that morning she saw Danby and Gilbert take off their aprons, wash their hands in the bucket standing outside the door, then, smartly attired, the master wearing a light cloak over his shoulders, and Gilbert with his blue one over his arm in partial concealment of his affliction, they left the workshop, crossed the yard and went out towards the street.

'Gone to St Helen's no doubt,' observed Tabitha, glancing out of the window. 'I'm off now as well. Are you going to accompany us, Sister?'

With a shock Hildegard remembered it was some time since she had attended a service and tomorrow would be the eve of Corpus Christi. 'You must be off to Lady Mass?'

'Just going. I'm accompanying yon cook of Edric's and the two little lads.'

'I'll come along in a minute. I've one or two

things to do first.'

Tabitha wrapped a scarf over her head and went out saying she would see her there. A few minutes later the troop of four set off.

With everyone out of the way it was an ideal time to check out a few things that bothered her.

After Jankin's alleged night in the stews at Baldwin's expense, he must have reappeared after Gilbert left that morning, and she wondered what had passed between him and Dorelia to persuade him to leave with her. Dorelia would have finally decided enough was enough after John Gisburne's visit and she must have appealed to her lover to help her escape an intolerable situation.

She crossed the yard and pushed open the door into the workshop. The stairs were off to one side next to the door into the living quarters. She peered inside. There was no one within. She turned to the stairs and began to climb. At the top the air was still as if unbreathed. It held a faint aroma of the flowery perfume Dorelia used.

A door to the right must lead into the chamber the couple shared, she supposed, while directly ahead was a stepladder. It would lead to the attic under the eaves where Jankin lodged.

She quickly pulled herself up rung by rung and arrived on a small landing with just one door.

She pushed it open. Gilbert was right so far. The attic had been cleared out. There was nothing here now except for a bed in one corner. The mattress was a thick straw bag, smooth as if newly turned. She glanced round.

A few hooks on the wall for clothing. A line

where a cloak might have hung. She peered under the bed. Bare boards. Not a sign of dust. That struck her as strange. Danby's housekeeper must be extremely thorough. Was it the deaf woman? she wondered. She doubted whether she was even able to climb the ladder.

Something wedged under the foot of one of the legs of the bed caught her eye. She reached down. It was a small feather. Pure white, as if from the breast of a swan.

A chuckle behind her made her swivel with a startled gasp.

Standing in the doorway was Master Baldwin. He came inside, kicked the door shut, then leant against it with folded arms.

'So…' he ground out, 'what have we here?'

Chapter Twenty-Five

He moved swiftly across the chamber until he was standing over her. 'Snooping, are we, Sister?'

In the face of aggression she thought it best to be bold. 'I suppose I am.' She slipped the feather secretly into her sleeve as she spoke.

'And what do you hope to find in here?'

'Some clue to Jankin's whereabouts, perhaps.'

'He's run off with my brother's wife. That's all you need to know.'

'Aren't you worried he's missing?'

'What's it to me?'

'He's your brother's apprentice. That should

make it something to you – even if a missing person means nothing else. And where he is, your sister-in-law is also, or so it would appear. Surely you would like to know she's safe and sound?'

Her questions seemed to unbalance his composure, as if he had expected her to bow her head under his hard stare. Now he seemed to realise that he had not got her measure after all.

He shifted his stance. 'I've told you, they've run off. Nobody's seen them since.' He did not meet her eyes.

'In a town like this it should be easy enough to track them down,' she replied. 'I'm surprised nobody's done so.'

'They'll be long gone. Passing themselves off as man and wife in a place where nobody knows them.'

'They could still be somewhere in the town,' she replied stubbornly.

'And where would you reckon to start looking? In a nunnery, mebbe? In the stews? Aye, that's an idea. Mebbe we should send somebody to search the stews.' He gave a sniggering laugh. 'Unless you yourself would like to go down there, of course. Doubtless you wouldn't be able to get out quick enough, seeing all that naked flesh.' He licked his lips and gave another laugh. 'On the other hand, Sister, we might never see you again either, so taken with the rapture of what you deny yourself!'

This idea amused him. He looked her up and down, his shoulders shaking with exaggerated mirth. Then he said, sharp-toned, 'I've often wondered what makes you people get up in a morning. What do you get out of life?'

She returned his stare. 'More than you'll ever know, sir.'

'Oh yes? Like living in the fear of hellfire? Or is all your talk of sin just a sham, as is so often revealed? Something designed to spoil our fun while enjoying all the pleasures of the flesh yourselves?' His expression was full of contempt. 'The Church is after worldly goods like everybody else. It'll do anything for gold. It's the greatest whoremistress of us all. And you monastics do well out of it.'

'You sound like an expert on whoring, master. No doubt that pleases your wife.'

A look crossed his face.

'Me?'

'I understand you're seen in the stews often enough, among the purveyors of flesh?'

She couldn't guess how he would react. He gazed at her without speaking, his eyes flickering over her as if trying to read her mind, but then he surprised her by lowering his voice to an intimate level.

'As a matter of fact, Sister, I did do some work for one of them houses not so long ago. They wanted a piece of fancy glass in one of their chambers, to raise the tone of the place for their wealthy customers.'

As he said this he tried to outface her but she would not drop her gaze.

She could not tell whether he was lying or not. It sounded feasible. It could be Gilbert who was lying for all she knew.

That shouted question she had overheard was

338

ambiguous: *Come for your money already, Baldwin?*

It could have referred to an innocent payment for some glazing. She had already considered this herself. She didn't like the man, but it didn't mean everything Gilbert had said about him was true.

'Julitta doesn't like me working down there,' Baldwin continued, keeping his voice low as if his wife might have extraordinary hearing. He gave an intimate smile. 'I can understand her point of view. I wouldn't like it if she had some young lover-boy. I didn't want to turn work away but I didn't want to upset her neither.' He lowered his voice still further. 'I hope you won't let on? Just a secret between you and me, like?'

She started to walk towards the door, to get out, to get away, to free herself from what might be a web of lies, but he didn't move out of her way so when she was standing right in front of him she asked, 'And Dorelia? Do you think she's gone back to Wakefield?'

About to let her pass he slammed the flat of his hand against the door, shutting it with a bang. Rage flared in his eyes before being obliterated by a recalculation of how matters stood.

'If you know anything about Dorelia you'd better tell me,' he ground out.

'I don't know anything. I just wondered if you thought she might have gone back there?'

'Is it Gilbert? Have you been giving Gilbert an inquisition? Is that it? You want to watch him. He's a bloody liar, a little snake in the grass.'

'All I've heard is she comes from Wakefield. That's where you met her, isn't it?'

'Who told you that?'

She shrugged. 'I can't remember. Maybe she herself did. It wasn't Gilbert. I assumed it was common knowledge.'

'It is true I met her over there. So what?'

'When you were working?'

'Did she tell you this?'

'I've told you I don't remember.'

'More likely that little rat's been talking!' He brought his face close to her own. 'You know he's obsessed, don't you? He'd say anything against anybody out of spite if he thought she had a glance for them instead of him. He's pathetic. Have you seen his drawings? Hundreds of the things. The little toad's mad in the head.'

She stepped back and he gave her a sharp glance. 'It is him, isn't it? He's been shouting his mouth off, spreading lies. It wouldn't surprise me if–' He broke off.

She watched him fiddle with the large jewel. It was now pinned to his capuchon. Always on display.

'If what?' she pursued.

Head down he mumbled, 'If he did something to her one day...'

'Like what?'

'Shut her up for good.'

She made a movement and his head shot up. 'And you, Sister – just what are you trying to make of all this?' He took a step forward, so close she was swimming in the sickly scent of attar of roses. 'This is a family matter,' he grunted. 'What's Dorelia got to do with you?'

For a moment she thought he was about to

strike her but his glance fell to the small wooden cross she wore and he stepped to one side.

'This is my brother's house. You come in here, into his private chambers, as if you have a right. He's too easygoing, Edric, always has been.' He pulled the door wide. 'You can find your own way out.' He made an elaborate and mocking bow.

She walked swiftly past him and as she set her foot on the first rung of the stepladder she heard him mutter, 'And don't come back.'

Fuming at her inept handling of the situation she made her way across the yard into Tabitha's house. The others had not yet returned from Mass. It gave her time to decide what to do next.

Baldwin came out of Edric's workshop and stood, arms folded, in the doorway. It was plain he was going to make sure she knew who was master.

The annoying thing was she had got nothing from him that she didn't already know, except for that slanted view of Gilbert. It shifted suspicion onto him. And yet it might be a hint that Baldwin had something to hide. It was as good a move as any to implicate the journeyman.

Another thing that rankled was his question: what do you get out of life? His unspoken assumption was so wrong that she didn't know where to begin.

Brother Thomas sent a note. It was delivered by one of the boys kept by the friars. It told her he had been instructed by Brother Alcuin to return to Meaux at once, now the business connected to the prioress of Swyne had been concluded.

Hildegard regretted that she would now have no chance to talk things over with him and maybe get a different perspective on Dorelia's disappearance.

She sent the boy back with a penny for his trouble, the information that she was waiting to find out what the prioress wanted her to do with the cross, and her best wishes to the monk himself.

After the boy ran off – another barefoot child, she noticed – she went up to her sleeping chamber and rummaged in her bag for her knife.

It was kept in a leather sheath and used mainly for eating. Now she took it out and inspected the blade. It looked wicked enough to scare off anybody if used in an appropriate manner. She replaced it in the sheath and strapped it to her belt underneath the light cotton mantle she had on over her shift.

Then she removed her black veil and the conspicuous white gorget and found a piece of cloth she had been using to wrap things in. She held it up. It was an ochre linen square. Worn as a headscarf it would be commonplace enough to allow her to pass unnoticed in the street.

After rinsing it out in the pail downstairs she hung it on the line inside the kitchen. It would dry quickly. Today was already another scorcher. Even though it was early, when she threw the dirty water outside it dried at once on the hot flagstones.

She went to the well to refill the pail.

Baldwin was still lounging around his brother's doorway. He had a drink in his hand now and gave her a baleful glance as she came out. She had to let the rope down an ell or more before she heard the wooden bucket hit the water. She hauled it up and carried it back indoors.

Baldwin watched without comment.

Bareheaded, she felt the heat of the sun on the back of her neck in just those few minutes. She would have to replace her straw hat with a new one from the market, she decided. She went back upstairs, changed her boots for a pair of cork-soled scarpollini and went back down. The head-scarf was dry already. She put it on, winding the two ends round the back and knotting them at the front.

When she popped her head outside Baldwin had disappeared.

The widow returned from Mass with the boys and the deaf cook and made no comment about Hildegard's non-appearance at church. She began to busy herself with a few chores.

Hildegard went to Edric's door and called inside for Kit. He came bounding out from the back kitchen with eyes agleam.

'Have you fed and watered my hounds for me?' she asked.

'Yes, Sister,' he answered smartly, giving a little flourish like a regular page.

'Then you may have the rest of the morning off. But don't get into mischief. I have to go into the town.'

'I'd be honoured to come with you, Sister.'

'You would?'

He nodded.

She weighed him up. 'All right then. Let's go.'

She whistled for the hounds and they bounded out of the shade with as much alacrity as Kit had done and she marvelled at the energy of her escorts in this vile heat. Her headscarf was no protection against it.

'We're going to the market so keep a tight hold of them both,' she told the boy, handing him the leash. When she glanced back into the yard as they turned the corner there was no sign of Baldwin. His house had its shutters closed again.

Kit was in a ferment of excitement. He squawked with glee every time a hand of pageant players went past. 'Look at them little devils!' he shouted, tugging on Hildegard's sleeve when a band of children of his own age wearing red suits went past brandishing miniature pitchforks made out of boiled paper and glue. Their parents would be guild members, she guessed, with prospects far beyond Kit's meagre little dreams.

Some shepherds sauntered by carrying painted sheep under their arms and Kit chortled again and, making little bleating sounds, pretended to stroke them.

'I'll never keep these bloody wings in place,' a fat man was grumbling as he trudged along with a couple of companions in long nightshirts. They all stopped and tried to hoist the wings back over his shoulders. 'You'll have to unfasten the strap to tighten it up a bit,' one of them advised.

The one in the lead roared back down the line, 'Come on, lads, no dallying! Rehearsal on the dot! Or are you aiming to land yoursens with a fine?'

344

'Pageant master's still at his prayers,' somebody retorted.

'Just because he's slacking there's no need for you to follow suit!'

'He's wettin' 'isself over your lines, brother, begging Our Lady to help you out,' one of them quipped. The bevy of winged men broke into guffaws.

They were accompanied by a friar wearing a brown habit. A woman tried to press some coins into his hand as he went by but he gave them back. 'No, mistress, I'm only a player.'

She insisted, confused, perhaps, by the heat and the crowds and the authenticity of his costume, so with a smile he accepted. 'Oh, all right then.' He made the sign of the cross. 'Bless you, my child.' Catching up with his companions they had another laugh over his earnings and one of them slapped him on the back with the words, 'You've got yourself a new job, lad, for when you're booted out o' t'guild!'

The booths were almost impossible to see over the heads of the crowd. Now and then a few coloured balls rose up, glittered briefly in the blue sky, then fell again as an unseen juggler went through his paces. A horn band started to play a jig and soon a hurdy-gurdy struck up in competition on the next corner. Hildegard managed to find a capper in among the fray and forced her way to where he was selling his wares. When she emerged she was wearing a wide-brimmed straw hat and carrying a smaller one for the boy.

'Now for a pair of pattens for your poor feet, and then to the first station outside Holy Trinity,' she told him.

The stand was finished but for its decoration. The open spaces underneath the scaffolding where the servant from the nunnery had dragged her were blocked in now with canvas painted to look like the walls of a castle. Roughly daubed flowers crawled up the sides and merged with trails of real flowers set along the edge of the platform where everyone would sit. In front was a rail for the armed guards.

Ulf was bareheaded. The hot sun had transformed him over the summer months, bleaching his hair, gilding his features, emphasising the blue of his eyes so that they looked like the cobalt glass in one of Danby's windows.

When Hildegard and little Kit, now making a clatter in his new pattens, strolled up the street, he was striding about in the company of a couple of clerks and a master carpenter. They appeared to be carrying out final checks on the structure and Ulf took hold of one of the struts to give it a good shake. It remained firm.

'Excellent work, master,' they heard him say to the carpenter at his elbow. As he turned he caught sight of Hildegard. Or rather, he seemed to recognise her two hounds and, peering at Kit, shifted his glance to the person beside him. He looked twice.

'It is me,' she called, going over and sweeping off her hat for a moment to prove it.

'Well garbed for this hot weather, Hildegard. It's driving me inside for a cool stoup of ale right now. Are you going to join me?'

346

He led the way to an imposing house a little way down the street from the pageant station. 'Roger's requisitioned the house of Robert of Harpham,' he told her. 'There was no way he'd get Melisen to come out in this heat without somewhere to refresh herself and do some entertaining. They're coming in shortly with a host of guests.'

'Where's her baby?'

'Back with his wet nurse at Hutton where he can bawl his little head off to his heart's content.'

'Is Melisen bringing the girls with her?' she asked.

He nodded. 'That Petronilla!' he exclaimed. 'She's made herself at home. Melisen swears she can't do without her. I didn't think it would work out, with them being so alike,' he exchanged a knowing smile, 'but they get on like a house on fire.'

'What about Maud?' she asked.

He frowned. 'Still goes around with her little hood up and that bundle she carries everywhere. Looks as if she's about to abscond all the time but I don't think she will. She spends a lot of time sitting on the riverbank with a line in the water.' He smiled. 'There's nothing like a spot of fishing to soothe away your troubles.'

'The river?' exclaimed Hildegard, imagining the danger.

'She's safe there. They're looking after her. The cook's daughter sneaks fresh bread out as a treat, thinking we don't notice. Lord knows, she's had enough opportunity to run away with the place in such chaos. I'm never off my horse, riding back and forth to Naburn,' he added with satisfaction.

'So long as somebody's keeping an eye on her.'

'Don't worry. They've taken her to their hearts. I assume nothing else has happened since I last saw you?' he added on a different note.

She shook her head.

'So how are you feeling?' He peered into her face.

She told him she was all right after a good night's sleep but that Thomas had been called back to Meaux. Then, making sure they could not be overheard by the many servants passing back and forth, and having sent Kit off to the kitchens for a morsel to eat, she told him about Gilbert's suspicion of Baldwin and how Baldwin just now had called Gilbert a lying little rat.

'No love lost there, then.'

'What's more important is we saw Baldwin disappear into the woods near Two Mills Dale. According to Gilbert he's been out that way for several consecutive evenings.'

'Probably got a woman out there,' Ulf said.

'Who? The miller's wife?'

Ulf shrugged.

'I couldn't see any reason for Gilbert's unease,' she continued, 'but now having spoken to Baldwin, I thought I'd take a stroll out there this morning. Have a word with the miller. Just to see how the land lies. It may simply be that the miller's a friend of Baldwin and Gilbert's trying to stir trouble.'

Ulf looked thoughtful. 'Did Baldwin say anything definite to make you doubt Gilbert?'

348

'He said he was mad, obsessed by Dorelia, and that he feared he would do something to her one day, out of jealousy as he hinted, and, I suppose, frustration at not being eligible enough for her.'

'It's a curse, looking the way she does. Both of 'em are jealous, I'd guess. Baldwin could scarcely take his eyes off her when we were talking about the glass. He and Gilbert probably hate each other's guts. Rivalry in love's a terrible thing. Especially when neither side can win.' The bright blue of his eyes kindled with some deep thought and he touched her on the back of the wrist. Pulling himself together he said, 'Hildegard, promise me you won't go out there until I can come with you? I can't get away from here till later on.'

'I only thought I'd go to Low Mill. I'm not going anywhere else. Besides, it's broad daylight – and I have my three escorts.'

'Come back here straight afterwards, then, and tell me what happens. Even if it's nothing at all.'

She smiled. 'I will.'

Hildegard and the boy made their way back down Micklegate towards Ouse Bridge on their way to Low Mill. It was here on Micklegate that she had been carried to safety in the company of the college of cardinals.

Now the entire width of the street from shopfront to shopfront was full of popes, shepherds, prophets, cherubim, devils, monks who were not monks at all but cordwainers and pewterers, and, processing towards their pageant house, three resplendent orient kings, goldsmiths in real life,

349

glittering and sparkling in their paper crowns and coloured glass jewels, parting the waves of sightseers with gold-painted staves.

It was just as busy when they eventually arrived at the riverbank outside the postern on the other side of St Mary's.

The camps on the common seemed to have doubled in number. Fires sent lazy curls of smoke into the stillness as the visitors cooked pottage and fed themselves and their hordes of children.

There were more people than ever in the water. Gangs of boys had been jumping off Ouse Bridge as they passed and Hildegard had to restrain Kit's desire to do likewise. Here swarms of people were swimming and splashing each other with raucous shouts or lying prone on the bank in the trampled grass. It was only as they proceeded along the river path that the crowds eventually thinned, and by the time they reached the woods there was hardly anyone about.

Duchess and Bermonda ranged ahead, fanning out on both sides and looping back again and again. She called them to heel as they entered the cool space under the trees. A path wound its way along, roughly following a line with the river. They caught a glimpse of water now and then like a ribbon of light behind the boles. When the path dipped down into a dell they continued until it brought them out into a wide, sunlit clearing with Low Mill on the other side.

The geese were still strutting about the yard and gave an excited gabble when they saw strangers. Hildegard told Kit to slip the leash onto the hounds' collars. There were still seven geese, she observed. So much for her supposition about the miller's Corpus Christi feast. The small child with the thatch of hair came bursting out through the back door, then skidded to a halt when he saw them. A woman appeared behind him in the doorway.

After a few pleasantries which Hildegard opened with a hope that she could buy a few goose eggs, the miller's wife offered them drinks of water and invited them into the kitchen. The wooden wheel was turning with a regular, soporific beat. She laughed when Hildegard remarked on it.

'No time for sleeping here,' she said, 'what with corn having to be ground and young master to attend over there.' She indicated a baby in a cot under the window. 'I don't get a spare minute!'

Hildegard went over to have a look at the baby. He was no more than three weeks old. The miller's wife confirmed this. Hildegard said, 'I expect you get plenty of visitors from the town, being so close?'

The woman shook her head. 'They come when they want their corn ground and that's it. Millers are never popular. They think we make a profit over and above what we should but I can tell you, we don't.'

They sat down in the cool, tidy kitchen. 'Is this your lad?' asked the woman, indicating Kit.

Hildegard nodded.

'He's a fine boy.'

She realised that her headscarf had given the wrong impression. It was needless to correct it. 'I thought I saw somebody from our lane coming out this way yesterday evening,' she remarked. 'It's not the first time he's been out in this direction. Friend of your husband, I expect?'

'He's a loner, Jack is, millers have to be. No visitors for us. We turn in early, we do. Rise with the lark. Keep the hours of the sun. I'm looking forward to the mystery plays, though. It's going to be a pleasant break, especially if this weather keeps up.'

They finished their transaction over the goose eggs. Hildegard and her boy took their leave.

So where had Baldwin been going to in the evenings? It certainly wasn't here.

As they reached the path back she looked off to where it continued to High Mill. It wasn't much further on. She gave a glance at Kit. 'Feel like walking on, young sir?'

'I do, Sister. It's like paradise to be out of that stinking town, though it's not so bad just now,' he added, 'with them players and all.'

There was a man sitting on the ground outside High Mill. Although the place was derelict, the door, she noticed, was in place and had a bar across it which she had failed to notice when they passed this way before. The roof too, although caved in on one side, still had its wooden shingles on the other. The wheel had been dislodged and must have been removed for its timber since they were last here.

The man wore a leather casque despite the heat and had a broadsword in his belt. That was legal. He was outside the city walls. He must have been posted to guard the solid timber of the mill by its current owner, aware, no doubt, of the need for wood by the strangers camped on the common land. He was whiling away the time by throwing stones into a clay-pot.

One. Two. Three.

The fourth one bounced off the rim and he cursed, emptied the pot and started again.

Kit had come to a stop in the undergrowth just as she had and seemed to understand the need to keep out of sight.

When her eyes got used to the dancing light filtering through the canopy of leaves overhead she noticed again the single causeway to where the man sat, and on one side the lush marsh meadow, rife with kingcups and bulrushes. On the other, the bright green, weed-covered mill-pond. The river gushed and flowed dark and deep farther off. Birdsong filled the glade just now, but the mill itself was silent with a brooding aspect, as if past defeats had tainted the timbers with poison.

Kit tugged at her sleeve. 'I don't like it here. This is where that miller hanged himself in the olden days,' he whispered.

'He did?'

'Nobody comes up here, because of his ghost.'

'Hm,' she replied, 'I'm not sure I believe in the ghost part of your story but it's a sad thing if the miller ended his life like that.'

'Can we go, Sister?'

She put her hand on his shoulder to turn him back the way they had come, when something made her stop. In the mosaic of leaves further off a human face had taken shape. It was in profile, motionless, turned towards the mill. Bright hair was splashed with sunlight making it brighter still.

Gilbert.

He had not seen them. While Kit, unaware of another's presence, melted slowly back along the path with the hounds, Hildegard hesitated. She rubbed her eyes as if not believing what she saw. It was definitely Gilbert. He had gained some courage from somewhere, then. Jealousy was a powerful motivator.

He was watching intently, waiting for something to happen.

She watched too.

Nothing did happen.

She waited for a few minutes but everything remained the same.

The guard continued to throw pebbles into the cup.

The birds sang.

The river rattled over the broken mill-beams.

Chapter Twenty-Six

There was a discussion going on outside the passage on Stonegate when they arrived back. It had attracted a large crowd of onlookers. They formed a circle round the disputants as if readying to watch a fight. More crowds were backed up along the street, unable to get past, and people craned their necks to see what the obstruction was. Caught in the press, Hildegard and her small retinue could only do likewise.

To her consternation she saw that Danby was involved.

Three men in mail shirts under scruffy tunics were opposing him. Danby, however, was not outnumbered. The dispute had attracted a posse of burly-looking angels. They stood shoulder to shoulder with the glazier, their arms folded in a manner that could only he described as truculent.

The spokesman for the three in mail had taken note of them. He was a handsome, rakish sort of knight with an easy manner and shoulder-length dark hair. 'We're visitors, here for the Corpus Christi feast,' he was now heard explaining. 'I apologise most profoundly for the ill-mannered nature of these brutes.' He indicated two muzzled hounds with the kick of a boot. 'I brought them with me for the purpose of sport and for some reason they were excited by the passage into your yard.'

He was clean-shaven except for the hair on his upper lip which was plucked to a thin line and he gave it a swift caress as he finished speaking. When he smiled as he did now he revealed a broken tooth.

Hildegard stared.

'Call the brutes to heel!' he ordered his men.

Plainly in awe of their lord's authority, the men whipped the hounds in at once. Without swords, empty scabbards swinging uselessly at their sides, they fidgeted awkwardly with their hands while they waited for further orders. He nodded to

355

them and they began to carve a path for him through the crowd.

The knight touched his fingers to his forehead and said to Danby, 'My sincere regrets, master.' He moved off after them.

For some reason one of his men peeled off from the others and in a casual fashion began to finger the goods displayed at a nearby stall. When he remained there Hildegard assessed him as a lookout. Meanwhile Danby was saying something to his supporters and a few black looks were sent after the knight. The crowd, disappointed in this mild outcome, dispersed.

Kit pulled on Hildegard's arm. 'Sister! That's them fellas did the hiring yesterday, the ones I told you about,' he whispered excitedly. 'Brought them hounds with him? What a lie! He hired 'em for six pence each.'

Taking Kit by the hand Hildegard followed Danby into the yard and when they caught up with him he turned to Hildegard and demanded, 'Did you see that?'

'I saw the last little bit. What happened?'

'Caught them sauntering around my yard!' he told her, sounding scandalised. '"Bloody cheek!" I said. "This is private property!" Smarmy knave. They were casing the place to see what they could knock off! They'd be after the lead we use for calmes and them tablets of Rhenish glass. It's costly stuff. The bloody thieves. You get all sorts at this time of year.'

Still grumbling, he went inside and before Hildegard had settled the hounds he was out again. 'Lucky I left my pageant sheets behind!'

He waved a sheaf of vellum pieces. 'My mind's on that window for Lord Roger!'

His spirits seemed revived after the shock of Dorelia's disappearance, but watching him go out into the street again, Hildegard wondered whether he was merely putting a brave face on things. Grief can break a man, he had said. He was, it seemed, refusing to give up the final sliver of his self-respect.

Kit took her by the hand, excitement in his voice. 'Gilbert showed me the glass he's painting. Do you want to come and see? It's brilliant!'

Before she could excuse herself, not wishing to be caught prying again, she found herself being pulled into the workshop and through into the inner chamber.

The work had come on a lot since she had last taken a good look at it. The pieces of coloured glass had been cut to shape and laid in place on the drawing underneath and work had started on the details of hair, the texture of the angels' wings, the folds and shading to suggest the drape of fabric, stippling to denote patterned velvet or the diaphanous quality of a silk sleeve. Melisen would complain that the faces were not yet drawn in.

'That white glass is what Gilbert's going to paint the faces on,' Kit told her when she re-marked on this. 'Then it has to go in the kiln to be fired at tremendous heat!'

He was obviously delighted with the whole thing. 'See this little bird here? That's a cuckoo. And this'n? An owl. Gilbert told me a story about owls. He said, "The lady owl is put in a cage and her hooting draws other little birds into the bird-catcher's trap." And look at these red feathers here. That's the archangel's wing coming all the way down one side of the picture to frame it. It brings everybody into its power.'

'Is that what Gilbert told you?'

'Yes. It's good, isn't it?'

'Very good,' agreed Hildegard.

Kit poked at a collection of drawings on a bench along the wall where the instruments of the craft were kept. 'And this is 'is pattern book. I'm surprised he's left it behind. He even takes it to bed with him, he said.'

Hildegard recognised it as the one Gilbert had shown her down by the river the evening they had seen Baldwin heading towards the woods. On a shelf under the bench was another book. Almost before she knew it she had reached for it and flicked it open. She stopped after a page or two.

She was stunned.

Baldwin was right.

Sheet after sheet was covered with drawings of Dorelia. Some were of her face, from every conceivable angle. In others, she was drawn full-length, standing at a door, sitting at a table and, in many, many more, she was lying on a bed, as Roger would have said, 'babe-naked'.

Startled, and about to snap the book shut, she heard a voice exclaim, 'What the bloody hell's going on now?'

Danby came blustering in. He stopped on the threshold. 'Forgive me, Sister. For a minute I thought it was that knight back again, seeing the door wide open. Have I left a page of my–?' Then his glance fell to the pattern book and as she closed it he stepped forward. 'What have you got there?' He peered into her face. 'You look as if you've seen a ghost.'

'Just something I shouldn't have seen.' She tried to put the book back on the shelf but Danby reached for it. She said, 'I'm sorry. I should never have opened it. I did it without thinking.'

Danby was turning the pages with a puzzled frown. When he came to the drawings of his wife in the nude his frown deepened. He looked at every page all the way through to the end without speaking, then carefully pressed the pages together and held it between his hands for a moment.

'I had no idea,' he said in a roughened tone. For one startling moment his eyes filled, then he turned briskly away. 'Thank you, Sister. It's a timely reminder of one of Gilbert's sayings: "truth will out". Now I know what he means by it.'

He left the workshop. His footsteps could be heard going upstairs into his private chamber.

Hildegard took Kit across the yard into Tabitha's, where the widow made a great fuss of him. She kept commenting on his skinny arms and eventually Kit said, 'I'm not a goose to be fattened up for a feast, widow.'

She laughed and said something about him not wanting another of her scones, then, to which he replied he'd rather be a plump goose than a 'skellington'.

Hildegard saw Danby come down and disappear into his back kitchen and a moment later the little scullion emerged looking important and sped off down the passage.

Danby appeared in the doorway and stood gazing across the yard.

She went out to him.

'I've sent the lad with a note to say I'm copping out of rehearsals.' He still had the book in his hands. 'I don't know what to think,' he told her. 'I'm poleaxed.'

He held the book as if he didn't know whether to throw it across the yard or open it again and have another look at the drawings. His eyes watered. 'It's a rare skill. He draws like an angel. How can I blame him – she's a beauty. Anybody with the art would want to capture that. I've got drawings myself – though not so skilled.' His eyes filled again. 'When he comes back in will you come over?'

'Are you sure you want me to?'

He nodded.

While she was waiting she took out the feather she had found in Jankin's sleeping chamber and looked closely at it.

The talk of geese had reminded her of it. The mattress on the bed was made of straw. When she inspected it she saw it could be the breast feather of a goose or a swan. It wasn't a wing feather like the ones used for writing or drawing. There was a brown stain of some sort on several of the fibres. The pageant angels wore wings made of feathers. Some had feathers painted on them, others, the ones with more important roles or in

360

the poulterers' or the wealthier guilds, had wings sewn with hundreds of real feathers. The Glaziers' Guild were going to perform the play called *The Harrowing of Hell.* Jankin was cast as the Archangel Michael.

The feather must be off his costume, she decided. But why had be risked a fine and brought it from the pageant house?

And, more importantly, where was it now?

She would ask Danby when the opportunity arose.

Gilbert trailed back to the yard a couple of hours later. Apparently, after his secret vigil at the mill, he had gone straight to a rehearsal, because he was wearing a haphazard garment of fustian and carrying a wooden stave like a crook. He came straight into the workshop and threw the crook into a corner, then lifted his head, having suddenly noticed Danby standing like a statue by the far door.

He raised his eyebrows as if about to ask his master what was wrong, when his glance fell to the bench and on it, prominently displayed, his own open sketchbook with a picture of Dorelia, naked, lying on what was presumably the marital bed.

He went over and looked at it.

For a long moment he didn't speak. When at last he did he simply said, 'I see.' He looked across at Danby. 'So...' It wasn't a question. It was more like *so there it is* or *that's that, then.*

'Where was I when all this was going on?' Danby asked in a hoarse voice. Hildegard was

361

surprised at how calm he sounded.

'You were off on guild business mostly. You've been busy with planning for the pageant these last few months.'

'I thought I could trust you.' Danby gave him a look of profound disappointment and added, 'I thought I could trust her.'

Gilbert made no reply but turned and went through into the small workshop. Danby followed him and stood in the doorway while the journeyman took a brush from a pot, a few pieces of charcoal and some sheaves of used vellum and put them in a leather bag he unhooked from a peg on the back of the door. He limped over to where his cloak was flung on his mattress in a corner of the workshop and picked it up.

'What are you doing?' Danby asked.

Gilbert straightened. 'You don't need to put it into words.'

'What?' Danby took a step forward.

'It's the end. I don't blame you. Just let's not say anything we'll hear in our minds for the rest of our days.'

'Stop a minute. Where are you going?'

'I'll find somewhere.' Gilbert's head was down and his hair shone like a blazing veil, hiding his face. His fingers were shaking as he fumbled with the strap of his bag.

'Gilbert, stop!'

Danby could still show some authority even though he was a broken man and Gilbert jerked his head up in surprise. His face was stiff with misery but his eyes flickered over his master's face with no sign of submission.

'You think you're just going to walk out?' asked Danby.

'I won't make you say what I don't want to hear. What's the point? I know what you'll say. It'll be what I've said to myself time after time. But it was too good a chance to miss. She's perfect. Her beauty at its height. I had to record that. Soon time will make a mockery of her like it does with all of us. But until then...' He shrugged. 'I had to record it. I can use her looks for the rest of my life.'

Danby was silent. There was a mixture of emotion on his face, none of which Hildegard found easy to name. Rage, certainly. Grief, without any doubt. But there was something else, a kindness of sorts.

When he spoke she knew it was also admiration, the respect of one craftsman for another.

He went over and clamped both hands down hard on Gilberts shoulders and forced him to stop trying to stuff things into his bag. He banged him back hard against the wall and for a moment Hildegard thought he was going to strike him.

'You're going nowhere!' he growled instead. 'I'm master here. I don't give permission for you to go. You work for me. Nothing's changed. If you walk out now you'll be well outside the law. You know that. You won't have a future. They'll hang you. You came to me begging me to save you and you gave me a promise. A year and a day. Well, your time's still to run. I'm not releasing you.'

Gilbert's lips parted in astonishment. 'I betrayed you. There's no two ways about that.'

'I know it. I feel it. God, you don't know how

363

much I feel that. It's a wound that will never heal, you little bastard. But she betrayed me as well. And,' he added, 'she was also betrayed.'

'How so?'

'By her beauty, you fool. It led her along a path she would never willingly have chosen. She has more temptations than most women. I have to forgive her for straying. Isn't that what Our Lady tells us, Sister?' He turned to Hildegard at last, as to a witness.

She came to herself with a start. It was like being spoken to by one of the players on one of the pageant wagons. 'That's what she tells us, yes,' she agreed.

Danby put his arms round Gilbert in a brotherly hug and after standing stiffly for a moment the journeyman rested his forehead on Danby's shoulder and muttered, 'I didn't mean anything against you. You know that, Edric. She broke no vows with me. She simply let me draw her.'

Both men stepped back.

Danby gave a strange sort of laugh, almost a sob. 'I expected to be shouting you out of town, exulting in your pursuit by hand and horn, dragging you before the justices, cheering as they hanged you from the gibbet,' he said. 'That was my first intention. To see you swing!'

Gilbert looked frightened. 'If you want I'll–'

'Go? Never. You stay. My dream is this. Dorelia will think better of her running off and she'll come walking back in here as if nothing's happened. Where else could she better be than in a workshop where her beauty is revered for its true value?'

Hildegard spoke as if from the prompt box at a play. 'We have to find her now. I think Gilbert may have some ideas on that score.'

So Baldwin was wrong, she thought. Gilbert was not a man obsessed by love of a woman he could never have. In fact, it could be said he had her in a way that Baldwin, for all he was in the glazier's trade, would never understand.

Danby decided they would go out to Two Mills Dale later that afternoon to give themselves time to get into position before Baldwin arrived. They could observe the situation and, if necessary, confront him. 'If we surprise him he won't he able to talk his way out of it.' It was evident he was used to his brother's glib tongue.

He was clearly unconvinced that there was anything in Gilbert's suspicions but to set his mind at rest he said he was willing to go along with things and put him to the test. 'He can't have abducted her. Why the hell would he do a thing like that? Is he after a ransom? I've had no note. And to keep her at that old mill? I don't believe it! And what about Jankin?'

He was scathing but there was no other option but to check out the facts. His wife was missing. He had to follow every trail, however slight. They would go to the mill and lie in wait for Baldwin when he put in an appearance before vespers.

'My own brother?' He gave Gilbert a hard glance. 'If this turns out to be a pack of lies I'll not find it so easy to forgive. Once yes, but twice? Never.'

Hildegard suggested taking some supporters. The guard was armed, after all, but Danby shook his head. 'I've made enough of a fool of myself over this. I want to keep it quiet. If I can't take on my own brother, then so be it. But it won't come to that.'

'What about the guard?' Hildegard insisted.

'I'm not helpless,' said Gilbert.

She decided to take her hounds.

Hildegard already knew that waiting for the prioress's letter to arrive would be like waiting for an axe to fall.

And then at last, before they left for the mill, a courier hurried into the yard, confirmed her identity, then thrust a sealed letter into her hands, and she knew this was it. She took the letter straight up to her chamber.

After the usual greetings the prioress came to the point:

By now it will be well known that you possess what some desire. My suggestion is that you do not conceal your whereabouts. When they come for it, as they shall, their identity will be revealed. Inform His Grace at once. He can then do as he thinks fit.

There were a few general wishes of a solicitous nature which cut no ice with Hildegard.

The prioress was instructing her to be a decoy.

When they come for it. And what was she to do when they did? Discuss the matter of the cross with them? Ask for payment? With a sword in her ribs?

366

She gazed in disbelief at the letter and read it twice more.

No word about what she was to tell the canons in Florence, who had entrusted her with the cross, if it fell into the wrong hands again.

No word about what she was to do if confronted by a band of rebels with nothing to lose and everything to gain by wresting it from her possession.

No word about what to do if it was Bolingbroke who had instigated the theft and was now trying to get the cross back in order to bolster his claim to the throne of England. No word if it was the Earl of Douglas or even King Robert of Scotland himself who was after it.

No hint, of course, about a knight in black strolling at large round Danby's yard apparently on the lookout for lead.

The prioress may suspect that it was no parochial theft. That there were people with power involved. But whoever they were they had no qualms about cold-blooded murder. The butchery of the rebel band swam before her eyes.

Placing the letter into the pocket in her sleeve she remained at the window until she saw Danby and Gilbert come out into the yard. There was a suspicious-looking bulge at Danby's side, poorly concealed under his cloak, and Gilbert had a determined mien, though not much else. She couldn't see Danby wielding a sword and Gilbert wouldn't frighten a flea.

Putting her own personal predicament on one side for the time being she went outside to meet them.

Half an hour later the three of them, accompanied by the two hounds, Duchess and Bermonda, were approaching High Mill through the water meadows.

It had been as busy as ever in the town and as they came out of the passage into the street Hildegard had noticed that the henchman belonging to the smiling, broken-toothed knight had gone. Evidently they had decided it wasn't worth burgling the glazier's workshop after all. If, indeed, that had been their intention.

Further down Stonegate the entertainers were doing brisk business and their assistants were taking the hat round with grinning faces. In among them all a familiar figure was rattling through his patter about love potions, but when he noticed Hildegard in the crowd his eyes widened and, taking in the sight of her two companions and the hounds, he broke off and stepped down from his stage with a nod to a bare-chested young man standing by holding a firebrand and what looked like a bottle of water.

Hildegard threw a glance over her shoulder and the mage read it aright, and from then on kept his distance. Behind him the young fire-eater had taken over his pitch and was already spitting flames into the air, to the joy of his audience.

The mage followed all the way to the edge of the woods without being noticed by the two men and now, as they left the heat of the sun and entered the shade, he was still there, slipping along like a fleet shadow behind them.

Danby was getting cold feet already. 'Besides,'

he was saying, 'we don't have any reason to think she's here, do we? Why should she be? We're going to look right sot wits. It'll be some deal he's made. Stored goods, exempt from tax. Always been a bit of a rogue, my brother. I'd be the first to admit it.'

Gilbert said he wasn't sure whether he hoped she was there or hoped she wasn't. As for Jankin, where was he, poor devil? Nobody seemed to give a damn what had happened to him.

Danby shot a sidelong glance when they came to a halt to get their bearings in the confusing pathways of the thicket and said, 'Don't think I'm not worried about Jankin. Of course I am. But he's not my wife. It's a different thing altogether. And if he's been taking advantage he deserves all he gets.'

Gilbert said nothing.

'Do we have a plan?' asked Hildegard.

'Yes,' replied Danby. 'We lie low until Baldwin appears. When he's gone inside we enter and demand to know what the hell's going on. Then, when he's defended himself with an explanation we should have thought of ourselves, we all shake hands, hope he doesn't bear a grudge, and go home.'

He reminded Hildegard of Roger de Hutton. Except for Roger's immense wealth they had a similar straightforward, some would say naive, belief in human nature and their own power to dictate matters.

They emerged at the edge of the clearing with the mill in front of them and, well concealed, settled down to wait.

Somewhere in the thicket of hawthorns and flowering ash the mage was watching too. When a cuckoo started up close by it seemed to Hildegard to go on past all belief. The others, however, were intent on the mill and clearly thought nothing of it.

By the time the shadows had lengthened somewhat, casting the clearing into deeper gloom, it began to seem that, maybe, they were going to be disappointed, and Baldwin was not going to show up after all. The guard was still sitting outside, however, and both she and Gilbert had to dissuade Danby from bursting forth, hailing him and demanding to know his business.

Time passed. The scene looked particularly desolate when they knew that outside the dark focus of their attention it was another hot afternoon, the meadow awash with families gathering for the festival, children still playing in the river to their hearts' content, excitement at the impending pageant palpable.

Hildegard contemplated the nature of the miller's feelings when he lost his livelihood. The location must have added to his despair. The thickness of the trees kept out the sun. Even the hidden nature of the place, with the steep bank on the opposite side covered in rotting, moss-covered trees crumbling into the dark flow of the waters, must have been confirmation of the futility of hope.

Another bird, one Hildegard could not identify, started up a rapid warning note. It was enough to make her freeze. 'I think someone's coming,' she whispered.

The two men peered through the leaves onto the path. Sure enough, with no attempt to conceal his presence, Baldwin emerged from out of the bright greenery and came swaggering purposefully towards the mill. Danby seemed to hold his breath.

They watched in silence as he crossed the causeway. His henchman rose stiffly to his feet.

Baldwin's voice floated loudly across the clearing. 'All quiet?'

'Not a murmur.'

'Gisburne's coming up later.' Baldwin strode over to the door, heaved up the wooden bar, and went inside.

The three watchers hesitated for a moment.

Danby's face was white. Then he muttered, 'Let's go and find out what the devil's up to.'

He moved stealthily out of the thicket and began to make his way across the clearing. He was halfway over the causeway when the guard happened to glance up and catch sight of him. He stepped forward and drew his sword. Then, changing his mind, he turned back towards the mill.

Danby was surprisingly quick. He was across the causeway and had hurled himself onto the man's back in a flash. He was a heavy weight and had the element of surprise. There was a brief struggle. Danby got his hand clamped over the man's mouth to stop him shouting a warning and with his supple craftsman's fingers managed to claw the guard's hood over his face, half suffocating him. Then with a boot in his back he jerked him off the causeway right into the swamp on one side. Dusting his hands he marched up to the door of the mill.

'Come on,' said Hildegard. With the hounds on a tight leash she ran with them towards the causeway. The guard was floundering about, up to his waist in sticky slime, his face covered in it, while he tried to keep his footing.

A word to Bermonda made the kennet crouch on the edge of the path with a threatening growl, teeth showing, claws stretched as a warning not to climb out.

By now Danby was inside the mill. Hildegard ran to the door. Gilbert came limping up behind her. 'Are they here?' he demanded.

There was a shout from inside. Two struggling figures came rolling down a short wooden staircase and landed in a heaving mass of flying fists. First Danby was on top, banging his brother's head against the wooden floor, then Baldwin was uppermost doing likewise.

Gilbert limped forward and there was a flash of silver. Hildegard saw him wave a narrow blade near Baldwin's face. 'Tell me where they are, you bastard, or I'll use this.'

Danby knelt over his brother, pinning him to the floor. 'Is she upstairs?'

'I don't know who you mean,' snarled Baldwin.

'Let me slit his throat if he's not going to tell us.' Gilbert gripped Baldwin by the hair, yanking his head back to expose his throat. A vein pulsed in his neck.

Danby stayed his hand. 'Keep him here. I'm going up.'

Hildegard loosened Duchess's chain. The lymer knew from long practice what to do. She loped over and opened her muzzle, allowing it to close around Baldwin's throat to keep him still.

Gilbert sat back on one heel with his lame leg twisted to one side but his stiletto still firmly grasped in one hand. He glanced up. A figure had appeared in the doorway.

'Is it to do with Dorelia?' It was the mage.

'Danby's gone up to look for her,' Hildegard said.

The mage climbed the stairs two at a time on his long legs.

'What's he doing here?' asked Gilbert.

'He knew Dorelia in Wakefield before she fell into Baldwin's clutches.'

There was noise from upstairs. A whimpering sound followed. They could hear the two men softly murmuring. Then a cloud of feathers came billowing down from the floor above.

The mage emerged, covered in feathers and walking slowly backwards down the steps to guide someone descending. The hem of a sheet came into view. It was blood-stained, torn, with other stains on it. Then a bare foot appeared, feeling shakily for the treads of the stairs, one step at a time.

Eventually she stood before them. Dorelia.

Danby had followed step by step, scarcely touching her, as if she was too fragile for human contact.

She swayed on the point of collapse with the sheet held closely about her. Still beautiful, her face was paste-white, her eyes dark with pain, and her hair fell in tangled tresses to her waist. She had bruises on her mouth and neck and now put out a hand as if she could not see. She took a step forward and stumbled.

The mage put an arm round her waist. 'Dorelia. It's me. John of Berwick. Your uncle's friend.'

She put out a hand and her fingers searched for something they might recognise. 'Berwick? How can it be? Is it really you?'

He took her hand and kissed the palm. 'You're safe now, precious girl. Here's your husband. We're all here. All friends. We've come to take you home.'

'I tried to run away. I went into the woods... I got as far as the meadows and saw your little daughter, Edric, but she was frightened and daren't help me... Then Baldwin caught me. He ... he brought me back.'

Gilbert struggled to his feet. He still held the knife. 'Where's Jankin?'

At his name Dorelia gave a cry and put her hands to her face and began to sob hysterically.

Gilbert took a painful step forward. 'Ask her where he is!'

They had no need. She answered his question herself, pointing with a shaking hand towards the door.

'He's out there!' she cried.

Chapter Twenty-Seven

Supported by her husband and the mage, Dorelia took faltering steps towards the threshold. Before going into the open she hesitated. Both hands went to her eyes. 'The light,' she whispered. 'I can't see! They kept me in the dark–' She began to sob.

'Where is he?' Danby asked gently. He glanced round the clearing as if looking for a mound of freshly dug earth.

'They tied him to the mill wheel.' Dorelia started to tremble. 'He was still alive. They put his angel wings on him and found a way to turn the wheel. They made me watch. They tied my arms behind my back and made me watch. Oh, Edric...'

Leaning heavily on the two men and shaking uncontrollably, she allowed them to help her down onto the causeway and there came to a halt. She pointed towards the millpond.

It was a bright green expanse covered with duckweed. It looked as solid as a clipped lawn. Gilbert got a stick from somewhere and reaching out parted the carpet of weed. They all came to the edge and looked down.

There, under the surface, was an angel, feathered wings drifting in the eddies, the tendrils of bright hair furling and unfurling, skin an unearthly greenish gold stippled with shadows. His eyes were open.

The vision rose towards the light then sank again, finally disappearing from sight as the weed drifted back.

Gilbert stood up and let the stick fall from his grasp.

Nobody spoke.

Danby held Dorelia in his arms. The mage looked solemn. No one crossed themselves. In the woodland on the other side of the water, nature continued as joyful as in another country.

Hildegard went back inside the mill.

There were all kinds of broken things scattered around. Shards of pottery. A broken millstone. Pieces of wood, their purpose long forgotten. What she was looking for was some rope and after a moment she found some. She went over to Baldwin who was lying in fear of his life under the focused attention of the staghound. As she was beginning to truss his arms, Gilbert came in. He bent down to help her. Neither of them exchanged a word.

Eventually when they were satisfied Baldwin could do no more harm they went outside. Danby said to them, 'We're trying to work out how to get her home. She can't walk all that way.'

'Maybe the miller at Low Mill has a cart he can lend us?' Hildegard eyed the man trapped in the swamp. 'And what about him?'

'Needs his throat cutting,' said Danby. 'He knew all along what they were doing to her.'

'Leave that for the justices,' advised the mage. 'You don't want to bring more trouble on yourself. Dorelia's going to need you.' He looked grim. 'I'll

376

go back to the other mill and see what I can organise.' He strode off through the trees.

Hildegard and Gilbert sat down on the steps after they'd put the bar across the door just in case Baldwin found a way to untie his bonds. The other man they had trussed up in old rope and returned to the swamp.

Gilbert shook his hair out of its tie and let it fall over his face. Above them, in the oval formed by the tops of the trees, the sky was an ever deepening shade of blue. A shaft of light penetrated the clearing between the boles of two oaks. It lasted only moments and then faded. The sun was going down.

At last Gilbert said in a muffled voice, 'He was a bloody useless glazier. And he couldn't act. Four lines he had to learn and he couldn't even get them into his thick skull.'

The sound of people in the woods from the direction of Low Mill alerted them. Hildegard stood up. Danby said, 'At last. Now we'll get her home where she belongs.' He stepped forward.

Several men entered the clearing. It was still light enough to see that they had no cart with them. One of them came towards the causeway. It was Gisburne.

For a moment Danby stared at him. Then without a further thought he walked across, drawing his sword, but before he could use it Gisburne's two henchmen pounced. They grabbed Danby by both arms. His sword fell into the grass.

Gilbert made a move but Hildegard put a hand on his arm. 'They'll strike you down. We'll think of something else.'

Gisburne was laughing quietly and began to circle Danby. He looked mystified, however, and kept glancing at the mill. From the swamp Baldwin's man gave a shout. 'Get me out of here, Gisburne. I'm drowning in this stinking mud.'

Gisburne gave him a brief glance. 'Learn to swim, then.' He turned back to Danby. 'Come to fetch her home, have you? Where's Baldwin?'

'You'll pay for this a thousand times over,' gritted Danby. 'Kill me. I don't care. But let her go. And the others. Only whatever you do, you'll rot in hell. And that's a fact.'

'A fact, is it? Well, you'll see how much I care when I slit your throat. But mebbe we'll have a bit of fun first, eh, lads? What do you say?'

One of his men heard it as an invitation to give Danby a punch in the ribs. Dorelia reached out as if to put a stop to it, then slid slowly to the ground. Hildegard bent over her. The girl had fainted.

Gisburne took out a lethal-looking knife from his belt and waved it in front of Danby's face. 'The eyes? No, not yet. I want you to see what comes next. The ears?' He grabbed one and twisted it. 'No, I don't think so. You'll want to hear her screams. What about this?' He held Danby by the balls and squeezed. Danby gave an involuntary gasp but refused Gisburne the gratification of hearing him howl.

'I'm going to enjoy this,' Gisburne put his face up to Danby's. 'You and that White Hart scum deserve all that's coming to you.'

'Were you behind that ambush out at the

coast?' Danby managed to gasp.

'Not I, said the fly!' Gisburne roared with laughter. 'Somebody bigger than me. You sot-witted fool. Do you think you can take on a duke and all his army?'

'Gaunt?'

'You'll all be singing another tune before long. God save the King! Which king? Not bloody Richard, for sure!' He walked about brandishing his knife in front of Danby's face. 'You and de Quixlay. Mayor? Him? I wouldn't wipe his arse! He might have got his shopkeepers and his tame guildsmen to run me out of town, but I'll be back! You can count on it, Danby! The only thing is, you won't be there to see it!'

'Won't he?'

Everybody turned at an unexpected voice from the trees. Striding across the clearing, his mail shirt glinting in the fast-fading light, was Ulf followed closely by a band of armed men. 'Drop that knife, Gisburne!'

From all around the grove men appeared in the livery of Roger de Hutton. Gisburne took one look, then backed off. Danby shook off the slackened grip of his captors and hurried over to Dorelia to cradle her in his arms.

Gisburne started to run but had gone no more than three paces when he was brought down in a tackle by one of the Hutton men and they landed in a noisy skirmish of metalware. Gisburne was held flat on his back with a knife at his own throat. It was clear the game was over.

Hildegard walked across the causeway to the other side as in a dream. 'How did you manage

379

such good timing?' she asked Ulf.

He adopted a long-suffering expression. 'This morning you told me you'd come straight back and tell me what you found here. You said you would come up to tell me. When you didn't show, what was I to think? You always do what you say you'll do.'

She put a hand to her mouth. 'I completely forgot.'

He looked at her in astonishment. 'You never forget anything.'

When Hildegard and Gilbert came back later that night after giving their deposition to the bailiff and his serjeant-at-arms, Brother Thomas was lurking at the entrance to the yard. Danby had arrived before them and gone straight into the house with Dorelia. An apothecary had been sent for. The mage, having reached the mill with a cart, later, for reasons best known to himself, disappeared as soon as the law arrived.

The serjeant-at-arms had been a different one to the man who had questioned Hildegard about the firing of the booths, but he insisted in going over all the ins and outs of the accusation several times before he was satisfied that he had an accurate account. Ulf and his men had been requested to stand guard over the prisoners and it looked as if they were going to be in for a long night. The jail was full of riff-raff drawn to the city for Corpus Christi day, said the constable in charge, and the problem was where to put the accused so they wouldn't abscond. Hildegard and Gilbert had left when it was clear they could be of no further use.

Thomas looked relieved to see them both. He stepped from the passage with a whispered, 'There you are! I'd no sooner got to Meaux than they sent me back here again. I don't know where I am. Something's up, isn't it?' He scanned Hildegard's expression. 'What's going on, Sister?'

She told him about events at the mill. He looked shocked.

'It's difficult to take in. Such cruelty.' Averting his face, he walked off a few paces and then, having recovered himself, turned back.

'I saw them return to the house.' He frowned. 'Dorelia seemed in a bad way. She was lying on a litter. I wondered what was wrong. But it wasn't because of that I was told to come back.'

'No?' She glanced swiftly at Gilbert. He was listening with interest.

Thomas intercepted her glance. He bit his lip. 'It's just something to do with Brother Alcuin,' he said weakly with another glance at Gilbert. 'He came flying out of his chambers saying, "I've got instructions from the prioress at Swyne that you're to go back to York at once to attend Sister Hildegard." Then he muttered something about women and stormed off. I think the job of trying to fill Abbot de Courcy's shoes is getting too much for him. So here I am.' He didn't meet her eye. 'For what use I am,' he added in a mutter.

'Thomas,' she took him by the elbow, 'you are some use and most welcome. It wasn't your fault things went wrong at the rebels' camp.' Gilbert was still listening. 'Are you staying at the friary again?'

381

He grimaced. 'Back with the Franciscans, being enticed into endless dicing, yes.'

'I hope you win. We can't have a bunch of mendicants running rings round us, can we?'

Her remark brought a tentative smile to his face. 'I do win often,' he admitted. 'My belief must be stronger than theirs.'

Gilbert went into the house.

When she was sure he was out of earshot Hildegard said, 'There is something, Thomas. It's probably the reason they sent you back to me. I had the most extraordinary letter from Swyne. The prioress wants me to act as a decoy for the men behind the theft of the cross.'

'Decoy?'

She nodded.

'But I don't understand. It was the White Hart rebels who stole it. Does she expect them to enter the city to re-steal it?'

'They stole it – but who gave them the information?'

'It was a set-up as we surmised?'

'We'll have to wait and see – but that's the drift of her thoughts on the matter.'

He rubbed his forehead. 'Thus the trail will lead back to the originator of the theft?' He gave a faint smile. 'And I've been sent ... to protect you from him?' He gave a rueful smile. 'Let's hope I can make a better showing next time. But what are we going to do?'

Hildegard was still awake when, a couple of hours later, there was the sound of armed men stealthily entering the yard. With a groan she dragged herself to the window.

By the light of several flickering cressets she was surprised to see Ulf, accompanied by a dozen men, leading Baldwin of all people towards his house at the far end. At least the man was a prisoner and in chains. It was the sound of their rattling on the flagstones that was making the most noise.

She watched as he was hustled inside his own cottage by an armed posse. The door slammed shut.

As he left, Ulf glanced up at her window. She leant out. 'That was never Baldwin?' she called down, still not quite believing her eyes.

'It was. The jail's overflowing. He's under house arrest. He won't get far with those irons on his arms and legs and my men in charge. He'll stay here until after the feast, when they'll empty the jails again and put him where he belongs.'

'Is Mistress Julitta in there?'

Ulf raised his eyebrows. 'Is she! I'll say! Baldwin seems to fear her more than the prospect of hanging.' He gave a salute. 'I'll see you tomorrow at Harpham's?'

Hildegard was still yawning when Brother Thomas returned next morning as they had arranged. She offered him a drink. 'I did finally get off to sleep but it feels like only five minutes ago,' she explained, yawning again.

'What's your plan?'

They hadn't got far the previous night.

'Any ideas yourself?'

'Apart from walking you around the town with

383

the cross on display to lure them out into the open, none.'

'Let's go outside. It's another stifling day. What time is it?'

'Near on tierce.'

'And it's hot already. It's going to be hellish later on. Are the streets busy?'

'Thronged with early risers. People still drinking from the night before or sleeping in gutters. The peddlers and entertainers out in force.'

'The drunks are probably what Roger's mason Master Schockwynde refers to as "the Saxon element".' She smiled. 'But he always adds, "What would we do without them?" Of course, I'm partly Saxon myself, so I try to defend them. They do drink a lot, don't they?'

'I thought you were Norse?'

'That as well.'

'That must be where you get your hair colour.'

'I'm sorry. I haven't managed to keep it covered. Does it offend you?'

'Not at all. It's most striking. Especially with that coloured headscarf. It's the colour of sunlight.'

They went outside to sit on Tabitha's bench. The widow was over at Danby's. The murmur and fall of voices came from an upper chamber.

Hildegard stretched out her legs and gave a long sigh. Then something caught her eye and she jerked upright. 'What on earth's that?'

Thomas followed her glance. 'It's a hat,' he said.

'Yes, but–' She got up and went over to the well. On the parapet was a straw hat. She picked it up. After staring at it she said slowly, 'This is the hat I lost when that go-between whipped my pony so unexpectedly as we set off for the camp.'

'Is it?'

'Did you find it?' She came back with it and sat down, turning it between her fingers. It was more battered than when she had last worn it.

'Not me,' said Thomas. 'But I saw it fall. Then some servant dashed forward and picked it up. He handed it to his master, I didn't think it worth getting into an argument over. My only thought at that moment was to get back here, tell Danby what had happened and find out if he knew where they were taking you.'

She picked at the straw with a thoughtful expression. 'What livery did the finder wear?'

'I didn't notice.'

'And his master?'

'Some visiting knight by the look of him. Astride a rather fine-looking horse.'

'And I suppose you wouldn't have noticed whether they followed you back here or not?'

He paled.

Hildegard dropped the hat onto the ground. 'They've found me.'

Chapter Twenty-Eight

'What I don't understand,' said Thomas after he had got over a spell of calling himself all the names Hildegard had assumed he had never heard before, 'is who they are. Clearly they're not rebels, coming and going through the town gates. And why follow me rather than you and the rebel fellow on the pony?' He frowned. 'Why leave the hat here as a sign? Is it a warning? And, what's more, if they're really after the cross, where do they imagine it is?' He gave her a sharp glance. 'It is safe, I assume?'

She nodded. 'Utterly.'

'They've got some cheek entering the yard,' muttered Thomas. 'The whole thing's sneaky.'

Not only that, she thought with a shiver, they had entered the yard that very morning while she slept and nobody seemed to have noticed. For sure Danby would have been up in arms if he had caught sight of more strangers violating his private sanctum. His noise would have woken her up at once. She rose to her feet. 'Let's go and show ourselves in the town and lure them further into the open.'

Duchess and Bermonda were ever ready. Hildegard poked her head into Danby's kitchen and told Kit she was taking the hounds out herself and for him to stay where she knew she could find him. He looked disappointed at not being invited to accompany her but accepted the decision with goodwill. After a word with Danby about Dorelia they left him and Tabitha to their ministrations.

When they reached the end of the passage leading onto Stonegate they were met by a wall of pedestrians shuffling along towards the market square. Nobody would see them in all this mass of people. It was probably a ridiculous plan.

'I thought that knight having the argument with Master Danby was Norman,' Hildegard began, thoughtfully. 'He was arrogant enough underneath his smiling manners. It's a pity you didn't see him. You might have recognised him. I wonder if he's involved in some way? But if so, who is he?'

'What was he like?' asked Thomas.

'Smooth-talking, long dark hair, a thin moustache scarcely visible, a broken front tooth.'

'The fellow I saw wore a casque. I didn't notice his face.'

Still thinking about the knight who had been somewhat discomfited by Danby's angelic guard, she said, 'At the time I thought he didn't look like your usual sneak-thief. Too well set up. There was something else about him as well – I can't put my finger on it. I suggest,' she continued, 'that we walk up towards Micklegate and present ourselves to Roger and Melisen. If there's a fellow magnate of any note in town they're bound to know who he is.'

As well as a miscellany of jugglers, fire-eaters, minstrels, fortune-tellers, acrobats, and a man with a marmoset, who expected payment for a peep at the creature hidden inside his sack, there were preachers of all persuasions selling their beliefs, or sometimes offering them for free. With the crowd so tight around them there was no choice but to move at the same snail's pace. It gave them an opportunity to hear a good part of what was being declaimed. Two preachers in particular had set up within speaking distance of each other and their opposing views drew the crowd into rivalry.

Hildegard recognised the one in the russet gown. She had heard him a few days earlier, before she had met his similar, Will Thorpe. He was saying much the same thing about the Eucharist as before. It was topical on this day of all days and the crowd was standing six-deep around him.

'How is it that the body of Christ can reside in a piece of bread?' he was asking. 'Does that make sense to you? But this is what we're told when the priest lifts the host and mumbles his pig Latin. I've even heard people admonish others for throwing away a scrap of wastel, on the grounds that they are throwing away Christ's body! What nonsense is this? Do they believe Christ can be discarded? If so, where does he go? Similarly, if a mouse eats a crumb of consecrated wafer, is the mouse, then, having partaken of Christ's flesh, as holy as Christ himself? Should we worship mice? This is a view to which we have not yet been coerced by our Holy Father sitting on his golden throne in Rome! But friends, give him time!'

There was laughter.

'Surely, dear brothers and sisters,' he continued, 'if Christ is in all things, the Host is no different from any other piece of bread. We can throw it away willy-nilly...'

There were murmurs of agreement from those who had not grasped his argument. He looked askance before giving an engaging smile. He held up a hand. 'Good friends – those who understand – we do not have to believe in magic as the authorities insist. Instead we can live out our days in truth and simplicity, trusting in the evidence of our own common sense, safe in the knowledge that Christ is an idea – a symbol of all that is true and good and most optimistic in human nature – and on those grounds only, worthy of our interest. Truth, goodness, now, in this moment – the bread only a symbol to remind us of true brotherhood, and the wine likewise. And who needs a priest to tell us that? Dear friends, this is all we need to know, the beginning and the end, amen.'

Before he could continue, from across the street came the Dominican view. In thundering tones one of the mendicant friars was exhorting the crowd not to listen to the heretic opposite for fear of hellfire.

'Come the Day of Judgement – which we shall shortly see enacted by the pageant players – every one of us will stand naked before God. Our faults will be weighed in the balance and those found wanting will be cast into the eternal flames of damnation to burn in the most excruciating agony throughout the rest of time. Repent, repent, oh sinners! The Last Days are upon us! The

Antichrist stalks the earth! The Apocalypse is nigh!'

At the sound of objections he leant forward and demanded, 'Why the Black Death? Why the floods last year? Why the earthquake at Wycliffe's trial? Why this infernal heat like the fires of hell itself? Think on it, sinners – heed the signs and heed the portents!'

'And so forth,' said Hildegard turning to Thomas as they were carried out of earshot in the stream of people passing by. 'You've read St Bernard?'

He nodded. 'I've also read that the murder of heretics is like the killing of birds. A necessity.'

'Can you see us in England taking his words literally as they do across the water?'

'I fervently hope not.'

'The Saxons are our saving grace, perhaps? They'll laugh the idea into oblivion.'

'Or get their fists out...' he looked back at the russet-robed preacher '...after enjoying the argument for its own sake, perhaps.' He gave a half smile. 'Even so, no one should lose his life for taking up an opposing view to the one that happens to prevail. Our understanding of the truth is too shifting for that.'

They had reached the end of the line of entertainers and now Hildegard gave him a puzzled frown. 'I see no sign of Theophilus today, or John of Berwick as he calls himself. I'm surprised he's letting a chance to add to his fortune slip by.'

'I see no sign of our friends with a penchant for returning lost hats either.'

'Let's try to force a path to Harpham's, then.'

Thomas needed no encouragement. Making full use of his height and presence he carved a way for Hildegard through the crowd, and she was surprised to discover that people were impressed enough to get out of his way as well as they could.

The house of Robert Harpham was a substantial residence as befitted the dwelling of a wealthy merchant. It had three floors, the middle one with a wooden balcony, open like a loggia on two sides overlooking the courtyard.

It reminded Hildegard of the house of the Florentine merchant Ser Vitelli where she stayed when she went to bring Constantine's Cross back from Tuscany.

A number of well-tended horses were at present being led into the stables on the third side of the building. A wooden stage had been erected and the cobbles round it strewn with rushes. A servant was following behind the horses, shovelling up manure, and a second one followed, throwing down sheaves of fresh rushes as he went.

From a balcony draped with embroidered hangings Lady Melisen was looking down on this scene. She was wearing a garland in imitation of wild flowers. In fact it was a masterpiece of the goldsmith's art. Even from a distance it could be seen that it was made of filigree silver and gold twining like vines, with precious stones to simulate flowers. It twinkled as she leant out of the shade into a shaft of sunlight. A pretty young girl attended her. She too was crowned but this time the flowers were real.

Hildegard had to look twice before she realised the girl was Petronilla. Suddenly catching sight of the nun she leant excitedly over the edge and fluttered a scarf in greeting. 'Come up, Sister. We'll have the best view of the players from here.' Melisen beckoned.

Accompanied by Brother Thomas, Hildegard made her way up a flight of stone stairs off the yard and was ushered along a wooden corridor into the loggia by a servant. Roger was nowhere to be seen but Melisen and a handful of guests were already seated.

'The players are going to give us a special performance,' she told them when they appeared.

'I'm to be their queen!' Petronilla broke in delightedly.

'I've told you about that,' Melisen reproved her.

She waited until Petronilla got to her feet to make a deep curtsy of apology. 'I beg the honour of being forgiven for being too forward and speaking out of turn, My Lady.' She bent her head.

Melisen's lips tilted in amusement before she straightened her expression as the girl rose. She told her she might go down now and assume her queenly duties. When she ran off Melisen turned to Hildegard. 'I fear you may lose her,' she said. 'The allure of becoming a nun has somewhat faded in recent days.'

'I doubt the prospect was alluring at any time,' agreed Hildegard. 'It seemed to me she was choosing the lesser of two evils. But what about Maud? Is she being crowned as well?'

'She refuses to put off that ridiculous hood,'

Melisen told her. 'I've tried every ploy in the book. It's as if she's afraid of being seen to be pretty.'

Thomas, who had heard Maud's confession and probably knew more about her than anyone else, said, 'It's a fear of God's judgement. Give her time. If what she told me is true she may go on wearing it for some time yet.'

Melisen looked at him as if hoping to prise forth a secret but his expression was enigmatic.

'We were hoping to ask Roger what he knows about any noble visitors to the city,' Hildegard began.

'He'll be along soon. It's no good asking me. I know hardly anyone in York.' Melisen came from Kent and since her wedding to Roger and the birth of her baby rarely left Castle Hutton.

'These players, then? Tell us about those,' Hildegard invited, to pass the time.

Melisen went on to explain that the travelling players who were commissioned to take the leading roles in the pageant also had a play of their own which they liked to put on whenever they had the chance. 'It's some nonsense about the Green Knight, but they're a droll lot and there are some good musicians among them, so it should be worth watching. They'll be along soon. We're still waiting for some guests to arrive.'

Wondering if they were about to behold Gaunt's son once more, Hildegard gave Thomas a look. The place, though grand in its way and decorated with great style, presumably at Melisen's request, was hardly sumptuous enough for someone like Bolingbroke, the Earl of Derby.

Presumably the horses that were being taken to the stables belonged to the guest, however, and it was obvious they wore no royal caparison.

Maud appeared. She gave a startled glance when she saw Brother Thomas but smiled shyly when he gave her a friendly greeting, then she slipped onto the bench between him and Hildegard. She gripped the nun by the hand. Hildegard said, 'I am glad to see you, Maud. I hope you're happy here. Are you looking forward to the play?'

Maud nodded with her hood half obscuring her face as usual. She sat close, as if glad to see Hildegard, but remained as silent as ever, only getting up to offer a dish of sweetmeats when the servants started handing them out.

The arrival of more visitors to the loggia was drowned out by the racket of the players processing into the yard escorted by a group of musicians.

Maud leant over the edge of the balustrade to watch. Her small face held an unexpected look of wonder as the actors burst from behind a curtain onto the wooden platform erected directly below them.

A tabor struck up a loud jig and, gaudily dressed in cap and bells, two actors began a long, declamatory and mostly ribald account of what was to follow.

Wine was brought in to the guests and an aquamanile appeared for the washing of the noble hands. An exotic Eastern scent wafted from a brass burner nearby. Hildegard settled back to enjoy the show with the feeling that at last here was a moment's respite from the terrible events of the previous days.

Maud was engrossed in the performance. It was probably the first time she had ever seen a play. When the acrobats came in she clapped her hands like any child. The fire-eater brought a gasp of astonishment as flames plumed from his mouth into the air.

She turned excitedly to Hildegard, for a second all signs of woe leaving her face, then, as Hildegard smiled back she saw the child's face blanch. Her eyes dilated in what looked like horror.

Hildegard's lips parted, about to ask her what on earth was the matter, but before she could frame the words Maud sprang to her feet, pulled her hood over her face and fled from the loggia by a side door.

Hildegard rose to her feet.

Lord Roger had appeared and was inviting three guests onto the balcony. Hildegard gasped. Thomas noticed something amiss because by the time she got outside he was right behind her.

'It's Maud!' she told him. 'Those visitors have sent her out of her wits with fear!'

By now the girl was at the top of the steps to the yard. 'Maud! Stop!' she shouted. But the frightened child took to her heels.

With Thomas following, Hildegard descended two at a time, but by the time they reached the bottom Maud was haring across the yard towards the street. 'Stop!' she shouted again. But the girl ran on.

Chapter Twenty-Nine

It was easier for a girl driven by desperation to squeeze her way through the crowd than for two adults who had been taken by surprise to do so. They could see the brown hood weaving all the way down to the bottom of Micklegate, but when they crossed the bridge into the town centre and the street split three ways they lost her. They were both out of breath.

'She seemed to turn into Conyngsgate,' said Thomas, peering over the heads of the crowd.

'What's down there?'

'Victualling stalls?'

'What's the only place she's likely to know in the whole of York?'

'The minster?'

'Exactly. She must be trying to make for that.'

'You go straight there. I'll go round the other way just in case she's gone by another route.'

They split up.

Hildegard tore along through the crowd, eyes peeled in case Maud had stopped elsewhere, but she arrived in the minster yard without seeing her.

There was a massive crowd round the open door, craning their necks at a notice fixed to it. No doubt they were hoping to get inside to view the Host, she thought. Early tomorrow it would be taken in procession round the town under a gold-stitched canopy with the archbishop in attendance. She started to push her way through, ignoring the shouts that followed in her wake.

Inside it was just as crowded. A choir sang somewhere and the shuffling of soft leather-soled footwear set up an echoing susurration that sounded like an invisible army on the move. Remembering where she had taken the girls when they had visited before, she hastened into the north transept.

There was no sign of a girl in a brown cloak. In the present weather such a heavy garment would have stood out.

At a loss to know what to do next she made another circuit, still hoping that she had simply missed her behind one of the massive stone pillars, but again she drew a blank. The silvery expanse of Gilbert's favourite window, the grisaille of the Five Sisters, let in a lustrous north light but it revealed no runaway.

Their guess as to her destination must have been wrong, then.

Hurrying towards the queue outside the sanctuary, Hildegard happened to notice some sightseers pointing up towards one of the galleries that ran around the minster walls underneath the great window. To her astonishment a small figure had appeared high up, moving like a sleepwalker between the stone buttresses. On this narrow ledge round the circumference of the church it was a familiar figure.

It was Maud.

Hildegard watched in horror as the child stared down with a fixed expression into the nave. She seemed to be mesmerised by the distance to the ground.

Without a moment's hesitation Hildegard ran into the nearby tower entrance and raced up the spiral stairs until she came out onto the ledge herself. She glanced down once and then averted her gaze. It was a long way to the ground.

Fearing that if she made any sudden movement the girl would jump she began to edge between the long drop and the wall on the other side. Close up to the windows the light streamed in with an overpowering glare. Feeling dizzy she stopped for a moment to regain her balance.

Maud was sitting down now with her legs dangling over the edge. People below had noticed her and a crowd was gathering. Everybody was gazing up in horrified suspense. Hildegard inched closer. When she was a couple of feet away she called softly, 'Maud, I've come to join you.'

Maud's head turned in surprise. Her hood fell back revealing an abundant tangle of red curls. Her expression was one of dazed horror. Hildegard shuffled closer.

'You gave Brother Thomas a shock. He'd hardly had chance to greet you before you ran away.'

'Has he been telling you things?' Maud demanded with a catch in her throat.

'Not about you, if that's what you mean. He keeps his word and I'm sure he told you he would tell nobody what you confessed to him. Is that right?'

Maud said it was. She gave a quick glance at the floor far below. The individual tiles were indistinguishable from this height but the lozenge-shaped pattern was clearer. Maud was staring at it again as if entranced.

Hildegard edged a little closer. 'I was wondering what it was that made you run off when you were enjoying the jongleurs so much.'

Maud was silent.

'Was it one of the guests who arrived as the play was starting?'

Maud said nothing.

'I think it's probably me they're looking for – or at least I have something in my possession they want.'

'No!' After that one cry Maud gripped the edge of the parapet and gazed fixedly at the floor many feet below.

Hildegard edged closer. She was still not close enough to catch hold of her if she made a sudden move and if Maud struggled they would both go pitching over the edge to their deaths. She said as reassuringly as she could, 'You seemed frightened of them. Did you think you knew them?'

Maud put up a hand in a mechanical fashion to her face. 'Do you believe in ghosts, Sister?' She turned her head to look into Hildegard's face.

She shook her head. 'Not at all. They're something we invent to explain what we don't understand.'

'I thought I'd seen a ghost. But he was real, wasn't he?'

'Dear Maud, who is it who's given you such a fright?'

'Who do you think?' Maud's face was white.

Roger's guest had been none other than the knight who had been sauntering round Danby's yard. He was clearly after the cross. He could have nothing to do with Maud.

Her thoughts in confusion, Hildegard edged closer. 'Tell me–' she coaxed.

'Nobody will believe me,' Maud mumbled. 'He's a great lord. You could see that for yourself. They'll believe him, not me. They'll call me a liar. They'll say I'm a witch. They'll hang me.' Her knuckles were white as she gripped the edge of the parapet with more force.

'I'm not going to call you a liar. Nor is Brother Thomas. And nobody is going to hang you.'

Maud put both hands over her face and for a moment Hildegard thought she was going to allow herself to slip over the edge. Instead she muttered, 'I thought he was dead!'

'Was he the same man who killed your little brother?' she asked softly.

Maud gave a moan and then Hildegard moved fast, stretching out with both hands to grab the back of her gown, dragging her so that they fell back against the wall, and Hildegard did not dare release her grip but hung on as tightly as she could, saying, 'Maud, you're safe. Whatever you've done, you're safe with me and Brother Thomas. I promise.'

Maud gave a stifled sob and buried her face in Hildegard's sleeve. 'You can't stop the fires of hell. Nobody can. Not the pope. Not the arch-angels. Nobody. And I don't know now whether I'm bad because he's alive or if I'm still to be punished for what I thought I'd done. He killed my brother and then he came back to take me with him...' Her words became inaudible and she began to sob without control.

'It's all right now, it's over,' Hildegard murmured, stroking the springing red curls. 'You're safe. It's over. He can do nothing more to you.'

'But you don't know what I did, Sister. I took his knife from his belt when he was asleep,' Maud whimpered, 'and I stabbed him in the neck and he gave a great shout with the pain of the wound and it was night and I couldn't see and I just ran out of the barn and I still had his knife and I hid and then I found a cart and hid in that and I slept under hedges and I kept on walking and then I was walking along the lane when Petronilla came up to me and asked me about the egg... I thought I'd killed him!'

Hildegard held the girl tight. 'You're safe, Maud. It must have been frightening to believe you'd killed someone–'

Maud face hardened. 'But I wanted to. I told Brother Thomas so. I told him I had murdered a man and he listened to me and said I would be forgiven. But I told him I wanted with all my might to kill him. And that means I'll burn for it. Brother Thomas said if I truly repented I would be forgiven. But I can't repent. I hate him. And now he's alive and I still want him to be dead...' She seemed to brace herself as if to scramble back towards the parapet but Hildegard held her still.

'Let's go somewhere less dangerous than this high perch where we can talk properly. Nobody will blame you for defending yourself. And he's not dead so you're not a murderess after all. There is nothing to forgive. We're allowed angry thoughts without fear of punishment. No priest, and certainly not Brother Thomas, would ever tell you otherwise.'

Maud took a long time to consider matters.

Aware that she could slip over the parapet at any moment taking both of them to their deaths, Hildegard said again, 'Let's go somewhere else – away from all those people staring up at us.'

Maud peered over the edge and for the first time seemed to notice the sea of faces turned up to watch. It acted as a brake. 'Get me away from them, Sister,' she whispered.

She scrambled back behind one of the buttresses and Hildegard followed, still keeping a tight hold on the back of her garments until she was sure she had changed her mind about jumping. Then it became a question of edging back along the gallery towards the tower steps. Even then she kept a tight hold of her under the pretence that the girl was helping her maintain her balance. It wasn't until they reached the safety of the doorway that she released her.

As they entered the tower an outbreak of applause came from the watching crowd below.

Hildegard held Maud by the arm. 'You see, my pet. They want you to live safe and sound. We all do.'

Trembling with relief that it was over, Hildegard went first down the narrow spiral. Maud was holding tightly onto her sleeve making it difficult to descend. Hildegard looked back at her when she reached the bottom of the steps and held out her arms. 'You're safe now, Maud.'

'Sister, permit me,' said a voice behind her. She turned.

It was the knight in black. The one who had sauntered onto Roger's loggia. The one who had been stopped by Danby from filching lead from his yard.

He wore a mail shirt underneath his black linen tunic and a white cloth was tied round his neck. Hildegard realised now it was a bandage. She gazed at it in astonishment. Maud had inflicted a knife wound. She had confessed to it.

What was more, underneath the bandage in the opening of the man's shirt was an emblem on a silver chain. He was standing so close she could not fail to recognise it this time. It was a silver swan. It was the one that had slipped through her fingers at Deepdale.

With no time to work out what it meant, she turned as Maud, lifting her head after jumping down the last few steps, let out a shriek. The knight in black was already reaching out to her.

'And little Maud,' he was saying smoothly. 'You've led me a merry dance and–'

At that moment Brother Thomas materialised from somewhere in a flurry of white monastic robes, his strong face suffused with alarm. 'These two are with me–' he began.

The knight swivelled, one hand already reaching to his belt. When the monk leant forward to grasp Maud by the other hand the knight pushed him hard making him stumble. Thomas jerked his head up with a look of astonishment. 'My Lord, I–'

He spread his arms to demonstrate his good

403

intentions but the knight took it as an opportunity to produce a knife and before anybody could move he stabbed Thomas in the chest.

The onlookers gasped. A woman screamed.

Hildegard gazed in horror as Thomas fell back with both hands to the wound. The knight still held the knife and now slipped it back inside its sheath and reached again for Maud.

Gasping with pain Thomas managed to shout, 'Run for it, Hildegard. Take her to safety!' before sliding to the floor.

For a moment Hildegard was torn. Then two vergers hurried up and a woman stepped from the crowd saying, 'I'm a leech. Quickly! Let me attend him.'

Without waiting Hildegard pulled Maud into the thick of the onlookers and grasping her by the hand, ran with her towards the minster doors. Shouts broke out behind them. A glimpse over her shoulder gave an impression of people stumbling out of the way of the knight in black and yet others reaching out to detain him. It was enough to make her rush Maud outside without further hesitation.

They ran across the minster yard towards the gates, then made a left turn onto Petergate where the crowds were thickest. If they could lose themselves in the throng they might give him the slip.

'Where are we going?' panted Maud. 'Just tell me where we're going!'

'We'll go back to Harpham's house. Ulf and his men will protect us.' But first, she thought, we have to elude our pursuer, otherwise we'll never make it across town.

She urged Maud into a back lane that led off the street they were on. It ran parallel to Stonegate. Assuring her that it would take them in the direction of Conyngsgate, she explained that they could eventually cross the river by Ouse Bridge and run up to the safety of the house.

When they arrived panting at the top of the street, however, one of the knight's henchmen was there before them. He must have been with his lord in the minster and taking notice of what had happened had gone on ahead.

He was a stocky, thickset fellow and was having difficulty looking over the heads of the crowd. So far he had not spotted them. When she glanced over her shoulder she saw the knight himself just sprinting round the corner in pursuit. The lane was narrow, thick with revellers. The knight pushed his way with difficulty towards them.

Near at hand were the back doors to the shops that fronted onto Stonegate and, dragging Maud with her, Hildegard plunged through one of them at random. A leather worker at his bench glanced up in surprise when they barged in, but with no time to explain they ran straight through his shop and out into the street on the other side, his shouts fading as they ran into a yard directly opposite.

A church, its doors open, swathes of incense sweeping out in a dizzying scent and a glittering array of candles visible on the altar within, was the only refuge. All the churches will be open now, she realised, the guilds processing around the town already before beginning their vigil on the eve of Corpus Christi. Unseen by their pursuers, they ran inside.

'There must be another door,' Hildegard told Maud, hurrying her down the short length of the nave and ignoring the startled glances of a scattering of worshippers. They reached the altar but there was no door behind it, merely a smooth sweep of painted wall with an aumbry and a curtain slung across an alcove where presumably the priest kept his regalia.

The sound of jangling spurs in the doorway brought Hildegard's heart into her mouth. 'Quick, in here.' She pushed Maud behind the curtain and followed after.

A voice from near the door was heard to ask, 'Did two miscreants just run in here?'

'No, sir, no one like that,' replied an unfamiliar voice. The jangling spurs receded. After waiting a moment Hildegard looked out. There was no sign of the knight or his henchman, but a stranger in the robes of a guildsman was hurrying down the aisle towards them.

He pulled the curtain aside. 'You're clearly in distress. Do you need help, Sister?'

'We do. No time to explain further, master. Is there a way out of here? We need to get into Micklegate.'

'Follow me.'

He led them briskly to the back of the altar and moved the aumbry to one side. Behind it was a door painted to fit in with a scene from the Garden of Eden on the wall. 'This is the Mercer's Guild church,' he told her as he opened the door. 'Follow the passage. It'll bring you out on the riverbank not far from the bridge. It's dark in there,' he added, 'so watch your step. Wait a moment...' he disappeared round the front of the altar and returned with a candle. 'Take this. St Benet be with you.'

Thanking him and with Maud already groping her way in terror down the narrow tunnel she set off. When the secret door closed their only light cast jumping shadows along the walls, bringing Maud to a sudden halt.

Hildegard urged her on. 'Go on, Maud. We have to get to the bridge before the knight does.'

The walls were running with water and there was a scuffling sound like rats. After a seemingly endless few minutes, slipping over wet stones, they came to a further door. Not knowing what was waiting on the other side, Hildegard pushed it open an inch or two and peered through. The lifted candle revealed a bare, windowless chamber with another door at the far side. They could hear the sound of many footsteps shuffling past with a sound like waves breaking on a beach.

She said, 'We must be below street level in a cellar of some sort.'

'I'm frightened,' whispered Maud. 'Can't we just stay here?'

'We must get to the bridge first, otherwise we won't be able to cross the river to Harpham's without being seen.' She only hoped that the knight's retainers were not already posted at the bridge. 'Come on, Maud. Be brave,' she urged. 'We'll tread with great caution.'

The empty chamber must have been a storeroom

at some time. The faint scent of grain lingered. It reminded her of the kitchen at Low Mill. They had no idea where they were when they opened the far door, but to their relief they found themselves in the open air at the back of a row of booths fronting the river. The latch snapped as it shut behind them. Pinching out the candle Hildegard slipped it into her sleeve.

'Which way is the bridge?' asked Maud, clinging onto her like a limpet.

Hildegard hesitated for a moment until she got her bearings. There was a staithe to their right with a couple of barges moored beside it, and further downriver to their left the rows of booths continued along the hank for some way.

'It must be down that way,' she said, pushing Maud to the left with a firm hand on her shoulder. No one paid any attention to them and the bridge soon came into view. Then Hildegard felt Maud give a shudder of alarm.

'That's the one called Hogg,' she exclaimed, drawing back.

Hildegard peered towards the bridge. A man-at-arms was lounging at the steps and giving the faces of the crowd a careful scrutiny. He was thickset, wearing a mail shirt and paring his nails with a knife.

Such was Maud's fear, she was standing as if transfixed. Then her eyes darted to the water. It was a heaving mass of swimmers. Every few moments a boy would jump off the side of the bridge and land with a great splash. 'I can't swim,' she said, as if an already frantic train of thought had been followed.

'Tell me something. Who is that knight?'

'He's just called "my lord" by his men. I don't know who he is. He said he claimed our manor by right of arms and to hell with law. That's what he kept saying. But what are we going to do now, Sister? We're trapped.'

'Not a bit of it.' She sounded more certain than she felt. It would only take the appearance of the other men to put a permanent guard at the bridge. Even if she tried to get Maud across by boat they would be clearly visible as they climbed up the embankment on the other side.

The mystery of the knight's apparent interest in the cross could be solved later.

Pondering the possibilities open to them Hildegard considered searching out a constable and putting their lives in the hands of the law, but what Maud had said about no one believing her, as a bonded maid, rang true. She could easily imagine the charm the knight in black would switch on, and the ease by which he would talk his way out of the situation and reel Maud back into his clutches. The law was tough when it came to a matter of runaway bonded labourers.

'I'm going to send a message to Sir Ulf,' she told Maud, mainly to keep the girl's spirits up. There was the problem of finding a reliable messenger, of staying out of sight of their pursuers until help arrived. It wouldn't do. 'Meanwhile,' she continued, playing for time, 'we'll make it more difficult for them to recognise us in the crowd.'

She hurried Maud into one of the nearby booths where a woman was selling a range of clothing.

There were rough cotton kirtles, tunics in various weights of fabric, cloaks and capuchons of every colour. Selecting a light-green summer cloak for Maud, she advised her to leave her brown one. 'Leave that one here. We can come back for it if you want it.'

Maud did as she was told. As she straightened it for her, Hildegard asked, 'What's in this bundle you always carry, Maud?' She indicated the cloth tied in a knot over Maud's shoulder.

'It's what I did it with,' she mumbled. She hung her head.

'What?'

'Killed him. Or thought I had.'

'You mean it's a weapon?'

Maud nodded.

Hildegard was aghast. 'You mean you smuggled that through the Bar when we first came here, despite the warnings?'

Maud nodded again.

'But why? You could have got us all locked up.'

She shook her head. 'I daren't leave it any-where.'

They moved away from the booth. Hildegard had tied on a dark-ochre kerchief that she pulled low over her brow, and Maud's abundant and eye-catching hair was hidden under another one. They took shelter behind a stall selling pancakes. The smoke from the vendor's brazier billowed out in thick blue coils, but at least it served as some concealment.

'Now,' she said, 'will you show it to me?'

Nervously Maud undid the knots that tied the bundle to reveal a long-bladed dagger. It was

410

expensively crafted.

The hilt was worked in silver and studded with what looked like diamonds, and the blade was well honed, a narrow and sharp instrument of death.

It seemed astonishing to Hildegard that such a lethal-looking weapon had not killed the knight outright. Maud must have stabbed out so wildly in her panic that she had missed her target and merely drawn blood. The knight no doubt considered himself fortunate to have his life.

Maud rewrapped it.

'Wait a moment.' Hildegard asked to have another look. 'What's this?' The pattern on the halt was not some abstraction created by the silversmith. It was a recognisable shape. It was a swan, its wings studded with small diamonds and its feet marked by sapphires. It was the same emblem the knight wore in silver round his neck.

Maud was staring at her as if afraid of what she would say next.

'Do you realise who he is?'

Maud shook her head.

Hildegard's head was swimming with the knowledge. This proved the identity of the man who had destroyed Maud's manor, killed its inhabitants, and also devastated Deepdale. It would stand as evidence in a court of law.

The reason for his ruthless pursuit fell into place.

It wasn't the Cross of Constantine that interested him. Nor – even – was it an absconding servant. It was the incriminating evidence of the embossed dagger. It was a direct link to the massacre of the villeins near Pentleby and the devastation of the Cistercian grange at Deepdale.

More and more people were coming out onto the streets as the hour of vigil approached. Groups of twenty or so were gathering with lighted candles. The air was sweet with the scent of beeswax.

For most of the next hour Hildegard and Maud remained on the bank of the river, far enough from the bridge to pass unnoticed but near enough to observe the eventual arrival of the knight and two more of his retainers. The men stood around, evidently discussing matters, and the one guarding the bridge was shrugging and shaking his head. The three of them fanned out again to trawl the streets in different directions. To Hildegard's consternation one of them started to advance along the river towards their hiding place.

Warning Maud to keep her wits about her Hildegard led her back along the river path towards a house with a bunch of broom tied to its gable. There they mingled with a crowd of people drinking outside. The ale-wife whose house it was looked red-faced and happy at the profit she was making, and Hildegard added a little to it by pressing some silver coins into her hand and asking if her child could sit in a private chamber for a little while as the sun had been too much for her that day.

When they came out later the man had gone, but there was another one standing at the bridge.

'That's Ivo,' said Maud.

'It's a pity you can't swim,' said Hildegard

trying to lighten the girl's fear.

'With all those rats and dead dogs,' said Maud. 'I wish I could. Better than the rats on that bridge. Oh, Sister, what on earth are we going to do? I'll give myself up. That's the best. Then you can get away with the knife and I'll jump into the water and end it all.'

'You do give up easily, Maud. I think it looks as if we'll be able to get a boat from somewhere now the light's beginning to fade. That should save you getting your new cloak wet.'

By this time the riverbank was in shadow, its only light the intermittent flare of cressets along the line of booths. It made it safe enough to approach one of the watermen who had been ferrying passengers back and forth all afternoon. He agreed to take them to the other side for twopence, which Hildegard thought exorbitant for the distance he would have to row but she accepted without quibble, eager only to make their escape without drawing attention to themselves.

He held the boat steady while Maud climbed in.

About to follow, Hildegard heard a shout from the bank. She found herself being grasped roughly from behind and she was dragged back off the boat onto the shore.

Looking up she noticed Maud's startled expression and her lips form a frightened cry as she rose to her feet. The boat rocked.

'Go!' she shouted to the ferryman. 'Take her across. Go to the steward, Maud, give him the knife! Hurry!'

The ferryman looked undecided until she shouted at him that it was a matter of life and death and to fetch Roger de Hutton's steward at once. Maud, she noted with relief, sat down in the boat and the ferryman began to ply his oars with strong, quick strokes towards the opposite side.

Hildegard swung round to face her attacker, and expecting to see the knight or one of his henchmen, gave a gasp of astonishment. It was the brutish, bald-headed servant from the convent of the Holy Wounds. The one they called Matthias.

Chapter Thirty

He pushed his face close to her own in a stench of sweat and human ordure that made her gag. Brutally strong, he gave her no opportunity to slip free, but dragged her to a stone jetty out of range of the cresset lights a few yards along the bank where nobody but prostitutes and their clients lurked. He pushed her down among the high weeds on the wasteland below the flood wall and held her down.

'Whore of Babylon!' He thumped her on the head. She saw stars. 'Punishment!' he mumbled. Slow-witted, he looked as if he was working out what to do with her now she was in his power. Pinned beneath his beefy thighs she was unable to move. Distantly she could hear the hymn singing that marked the beginning of the night vigil.

Her captor raised his fist again but before he could smash it into her face she put as much fear into her voice as she could and whimpered, 'Please, great sir! Punish me as I deserve. But I beg of you – don't take me back to the convent, whatever you do!'

He paused, his fist in the air. His garments gave off the rancid odour of animal wax.

'Please,' she said again, 'don't let your mother superior punish me herself! I beg of you, kind sir!'

'Holy Mother?' His eyes gleamed with the sudden possibilities her words opened up.

'She'll punish me most horribly, sir, and for sure she'll reward you for taking me back to the convent as your prisoner – but resist, I beg you, resist!' She gazed imploringly into his piggy little eyes. 'She'll torture me,' she continued. 'She'll whip me! She'll cut my flesh! She and all the other holy sisters. And Sister Michael,' she added, remembering the large woman who had tried to keep Maud prisoner. 'She'll wreak a vile vengeance on me, most holy sir!'

The brute gripped her by the jaw and stared intently into her face. He seemed to be trying to read something in her expression. His animal gaze held no trace of rational thought. She could hear his breath rasping in and out, wrapping her in a miasma of rotten food that was enough to make her faint in itself.

'Please don't take me there, good sir, they'll pain me beyond endurance,' she pleaded again as he seemed to waver.

415

His eyes had a veiled look, half mad, and then she observed a shift in the mud of his thoughts that forced a grunt from between his blackened teeth.

'Take you there? To the convent! Yes! Me do that. My lady well pleased with Matthias. Get up, heretic!' He lifted himself off her and began to drag at her clothing to force her to rise.

Shakily, amazed she could still stand, Hildegard stumbled to her feet. There was no opportunity to make a run for it. He maintained his oafish grip on her garments, and when she swayed, about to fall, he merely wrapped one arm round her waist and hauled her along beside him, ignoring her feeble attempts to resist. In the confusion of the moment – lights glittering from the riverboats, cressets like stars along the bank – she had chance to wonder what would happen when they reached the guard on the bridge.

They approached. The knight's esquire was looking for a nun, not a drunken baggage being carted home for a beating by her man. They passed over without hindrance.

Praying that Maud had managed to get across to safety and had enough common sense to make straight for Harpham's house to tell Ulf what had happened, Hildegard found herself being dragged in the direction of the convent.

By tricking Matthias into leaving the isolation of the riverbank she had hoped that she could escape once back in the mainstream of the crowd, but she had reckoned without his brute strength and the drunken indifference of the revellers. She regretted the absence of her hounds with all her might. Her only hope was the knife in the sheath on her belt. As he dragged her along she began to jerk it free with small, surreptitious tugs on the haft.

They reached the corner that led into the stews. After that the lane was relatively empty as it went on only to the nunnery and the warehouses where the barges were moored. As they reached the lane end she pretended to stumble.

Momentarily free of his grasp she pulled the knife right out of its sheath and got it in a good grip with both hands. Her captor's small eyes probably caught sight of the blade as she thrust it upwards under his filthy cloak because he lurched to one side with a grunt of surprise. She felt something sticky on the backs of her hands. She had drawn blood. The knife remained stuck for a moment until she managed to twist it free. Matthias stared at her, a spark of red rage flaring in the depths of his eyes.

By then she was off, running, running fast into the network of alleys that formed the stews, running in the knowledge that a madman was in hot pursuit.

She was deep in the labyrinthine alleys of the stews, not knowing which way to turn next. The doors of the houses stood open and spilling out onto the street was a raucous gathering of musicians, prostitutes, customers and hangers-on, people coming and going all the time. Without looking back she flung herself inside the first door she came to.

No one noticed her. Panting, she glanced wildly

round for somewhere to conceal herself, reaching for a stoup of ale from one of the foaming jugs that were going the rounds, burying her face in the flagon and quickly finding somewhere to sit. A couple of men flung themselves down on the bench next to her almost at once and tried to fix a price. She deflected their interest for a moment by pointing to a woman who was doing a seductive dance to the music of a couple of knacker-men and a gittern player. Dancing for money, she encouraged the men to stuff coins into the partly unlaced opening of her bodice and had plenty of customers.

One of the men, who only moments before had competed with his companion over Hildegard, took a fancy to the dancer, especially when she bestowed a flirtatious smile on him. He got up and she moved off out of his reach, but kept looking back to encourage his interest, and when the music changed he danced a few drunken steps in an attempt to copy her.

Just then a woman accompanied by two armed men arrived and was conducted through the crowd to a room at the back. She was welcomed with some deference by the doorman. Hildegard's glance followed her in astonishment. It was Mistress Julitta, Baldwin's wife.

The entrance to the private chamber was briefly obscured when one of the pimps stepped up to the dancing drunk as he got too close to the girl, and hauled him back into a corner with some commotion. By that time the door had closed and Julitta had disappeared inside.

It was then that Matthias pushed his way into

418

the building.

His shaven head gleamed under the light of the cressets as he searched the faces of the crowd. Evidently he was well known and one of the women went over and put her garland round his neck. It was too noisy to hear what was said, but he pulled back his cloak and pointed to the blood on his chest and then lurched further onto the dance floor. There were cries as people noticed the blood. He ignored them and with a wild expression searched the faces of the onlookers for Hildegard. He had obviously seen her flee into the house and now lurched round the crowded chamber, peering into people's faces, exciting a lot of attention and some hostility.

'Get out of it, you drunken sot!' Somebody gave him a push and Matthias turned on his attacker with a snarl.

Hildegard whispered to the man next to her, 'Would you like to go outside, lover?'

'Would I! Come on, sweet!' With a laugh he pulled her into his arms and leaning heavily against her staggered towards the exit.

Matthias was approaching the dancer now, distracted by her naked breasts as she emptied the coins out of her bodice into a pouch held out by her pimp, and with an inane grin he took a step towards her with his hands outstretched. The blood on the front of his tunic made her recoil. The crowd jostled round to have a closer look.

Hildegard didn't linger to see what would happen next. As soon as they got outside she broke away.

'Hey!' the man called, stumbling after her, 'I thought you said—'

She was already halfway up the street when her potential customer gave up. She heard him shout after her. 'Come back if you change your mind!' When she risked a glance over her shoulder he was standing under the light over the door scratching his head and gazing up the street after her. Then, with a mystified shrug he went back inside.

Confident that Matthias had not noticed her exit, she didn't look back again. The strident sounds of the stews gradually faded as she ran on up the hill to the more respectable part of town.

Once more she found herself outside the French priory near the church of the Holy Trinity. A last group of travellers were arriving at the postern at Micklegate Bar before it was closed for the night. One of them stood out from the rest. It was a pilgrim in a broad-brimmed hat, white robes and a stave in one hand. He stood at the top of the street drinking in the sight of the city lower down as if it had been some time since he had last seen it.

Harpham's house was on the opposite side of the street and she was about to cross over when Ulf and a dozen men-at-arms carrying flares came clattering out from the inner yard. She fled towards him and saw him check himself in mid stride. Then he came towards her.

'Hildegard!' he exclaimed, grasping hold of her as she fell into his arms. He held her tight as if unable to believe his eyes.

420

The security of his rough mail shirt pressing hard against her made her feel like fainting with relief. Safe at last. With his strong arms wrapped round her in an embrace she rested her head against his broad chest with a sob of relief.

He held her until she was steady, murmuring, 'Hildegard, Hildegard, my dear Hildegard, am I glad to see you!'

He stroked her head, murmuring endearments, then he started to tell her what had brought him and his men pouring out of their quarters just now. 'Little Maud came running in, shrieking her head off, saying you'd both been pursued by a knight and two henchmen and then you'd been kidnapped by a servant from the Holy Wounds. And now look at you!' He gently fingered the side of her jaw where it was beginning to swell. 'What did that animal do to you?'

'He got the worst of it.' She tried to laugh but it was halfway to a sob. For a moment longer she clung to him in sheer relief at having reached safety. Then she told him what had happened and where he might find Matthias. 'I've wounded him,' she admitted.

'He deserves it. I'll send men to turn the place inside out. He's not getting away with this.' He stepped back. With a concerned look he turned and issued a few orders, and a detachment of men set off with attitudes of grim purpose down the street.

Ulf led her towards the light of a cresset at the entrance to Harpham's house so that it shone full on her face. He peered at her bruises. 'He'll suffer for this.'

'It's probably worse than it looks. I just need some arnica.'

He lifted her chin. 'The fiend,' he muttered. 'I'll see him in hell!' He held her face gently between his palms and gazed deeply into her eyes. 'It's useless to ask why you can't stay safely in your priory, isn't it?'

She tried to smile but her face was already stiffening under the bruises. 'It seems circumstances would rather I was outside.'

His eyes, usually as vivid as a piece of cobalt medallion glass, were storm dark and he ran his hand gently over the top of her head, smoothing and comforting her, tucking a few stray wisps of hair back under her kerchief.

She dropped her glance under the intensity of his gaze. 'It's a wonder I didn't lose my kerchief.' She fingered the piece of linen and felt herself sway against him. Dear, capable Ulf. His kindness made her want to weep. 'If you don't mind,' she whispered after a long pause, 'I'd like a drink and something for these bruises so I don't look too monstrous tomorrow.'

'I know all about bruises.' He became brisk. 'But what about broken bones – you don't have any of those do you?'

Smiling, she shook her head. 'I don't think so.' She straightened.

'Come inside, then.' He took her wrists in his broad and dependable hands. 'We've plenty of cures for bruises if you haven't any yourself. And you'll be needing some of the Carthusians' special distillation from France. That'll fix you up in a trice.' He put an arm round her to assist her inside.

For a moment, over his shoulder, she saw the pilgrim she had spotted earlier. He was watching intently from the other side of the street from beneath his broad-brimmed hat. As she turned towards the house he, too, turned away and began to walk slowly down the hill towards the town.

Melisen insisted that a tub be filled with hot, scented water, and fresh garments laid out on a stool next to it. Now, lying back in the steam with the screen closed, Hildegard thought over what had happened.

Ulf had already told her that he had given the knife Maud had shown him to Roger. Apparently Roger had stared at the emblem carved into the silver handle in astonishment and then pronounced, 'Either he's a member of the Poulterers' Guild ... or he's a knight in the service of the de Bohun family.' He had paused. His expression darkened. 'If the latter – then he's my guest.'

One of his famous rages had followed. A de Bohun heiress was married to Gaunt's younger brother, the Duke of Gloucester. The other one was married to Gaunt's son, Henry Bolingbroke.

But the matter was now out of Hildegard's hands. The knight, which ever de Bohun noble he served, was Roger's responsibility.

Something was resolved, however. Lord Roger de Hutton now knew who had destroyed his property at Deepdale. He also knew, as would everyone else, who had wrought such devastation on a group of ordinary labourers and their families on a far-off manor in another Riding.

Matthias was not her concern now either, Hildegard realised, as she luxuriated in the steaming tub. He would get his just desserts.

The danger to the cross was over too, she realised. The knight in black had not been looking for it after all. Probably no one was looking for it. It must have been an opportunistic theft by the rebels. They had heard rumours of something valuable and taken their chance. Nobody was interested in it anymore. She would take it back to Swyne as soon as she felt rested enough to travel.

Only one thing disturbed her thoughts, but she was too befuddled by the combined effects of the Carthusians' cure and the hot, scented water to work out what it was.

Hildegard was still in the tub when Ulf was announced. She heard him enter the chamber and pull up a stool on the other side of the screen.

'The lads have arrested that knave,' came his voice. 'You didn't give him a deep wound. He had a hair shirt on under his outer garments along with various studs and leather bindings. It's best not to ask for more detail. When the lads arrived at the brothel he was just about to get a whipping for both his own pleasure and that of the customers.'

'I guessed they knew him,' she replied. She sank deeper into the warm water and allowed her limbs to float among the rose petals the maid had scattered. 'But what about Mistress Julitta? What was she doing there? Did you find out?'

'We did indeed. Apparently she was just coming out of the house next door when the men arrived. She'd been down there collecting her husband's takings. I doubt he'll ever see them.'

'Takings?' She raised her head out of the water. So Gilbert had not been lying.

Ulf's voice came. 'You don't need to know all this, Hildegard.'

'I think I do.'

'Are you sure?'

When she didn't reply he confirmed what Gilbert had told her. 'It's like this. Baldwin has a financial interest in several houses down by the wharf. He supplies the girls. Dorelia was just one of those he abducted from the West Riding. The others were set to work in the stews where he extracted the maximum profit he could get from them. It was a regular deal. He had an understanding with a crooked serjeant-at-law over in Wakefield who tipped him off concerning unmarried heiresses coming onto the market. Baldwin then stepped in to obtain maintenance which he sold on to whoever was willing to pay up. The girls, with no land and no fortune after all, and no kin who couldn't be bought off, were forced to make the best of things. Once they started talking,' he added, 'they couldn't stop.'

'Does Danby know what was going on?'

'I doubt it. He's on the level. He would never have condoned it.'

'But he must have wondered where Baldwin got his money from? Even I wondered that. He never seemed to do any work.'

'Remember what Danby told us? Baldwin had a longstanding commission at a church in Wakefield. I guess he can sound plausible enough when he wants to.'

Hildegard let herself slide down under the water to have it lap over the bruises on her face and when she emerged in a swirl of rose petals there was no sound from the other side of the curtain.

Ulf must have left. She sighed and closed her eyes. The Carthusian liquor was doing its job. Her limbs relaxed, floating on the surface of the water as her pain and fear began to drain away.

'Dearest Ulf,' she whispered, half to herself. 'Dear, sweet, beloved Ulf.'

There was a soft movement from the other side of the screen.

'I'm still here, Hildegard.' His voice was gruff.

There was a pause and then he muttered. 'Listen, there's something I want to say.'

There was another pause.

'Hildegard, what I want to say is this – give it up, all this. Buy your way out. Come back to a free life outside your Order.'

There was another pause before he added, 'We could have a life together, you and me. It's not too late...'

She held her breath.

There was silence.

She put one hand into the water and let it sink, dragging a trail of rose petals after it. When she lifted it the water dripped off it as if nothing had changed.

'Have you drowned?' he whispered.

'I'm still here. I'm just–' She slid under the water again. Her hair, which was longer than it

426

should be, floated round her face and when she emerged it flattened itself to her forehead and water drops coursed down her cheeks like tears. 'Am I to take my vows so lightly, Ulf?'

There was a brief silence, then the old Ulf spoke up. 'I would never have dared say any of that to your face. It's your choice to consider it unsaid – or not – when next we meet.'

She heard a stool scrape back and footsteps swiftly moving towards the door. The door opened. The door closed.

Bathed, wearing fresh clothes lent by Melisen, and with a good meal inside her, Hildegard was summoned to a meeting in Robert Harpham's hall.

Lord Roger de Hutton was sitting in state. That is, he was in a comfortable chair in front of his cloth of honour on an elevated dais at one end of the raftered hall, with his wife beside him, his chamberlain, his steward and his various yeomen in declining importance ranked along the walls and, just entering as Hildegard made her appearance, a man who, from the look of his overmantle, was a serjeant-at-law. A chair was brought for him and placed below the dais.

A maid entered with Maud, also freshly bathed and wearing a pretty gown of primrose yellow, and for the first time since Hildegard had known her, without her cloak and hood. Her abundant red hair which had been such a surprise when Hildegard first saw it in the minster was caught up in a silver clasp.

Petronilla took Hildegard by the hand as soon

as she appeared at the door. 'My lady wishes you to sit close by,' she whispered and led her down the hall where a vacant seat was found. Hildegard looked out at the sea of faces. It was either an audience or a showdown. There was no music, only the murmur of voices in expectation of some unspecified event.

The night was hot. The heat of the day lingered and the window screens were flung wide, allowing a breeze to ripple the tapestries along the walls and bring in the overheated scent of the nearby streets with their contradictory aromas of frying meats, honeyed fritters, incense, human excrement and flower water.

Wine was handed round. The chamberlain thumped his mace on the floor to engage everybody's attention. 'I announce Sir Alaric de Belfort.'

There was a flurry of interest. Smiling with somewhat surprised pleasure, the knight in black entered. He was accompanied by two men-at-arms. With some ceremony he advanced down the hall to the foot of the dais. Lord Roger was at his most benign.

'Greetings, sir knight. When your servant announced you earlier today I had no idea who sought my hospitality.'

The knight made a flourish. 'By chance in York for the Corpus Christi plays, we had no expectations that we would find such a generous welcome.'

'That's the way we do things up here,' replied Roger with a bland expression. 'And of course,' he added, 'I do know your liege lord and his daughter, the wife of Henry Bolingbroke.'

The knight shifted somewhat.

'I know your lord's entire family well,' Roger added with a smile. He stroked his beard, adding, 'And now I know all about you. Tell me, sir, what do you know of a holy relic now said to be back on the market?'

The knight looked startled. 'I know nothing of holy relics,' he snorted. 'I'm a knight, not a priest.'

Roger gave a thin smile.

The knight was beginning to look round as if expecting to be invited to take his place on the dais and, appearing annoyed that it wasn't immediately offered, failed to heed the harsh note in Roger's voice when he sat back with the remark, 'Your lord – somewhat misguided, you must agree?'

Sir Alaric de Belfort gave him a blank look. 'In what respect, My Lord?'

'In respect of his allegiance to those who would overthrow the king,' replied Roger with a genial smile. 'As you might have realised, some of us are of a different persuasion north of the Trent.'

For the first time the knight looked alarmed. It was as if he had suddenly realised he was in a foreign part of the country where perhaps certain rights which he had taken for granted and which served him well in his own region, did not now apply.

'A fine county it is, My Lord,' he replied cautiously.

'Indeed. And it's a county where we treat our womenfolk with some courtesy as far as we're able. This little maid, for instance.' He beckoned to Maud who, biting her lip but with a brave look of defiance on her face, stepped forward from behind Roger's chair.

The knight gave a confident smile. 'So, Maud, you elusive little creature. They've found you for me again, have they?' He turned to Roger with a smirk. 'I've been searching high and low for her for some time–'

'Not found,' corrected Roger. 'She recently threw herself on our mercy, having suffered unspeakable terrors at the hands of a gang of armed brigands who not only laid waste her manor in an attempt to wrest it from its rightful lord, but also killed her father and her brother, raped and killed her mother, and did many other things which it is beyond the bounds of delicacy to record here in public. The man responsible,' he continued in an implacable tone, 'will pay for it. Do not doubt me.'

'I say, this all sounds most unfortunate,' began the knight. 'Who the devil would do such a thing?'

'The owner of this,' said Roger. With a flourish he produced the knife.

His retinue gasped. Well used to Lord Roger's theatrical gestures they never failed to be impressed by them.

The knight looked at the knife but did not reach out to inspect it.

'It has on it, for your information, an emblem. I notice you wear the emblem of the de Bohuns, a white swan?'

The knight's hand flew to the silver chain round his neck.

'I also notice you have a neck wound. Chamberlain,' commanded Roger, 'read the motto on the hilt of the dagger.'

Patting his houpelande into place, the chamberlain stepped forward, but by now the knight was walking away. 'I don't need to hear the testimony of a mad and vindictive bonded servant,' he called back over his shoulder. 'The knife proves nothing beyond the fact that she stole it from me and then absconded. My wound I acquired in battle.'

When he reached the door the men lounging there as if watching a play suddenly came to life. Their pikes clashed, barring his way.

'Oh now, this is beyond reason!' protested the knight.

Roger had risen to his feet. 'I'll tell you what's beyond reason, sir.'

The knight turned.

'What is beyond reason and humanity and compassion and all the bounds of decency and civilised custom is that a servant should be subjected to the treatment meted out to her by you and your men.'

Without trying to protest his innocence Sir Alaric took a few steps forward towards the dais. 'I admit I took back the manor. It should never have been stolen from me in the first place. Naturally the peasants there suffered. The men were loyal to the rebel cause for a start, and all the more reason to stamp them out. But she...' he pointed to Maud, 'she's nothing but a Saxon serf, My Lord. Not of our stock. It's the treatment they expect.'

Roger leant forward and all his affability had vanished. 'I'll tell you what she is, sir, she is my ward. I will have redress for this outrage.'

Sir Alaric went pale. 'Your ward? But how is it possible?'

Roger gestured to the serjeant-at-law. 'He has the documents if you wish to read them.'

'But I couldn't have known that! How could I have known? It's grossly unfair. Let's talk it over like brothers-in-arms—'

'I've said all I want to say.' Roger turned to Ulf. 'Make sure he stays here until the justices can fetch him. I expect the manor lord whose property he laid waste will have something to say to him, as have I over the destruction of Deepdale.'

A group of armed men surrounded the knight and his henchmen and, aware that there was no point in protesting unless they preferred to put themselves forth as martyrs, they were marched from the hall to a boisterous cheer from the entire household.

'Now,' said Roger, 'let the music begin!'

It was midnight when all those who wished to attend the vigil for the feast of Corpus Christi processed out of the hall to join the crowds already thronging into the candlelit churches.

Hildegard, feeling weakened by her ordeal, retired to the chamber allotted to her and spread her aching limbs on the bed. Roger's generosity to Maud was a cause for deep satisfaction. In addition, a message had come through from St Leonard's while they feasted. Thomas had been

432

conveyed to the hospice where his wound had been stitched up – and he was already pleading to be let out.

She closed her eyes.

Throughout the feasting just now Ulf had made sure their paths had not crossed. She had seen him take a partner or two onto the dance floor. The rest of the time he had been surrounded by a laughing, chattering retinue.

Except for one thing it was almost as if she had dreamt those words whispered in the steamy alcove while she bathed. It was when she rose to leave. His glance immediately swung her way as if he had been aware of her out of the corners of his eyes all evening – just as she, full of compassion, had been aware of him.

The dawn sky had a lustre like the inside of an oyster shell. Those who had returned early from the vigil now roused themselves again to prepare for the first pageant play, *The Creation*. A fanfare of sackbuts from nearby Pageant Green announced the start with enough volume to waken any who imagined they could ignore it. The first wagons rumbled onto the street hauled along by men from the Guild of Barkers.

The steel-shod wagon thundered over the cobbles and came to a halt outside the church of the Holy Trinity. The drumming of nakers and tabors started up, almost drowning out the shouts of the pageant master as he ordered his actors into place. Then came the chatter of timbrels and the skirl of pipes and after that the low-pitched murmur of an approaching crowd from lower down the street.

Hildegard hauled herself out of bed and pulled on her freshly laundered summer habit before stumbling over to the window and looking down. From one end to the other Micklegate was a river of light.

Townsfolk, hundreds of them, were streaming up the hill towards the first pageant station. She watched them emerging out of the morning mist with lighted candles in their hands, men and women, young and old, children carrying small tapers, babes in arms, entire families, all walking up the hill to join the worshippers still swarming out of the priory church opposite the house. The two groups merged and eventually gathered at the foot of Holy Trinity steps in a blaze of light.

Throwing tiredness aside, Hildegard hurried down to join them.

An army of burly guildsmen had already manhandled the first of the two-tier wagons into place when she arrived.

An awesome silence fell before the first words to herald the creation of the world were spoken. Candlelight flickered over upturned faces. Dawn began to break, piercing the mist with a shaft of light. On the stage with its painted clouds the angels and the archangels were ranged in order, as still and bright as figures painted on glass. Then the pageant began. God spoke:

'Ego sum Alpha et Omega vita via
Veritas primus et novissimus...'

His voice rang out over the upturned faces of the crowd.

'I am gracious and great, God with no beginning,
'I am maker unmade, all might is in me,
I am life and way unto wealth wynning,
I am foremost and first – as I bid shall it be...'

The audience stopped fidgeting and became absorbed in the unfolding story. The actors were guildsmen, more used to trade and manual work than acting, but they had learnt their lines well and, proud of their roles, put all their energy and skill into this first performance. If anyone had fears about the explosions earlier in the week they were forgotten now.

Chapter Thirty-One

From her position at the side of the audience Hildegard could see the machinery behind the wagon where the apprentices, working as a team, were hauling ropes to move the painted clouds across the sky, conducting the actors on and off stage at the right moment, and handing up props on cue.

One apprentice was preparing some concoction in a clay pot and handed it to an assistant. When Lucifer appeared it emitted a flash of light that made the audience draw in its breath.

Hildegard watched as the pot was stuffed in

with the other props to be used again at the next station.

The Fall came.

It was Lucifer again who slid spectacularly down a rope to land with a howl of defiance in the middle of the audience, making them scatter, and somehow letting flames spout from his scarlet mouth. His face was blackened by the smoke. With curses on heaven and all its denizens, he raged for quite some time. It sent those at the front shuffling back out of his way with mock cries of alarm for fear of another spout of flame. Then a woman's hair caught fire on her neighbour's candle and more scuffles followed to put it out.

God spoke again.

Despite the mask, his words were perfectly audible. A child held aloft at the back of the crowd mimicked him in a false, deep voice, making the audience roar. Unperturbed, he ground out his curse, and the angels, ranged along the back of the wagon, exchanged smug glances.

Hildegard remembered how Jankin had cast doubt on the audibility of God in a mask. Now the thought seemed a pathetic memorial to him. Tears filled her eyes. She saw his face underwater. It was as if he floated on the green air, weightlessly borne aloft on his wings.

The wagon of the Barkers' Guild rumbled away down the street to the next station. Its place was taken by the plasterers. In a short knockabout piece the entire earthly world was built in moments – drawing jibes from the crowd about

436

the plasterers' uncustomary speed – then the next wagon lumbered into place. The speaker stepped forward to a fanfare and with a sweep of his arm announced: 'Scene: The World.'

Despite the ambition of its setting it had only three characters. The boy who played Eve wore a skintight leather suit like the one Melisen was supposed to have worn for Gilbert's drawing. His wig of long flaxen hair was garlanded with real flowers and brought whistles of mocking appreciation from the apprentices at the front whenever he tossed his head. This time God had so many lines Hildegard suspected that the Cardmakers' Guild was employing one of the professional players who travelled from town to town; either that or he was an amateur with a prodigious memory.

The scene changed again and another wagon rolled up, this one carrying the Garden of Eden complete with tree. One of the stagehands shook it to make its leaves tremble and there were cheers, but the biggest cheer came for an actor in a serpent suit who leapt on stage clutching an enormous red gourd.

'And an angel with a sword!' announced the narrator. 'To drive the sinful pair from Paradise!' Booing followed.

Attached to the angel's shoulders were wings of cloth and paste and, brandishing a toy sword, he was let down on a rope to 'fly' across the stage to a wooden perch at the back. The audience decided to give him a rousing cheer for his daring, even though he was against the transgressors whom they clearly favoured. With a sardonic flourish the narrator withdrew.

Despite the ribald jokes that continually interrupted the actors, Hildegard was only half listening. She was haunted by more sombre memories.

Jankin.

He would have loved the show. He had been so young, so full of life – so unwitting of his bloody destiny.

She decided to head towards the de Hutton stand. The sun had already burnt away most of the mist. It glittered off the spangled costumes of the actors, making her eyes water. Dashing the back of her hand over them she wove through the fringes of the crowd and started across the street.

Before she reached the other side there came the sound of a massive explosion. A rush of alarm coursed through her and when she turned she saw a pall of smoke rising from the pageant wagon. Then she gave a shaky smile. It was only the serpent demonstrating his power over the hapless couple in Eden. Now everyone had recovered from the shock of the explosion he was drawing roars of protest from the onlookers. Cries of 'Shame!' and 'Leave them alone!' arose on all sides.

Backstage, the hands, apprentices by the look of them, were standing about with buckets of water as a precaution against fire. They had broad grins on their faces and were obviously itching to let loose with the water over each others' heads. There was another flare of flame as the serpent vanished into his tree.

She reached the stand. The de Hutton contingent were already in their seats. They looked as engaged as the townsfolk by the performers.

Petronilla and Maud, wearing little chaplets of fresh flowers, were sitting next to Lady Melisen who herself wore a startling mantle of shimmering silk worked in silver filigree that would not have been out of place onstage. Roger, much as usual, had a stoup in one hand but had at least donned a tunic with his red and gold emblem on the front. His chamberlain, wrapped up against the dawn air in his black velvet houpelande, looked as if the hot weather was a myth. He's not taking his cure for melancholy, observed Hildegard as she climbed up to take a seat beside him.

Below them, a row of men-at-arms, broad-shouldered and alert, were leaning against the rail across the front of the stand and pretending to keep an eye out for possible malcontents, but even they were as engrossed as everyone else in the plays.

Ulf, she noticed after a careful scrutiny, was nowhere to be seen.

In the break while one wagon was hauled away to the next station and another one was trundled into position, Hildegard got up again. She felt unsettled. The continual explosions onstage were rattling her nerves with their reminder of the threats made earlier in the week. She decided to see how things were going with Danby and his company in the pageant house. It would be some time before the Glaziers' Guild were due to perform.

They would have had to find another archangel,

439

she thought as she descended to the street. No doubt they had been hard put to find one who looked as right for the part as Jankin. She wondered about the wings and if they had managed to find a substitute for the ones that had ended in the millpond. That one feather, discovered under Jankin's bed, had been the only sign of his abduction. She wondered who had scrubbed the place clean and later disposed of his possessions and guessed it must have been Julitta.

The glaziers' wagon was already standing outside the warehouse where it had been stored during the preceding weeks, and the painted flames that had caused her such fright as she groped her way inside the place at dead of night had already been erected. Now she saw again that they were crudely painted, the brushstrokes obvious in daylight. No doubt when they were pulled about on ropes to simulate the fires of hell during the harrowing, they would be convincing enough. Judging by the singing that kept breaking out among the crowds, the audience would soon be in a state to be convinced of anything.

'Is your master around?' she asked a busy apprentice as he was heaving a load of costumes into the apparelling chamber underneath the stage.

'In there, Sister.' He gestured towards the pageant house.

She went over. Almost empty, it was still gloomy and shadow-filled despite the sunlight pouring through the door. Danby was standing over by the far wall talking to Master Stapylton.

Both wore worried expressions. When Hildegard appeared Danby gave a startled glance and put a hand on Stapylton's arm. Then he called out, 'Over here, Sister. Something I'd like you to see.'

When she approached he held out a piece of vellum like the ones Gilbert used for his pattern book. It was much scored and scratched. 'What do you make of this?'

She took it and peered at the words with a feeling of alarm. Written in a clear hand it was a proclamation warning of the approach of the Antichrist and the imminent death of the town's mayor and civic dignitaries. It was unsigned.

'Is it a joke?' she asked.

Danby turned away as if to conceal some thought that was too painful to bear and when he turned back he said, 'Joke or not, I found it in my own creel where we put all the waste.'

She turned it over. There were some notes on the back, a random list of colours and quantities of pot metal, some crossings out, ingredients for a rabbit pie, a few sums totted up, and when she read the proclamation again she saw that a word or two had been changed. Instead of 'the mayor and his aldermen', it read, 'the mayor and his aldermen and all the guildmasters'. Someone who liked to get things right, then. Someone focused in their threats.

'Clearly a devil out there thought it worth making a rough draft of his intentions before pinning his copy to the minster doors,' Stapylton said. 'We're treating it as a serious threat. It's the same as that proclamation that got everybody talking yesterday, the one nailed to the doors where everybody could read it.'

Hildegard remembered the throng clustered at the entrance to the minster when she had gone in pursuit of Maud. So that was what they had been doing, reading a death threat.

She asked the obvious question. 'Who do you think put it in your waste, master?'

Danby's expression was bleak. 'Who else is at liberty in that back workshop...?' He didn't need to utter Gilbert's name.

'Have you spoken to him?' she asked.

Danby shook his head. 'I'm in a flat spin.'

'Keep a hold on yourself, Edric.' Stapylton put a consoling hand on his arm. 'I know I've got my suspicions but he's not the only one around. No point in accusing the devil to his face until you've got more proof. You've had folk in and out of your workshop with this business over Dorelia ever since you got back with her.'

'I know, I know,' Danby was shaking his head, 'but nobody goes through into that little back workshop without me or Gilbert with 'em. It's his own domain. I went in there to cool down after...' He was shaking his head again as if to free it from a restraint.

'The thing is,' he gave Hildegard a suffering look, 'Dorelia's been in such a bad way, sobbing her heart out, and I've been at my wits' end to know how to console her, and she was crying out for somebody in the night, the name of some fella, and when your friend Theophilus happened to hear tell of his name, he knew at once who he was. I never knew,' Danby went on in a parched voice, 'but she was betrothed before Baldwin

442

offered her to me – I just didn't know! How could I have known a thing like that? She should never have married me, being hand-fast to another! Now it seems he's all that might bring her back to her senses. Yon Theophilus has sent to fetch him.'

He finished and abruptly walked away.

Stapylton said, 'His heart's in tatters. He doesn't know which way to turn.'

Danby gathered himself and came back, saying, 'I was so enraged by it all I went into Gilbert's workshop and gave a good kick at that creel where nobody could see how it blasted me. Then I bent to pick up everything I'd spilt and there it was! From one catastrophe to another. I almost wish I'd kept a leash on my temper and stayed in ignorance.'

'Come on now, Edric, it's better to know the truth than to live like a child knowing nowt.' Stapylton put a hand on Danby's shoulder. 'Any man would have done the same as you and likely worse, even. You've had more to put up with than anybody should have to bear. It's a good thing we've found out what they're planning. At least there's a hope we can put a stop to it.'

'So you really think there are going to be more explosions?' Hildegard looked from one to the other.

Stapylton grimaced. 'Today. Of course. When better? If it's their evil intention to kill and maim, this is the time to do it.'

'But as you said, you can't be sure...' Hildegard frowned. Of course they couldn't be sure. Nobody could until it happened. Carefully she said,

'Gilbert must be confronted if you suspect him.'

Stapylton turned to her. 'For the rest of the day he's in the pageant. He's had to step into Jankin's place. With that hair of his he'll look the part. We've even rigged up a throne for him so he doesn't have to walk with his limp in front of everybody. He's where we can keep an eye on him at all times. We'll not be doing anything today.'

'But if he is involved,' she pointed out, 'it doesn't mean that he would be the one to plant the explosives. He'll have accomplices.'

'We've put word out. The guildmasters have been informed. We're keeping a close watch on our lads. If there's trouble, that's where it'll come from – from them. The mayor and aldermen have got their men to police the crowds. The bailiffs are on full alert, the constables out in force. Nobody can possibly get away with another explosion. We'll catch them with the touchpaper in their hands if there's a next time.'

Danby took the fragment of vellum from Hildegard and stared at it as if hoping the words had been misread. Then he folded it into four pieces and put it in his pouch. 'Can you believe he'd plot such a wicked thing?'

His expression was bleak. Head bowed, he left them. As he went his shoulders seemed to heave with a spasm of repressed grief, but by the time he got to the door he had forced them back. Head erect he bellowed to the actors outside. 'All right, lads! Get to it! Are we glaziers or sot-wit tanners? Let's get this show on the road!'

444

Chapter Thirty-Two

The apparelling house was a cavity built between the wheels of the wagon under the acting area. Its contents were concealed by a curtain. Inside were the props, and if there were any devices being used, that's where they were stored.

The glaziers' play was fortieth in the sequence. The actors were not required until later in the morning and now they hung around the wagon on Pageant Green, suffering various degrees of anxiety over their lines.

It was a large cast of fifteen actors for *The Harrowing of Hell,* Satan, Jesus and a small part of four lines that had belonged to Jankin, now to be spoken by Gilbert as the Archangel Michael.

He was at present sitting a little apart from everyone else. As a militant angel wielding a fiery sword he was unconvincing. Hildegard wondered if he guessed he was under suspicion. Danby was putting up a good show in the role of genial guildmaster, swapping jokes with the leads, ribbing John the Baptist about the smell from his animal skins, and handing round a flagon of what turned out to be good Rhenish from his own cellar. She handed the flagon on to Gilbert after she had had her turn.

'Word-perfect?' she asked.

'I was word-perfect weeks ago,' he said, 'having to listen to that sot wit trying to get his few lines into his thick skull.' His face was pale, devoid of any expression. Outlined in black charcoal his eyes appeared even more translucent than usual. Despite the harshness of his tone she found it difficult to gauge his mood and suspected that it concealed more emotion than he was willing to admit openly.

'How's the window for Lord de Hutton?' she asked.

'Nearly finished. As soon as this bollocks is over I'll paint in the faces, get them fired, and fit them in. Job done.' His eyes briefly sparked. 'I should be working on it now instead of indulging in all this,' he added.

'Don't you believe Corpus Christi should be celebrated?' she asked.

'What do you think?'

'I take that as a "no" then.' It was a common view that the Church put on these holy days to keep everybody in their place. Bread and circuses, just like the Romans.

'At least it gives folks a chance to have a day off from the daily grind.' He nodded towards the cheerful crowd behind the barrier. 'I would never begrudge the poor fools that.'

'What time are you setting off?'

'Ages yet. Time for stage fright to settle in and get a hold.' He handed the flagon back and she drank and passed it on to one of the nearby devils.

To answer Danby's question: no, she couldn't believe Gilbert would do such a wicked thing.

And yet – there was that handwritten warning of the wrath to come.

Ulf's absence had been explained. That was one bright spot in the current situation. He wasn't trying to avoid her because she had broken his heart. According to Danby he was working on security, not lounging around with his lord and guests at the first station enjoying himself. Now it had been drawn to her notice she perceived that the street was full of men wearing the city's blazon of leopards. Once you suspected weapons you could see them barely concealed beneath their cloaks.

The de Huttons were still in the stand and had been joined by several gaudily attired visitors. They looked like local merchants, small land-owners, wealthy burgesses. Food was being handed up on platters from a portable kitchen at the back. The Tuscan chef was shouting orders in the sort of English that sent the yeomen of the board into stitches, but it was all good-humoured and everyone was pulling together.

The cooking was being done on a makeshift brazier, and a spit of roast pheasant and other fowl was turning above the flames, giving off an enticing aroma. A boar's head, as yet uncooked, stood on a trestle close by.

There was a lot of fire around, not only here with the brazier, but on the pageant wagons them-selves. Hildegard considered what it had taken to set alight the market booth with its terrible out-come. She recalled Stapylton's outraged descrip-tion of the attempted firing of his workshop and his mention of the brass bowl, presumably containing the wax common to both outbreaks.

447

When she considered the matter she realised that almost every play she could think of had its possibly lethal ration of flame – *Lucifer*, obviously, as she had just witnessed, *Abraham* with the sacrificial fire for his son, the thunder and lightning denoting the wrath of God as the flood swept all but Noah and his family from the world, *The Annunciation*, *The Holy Light* seen by the shepherds, the flames of hell in *The Harrowing*, not to mention *The Last Judgement* with its fiery glory hole into which the damned were hurled.

Fire was a favourite device, thrilling the audience, with every burst of flame set to outdo the preceding one, and safe enough when confined to the wagons. The apprentices were well advised to stand by with buckets of water and the players themselves would be alert for their own safety, exposed upon the open stage.

But what about the crowds? she wondered now. What if fire broke out in the thick of it? There would be panic. Children would be trampled, the old and infirm would be injured, people might finish up like the poor woman who had died with that long drawn-out scream of agony, devoured by a ball of flame in the fabric booth, or delirious with blackened skin and talking of crocodiles like her husband in the hospital of St Leonard.

Drunkenness would make the situation worse. With minds bleared by alcohol, nobody would notice a figure in the crowd putting a light to some device. They would take it as part of the entertainment. But then the fire-setter's own life would be at risk as well. It would have to be a timed explosion. It would need to be set up as at

448

the chandler's workshop and in the puppet tent – in such a way that by the time of its death-dealing the madman who had devised such a stunt would be away to safety.

A device like that would not be difficult to set. As Stapylton had said, any fool could do it. Even though it would have to be done in secret where it was likely to go unobserved until too late, it could be done.

She remembered how Stapylton had told them about the cloths hanging above the bowl of wax so that the flames set light to them and it was the cloths that were then supposed to set light to the beams above. An apparelling house would be the ideal setting except for the fact that there were always people on hand.

There were many other ways of making an explosion.

It need not be beeswax.

Saltpetre was easy to get hold of, as was brimstone.

There were other substances, imported from the East. There was the mysterious stuff called Greek fire, although nobody really seemed to know if it existed or not. There was even an experiment done with mirrors that was said to have set alight the sails of a warship off Constantinople. The sun was certainly bright enough today to experiment with such a device.

Stapylton, in his mood of black suspicion, had also claimed that there were some young rebels so enraged by their political impotence that they would even risk their own lives for the cause. She imagined how an explosive device could be

449

strapped to the body of one with such desperation in his soul.

In fear she went back under the stand to where the spit was turning. Roger kept a full complement of servants. There were people around all the time and none without his blazon on their tunics to declaim their allegiance. Unobtrusively she stood by for a while, observing what went on and ultimately deciding that if anyone tried to set up a firebomb here it would be noticed at once.

Even so, she climbed the steps between the strings of fluttering pennants to where everyone was still watching the plays and asked if she might sit next to Roger for a moment. The chamberlain moved up, scarcely taking his eyes off the stage.

She leant forward. 'My lord, a word?' When she explained her fears he nodded, then called for his kitchen clerk and whispered in his ear. Grim-faced the man went down underneath the stand. Roger put his hand over hers. 'Be reassured, Hildegard. If anybody can get away with it they'll have to make themselves invisible.'

Invisible. The only person she had met recently who could make themselves invisible had been the mage, Theophilus, otherwise known as John of Berwick, with perhaps other names besides.

According to Danby, he had sent word to Dorelia's betrothed to inform him of recent events. Today he had been invisible all right. She had seen no sign of him. It looked as if he had given up on a sure profit in the streets of York to take the message into the West Riding himself.

Still haunted by uneasy premonitions she again went down into the street. It was heaving with activity.

Aware that it was useless to try to second-guess the actions of the one who had written the threat on the minster doors, and conscious that poor Brother Thomas must still be lying in St Leonard's on the other side of town, she decided it was high time to pay him a visit. She had scarcely given him a thought in her fear of the fire-raisers.

At the same time she would keep an eye open for the mage. His view on things was often confirmed by the confidences he picked up.

The procession following the pageant wagons already stretched down the hill towards the bridge. It was another hot morning promising more of the same. It seemed as if the fine weather would never end. There was a new heaviness in the air, however, pressing down like the lid over a furnace. It was becoming uncomfortable, the sort of weather to bring headaches and ill temper.

The third pageant station was at John Gisburne's mansion near North Street. It was on the way to St Leonard's, so Hildegard made her way towards it in the wake of the followers.

Robert Harpham, in whose house Roger's party was staying, had had a simple balcony erected, on a level with his first-floor windows. It was wide enough for the old merchant to sit there in comfort above the street with a couple of body-servants and a few members of his family beside him.

451

Gisburne's viewing place, on the other hand, was an elaborate three-storey erection, hung with enough gaudy tapestries to make sure everyone knew he was a man of wealth. Not that it was doing him any good now, in prison.

Undaunted by his fate, his wife, accompanied by a handsome young man in lieu of her husband, was surrounded by servants and visitors. There was a charge to sit on the upper level and a household clerk was doing brisk business from a queue of people who had tired of the growing rowdiness of the streets and wished for a little privacy. As Ulf had said, now was the right time to make a killing. It was frightening to think that was what the fire-raisers might think too, in a different sense.

Hildegard continued down the hill. It was difficult to know what to look for, but she was alert for anything that seemed suspicious. The firebombings were seen as the work of the White Hart, designed to spoil the religious festival and put a question mark around the whole idea of the body of Christ being turned to bread and wine.

The last notice, however, the one pinned to the minster doors, had been different. It was a direct threat against the mayor and his men. It was common knowledge that the council was loyal to King Richard and openly stood against John of Gaunt and his allies. It made no sense for the freethinkers to threaten the council. The suspicion that Gilbert had written it only led to confusion.

Praying that their suspicions were groundless, she crossed the bridge. The route was being kept

452

open by the constables but it was thick with spectators on both sides. After watching the wagons go past they would gather to watch the procession of the Host after it emerged from the minster.

People were gathered at every station she passed, although they were at different levels of expectation. Those at the end of Conyngsgate were already cheering the arrival of the armourers' wagon, while at the sixth station on Castlegate the fullers were just bringing their play to an end.

Further on the performing space was taken up by entertainers – jugglers, acrobats, minstrels, sword dancers, fortune-tellers, a chained and muzzled bear, conjurors, card sharps and a ventriloquist or two – all making the most of a captive audience with money to throw at their feet in the time before the wagons appeared.

It was steamy down here in the heart of the town. The crowd was rougher, less well dressed, less polite and, inevitably, already drunk. Hildegard made her way to the end of Jubbergate and on to the next station, then wended back towards Conyngsgate towards the Common Hall.

There was no sign of the mage.

Regretting that she had made a detour away from St Leonard's, she headed back towards the river. In doing so she had to cross the square outside the Common Hall.

Here things were a little more decorous. The mayor, Simon de Quixlay, had just arrived and was about to climb the steps to take his place alongside his aldermen on the official stand.

Banners in the colours of the city livery adorned the platform and flags were strung from one side of the square to the other.

De Quixlay gave a genial wave to a crowd of supporters as he took his seat. He had guards, she noted, posted all the way along the front. Clearly his genial nature did not extend to welcoming possible fire-raisers.

She watched for a moment or two. The stand was similar to the one Roger had had built. The kitchens, however, were in the adjoining hall and there were guards posted on the doors doing an efficient job in preventing entry to anyone they did not recognise. Just to test them she made her way over and tried to get inside. She was stopped at once.

'Despite your Cistercian habit, Sister, I beg leave to ask for your avouchment.' The guard's manner showed that he didn't know whether she was genuine or had merely adopted the white habit as a form of motley.

'I have no proof of my identity,' she told him, 'other than my word.'

'In that case, with the utmost regret, I am forced to bar entry. Go and ask for permission from the aldermen if you know any of 'em.' He turned his attention to other matters.

The next station was somewhere along Stonegate. It was not too far out of the way to St Leonard's. With her linen undershift sticking to her in the heat she made her way slowly in that direction and had just reached the corner when a man she took to be a beggar stepped into her path. He wore a travel-stained robe of rough fustian and had leather sandals on his feet. Reaching for her pouch she extracted a few coins, then, as she tried to drop them into his palm, she glanced into his face.

Her lips opened.

It was a second or two before she managed to recover. Dropping to her knees at once and with head bent she crossed herself. 'My Lord.'

'Arise, Sister.'

Trembling, she straightened. Eye to eye, she saw she was not mistaken.

It was Abbot Hubert de Courcy.

Chapter Thirty-Three

His face was deeply tanned. He looked what he was, a man who had been honed by long hard months under the blaze of a desert sun. She lowered her glance. If the ground had opened up and swallowed her she could not have been more confused.

'So?' he prompted when she failed to speak.

She tried to gather her wits. When at last she raised her head she was surprised at how calm she sounded. 'I understood you were still on pilgrimage, my Lord Abbot.'

'As you see – I have returned.'

His eyes flickered over her face as if searching for something.

In a secret confusion of astonishment and joy she said, 'It gives me chance to thank you for the gift you sent...' and, unable to leave matters like that, she heard herself add, 'from Avignon.'

The expression in the remote depths of his eyes was unfathomable. 'It reached you safely, then.'

'I admit I was surprised,' she continued, with the feeling that she was suddenly unable to hold back the words. 'I understood your destination was Jerusalem?'

'And so it was. I returned by ship to Aigues Mortes and it seemed sensible to pay a visit to the papal palace...'

'To the palace of Pope Clement,' she added, to establish the fact beyond doubt.

'Indeed.' He gave a faint smile at her emphasis but at the same time seemed to draw back.

To compound her folly even further, she remarked, 'I trust your career has been enhanced by your visit to Avignon?'

It was cheap and she was immediately dismayed at allowing the words to fall from her lips, but they were out and, indeed, they expressed her confusion when the messenger told her where Hubert had purchased the missal he had sent.

His expression did not alter. The ambivalent manner with which he had greeted her was more confusing still. For a moment they stood without speaking as the crowd pushed them on all sides. It seemed as if the silence would go on for ever. Hildegard felt bereft of every word she had ever learnt. There was nothing. Just a gaping silence like the void in the beginning, before the first word was uttered.

Someone barged between them. She took a step back. More people followed, a long line of jigging fools with a hurdy-gurdy man egging them on. Hubert's face seemed to burn in the very air, like a ghost cast out from his nocturnal realm. The strangeness of seeing him again without warning and in this place, on this day, was beyond reason.

They were at the top of Stonegate, and suddenly from the far end came a sound like many hundreds of birds taking flight.

The soft flapping of wings was multiplied until it was a drowning wave, washing over them. The hurdy-gurdy fell silent in mid phrase. Stillness prevailed all the length of the narrow street. She saw the abbot sink to his knees, and those around him were dropping to their knees in that soft sound of fabric brushing on stone, of hats being removed. And then she understood that the Host was approaching.

Turning, she saw the glitter of the canopy first, and, because she could see unimpeded down the length of the street over the heads of all the kneeling people where only one or two men stood with arms folded in defiance, she could see the Host itself, borne aloft by two acolytes in its glittering gold pyx amid the shimmer of beryl and pearls and rubies and countless other precious stones adorning the chased silver and gold monstrance. The whole thing seemed to burn with an unearthly fire as the scarlet silk canopy embroidered in gold thread swayed and fluttered its tassels as it approached.

Slowly she sank down at Hubert's side.

The hems of their robes lay folded together, touching.

457

They stayed until the procession had gone past and then, as everyone around them rose to their feet and brushed themselves down and recovered their heads, the abbot stretched out his hand to her.

Feeling his touch for the first time in over a year, she froze in shock. Then she allowed him to raise her to her feet. They stood face-to-face, his lips, his mouth on a level with her own. She could feel the heat radiating from him. It carried the exotic scent of the East, suggesting distant places, the regions he had visited, the foreign lives that had touched his in the long year of his absence.

Her tears the previous night in the tub of rose-scented water had been for this moment – for the sense of loss she knew it would bring. It had been a forewarning of finding and losing in the same moment.

With an effort, to retain a shred of common sense – he could not know the impact of his sudden appearance – she forced herself to speak. 'Brother Thomas was wounded yesterday. He's in St Leonard's hospital.'

'Are you on your way to see him?'

She nodded.

Hubert looked grim. 'I heard about the attack. It's all over the archbishop's palace.'

'Are you staying there?' she asked. It was amazing how matter-of-fact she sounded.

'Last night and tonight only. Then it's back to Meaux to see what havoc they've created while I've been away.' For a moment there was something dancing in his expression. She put it down to his pleasure at taking up his duties again – well purged of all the sins of the past by his pil-grimage.

'I'm sure things have gone smoothly – though not,' she hastened to add, 'as smoothly as if you'd been there yourself.'

It was with a kind of private joy, fragile, not quite formed, with which she accompanied him through the crowds towards the river. He said nothing more to her. When they reached St Leonard's she felt regret that this silent com-munion was about to be curtailed, with no further indication of how things stood between them.

When they went inside and walked down the aisle between the cubicles they found Thomas lying on a bed. He was going through his beads. When he realised that his abbot had taken the time and trouble to visit him he was overwhelmed with gratitude.

He kept saying, 'I'm fine, My Lord. I really am. It was nothing. It was scarcely a scratch. A wonderful old leech-woman stepped out of the crowd and put me to rights. And best of all, Sister Hildegard took little Maud to safety.'

In the expectation that his Order would be footing the bill for his treatment, the monks had given Thomas the sole use of one of the double cubicles in the main ward of the hospital. It was private enough for him to explain to the abbot the circumstances that had brought him there. The story had to be told in all its detail.

'So,' Hubert summed up when Thomas finished, 'all's well that ends well?'

Hildegard reserved any comment and merely

made a fuss of Thomas and insisted on inspecting the bandages they had applied. 'I see they know their job, Brother. Thank heavens for that. I hated leaving you.'

'If you'd lingered, that knight – one of de Bohun's men, you say? – would have snatched Maud again. He had guards posted close by. You would never have got away if you hadn't left so quickly.' He looked serious. 'I hope I've made up for that other time when I behaved so cravenly?'

'Dear Thomas,' she said softly. 'Your behaviour is never craven.'

Afterwards he insisted he was well enough to get up, gathered his few belongings, and went to inform the almoner that he was leaving.

When he was out of earshot Hubert turned to Hildegard. 'I may as well tell you and get it over with. I saw you last night. I'd just arrived after the last day's long walk. You were crossing the street near a merchant's house. Is that where you're staying?'

'Only until I return to Swyne. There was some difficulty in getting Maud back to safety.'

'I didn't see her with you.'

'I had to send her back across the river by boat. Her pursuer had a guard posted on the bridge.'

Thomas had said nothing about what had happened to Hildegard afterwards, of course, as he knew nothing about it. Now she made no mention of it. Hubert would never drag that part of the story from her.

His tone was abrupt. 'No doubt it's pleasant to stay in a town house with your old friends.'

Thomas was still at the far end of the ward and

460

Hubert went on, 'As abbot, I will have to make a representation to our prioress on a question of discipline. It will be a matter for the Chapter at Meaux. Your conduct is scandalous. It goes beyond any bounds of decency. Frankly, you horrify me.'

Before she could ask what on earth he meant he turned with a sweep of his robes and headed towards the door. She stared after him in anger and astonishment. Thomas reappeared. He looked surprised at the haste of his abbot's departure but Hubert was already outside, striding along the path towards nearby St Mary's Abbey, and he hurried after him with a delighted glance at Hildegard, exclaiming, 'So our abbot is back! Praise the saints!'

'He's back all right.' She turned away, blinking at a sudden smarting sensation in her eyes.

When she looked again Thomas had caught up with Hubert and she watched them continue along the path, apparently chatting amiably, until they were out of sight within the precincts of St Mary's.

Chapter Thirty-Four

As she reached the street a few minutes later the Host reappeared on its meandering journey through the town. This time she stood in a doorway so she didn't have to kneel.

Other people were doing the same. Even a few

461

who were at the front of the crowd remained standing, despite objections from those behind. Harsh words were exchanged between spectators of different persuasions. Several people crossed themselves and looked askance. Others joined in the dispute.

'It's a free country,' somebody retorted. 'We can think what we like. We don't have to believe your popish lies.' More argument followed until the crowd, through sheer force of numbers, pushed the disputants apart.

Hildegard meandered back along the route of the pageant and eventually found a niche on a window ledge within earshot of the stand at Jubbergate. She didn't hear a word. All she could do was go over everything that had passed between herself and Hubert since she had handed him alms by mistake.

Every word he said burnt in her mind. She realised that she should not have spoken so critically. He was the abbot after all. But surely that wasn't a reason to be forced to stand trial in front of the Chapter of monks at Meaux

She went over her words again and again and could find no real fault in them. How could he take exception to the truth?

If they dare cross-question her she would stick by every word. He could not take offence at the truth. How could it horrify him to discover her shock at his visit to Avignon? He made no apology for his allegiance with the antipope.

This was England.

Clement was the French pope, known for his avarice and duplicity. And the king of France was again rumoured to be massing forces on the other side of the Channel ready to invade. The mother house of the Abbey of Meaux, what's more, was itself French. By putting a detour to Avignon above his immediate return to Meaux he had clearly shown where his loyalty lay.

How could Hubert defend that? It must be true what the prioress had hinted: he was in the pay of France. He was a spy.

Miserably she watched the plays from the street until the sun was nothing but a burning disc overhead.

Still no sign of the mage. Above the roofs the sky acquired a molten look. A strange light tinted with copper the underbelly of a single large cloud.

During the next half-dozen plays the cloud expanded and darkened and dropped lower. A deceptive breeze suddenly sprang up. It refreshed the air for a moment and then abated. The banners looped from balcony to balcony across the street had fluttered briefly into life and now fell still once more. People took off their straw hats and used them as fans, then replaced them for fear of sunstroke. An enterprising gardener brought out sheaves of rhubarb leaves and sold them for a farthing each. The water-sellers did a roaring trade.

Hildegard realised that she could be sitting in more comfort under the awning with the de Huttons – the old friends Hubert had referred to in such a scathing manner – so, heavy-hearted, with no idea whether the rumour of explosion was to be trusted or not, and with a headache just beginning, she made her way back across the river to Micklegate.

The sequence of plays was continuing as she took her place on the stand. Petronilla turned to her in excitement. 'You've just missed the glaziers' play, Sister. That beautiful man you know called Gilbert was the Archangel Michael. He was magnificent, even though they hardly allowed him to speak more than a couple of lines. I am so enamoured of him.'

Melisen broke in. 'Don't be such a ridiculous child. He must be at least twenty-six, even older than I am!'

Hildegard scarcely heard them chatter on. She was wondering if Danby had told Ulf of his suspicions regarding Gilbert.

As far as she understood him, he and Stapylton had merely agreed to mention the apprentices in general. There was the performance to consider, the humiliation of failing to provide a play to the necessary standard and the severe fine if they failed. No doubt Danby felt that as long as he could keep an eye on his journeyman, retribution could wait and the honour of the guild he maintained.

It was impossible to believe that Gilbert had planned to set an explosive in the crowd. Poor Danby, she thought. He looks on Gilbert as his son.

Unable to sit still she got up with a muttered explanation, saying that she needed something for her headache and, trailing back towards Harpham's, had just reached the gates into the

464

courtyard when a stranger stepped from out of the porter's lodge and planted himself directly in her path.

'Sister Hildegard?' he asked.

'Who wants to know?'

'I do. May we go inside?' He gestured for her to precede him into the lodge.

Inside she turned to give him a long look. He was an angular sort of fellow, tall and stooped, his face parchment coloured and grooved with worry lines running vertically down his forehead as well as on both sides of his mouth.

Jostling at his side were four little girls, ranging in age from around five to twelve or so. They were prettily if shabbily dressed and the man himself, their father perhaps, had on a worn tunic over darned brown hose.

He said to her, 'I believe you have custody of my daughter.'

Chapter Thirty-Five

She stared. 'Your daughter?'

His glance was eager as if she held the key to all his future happiness. 'I've just come from Swyne. The prioress there told me you brought her to York for safety? I mean my little Petronilla.'

'She's safe and well,' Hildegard told him evenly. 'If you would like to see her, come with me.'

'Hear that, girls, I think we've found her!' he exclaimed.

465

The children were standing in a chain of clasped hands and the smallest, a tousled moppet, anchored this little chain to their father's sleeve with a firm grip of her chubby fingers. The chain broke at these words, however, and the little girls surged round him so that he was suddenly knee-deep in a sea of piping children.

In one swoop Hildegard grasped the entire picture. 'It's not far,' she reassured him. 'Follow me.'

They practically had to fight their way through the crowds towards the stand.

Despite the evident delight of the little family, it didn't stop Hildegard from briefly wondering if he had been sent to kidnap Petronilla, just as the knight had tried to kidnap Maud, but she led the way to the pageant stand anyway. It was reassuring to note that there were plenty of guards around. When she reached the steps she said, 'If you wait here I'll go up and fetch her.'

Petronilla was leaning on the railing, her glance fixed avidly on another play. She was accompanied by Maud and one or two personal servants. Lady Melisen was lying back with her eyes half closed and seemed to find the heat even under the canopy too much to bear. Lord Roger was asleep.

Hildegard called over. 'May I borrow Petronilla for a moment, My Lady?'

'Oh do! They never stop chattering and I'm too hot to care about anything just now.' Melisen fanned herself with the edge of her veil. 'We're all about to decamp to Harpham's to refresh ourselves. I'll be delighted when the storm breaks.

466

This weather is intolerable.' She stretched out a languid arm. 'Run along, Petronilla, do as you're told.'

The girl got up and followed Hildegard down the steps. Hildegard was in front and temporarily blocked the view of the people below. When she reached the bottom she stepped to one side.

There was a gasp from the top of the steps. 'Father!'

'My little chick! My beauty! My little dove!' The stranger climbed swiftly up the steps to sweep her into his arms. He carried her down, then twirled her round in a flurry of skirts before setting her on her feet again.

Then he stepped back and tried to adopt a stern look that didn't quite convince. 'My angel, why did you run away without telling anyone where you were going?' he asked in hangdog tones.

'I didn't think anybody would notice,' Petronilla replied, giving him a wary glance from underneath her lashes.

'We've been out of our minds, pippin! Your sisters have been crying their eyes out ever since you ran away. Isn't that so, girls?' As at a sign the children gave little squeals of delight and threw themselves all over their sister.

Melisen appeared at the top of the steps. 'What on earth's going on?'

'This is Petronilla's father,' Hildegard announced. She stepped out of the way.

Melisen slowly descended the steps. When she reached the bottom her glance was on the stranger, but then it fixed on Petronilla. 'Your *father?*'

Petronilla stared at the ground.

467

'You told me you were an orphan. You told me your guardian was a wicked fellow who had tried to marry you off to an old man. You told me ... you told me a pack of *lies,* madam!' Melisen's voice had risen.

Petronilla began to cry.

Melisen was unimpressed. She used tears to good effect herself and was not moved by others adopting the same ploy. 'So you are not an orphan! Your inheritance has not been squandered by a profligate uncle! May I ask, has anything you told us been true in the slightest degree?'

'Everything was true,' blubbed Petronilla, 'except where I came from and why. That was the only lie.'

'It doesn't leave much out!'

'And London.' Petronilla glanced hurriedly at Hildegard. 'I've never been there, Sister. I'm sorry.'

She allowed her tears to trickle very slowly down her cheeks, then with a little anguished cry she dropped to her knees. 'I beg and implore you to honour me with your forgiveness, My Lady.'

'You should be kneeling to your father and begging his forgiveness,' Melisen reproved. 'If you were my daughter I'd give you a good whipping.' She looked the man up and down. 'Let me invite you over to the house, sir. At least we can get out of this infernal heat. Your little girls might like something to eat and drink. Is their mother with you?'

'Dead, My Lady.' The man quickly removed his cap and held it in front of him. 'I'm a widower. Have been now for some five years.'

He indicated the smallest child. 'I try to do what's best for them. But nothing seems to work out. We've been making toys for the Rhineland trade, very pretty things, the girls could scarcely bear to part with them, but it's come to nothing. I'm at my wits' end. She's a good little creature.' He touched Petronilla with great gentleness on the shoulder. 'Don't be harsh with her, My Lady. She's probably sick of having to look after so many little ones, being only fourteen herself.'

'*Fourteen?*' repeated Melisen in wonder. 'You had better come with me.'

Aware that matters had been taken out of her hands, Hildegard made off at once. While they had been talking something had occurred to her. By the time she arrived in Danby's yard she had pushed the question of Petronilla to the back of her mind. It was another young woman she wished to speak to.

The first thing she noticed when she entered the yard was the guard at the far end, and the second thing was that someone had rigged up a temporary shelter for her hounds outside the widow's door. Both animals were lying peacefully in its shade with a large bowl of water between them and some half-gnawed bones. They greeted her fondly and allowed her to pet them, and then she went on into the workshop and gave a call.

There was no response.

Poking her head round the kitchen door she saw it was empty. Even the deaf cook had gone. At the foot of the stairs she called out again.

The widow Tabitha appeared from Danby's

private chamber with a finger to her lips. 'She's up here, Sister. Come up.'

When she reached the landing Hildegard asked in a lowered voice, 'How is she? Is she able to talk?'

Tabitha put her hand to the door. 'She's much better since that mage said he'd have her betrothed fetched over.' She hesitated, then whispered, 'I may tell you this so you may better understand. She was with child. It was lost because of what happened – some would say it's probably for the best.'

Then, without waiting for Hildegard's response, she ushered her inside and in a bright voice said, 'There she is, Sister. I'll leave you both for a while. Cook is going to come in and sit with her later on.' As she turned to go she said to Hildegard, 'By the way, my nephew built a shelter for your hounds and now he's taken Kit and the kitchen lad to watch the pageant.'

Thanking her for looking after everything Hildegard went over to the bed.

Dorelia was lying back with one hand over her brow.

Her hair had been washed and brushed and was spread out in a silky sheen across the pillow. She wore a high-necked shift, but the bruises on her neck, blue, turning through green to yellow, were visible under the lace frill. When she heard someone approach she had opened her eyes and now, seeing Hildegard, she lifted one hand in greeting, but let it drop onto the counterpane almost at once without the strength to do more.

'So kind to come – master told me what you

470

did. Sit down and talk to me if you will...'

'I was rather hoping you would talk to me, Dorelia. That is, if you're well enough?'

'I'm as well as I can be at present. Berwick has sent for my betrothed. I thought all was lost ... if he comes ... though I reckon he'll want nothing to do with me when he hears the shame of what's happened...'

Her voice was a wisp of sound and faded completely, but after she closed her eyes for a moment she seemed to gather strength from somewhere and, opening them, revealing their startling colour, began to speak again. 'Poor Edric,' she said, 'I've brought him nothing but grief, and if I'd known how it was going to turn out – I don't know what else I could have done – will I be forgiven, Sister?'

'I'm sure He's already forgiven you. Master Danby too,' she added.

'I don't deserve it – he's a kind man...' Her voice faded.

'And Jankin?' Hildegard asked softly.

Dorelia's lips trembled. 'Dearest Jankin. He was a light in all the darkness – I don't know how I would have survived all this without him – there was no badness in him ... he did not deserve what happened...' Her lips trembled even more and her words trailed away again.

'Why would Gisburne and Baldwin do such a thing?' Hildegard asked as gently as she could.

'Jealousy,' she replied simply. 'Baldwin could not leave me alone. He was mad, obsessed. It made him want to drag me through the dirt because I couldn't love him back. He said he had

471

made a mistake–' She broke off.

'Mistake?'

Dorelia gave her a bleak glance. 'He said he sold me to his brother when he should have kept me for himself.' Her eyes brimmed. 'You see, Sister, I lost everything when my father died. I thought he had money but it seems he had nothing. My betrothed was travelling away at the time with his master. I didn't know which way to turn. Baldwin appeared and he was kind at first. I thought he was a refuge. And then – then I saw his true colours. By then it was too late...' She wiped her eyes.

'There is something more I need to ask you, Dorelia,' Hildegard murmured. 'I fear people's lives may be in danger – and you may be able to help prevent it–'

'Danger?'

'I'm not sure about any of this.' She paused. 'I wonder whether you can tell me anything more about Jankin?'

Dorelia widened her eyes. 'What sort of thing?'

'About his beliefs, for instance?'

She shook her head. 'What would I know? He was no different from any other apprentice.'

'Surely there's something?' Hildegard paused. 'Did he sympathise somewhat with the rebels?'

Dorelia looked confused.

'It can do no harm to him to tell me what you know,' Hildegard urged. 'Was he planning anything with the others?'

Dorelia gave a small sigh, halfway between fear and resignation. 'You're right. He can't be harmed anymore.' She glanced at Hildegard for

472

reassurance and, seeing her expression, said hurriedly, 'He was what the old-timers called a hothead. That's what you mean, isn't it? Them apprentices are all alike. Mostly it's just talk. They wouldn't do anything. They've their livelihoods to think of–' Biting her lip she broke off.

'So he was planning something?'

Dorelia gave a slight nod.

'With others?'

'No,' she replied at once, voice almost inaudible. 'Not with the others. And it wasn't so much planning as... I'll explain.' She took her time before beginning to speak and Hildegard wondered what she was about to reveal.

'As you've guessed, he sympathised with the brotherhood–'

'The Company of the White Hart?' Hildegard confirmed.

'Them.' In a rush she said, 'He used to listen to Gilbert spouting on and he became persuaded by him. He was eager to do something. "Anything," he said. "We can't live under their insults any longer. We're not serfs now." Everybody knew that Tabitha's son had been in the Company. He was one of those murdered about eighteen months ago over near Beverley. Six apprentices all told and the killers never brought to justice.'

Hildegard's eyes narrowed. She remembered that terrible event very well indeed. She had come across the gibbet in the woods with its grisly burden. And nearby she had found the body of an apprentice clutching one of the phials containing a scrap of cloth soaked in the blood of Wat Tyler. It was a sacred relic to the rebels, as

473

sacred as the blood of a saint to believers.

'Go on,' she urged.

'When Tabitha was upset one day, it being her son's birthday and him dead at eighteen,' Dorelia continued, 'Jankin found her in tears. She told him why. It made his blood boil. "I'll find his murderers for you, mistress," he said. "Trust me!" He had such a good heart. He would have found them, too, but he could never keep his mind on anything for long and...'

She began to focus with unnecessary attention on a loose thread on her sleeve. Hildegard gave her time to continue.

After a moment she looked up, blushing. 'Before he could think what to do Baldwin caught us both. And he found a way of turning it to his own advantage.'

'What do you mean?'

'Baldwin threatened to tell the master about us.'

'That you were lovers?'

Dorelia blushed. 'We were in terror lest it got out. He said to Jankin, "I've got a hold over you now. If you want to stay safe you're going to have to do me a favour or two." I was frightened he'd do something bad to Jankin if he refused, and I said, "I'm the only reason he's got a hold over you. We must stop. It'll be his word against ours." I didn't know then about the White Hart lads but Baldwin suspected Jankin of being a sympathiser like most of the other apprentices. I said to Jankin, "If he tells the master about us you'll lose your apprenticeship. We must stop." But he wouldn't give me up – and I...' she looked shamefaced, 'I

474

was too weak to resist.'

She closed her eyes and her lips trembled.

'What did Baldwin want Jankin to do?' asked Hildegard.

'He wanted chapter and verse about the Company of the White Hart, what they were up to. He wanted their names and the times and places where they met. He wanted Jankin to inform on his friends.'

'So what happened?'

'Jankin made stuff up. I warned him not to mess about. I knew what Baldwin was like. Jankin said he could handle it. He invented a pack of lies. Baldwin made him carry messages between himself and Gisburne.'

'What about?'

'They were trying to undermine de Quixlay. It wasn't just Baldwin and Gisburne. They had other supporters. Clerics. A few friars. A nun. Somebody at St Mary's. One or two guildsmen as well, them from the Lorimers' Guild, I think. He took messages between them but he wouldn't tell me much in case I let something slip. But I knew for sure Gisburne's lot were working against Simon de Quixlay. Gisburne wanted him out of office and himself put back in.'

This fitted in well with what Ulf had told her a few days ago about the long-standing rivalry between the two men.

Dorelia said, 'Jankin had no idea what an evil bastard Baldwin was. I warned him, "Once in his clutches you'll never escape." And that's exactly what happened. Baldwin would not let him go.'

'But why did Baldwin want Jankin dead if he

was willing to spy for him?'

'Maybe he knew he was being messed around.'

'How would he know that?'

'He could always winkle the truth out of a situation, Baldwin. It must have been when the firebombs were set off. Jankin heard what happened to that poor cloth-seller and her husband. He didn't know whether Baldwin was involved but he knew for sure it wasn't the White Hart. He decided he would inform on Baldwin to de Quixlay.'

She gave Hildegard a quick frightened look. 'It's more than just Baldwin and Gisburne. They're small fry. They have a master, one of the great lords, somebody close to the king.'

This all made sense. It was well known, of course, that Gaunt and his brother the Duke of Gloucester held land and property here in the Riding. Gaunt held a string of castles all across the region. He was even a major benefactor to St Mary's Abbey here in the heart of York itself.

'Jankin didn't understand the power he was up against,' Dorelia said, 'he was a child. But even I could see that. The next thing is Gisburne must have found out Jankin had been to see the mayor. He must have had an informer planted in the mayor's chambers. While master was out Baldwin and a couple of his cronies burst into the attic and–'

A tear started to trickle down her cheek. 'Baldwin forced me to go with them. He didn't need to take me. It was nothing to do with me. I didn't know anything. But he was mad. He planned to keep me a prisoner and do whatever he wanted

476

with me.'

'How did he manage to get you away without being seen?'

'They had a cart waiting in the street. It being pageant week with plenty of strangers around nobody was bothered at seeing a cart. The yard was empty – they timed it well – and they bundled me up in a cloak and dragged me out naked underneath it. I thought Jankin was dead. He'd broken the guild rules and brought his pageant wings to show me... Then blood. Everywhere.'

'But he wasn't dead?'

'They'd only wounded him. And that was worse. Because then he knew all the time what they were doing to him – and to me – and–' She broke off again and her eyes were brimming with tears again and she whispered, 'Can I tell you this? May I speak, Sister?'

'Go on, my dear.'

'They tied him to the wheel. They made it grind round. They were laughing and singing the rebels' song about the mill – *it grindeth small, small, small* – and his wings were ripped when he went under the water. The feathers floated away into the mill race. And then he came out of the water and they turned the wheel again and he went down underneath and they held him there and when they were sure he was dead they cut him loose and let him fall back into the millpond where you saw him...'

Hildegard took her by the hand.

Terrible though this was, it seemed to have nothing to do with the fires that had erupted, nor with the threat written on Danby's scrap of

477

vellum. When she asked whether she knew anything about the fires Dorelia's answer was to grip Hildegard by the arm.

'I don't know who did such a sinful thing against innocent folk, but I know one thing – they want to turn people against the rebels. They're trying to push the blame onto them. They hate the Company of the White Hart.'

'Why do they hate them so much?'

'The want bonded folk to remain in bondage. It's free labour to the landowners. And the Church wants to keep its stranglehold. They're frightened of losing power over us. They'll stop at nothing. Baldwin and Gisburne might be finished now but their master is still out there. And you can bet on it – somebody's keeping him informed even now.'

'And are they planning to set more firebombs like the ones at the booths and in Stapylton's workshop?'

'I wouldn't put it past them.'

Hildegard offered Dorelia a drink from a pitcher on the stand next to the bed and she watched the girl drink until the cup was drained.

'There is one more thing,' Hildegard murmured as she replaced the empty cup on the stand. 'Did Master Danby tell you he found some writing on a piece of vellum?'

Dorelia looked puzzled and shook her head.

'He found it in a creel in the small workshop,' she explained. 'It was a draft of the warning that was nailed to the minster doors yesterday.'

'I heard about that,' Dorelia replied. 'Wasn't it some threat to de Quixlay and his aldermen?'

Hildegard paused and then she said, 'It was almost certainly written by Gilbert.'

'*Gilbert?*' Dorelia's mouth opened. She stared at Hildegard in shocked silence.

'Have you ever had any suspicions about him?'

Dorelia shook her head. 'We trusted him.' She spoke as if in a dream. 'We trusted him,' she said again. Then her eyes blazed. 'But it must have been him who told Gisburne about Jankin's visit to the mayor.'

'He knew about that?'

'Of course he did.' She gazed at Hildegard in horror. 'Gilbert? I can't believe it! The deceitful little snake!' Unwittingly she echoed Baldwin's view.

Sinking back on the pillows she allowed her eyes to close. Her cheeks were as white as chalk. She would say nothing more.

Hildegard made her way downstairs. She was doubtful about leaving Dorelia in her present distress but Tabitha was waiting in the kitchen and went up straight away. Hildegard glanced in through the open door of the workshop as she was going out. But something stopped her. She was drawn inside to look at the glass.

It was at the stage where some of the pieces were already leaded and the rest were in place waiting to be fixed permanently within the calmes.

Even the face of the Queen of Heaven was in place.

A figure of enchantment encircled by stars, it was unmistakably Dorelia in all her youth and beauty. The image could be a token of Gilbert's obsession, a work in praise of the unattainable as Baldwin had tried to claim. It filled the centre of the glass, coloured fragments suggesting the graceful curves of her blue gown. On either side were smaller images of the donors. Lord Roger just as she had seen before and Lady Melisen, her long hair descending like a cloak with yet a hint of the voluptuous body concealed under its tresses.

At the bottom edge of the glass there was also the image of the little red fox, Gilbert's ambiguous signature, a symbol with many meanings. Although small it was plainly visible, looking up at the participants, half inside the frame and half outside. It aptly expressed Gilbert's place in the drama. A loner with no obvious affiliations. Unable to enter fully into paradise.

She gazed at the glass for a moment longer. Gilbert was well placed to know everything that was going on in the craftsmen's yards. Jankin, it seemed, had held nothing back. Dorelia said Gilbert knew about Jankin's visit to the mayor to warn him about the plot against him. Had Gilbert taken advantage of the knowledge to betray him to Gisburne? His espousal of the rebel cause might be sheer invention. A lure to draw the rebels to their doom.

What was the story he had told young Kit about the owl? She is put in a cage and her hooting draws other birds to the huntsman's trap.

She ran a finger over the glass. There was another way of reading the symbol of the little fox. It could be an ironic sign to demonstrate Gilbert's secret affiliation with the beliefs of Bernard of Clairvaux. The fox. Scenting out the heretics. Exterminating them as the saint instructed.

She moved a pot with a few grains of ground glass in it that had been left on a corner of the trestle, then leant down to have a closer look at the separate panels.

A border of leaves and vines enclosed the figures and within their convoluted shapes of green and red was the tiny white-robed figure of a nun. She saw at once that it was based on the drawing Gilbert had made in his pattern book when she had been sitting by the river. At first she did not recognise herself, so serene and strong was the expression on the face drawn in miniature on the glass, and yet, even within its limitations, she could make out her unsettled attention as she turned away from the world. She peered more closely and saw another familiar figure in its own separate frame.

It was an angel.

His wings were outspread. On his legs were quaint feathered breeches.

It was Jankin. He was smiling out of the glass as at a distant splendour.

She stepped away.

Whatever the nature of his other activities, Gilbert's work was magnificent. Master Danby's life, in many respects unfortunate, was now immortalised by his collaboration with an artist-craftsman. Their work would live for ever in the windows of the minster when their stories were long forgotten.

As she went out into the yard Mistress Julitta came out behind her from the direction of

Danby's kitchen. She carried some herbs wrapped in a rhubarb leaf. With a tight-lipped nod she carried on up the yard to where the guards were at their posts.

One of them spoke up. 'Still cooking for him, mistress?'

'Only doing what needs to be done,' she replied haughtily as she went on into the house.

Chapter Thirty-Six

By now the sky was the colour of a copper pan. Sheet lightning lit the sky. There was a close, dry, dusty feel to the air. It was weighted like something that could be cut by a blade. The whole town seemed to be on the point of erupting into flames. Hildegard's headache hammered at her temples with renewed force.

Before leaving Danby's yard she went to look at her hounds and thought about slipping their chains and taking them with her, but the streets were wilder than ever by now so she refilled their bowls, gave them a pat, and left without them.

The pageant wagons were still lumbering from one station to the next. The first half-dozen plays had already reached the twelfth and final station, but the rest continued to come down one by one over the bridge and into the town. *The Day of Judgement* would not arrive at the final station until midnight. By then the streets would replicate the fields of Armageddon.

Although it was still only mid afternoon it became so dark because of the brewing storm that people were beginning to carry flares. Lighted cressets were placed in the brackets outside the houses of the wealthy, and between the overhanging buildings people passed in a kind of twilight, their features lurid, like those of the players under the flickering pageant fires.

To make it even more confusing, many had gone to the trouble of painting their faces with violent-coloured dyes and most wore motley, an assortment of costumes in whatever bizarre form their imaginations could devise.

Some groups dressed alike as if having devised a common theme – a school of fish, for instance, their paste scales dislodged in the press falling like leaves in their wake, or a chivalry of knights with fake swords and armour leading a man wearing a horse's head, or groups of Saracens brandishing wooden scimitars, or teams of dragons, red, green, with paper flames spouting from between their jaws.

A gang in animal masks were threading their way through this mayhem, creating an even greater commotion. Nobody gave them more than a passing glance amid the confusion. A haze of lung-wrenching smoke from the torches they were carrying added to the smoke trapped between the buildings from the pageant devices. The dangerous scent of naphtha hung in the air. Hildegard tried to move out of the way as the animals came charging down the street but the crowd was at a standstill. Everyone was trapped.

To make matters worse, out of the heart of this tumult a pageant wagon loomed between the houses further up. It was trying to force a way between the onlookers from the previous station and it emerged like a behemoth, ungainly through the smoke. Hildegard flattened herself against the wall with everyone else as it trundled past.

At last it was the glaziers' wagon, with Gilbert himself sitting high up on a throne of clouds attached by stout ropes above the tilting stage. His throne was so elevated he was almost on a level with the first-floor windows of the houses and could have touched the sills as he passed. The whole top-heavy edifice was swaying from side to side as it rumbled over the cobbles.

The actors, Jesus, John the Baptist, Adam, Enoch, Seth, Simeon and the rest, were hanging onto the struts that held the scenery, singing various anthems with their flagons in their hands and now and then declaiming sundry lines as they lurched along. They looked unreal in the weird light. Gilbert's wings, crumpled by now, reached down to the stage in a fall of crimson paper feathers. What was it Kit had said? *So that they controlled everything.*

Gilbert didn't seem to be controlling anything at all just now.

He appeared to be trying to descend from his perch but everyone was too drunk or preoccupied to help him down. Or maybe Danby had warned one of the players he trusted to make sure Gilbert did not leave his aerial prison cell.

Banter passed back and forth between the cast and the crowds and the latter, pressing thickly in on both sides, continually handed up gifts of ale, cheering as they did so. Several brawny apprentices wearing nothing but cotton breeches were working as a team to heave the wagon forward. They were sweating and pouring ale down their throats to keep their strength up, their leader urging them on with a whip, but when he insulted their manhood they cursed back happily, impugning his own.

'Come on, you lily-livered losels!' he was roaring as they approached the place where Hildegard was flattened against the wall. 'Put some beef into it. Let's have a bit of effort! Where are your balls?' Tendons stood out on arms and necks as they strained to heave the loaded cart forward. The racket of the tabors was deafening in the confined space and seemed to obliterate all logical thought.

A guildsman was walking in front with a beribboned mace to clear the way of dogs and drunks. A child ran out from the crowd and was scooped up immediately and returned to its parents. So far there had been no fatalities. Now the mace-bearer said something to the wagon master and the whole swaying edifice groaned to a halt. The wagon ahead had not yet moved off from the front of the Common Hall. There was a snarl-up as the great vehicles blocked the street.

Watching Gilbert in the character of an archangel perched on high reminded Hildegard of the angel in the glass. Gilbert had talked about type and antitype. *The Harrowing of Hell* now due to be enacted before the mayor and his aldermen would be antitype. Its type was *The Massacre of the Innocents*. But that particular pageant had gone by long ago without incident. She shivered.

There were shouts from somewhere up the street and the wagon began to edge forward again. She followed in its wake, forced along with the rest of the crowd as far as the yard outside the Hall.

The mayor and his council rose to their feet with as much enthusiasm as everyone else as the wagon approached.

There were deafening cheers. A steward seemed to call for silence but it went unheeded.

Simon de Quixlay stepped to the front of the stand and appeared to make a speech, although nobody could hear a word he said. When he finished he waved a fist above his head in a sign of solidarity and it brought a massive cheer from the onlookers. Fists were raised in response and somebody started to sing the rebel anthem. The mayor regained his seat, smiling and shaking hands. Aldermen were slapping him on the back, everyone clearly delighted that today he was the man at the top.

Hildegard watched carefully. It was difficult to believe he was under threat. The townsfolk clearly adored him. Maybe it was all a hoax. There was no threat. It was only wishful thinking by his enemies. It was impossible to understand what had made Gilbert pen that warning.

De Quixlay, it was well known, had refused three times to be mayor. Only on the third vote had he agreed to stand. His reluctance might have been natural humility or it might have been caution – knowing as everyone did that Gaunt, the Duke of Lancaster, wanted to put his own man in charge of the city as he had done in Harrogate, Knaresborough, Ripon and elsewhere in the north. It would be a tough and dangerous prospect to stand against the duke.

Apart from the people he served, the only allies de Quixlay had came from the burgesses in smaller towns like Beverley and Scarborough, ones fined heavily after the Rising in '81 because of their support for it.

Even Hull, an increasingly important trading port, was run by a council who favoured Gaunt. No doubt this was because of the protection he offered in terms of trade with Flanders and the Hanse ports of the Baltic. Nobody else had the resources to protect their merchant ships from pirates and the excessive taxation the Hanse League tried to levy on foreign traders, so it was easy to see their point.

Gaunt: trading profit. No Gaunt: trading loss. Type: antitype.

But here in York de Quixlay had the free vote of the burgesses. He was no strong-armed autocrat with an army of knights at his back. He had started from humble origins and worked his way to the leadership by sheer ability. He was a vigorous supporter of the bonded labourers in their attempts to free themselves. He said, it was claimed, that they should be able to sell their labour just as the merchants sold their goods. He offered protection for those who were outlawed for their beliefs.

Surrounded by the love of his people it was difficult to work out how he could be in danger.

Engrossed by this problem Hildegard slowly became aware that there was an increasing commotion at the end of the street in addition to that caused by the glaziers' wagon.

The crowd seemed to bulge and fatten in the narrow artery leading out towards the back of St Mary's Abbey. The wagon was forced to a halt before it could reach the mayor's stand. People craned to see what had brought the procession to a stop.

'It's the Host!' a distant shout went up. 'They're taking it back to St Leonard's!' A column of blazing torches became visible crossing the junction ahead, and following the blaze of gold and silver came a cohort of hooded monks, carrying their own lighted candles.

There was more pushing and shoving as the crowd, forced by the procession of the Host up the street towards the stand, met a column of masked players trying to force a way down. They all carried lighted flares.

At first sight they reminded Hildegard of the jolly company of cardinals who had saved her from Matthias a few nights ago, but as they drew level she felt unsure. There was no pope at their head chuckling, 'See you in hell, fair lady.'

Instead the leader pushed with some violence through the crowd, arousing hostility as he passed. A woman standing next to Hildegard held a protective hand round the child at her knee. 'No need to be so bloody rough!' she shouted after them as they went on. One of them turned with a snarl but was urged on by the pressure of those behind.

488

'Who are they?' asked Hildegard. She followed their progress with a puzzled frown.

'Never seen 'em before in my life and when I see 'em next it'll be too soon,' the woman replied.

Hildegard watched them force their way down the street until they merged with the crowd near the mayor's stand. She couldn't see what the hurry was about. They were not in the glaziers' pageant and if they were hoping to join another wagon they were going in the wrong direction. When the glaziers finished here they would go on towards the house of old Adam del Brygges in Stonegate, and then on down towards the station at Minster Gates.

More and more people were trying to get into the yard outside the Common Hall by now, and it was beginning to be frightening. The constables seemed to have lost control. People were pushing and being pushed in all directions. Someone fell but was dragged to his feet before he could be trampled. There were calls for calm which no one was able to heed.

The masked men must be trying to join the procession of the Host, Hildegard decided. She felt troubled.

They had set off a minor stampede by the rough way they forced a passage through the otherwise good-humoured crowd and the thick smoke from their torches left a suffocating stench in the air.

The smell of naphtha was stronger still.

The crowd was forcing her towards the pageant wagon and by now she could see the Host being raised beyond it. A group down there started to

489

sing a *Te Deum*. At once it provoked opposition and one of the rebel songs could be heard in reply: *'Together we stand as brothers and sisters, one for all, all for one, strong we stand, never to fall, all for one, one for all.'*

It was like an antiphon or one of the Saxon poems, a line followed by a response.

The two rival groups increased their volume in an attempt to drown the other out. Everyone joined in. Neighbour vied with neighbour in a cacophony of sound.

Then something happened.

An alarm swept through Hildegard that was as sudden as a physical shock. It caused her to exclaim aloud. In a flash she recalled the man in the mask who had snarled at the woman and her child as he pushed past. That smell of rancid wax. She knew who he was. But it was impossible.

She stood on tiptoe to search the faces of the crowd.

The group were standing outside a house opposite the mayor's stand. It was the only one that had no spectators leaning from the windows. Inside, however, cressets blazed and there was an elderly porter standing on guard in the doorway.

She turned her attention back to the men in the masks. They wore cloaks. Only the fact that no arms were allowed inside the walls of the town during the festivities had made her think the danger would come from an explosion like the ones before. But anyone could conceal a weapon should they choose.

Now as she stared over the heads of the singing

mob the exact words scratched on Danby's piece of vellum flooded back: after the specific warning to the dignitaries came the words they had all ignored as being mere bombast. Now she ran them through her mind again: *Beware the Antichrist! He comes armed with a bow of burning flame!*

The pageant wagon reached its destination. It shuddered to a halt in front of the mayor's stand. Gilbert was struggling to get down from his throne in the clouds. Somehow he noticed Hildegard as she pushed her way to the front of the crowd.

She was staring up at him.

White-faced he stared back.

He had written the words. There was no doubt of that.

Now she thought she understood why: it was a warning not a threat. He knew something and for some reason this was the only way he could make it known.

Fighting her way through those thickest round the edge of the stage she managed to attract the attention of a group of apprentices leaning against the shafts of the wagon. Jesus and a couple of the others were playing dice in the pause before the performance started and she called up to them.

'Gilbert wants to get down!' she shouted above the chanting crowd. They had clearly forgotten he was there.

John the Baptist heard her first. He stood up and bellowed up to Gilbert, 'Want a piss, lad?' Shrugging his skins over one shoulder he began to slacken the ropes that kept the throne of clouds in place.

'Hurry, I must speak to him!' urged Hildegard above the commotion.

With a sudden pull the final knot unloosed itself, the throne slipped and Gilbert half fell, half jumped to land on the wooden boards. The audience cheered. The whole wagon rocked, making the actors yell in protest at having their dice disturbed. Somebody reached out to catch a toppling flagon and the apprentice boys jeered lustily.

When he stumbled towards her she demanded, 'Did you post that notice on the minster door?'

'Of course I did! I thought it was a clear warning. But look at de Quixlay. He hasn't understood, the sot wit! He thinks he's safe!'

He reached out and gripped her by the edge of her veil so he could be heard. 'Jankin hinted about their plans before they shut him up. He knew about the whole thing. I tried to get in to see de Quixlay but their security was too tight. They thought I was just another madman predicting the Last Days.'

'Is it to do with those players in the masks?'

'Who?'

'Over there!' she gestured towards the house opposite.

'They won't be players, they'll be the duke's men.'

'I know one of them.'

He stared.

'You wrote "He comes armed with a bow of burning flame." What did you mean?'

'That's the phrase Jankin heard them use. But it makes no sense to me.'

'It does to me.'

They were almost in front of the stand. It was surrounded by singing supporters. Hereabout the *Te Deum* went unheard.

'We've got to warn de Quixlay,' she told Gilbert.

It was all so obvious now. The guards standing along the front railing could be picked off one at a time by anybody with a crossbow – so long as they were suitably hidden above the crowd. The mayor himself and every one of his council could be shot by as few as half a dozen men aiming together.

If the attackers used fire to prime their bolts the entire stand and the Common Hall could go up in flames.

She glanced back at the line of players with their burning torches. In the present crush no one would be able to get away. People would be killed in the stampede to escape. The buildings all about would be set alight. The entire town could burn. Even if, by some miracle, de Quixlay was saved from the flames, it would be a sign to the superstitious that he was the herald of the Last Days, to others that he had no backing for his reforms.

Hurriedly peering over the heads of the crowd she saw one of the masked men who had been left behind in the crowd fighting to join his fellows. He wore some kind of animal mask like the ones she had seen earlier. When he reached them they began to push towards the house opposite the stand. Its upper floors hung out over the heads of the crowd on both sides of the main door. 'Whose house is that?' she demanded, tugging at Gilbert's shoulder to alert him.

'The mayor's.'

They saw the porter disappear from his station and the men went inside. Hildegard shouted that she was going over there but whether Gilbert heard her or not she did not wait to find out.

By the time she had forced her way through the crowd the men could be heard inside the building as they pounded up the wooden stairs. The porter was lying just in the entrance, clutching his ribs. 'Stop them!' he gasped when she bent down beside him.

'Are you badly hurt?'

'Stop them devils! They'll be ransacking the place. I'm just winded.'

'Call de Quixlay's guards at once!' Hildegard helped him to his feet, then ran two at a time to the next floor. She could hear the sound of boots in the solar above.

Without thinking she grabbed a cresset from the wall bracket on the landing and ran up the next flight of stairs and along the passage towards an open door.

It was the main reception chamber, with several windows overlooking the street. There was a clear view of the mayor's stand right opposite, the wooden roof beams of the Common Hall behind it, and below the window the swaying pageant wagon surrounded by a sea of faces.

Three masked men were in the process of opening the casements. They were dragging wound crossbows from under their cloaks. She could see at once that the bolts were primed with cloth and the smell of naphtha was stronger here than ever.

As soon as Hildegard appeared in the doorway they froze in astonishment. One of them strode at once towards her. He pulled his mask down. It was in the shape of a bear, the snout jutting forward. Behind it his eyes were small and darting. 'What the fuck do you want?' he snarled.

He bunched one fist but before he could raise it she said, 'I wouldn't touch me if I were you or the whole place will go up in flames!'

She lifted the cresset so they could see her clearly. 'Good disguise, isn't it? So is yours. But do I really look like a nun?' She turned to the man she thought she knew. 'You certainly fell for that one, didn't you?'

He stepped forward in astonishment but the leader pushed him aside. 'What's all this about, nun, or whatever the hell you are?'

'This is the day when you'll discover whether you have a judge in heaven or one in hell,' she said forcing a laugh from between her lips.

The sound stopped the bear in his tracks for a moment. 'What the bloody hell is this?'

'I know her! She's that whore who stole our martyr! Whore of Babylon! Out, whore!' The figure she had addressed earlier now pushed his way forward again. He ripped off his mask, confirming her suspicious.

'And you, Matthias,' she said. 'You escaped from custody, then.'

'No prison can hold the righteous–!' he began.

But just then music from outside announced the beginning of the play. It was *The Harrowing of*

Hell. Any minute now the actors would begin to speak their lines. The hell-gates would open up and the unsaved would be cast into the eternal flames.

Hildegard took a deep breath. If she didn't play it right, hell would indeed open up, but it would be the innocent to suffer.

'It's like this, my friends,' she began, thinking quickly. 'Strapped to my body – I have explosives brought to me from the East. The friend who brought them is a close ally of the pope in Rome. It's not only Pope Clement who arms himself with poisons and other secret defences against his enemies. Urban does so as well. In fact...' she paused, the men had fallen silent, 'this friend of mine has a contract with both popes to purchase explosives on their behalf. And he was good enough to give some to me.'

She moved a step closer. They were listening intently. 'I now wear this explosive underneath my gown. No doubt you've heard of Greek fire?'

There was an alert shifting and the bear poked his head forward. 'What?'

'One spark!' she declaimed. 'Just one spark will set this mysterious substance alight and send a ball of flame bigger than anything you've ever seen exploding through this house and destroying us all in an instant. I warn you...' she glared at one of the men who, pushing up a black and white badger mask, made a disbelieving step towards her, 'I will not hesitate to use it. I have nothing to lose. My sins have been confessed. I shall go straight to heaven to sit in glory at the feet of Our Lady. Now,' she gave each one of

496

them a slow glance, 'who's going to be the one to do me the favour of sending me there?'

The men milled about as if behind an invisible barrier and glanced from one to the other.

'Matthias?' she asked. 'Will it be you?'

He grunted but remained where he was.

'If any one of you tries to raise his crossbow I shall take it as a challenge. In fact,' she lowered her voice, wondering frantically why help did not come, 'I shall deem it a pleasure to blow you all to hell. And let the Devil deal with you as he will.'

'Are you for King Richard?' muttered the man in the badger mask uncertainly.

'And the true Commons!' she replied.

'If this is revenge for that massacre near the coast, it wasn't our doing,' the bear butted in. 'It was Gaunt's contingent from the castle at Pickering, acting on their own behalf out of a lust for gain…'

'They got wind of a barter for gold…' added the badger.

'Them thievin' pirates living down in that vill looted a cargo of arms from Acclom's ship and were due to hand it to the king of Scotland…' His words tailed off as if he had admitted too much.

There was silence.

'I'm not interested in your greed,' she told them. 'This is revenge for all the dead after Smithfield and Mile End. It is a just execution of the king's enemies!' What on earth am I saying? she thought, as the words tumbled out. I've become a player. None of this is real. Why does no one bring help?

The men were looking emboldened now that a

497

dialogue of sorts had been established. One of them made as if to reach for his crossbow. Ostentatiously she put a hand to the neck of her habit to pull something from inside and noticed that they all froze as if expecting immediate immolation. The bowman's hand dropped to his side after only one turn on the windlass.

'I see you understand me,' she remarked, wondering how long she could keep going. 'Perhaps you want to tell me who sent you to assassinate the mayor?' And when they refused to answer she said, 'You must be maintained by somebody, even though you're not brave enough to wear his badge.'

'Everybody's maintained these days. Nobody can exist without protection – what of it?'

'And it was Gaunt instructed you to set fire to the Common Hall.'

'Did he?'

'One of our sources said as much–'

'We've got a spy,' one of them cut in. He turned away as if that was the end of the matter and they could do nothing now but return to barracks.

'Who was it?' the leader demanded through his mask.

She couldn't tell him it was the slimmest of slim chances that had led her here. Trying not to look into the malign little eyes that peered out from behind his mask she ignored his question and continued, 'As I understand, Gaunt instructed you to rid York of its elected council and mayor so he could put Gisburne in the mayor's office?'

'What is this about Gaunt?'

'Everybody knows he instructs his son,' she added quickly.

This seemed to make sense to them. Even so the bear said, 'You can't stop us with your lies about explosives. Why should we believe you?'

'You don't have to believe me if you don't want to. I don't represent the Church with its demand for belief in the impossible. Believe what you want. You can even believe in the honesty of the duke and his son if you're so minded. Believe they're working for the good of everybody and not just for the House of Lancaster! Why not!'

She gave a crazed laugh to add weight to what they knew was true. Gaunt ruled by fear. They were well aware of that.

She said, 'This is making me tired. I thought only to destroy the Host as it came round. Now I find I can destroy a handful of our enemies as well! Fortune smiles on me and on the justice of our cause!'

She started to untie the neck-strings of her undershift beneath her habit, thinking that perhaps she could fool them into backing off into the adjoining chamber where she might bang the door on them, and as she pulled at the ribbon she said, 'Let's see what my friend in Outremer has brought me and whether it can fulfil his claim that it burns hotter than a thousand suns!'

To her astonishment there was a bang and a flash of light. The room filled with thick smoke. When it cleared a black-hooded figure stood in the doorway.

'Drop your weapons and get back against the wall!' he rapped.

Striding into the chamber with another burst of flame from between his hands he herded the startled men against the wall and kicked their weapons to one side. Matthias fell to his knees and began to pray, breaking off to curse the mother superior at his convent. 'She put a spell on me,' he jabbered. 'She said only I could save us from the Antichrist! Help me, Mary, Mother of God. All I did was obey orders. I am innocent! No fires, I beg your mercy. No hellfire for Matthias!'

From the stairs came the pounding of boots. At last a storm of armed men in the mayor's livery burst into the chamber.

'Over there!' The man in black gestured towards the outnumbered bowmen, then pushed back his hood.

Hildegard's mouth opened. It was the mage Theophilus, otherwise John of Berwick.

He came over to her. 'I caught sight of you in the crowd with Gilbert. You looked panic-stricken, it was clear something was up. Then I saw you rush in here but couldn't get through the crowd in time to find out what was going on. I stumbled over the porter, poor fellow, and got up here just as you were threatening some evil from Outremer. I only just managed to come in on time for my cue.' He beamed. 'What a performance, Sister. I'm inclined to offer you a job as my partner. Together we could make our fortunes.'

Hildegard let out a long, slow breath. 'I have to thank you for leading me to that ploy. I had no idea what I was going to do when I burst in here with nothing but a cresset as defence. And I'd just reached the end of my script.'

He offered her his hand. 'From one player to another.' He bowed.

Chapter Thirty-Seven

While the men were being disarmed and un-masked, Simon de Quixlay and a group of aldermen made their way over from the pageant stand. The mayor gave the bowmen a disappointed glance.

'I know a couple of you fellows. I thought I could trust you to obey the will of the people without further trouble. Now I see I was wrong.' He turned to the captain of militia. 'Take them away. This time they shall have no mercy!'

Shackled hand and foot they were dragged roughly out and could be heard clattering all the way down the stairs accompanied by a dozen or so snarling guards.

The situation was explained in more detail to the mayor.

Gilbert had managed to climb up onto the mayor's stand and tell him as coherently as he could what was suspected. Entering minus his wings, he was pushed to the front of the group and the whole thing explained again with additions from the mage. Matthias, it transpired, had been put in a cell at the convent after Ulf and his men had apprehended him in the stews. But he had at once been let go by the mother superior to continue his work as an assassin.

De Quixlay looked grim. 'The monastics have their own ways, curse them. They obey their pope, not our secular laws.'

Hildegard's contribution was to confirm that the men had an affinity with Bolingbroke if, indeed, they were not directly instructed by him.

'You would not know it,' de Quixlay told her, 'but one of those men was Gisburne's son. We shall soon have his confirmation that his father is in the pay of Bolingbroke.'

There were murmurs of satisfaction from the aldermen and one of them muttered, 'This nails the bastard good and proper.'

While they were talking the storm that had threatened all afternoon burst directly over their heads with a rumble like falling ale barrels. Lightning flashed along the walls of the chamber casting an uncanny glow that lingered for some moments after the first clap. Then there was a deathly hush followed by further detonations merging with the lightning flashes, one after another, and after this preliminary the rain started in earnest.

It fell as if it would never cease, straight, hard rods ramming viciously onto the spectators still thronging the streets. The crowds were trapped by sheer force of numbers under the deluge. Nobody could move but no one seemed to mind.

News got out about the near assassination of the mayor and his entire council, and aware that de Quixlay and his men were inside the house, they stood underneath the window, linked arms and started to sway in time to their own singing of the rebel anthem. Then they sang a hymn or two, then more songs.

Marooned in the mayor's chamber as if in a stormbound ship, de Quixlay and his supporters could only remain where they were and a sense of celebration set in. The mayor and his men were alive. 'All praise if there's somebody up there!' an alderman was heard to say.

Somehow food and wine were brought up.

Hildegard went to look out. There were cheers when she appeared at the window. Probably nobody had an idea who she was or what she was doing up there and they were all soaked to the skin and, in truth, had nothing to sing about, but no one cared. Word had got out about the plot to kill the mayor and that was enough. Whenever anyone else appeared at the window there were further roars of applause.

'Poor fools,' said de Quixlay looking down and acknowledging the cheers. 'They're drenched. Pity we can't fit them all in up here. Have we got spare sacks they can put over themselves maybe?' Somebody went to find out.

The pageant wagon was swimming with water.

The wings that Gilbert had wriggled out of as he fell to earth were lying in a bedraggled heap. Dye the colour of blood ran from them. Jesus and the rest of the characters sat under an awning they had rigged up. Rain fell off it like water through a sluice. Their game of dice continued.

The minster procession had hurriedly carried the Host back into the shelter of St Leonard's, where it would stay overnight, and a small section of the crowd had gone with it.

Hildegard let the men talk and went back to the window.

The storm was a sight. The whole sky was split by lightning with scarcely a pause between the flashes. In a gap near the Common Hall and the buildings next to it she could see the river darkly running, and every time the sky was riven by light the water glowed like phosphorous.

She glanced along the street. A figure at the far end was hurrying along through the crowds with hood pulled up, thick cloak over the shoulders, but underneath, the hem of a white habit.

A Cistercian brother.

She wondered if it was Thomas, but after watching for a moment decided it wasn't. Whoever it was had to keep stopping to ask directions. Thomas knew his way round the town. After a moment or two the figure halted outside the mayor's house and looked up.

She saw his face clearly in the light of the cressets.

There must have been somebody on the door because it was a moment before the newcomer appeared in the upper chamber. Already pushing back the hood of his sodden cloak he gazed in at the assembled crowd.

Hubert de Courcy.

He lingered in the doorway for a moment. It gave Hildegard time to observe him from where she stood to one side, His hair, still quite long from his travels, stuck darkly to his forehead. His cloak clung in wet folds from his broad shoulders. He said nothing but merely searched the chamber, noticed that Hildegard was stand-

504

ing over by the window, and then abruptly turned, as if to leave.

The mayor, however, caught sight of him. 'The Abbot of Meaux, I believe?' He made a small flourish. 'Welcome, My Lord Abbot. Please honour us by stepping within.'

Hubert looked wary as if suspecting a trap but de Quixlay showed why he was so popular by the easy manner with which he made a potential enemy welcome. His affable mood was explained when she heard him say, 'I have one of your Cistercians to thank for my life.'

Hildegard put a hand over her face. The mage noticed and came over. 'Are you feeling all right?'

She nodded. 'A momentary faintness, that's all.'

'I'm not surprised after what you've just gone through.' He bent his head close to her ear to make himself heard more easily in the hubbub. 'I've got a cure in my scrip.' She touched him on the arm. 'Thank you. I doubt whether there's a cure better than prayer for what ails me.'

She chanced to glance across the room and saw that Hubert was watching her over de Quixlay's shoulder. She remembered his inexplicable hostility the previous day. Clearly it had not abated.

The mage followed her glance. 'Ah,' he murmured. 'I told you so.'

Later, Gilbert and Theophilus, as they could not help but call him, accompanied Hildegard back to Danby's yard.

The pageant wagons were still going the rounds despite the rain. Angels' wings drooped, paint was

505

washed away, explosions failed to detonate in the wet, and the fires of hell were little more than a candle flash. Minstrels were bemoaning the damage done to their instruments and taking off their own cloaks to protect them. Yet despite all this, the town was still *en fête*. Instead of dousing their spirits, the opposition of weather, God, Saints Edmund and Benet and the entire hosts of heaven, and probably hell too, only urged everyone to a greater determination to enjoy themselves.

'I'm not sure I understand how those cross-bowmen set fire to Stapylton's workshop and the booths,' Hildegard said as they splashed through the puddles in Stonegate.

'I've had my ear to the ground,' replied Theophilus. 'It was the work of a free lance. They simply capitalised on it. They themselves had something bigger in mind, as we nearly witnessed.'

Gilbert frowned. 'Who set those smaller fires, then?'

'It was the work of that fellow working for the Sisters of the Holy Wounds, a fanatic, over from a house in Flanders–'

'Matthias?' Hildegard exclaimed. 'He blames his mother superior. He says he was only obeying orders.'

'But why Stapylton?' Gilbert asked.

'The Corpus Christi candles,' Hildegard suggested.

'And he hoped the White Hart fellows would be blamed because that's what happened in London during the Rising.' Gilbert wrinkled his nose.

'I doubt whether he could work out a bluff like that for himself,' said Hildegard. 'He needed

506

someone to suggest the idea to him.'

She recalled the virulence of the mother superior when she tried to prevent Maud, her little martyr, escaping her control. It was easy to see how she could have instructed Matthias to act on her behalf, or at least put the idea into his befuddled head.

'And then the bowmen joined forces for what was to be their final killing attack. There would have been no bluffing then.' It had come to be known that a river man had been commissioned to provide a boat so that the bowmen could escape by water when the town went up in flames.

Theophilus came to a halt in the shelter of the archway leading into the yard. Rain was still gurgling in the gutter down the middle of the street. 'I've already had a message from Wakefield, you know. Dorelia's betrothed is fetching a char in order to take her home. He's going to be a lad of some means himself now he's finished his apprenticeship as a goldsmith. He wants to take Dorelia back, as I knew he would.'

'Will she regain her inheritance?'

Theophilus shook his head. 'I doubt it. But some of us are determined to do our best for her. The law may yet be used for good. But you know what it's like – it could drag on for years. And no doubt Baldwin's wife will deny all knowledge of receiving any gain from the transaction.'

'She may have to explain where her husband got such a large and costly jewel from,' murmured Hildegard, suspecting now that it was genuine after all.

'He made a good living from his trade in girls,'

507

said Gilbert.

'Poor Danby,' she said. 'He'll be heartbroken over that and heartbroken when Dorelia leaves him.'

'It might bring him to his senses,' said Gilbert. 'He's got a little daughter who's been having visions of the Virgin Mary and creating a great furore down by the camps.' He turned to Hildegard. 'You saw her on the riverbank that evening when I first pointed Baldwin out to you on his way to the mill.'

'In the little boy-bishop's procession?'

'The girl was Danby's daughter. Remember when Dorelia said she tried to escape and a child saw her in the woods? That was Lucy. It must have been too much for her to understand so she convinced herself she'd had a vision.'

'Poor child.' Hildegard's voice was full of pity.

The mage said that seemed to tie things up and that he now intended to transfer as much silver as possible from other people's money-pouches into his own before they wasted what little they had left on ale. With a bow he turned to go.

'Wait a minute!' Gilbert had heard about the miraculous flame the mage had made appear. 'How did you do it?' he asked.

The mage tapped the side of his nose. 'I have a friend in Outremer.'

Hildegard and Gilbert went back to the yard. The guards outside Baldwin's cottage were in some turmoil as they approached. For a moment she thought Baldwin must have escaped.

'Sister!' one of them shouted when he saw her.

He hurried over. Rain was trickling down his face. 'It's the prisoner. He's been taken bad. Can you come?'

With Gilbert at her heels they squelched across the puddled yard, bending their heads under the lintel of Baldwin's front door.

He was lying on the floor in the kitchen, still wearing his manacles, and writhing about as if in pain. One of the guards was looking doubtful and his companion was holding him back saying, 'It might be a trick. You can't unlock him. He's a cunning bastard. This is probably all a show so he can escape!'

Mistress Julitta was sitting calmly on a bench against the wall. When Hildegard asked her what was going on she shrugged and made no comment.

Hildegard bent down to put a hand on Baldwin's forehead and found it burning to the touch, but there was nothing she could do without knowing what had caused his collapse. It was certainly no fakery. She opened his jerkin and at once closed it again.

She stood up. On the table was a half-eaten bowl of pottage. She went over to it, sniffed it, scooped some onto a spoon and inspected it by the light of the window. She gave Julitta a glance. The woman stared brazenly back.

'Did Baldwin eat this?' she asked the guards.

'Took half a dozen mouthfuls,' one of them replied. 'Is it poisoned?'

'Not exactly.'

Just then Baldwin gave another great roar of pain and thrashed wildly from side to side clutching his stomach. There was blood coming from his mouth and a terrible stench filled the chamber. Before anybody could think what to do for him he arched his back and, with a piercing scream, collapsed as if felled.

Julitta got up from her place by the wall and went to stand over him. She did not speak. After a moment she bent down and unclasped the silver chain carrying the jewel from around his neck. Without a word she pushed it inside her bodice and went out.

Hildegard picked up the mortar from the sill. A few shards of glass still glinted at the bottom.

'As one might say, all's well,' commented Gilbert harshly when they eventually took their leave.

Hildegard had explained to him what she thought had happened. The coroner had been called as a matter of urgency but had not yet arrived. The guards remained.

He turned to Hildegard. 'If you don't need me I'm going to sit with Dorelia for a while.'

'What about the play you're in?' she asked.

'Four lines? They can surely get somebody else to mouth them for the last couple of stations. They've got my wings, those glued-together paper feathers. Let somebody else put them on and play the fool!'

She noticed that when he went upstairs he left his pattern book and charcoal in the workshop. It was not to be a working visit, then, but social.

As for Baldwin, when she had bent down to see what ailed him a small piece of vellum on a cord lay next to his heart. On it was a drawing of Dorelia.

Julitta had seen it. That's when their eyes had met.

As Petronilla might have said, the angels punished him according to their law.

And none shall escape.

Around midnight Hildegard dragged herself out of her chamber at the Widow Tabitha's house in Danby's yard to see what was happening in the town. Gilbert saw her leaving and came out to join her.

After the storm the night was clear and cool. A moon rode high shedding a silvery light over the rooves. In the narrow streets the crowds were as thick as ever but they had mellowed now, exhausted after a day of indulgence.

A massive audience was gathering round the final pageant on Pavement. Master Stapylton and his guild had done well by the onlookers. The stage was ablaze with candles and on all sides hundreds of little flames glimmered like stars as if the heavens themselves had fallen to Earth Their soft glow lit up the faces of the people nearest the stage, gilding signs of poverty and ill health, of grief, pain, lack of hope and all the ills of being human, and for this short time everyone was bathed in their benediction.

Gilbert found a place at the back for them both, close to where Kit and Danby's kitchen boy were sitting on a wall from where they could watch the final scene of judgement. As they arrived Agnetha slipped in beside them. 'I knew you'd come. I've been watching out for you. There's Roger's stew-

511

ard with Maud,' she whispered. 'Look, down near the front.'

Ulf, with Maud perched on his shoulders, her hood back, her face alight, was attended by a retinue of de Hutton retainers with Petronilla in their midst. Their faces were turned to the candle-lit stage.

It was *Judgement Day*.

With anguished howls the bad souls were pitchforked into the mouth of hell. The good souls were lifted up by choirs of angels to a life of eternal bliss. And God intoned his final lines:

> *'Now is fulfilled all my forethought*
> *For ended is all earthly thing...'*

Gilbert caught Hildegard's eye. She thought he might be thinking of Jankin. Of Dorelia. Of his own strange and powerful gift and what he might do with it for the good of all, and she rested her hand on his arm.

> *'They that would sin and cease not,*
> *Of sorrows sere now shall they sing,*
> *And they that mended them while they might,*
> *Shall belde and bide in my blessing.'*

The actor drew in a deep breath after his last line and there was a pause as if the audience, too, was holding its breath.

'So sad,' Hildegard whispered. She meant life. Everything.

And it ended with the melody of angels crossing from place to place.

Epilogue

Hildegard emerged out of the morning mist under a sky as sheeny pink and lavender as the inside of a mussel shell. First into view was the tower above the trees, then the crooked roofs of the buildings, and finally the grey arch of the gatehouse. Not as grand nor as forbidding as the abbey at Meaux, the Priory of Swyne was a pleasing arrangement of turrets and trees. It looked deserted.

With no one to greet her, Hildegard took her hired ambler into the stables herself and saw to his needs. Then she fed and watered her hounds. Finally, she made her way over to the main building. The sound of singing came from the chapel, antiphon and response. Soft-footed she let herself inside and slipped into a seat near the door. The voices rose sweetly all around and she gave a long sigh. Home at last.

The prioress was standing up as usual, her gaunt frame still erect, but her face more lined in the twelve months since Hildegard had last seen her. The private chapel in which they stood was as cold and austere as ever.

Everything was explained, all questions answered, remarks on the way things had turned out had been offered and reciprocated. Her account was nearing its end.

Maud would remain as Roger's ward until fate maybe decreed a husband. Her persecutors had been brought to account.

Petronilla was to continue as Melisen's damosel of the bedchamber. Her father and his retinue of little girls had found a sponsor in old Robert Harpham, who, astute in the needs of the market, had backed his attempt to export his handmade toys to the Rhineland with hard cash and some useful contacts.

Even the fate of Kit had been settled. Hildegard told the prioress how, when she went to speak to Danby about his keep, the boy had been busily helping Gilbert in the workshop. Observing his dexterity and Gilbert's delight with his progress, she had not even mentioned her idea of bringing Kit to Swyne to assist their falconer. 'I believe he has found his life's work,' she said.

And Danby had invited his sister and her brood to come and live within the city walls in the now empty house at the top of the yard so that his daughter, his little Lucy, could live at home and still have the care and kindness of her aunt.

And finally, she told the prioress, Danby had made Gilbert his partner and they vowed to make their workshop the most famous glazier's in England.

By the time Hildegard concluded her story the prioress was looking thoughtful. Now she said, 'And the cross is safe. Despite the terrible events it brings in its wake you must be pleased it still survives after having gone to so much trouble to bring it back to York in the first place.'

She turned to look at the rough wooden relic

on her private altar. 'It was clever to hide it on full display in St Helen's Church,' she approved. 'Of course, if we were merchants we would now be sniggering into our money-pouches.' She sighed. 'It must be returned to its guardians in Florence. I imagine that journey across the Alps last year was something not to be endured more than once in a lifetime?'

'It wasn't as bad as it sounds. The tragedy was that my escort was murdered there.' She referred to a tourney knight, Sir Talbot.

'So you would do it again?'

'I imagine it would be pleasant enough in summer when the snows have melted.'

'Indeed?' The prioress gave a brisk movement of her hand. 'More of that another time. I have a matter of a different nature to bring to your notice.'

This is where she mentions the abbot's threat of punishment. Hildegard braced herself.

The prioress gave her a hard look. 'Yes. Abbot de Courcy.'

Hildegard's heart missed a beat.

'A serious matter of discipline, or so he claims.' The prioress sighed heavily. 'What seems to have urged him to press for censure is the fact that he saw you, as he puts it, "in the arms of that steward of de Hutton's", by whom I take it he means Sir Ulf. Is this true?'

'Of course not! Is the abbot mad? I'd just escaped from that brute employed by the Sisters of the Holy Wounds, barely escaping with my life I might add, when Ulf appeared outside Harpham's house having been told by Maud about the

515

brute's attempt to abduct me.'

'And?' The prioress gave her a searching glance.

'Ulf was merely inspecting the bruises on my face under the light of the cresset outside the house. It was a professional examination of my wounds, who better to do it? De Courcy must have just arrived through the postern at Micklegate Bar and was presumably already deluded by his travels. I gather he had just arrived from Avignon.'

The prioress raised her eyebrows. 'And you imagine that warped his judgement?'

'I would imagine it was already warped to make him choose to go there in the first place.'

'Ha!' Her eyes flashed with humour.

Hildegard knew she was stepping out of line but she had to speak honestly. The prioress continued to raise her eyebrows for a moment or two as Hildegard described in greater detail her ordeal just before coming across Ulf and his men in the street.

When she finished the prioress gave a grim chuckle. 'That sounds far more plausible than de Courcy's version. Leave it with me, Sister. I assume you told the abbot nothing of what had preceded this incident?'

'Wild horses wouldn't drag it from me.'

'In that case this misunderstanding might continue for some time, don't you think? As will yours over his reason for sojourning with Pope Clement until you discover the truth.'

She flapped a hand and Hildegard was dismissed.

Not much later, three days at most, Hildegard was summoned to the Abbey of Meaux. Expecting a harsh penance for her alleged activities she was surprised by the abbot's genial mood, if genial was a word that could ever be applied to so driven a man.

Nothing was said about Ulf. Indeed, the abbot invited her to sit beside him in his private garden after compline to watch the sun go down over the canal, as if a harsh word had never come between them.

She was careful to make no comment about Avignon. If the prioress considered him trustworthy, it would have to be good enough.

Instead, talk turned to Wycliffe, the sadness of these latter months when, forbidden to preach, he was rarely seen in public.

Then they turned to the border wars with Scotland and how it would be to everyone's benefit if both sides could shake hands and settle down to an agreement.

After that they covered the topic of how young King Richard was losing his popularity and whether the rumours about his erratic behaviour could be trusted, or whether they were stories spread far and wide by his enemies. Hubert then told her a little about his pilgrimage and his ensuing concern for the Byzantine emperor with his ceaseless efforts to maintain a Christian region in a hostile territory, and how no one in the West, 'neither pope, in Rome nor Avignon,' he pointed out, seemed at all interested in going to his aid. 'Despite all efforts to persuade them,' he added.

Then the abbot turned to matters closer to home, to the exceptionally dry weather and the effect it had on the crops, but how the sheep appeared to be surprisingly unaffected, and how the recent storms, sad though it was that they had drowned out the pageant, had not doused the town's enthusiasm.

'It was an evil thing for Mistress Julitta to put glass in her husband's food,' he observed. 'And how strange that the coroner took so long to arrive that she had already vanished.'

'If Petronilla's view of angels is correct,' she told him, 'she will not escape punishment.' She explained what the girl believed about the law of angels and they exchanged glances without comment.

And then, finally, Hubert mentioned the disappointment Hildegard must feel at having all the hard work at Deepdale come to nothing.

'I know how much effort you and that handful of nuns must have put in to establish the place while I was away. I've been given a most careful accounting of what you achieved over the last year. And then to have it destroyed like that...' He shook his head. 'It must be a grave disappointment.'

'I hope to return soon to see what we can make of it,' she replied. 'The bees were dispersed when the men put their swords through the hives. The geese will have flown. And no doubt the hens that survived will already be working hard for the inhabitants of the next vill. But there must be something we can restore.' She smiled ruefully.

'Of course, I will never give permission for you

to return there,' he told her emphatically. 'I remember clearly the first time we ever met...' he hesitated, then added, 'I remember how I expressed doubts then about your ability to defend yourselves against marauders. And how you assured me that you could take care of yourselves–'

'I doubt whether even you or your brothers could have defended yourselves against those armed men. Unless you had been willing to take up arms yourselves.'

She turned to him quite fiercely but to her surprise he was smiling.

'You're probably right. It's the nature of the times that men of violence can wreak havoc with impunity.' He held her glance for a moment but then he hesitated again.

Many things lay unspoken between them and he seemed to be on the brink of laying them bare. She had a vision of the soaring pillars of Beverley Minster and the abbot's confession during their night of vigil at the sanctuary of St John last year. Her lips parted. She both desired him to speak and feared where it would lead them. His dark eyes seemed to reach into her soul. She put up a hand as if to ward off some unseen force.

His voice was soft. 'It must have been an ordeal to face those men in the mayor's chamber with their crossbows primed with naphtha,' he murmured. 'How did you manage to remain so calm?'

'I felt neither calm nor sure,' she told him, leaping at the chance to talk of something that would lead them away from danger. 'The idea of Greek fire came to me out of nowhere – or rather, it reminded me of the mage at the booths and how he kept talking, saying the most outrageous things, even when he suspected he was being targeted by cut-throats.'

Hubert smiled at her, watching her lips. 'And that gave you courage?'

'I thought that if I kept talking it would give the porter time to fetch help. It was strange, though. As I spoke about my willingness to die for the right of ordinary people to be free from feudal bonds I...' She paused. 'The massacre at the coast has shaped my views. They have a stronger focus now.'

'But what made those men-at-arms take you seriously?'

'As luck would have it a ribbon had come loose at the neck of my undershift. They seemed to think it was attached to a device that would unleash the fire.'

'Was it this one?'

He reached out and held a thread of twisted silk between his fingers.

She could have lowered her lips then and brushed them across his fingertips.

Moving hurriedly back she tucked the ribbon out of sight.

Noticing her expression he said more briskly, 'All that's by the by. I have had an idea, one that I hope will please you as much as it pleases me.'

Saying nothing more, the abbot reached inside the scrip that lay beside him and took from it a parcel of documents. He held them out. 'These are yours. They come with my blessing.'

Curious to see what it was, she took hold of a

winding of new vellum and began to unroll it. It turned out to be the deeds to a vacant grange on the other side of the canal, opposite the Abbey of Meaux.

And so one way of life ended.

And another began.

Meanwhile, the castle at Pickering in the royal forest, less than thirty miles away as the crow flies, has a visitor. The great hall is royally adorned. Three men are sitting on the high dais eating venison from a great silver platter. A constant stream of servants attends them. Musicians play in the gallery and down in the mesh the retinues of three households laugh and joke in amity.

The guest of honour is telling a story, outrage in his voice but also a tone of mockery as at some scandalous behaviour he, as a man of reason, is at his wits' end to explain.

'So there I was,' he is saying, 'summoned to Sheen. And on no account would he let me leave. That's the reason I'm late. And then a detour to York, of course, avoiding the players by many devious and cunning excuses which My Lord Archbishop was too tactful to reveal for the pack of lies they were. But Sheen!' Despite his levity he frowns now. 'God and St Benet preserve us! Same as ever. The court monkeys nimbly jumping through the hoops. The lovely Anne being lovely. And he in his little chamber with the one door in and out for fear of assassins.'

'Which he does rightly fear,' points out his host.

'Which he does, rightly,' agrees his guest with contempt. 'So what does he say to me when I'm eventually called? First, he pretends he doesn't know I've entered and he goes on sitting there on his velvet cushion – and will you believe this? – with the crown between his hands. He was hunched forward, staring at it. Eventually I cough and he gives a little start and looks up. "Oh!" he says in mock surprise. "You, coz, do you want me?" "You summoned me, Majesty," I say. He looks vague as if with something heavy on his mind. "I was looking at my crown," he says. Then – I tell you no lies – he lifts it so that the sunlight strikes the jewels – all that, a great blazing show – and he says, "So beautiful. My beautiful, bloody crown." Then he stands up and places it on his head! "You may go, coz," he says. "I forget why I summoned you." And he flicks his fingers and I'm dismissed After all that waiting about! Can you beat it?'

His companions growl something that might be sympathy and one of them stabs his knife into the haunch of venison and hacks some off. The guest, his story finished, fills his mouth and chews thoughtfully until his host says, 'I gather, My Lord, that your time in York was not entirely ill spent, for I hear you purchased something of extraordinary power?'

'You hear wrong, sir. But at least I now know where I can lay my hands on it should the need arise.'

The guest gazes out over the tops of the trees that are just visible through the arrow slit. The forest stretches for many leagues to the horizon and beyond. Then come the northern marches and after that France's great ally, the separate

522

and turbulent kingdom of Scotland.

But in the opposite direction, before one reaches the great river that divides England north from south, lies a modest priory called Swyne.

The publishers hope that this book has given you enjoyable reading. Large Print Books are especially designed to be as easy to see and hold as possible. If you wish a complete list of our books please ask at your local library or write directly to:

Magna Large Print Books
Magna House, Long Preston,
Skipton, North Yorkshire.
BD23 4ND

This Large Print Book for the partially sighted, who cannot read normal print, is published under the auspices of

THE ULVERSCROFT FOUNDATION

THE ULVERSCROFT FOUNDATION

... we hope that you have enjoyed this Large Print Book. Please think for a moment about those people who have worse eyesight problems than you ... and are unable to even read or enjoy Large Print, without great difficulty.

You can help them by sending a donation, large or small to:

**The Ulverscroft Foundation,
1, The Green, Bradgate Road,
Anstey, Leicestershire, LE7 7FU,
England.**
or request a copy of our brochure for more details.

The Foundation will use all your help to assist those people who are handicapped by various sight problems and need special attention.

Thank you very much for your help.